SUMMER
at
MOUNT HOPE

ROSALIE HAM

First published in Great Britain in 2016 by Serpent's Tail,
an imprint of Profile Books Ltd
3 Holford Yard
Bevin Way
London
WC1X 9HD
www.serpentstail.com

First published in 2005 by Duffy & Snellgrove, NSW, Australia

Copyright © 2005 by Rosalie Ham

1 3 5 7 9 10 8 6 4 2

Printed and bound by
CPI Group (UK) Ltd, Croydon CR0 4YY

The moral right of the author has been asserted.

The characters and events in this book are fictitious.
Any similarity to real persons, dead or alive, is
coincidental and not intended by the author

A CIP record for this book can
be obtained from the British Library

ISBN 978 1 78125 739 5
eISBN 978 1 78283 301 7

Mixed Sources
Product group from well-managed
forests and other controlled sources
www.fsc.org Cert no. TT-COC-002227
© 1996 Forest Stewardship Council
FSC

ROSALIE HAM was brought up in the Riverina, New South Wales, and now lives in Brunswick. *The Dressmaker*, her first novel, was an international bestseller and became a major motion picture.

Praise for *Summer at Mount Hope*

'There is a hint of the Jane Austens about Rosalie Ham's new novel' *Sydney Morning Herald*

'While it's the social and romantic intrigue that carries the story, it's Ham's wickedly black humour and finely researched social observation that deliver the real joy of the book' *The Australian*

'The novel is a delight. Complex beneath its witty surface, and one of the surprising fictional treats of the year' *The Bulletin*

Praise for *The Dressmaker*

'Wickedly funny and glamorous … an irresistible, gripping read' *Essentials*

'There's almost a fairytale aspect to this story of the prodigal returning, in this case the prodigal daughter … Tilly is a fun and dark creation' *Sunday Herald*

'Blessed with an astringently unsentimental tone and a talent for creating memorably eccentric characters, Ham also possesses a confidently brisk and mischievous sense of plot' *Sydney Morning Herald*

'Ham writes delightfully rich set pieces and descriptive passages … her eye for the absurd, the comical and the poignant are highly tuned … one to savour and enjoy' *Weekend Australian*

Thanks to Varuna Writers' Centre, Gail MacCallum,
Michael Duffy, Ashley Hay; also Neville Ham,
Terry and Ian.

Sunday, December 31, 1893

I t was the last Sunday of the year, blazing hot, and Phoeba
Crupp was squeezed next to her stout mother and slim
sister on the narrow bench of the family sulky in the middle
of a low dam. Their boots were on the dash, their skirts were
bunched in their laps exposing the lacy trim on their bloomers,
and slimy green water swirled just below their bottoms. Lilith
snivelled while her mother, Maude, eyed the stagnant water. In
front of them the black tendrils of Spot's tail floated like yabbie
whiskers. His nose rested lightly on the water and he blinked flies
from his eyes.

The day had started well. The trip down Mount Hope Lane
had gone without incident until they got to the intersection,
where Spot had stalled, looked sideways at the dam, lifted his
tail and expelled a pile of warm manure. They sat, they waited,
willing him to move off again, but he had lowered his head and
leaned back.

'No Spot,' Phoeba said firmly, but he creased his ears flat.
She pulled the brake lever; he trudged off the lane and across
the stock reserve, the locked sulky wheels leaving gashes in the
tufty, punctured ground. And although she leaned back on
the reins with all her might, the sulky slid down the low bank to

1

the muddy edge and splashed into the thick water.

'Lord save us!' Maude cried, while Lilith squealed and waves sloshed to the bank, sending the ducks flapping.

And now they waited, their wide hats tilted to the hot breeze. A crow cawed at them from the signpost on its island of thistles in the centre of the intersection. When travellers arrived here from Bay View – a settlement of just three structures hugging a salty slice of seaside mud that was fondly called 'the beach' – they were directed south to Elm Grove, a mouldering property belonging to the Pearson family, or north via the pass to the vast plains of Overton Station. Most people – swaggies, shearers, travelling merchants and itinerants – knew to take the short cut through Crupp's place and so continued to the west towards the outcrop and Mount Hope, although some wag had added a few letters to the end of the sign and it read, 'Mount Hopeless'.

'I've been asking your father for decent transport for years,' said Maude, 'and I have never understood the vengeful nature of this horse.'

'Take no notice of them, Spot,' said Phoeba, rattling the reins softly over his black rump. She'd fallen in love with Spot the instant she first saw him, a skinny black yearling with huge feet and a head like a plough blade, loping up the lane behind her father. Phoeba was ten at the time; they had just moved to the country and Spot was the first animal her father purchased. Phoeba fed him, washed him in the dam, trimmed his mane and fringe, plaited his tail and polished his hooves. She snuck him apples and confided in him, and every day Spot transported her to and from school. He had graciously accommodated Lilith when she started school too; she'd clung to Phoeba's waist while her small feet bounced against his ticklish flanks. Phoeba still rode him everywhere, astride and bareback.

'This is your fault, Phoeba,' said Lilith.

'Of course it is,' she replied. 'So is the recession and the drought.'

'I'll get to church all red, wet and smelly, and we have a new vicar today.'

'I haven't seen a rich, handsome vicar yet, Lilith.'

'A vicar's wife is an admirable position to have in any community, Miss Pertinacious Phoeba,' said her mother, slapping at a fly with her hanky. The ostrich feathers above her shifted like kelp: Maude always pinned far too much plumage to her hat. 'It's you father's fault,' she continued. 'He should never have brought us here.' She recoiled as a small beetle swam past.

When Maude had stepped from the train onto the siding for the very first time fourteen years ago, she had looked up at her new home and the surrounding countryside and declared, 'This is a wretched place.' Lilith had been a sickly, whining four-year-old at the time but Phoeba, at ten, liked the outcrop and the bay immediately. She relished helping her father establish the vineyard, and on her first day at school she had made two best friends – Hadley and Henrietta Pearson. They would be at church now.

A breeze skimmed through the dry heads of acres and acres of ripe wheat, and a distant sheep bleated. The crops were thin because of three dry years, and the air smelled of hot sun, of dust and baking grain and manure. The Melbourne train was approaching the Bay View siding, a low square platform made from sleepers, and slowed down. The mailman leaned from the goods van but no mailbag waited, so he waved his flag and the train whistled like a wailing child and accelerated away, curling a plume of black smoke across the foreshore.

'We're late,' said Lilith gathering her skirt higher.

3

'Sit still,' said Maude. 'We'll sink and our bottoms will get wet.'

'If we sink, mother, it will be because of your bottom,' said Phoeba.

Her mother opened her mouth but the approaching clatter of steel-rimmed wheels silenced her. Phoeba turned and saw a slim, four-wheel carriage coming along the lane. It was dark blue with a golden 'O' painted on the petite door, and lacy golden steps. The driver, Mr Titterton, was perched on a blue velvet bench high above two shining, chestnut Hackneys, and behind him in the carriage sat two well-dressed passengers.

'The britzka,' said Phoeba.

'Not Mrs Overton!' moaned Lilith, sinking further under her hat brim.

Maude stole a quick look and gasped, 'And Marius!'

No one had seen the Overton's son since the death of his wife seven months before.

Lilith buried her face in her gloves.

'They may not notice us,' said Maude hopefully. Mrs Overton swung her parasol behind her to see who was sitting in the dam.

Robert Crupp was sitting peacefully on the front veranda at Mount Hope sipping a glass of last year's vintage and puffing on his pipe – two pastimes his wife disapproved of, especially on Sundays. He was admiring the green, leafy sweep of his neatly serried vines, his best crop to date. While the farmers around him struggled through the dry year Robert's grapes, sustained with dam water, thrived. It was the only vineyard in this sheep and wheat district, and no one believed he could make a living from grapes. But Robert knew he was poised to reap the benefits of many long, hard years.

He raised his Collector, a small .410 gauge double-barrel gun specifically designed for orchardists, and focused on a bird as it pecked at a bunch of his bursting grape flowers. Beyond, at the intersection, he saw the Overton carriage stopped at the dam.

'Bloody heck,' he said. He reached for his looking glass and it was then he saw Spot, chest-deep in the dam, and his wife and daughters perched in the partially submerged sulky.

He drained his glass of wine, picked up his hat, and made his way to the stables.

Spot raised his head and water dripped from his muzzle as he pricked his ears towards the shiny chestnut Hackneys. The slim, blue britzka drew to a halt on the lane.

'Good morning,' called Phoeba brightly, raising her whip to the people who stared at her from the elegant carriage.

Marius Overton stood up, his hands on his hips, pushing his coat-tails back to show a braided waistcoat and a gold fob chain.

'Ladies,' he said.

Lilith dabbed at her cheeks with her handkerchief.

Mrs Overton, regal and lily-white under a city parasol, stared at them while the driver tied his reins firmly to the brake handle, removed his hat, placed it on the seat, and climbed down. As the stock overseer at Overton Station, and the owner of a top hat, Mr Titterton was very important. He had caused controversy recently by sacking most of the drovers, buying an enormously fat boar and ten sows, and threatening to switch from sheep to pigs, but the thing he was most famous for was his Crimean teeth – said to be taken by Russian women from corpses on the war fields and sold to enterprising dentists who glued them to wooden plates.

Removing his boots and socks and placing them neatly on

the dam bank, Mr Titterton paused while Phoeba prodded Spot again. The horse didn't move, so he pinched the crease of his trousers and waded gingerly into the slimy mud.

'I am sorry,' said Phoeba.

'Not to worry, we all know old Spot,' said Mr Titterton sinking up to his thighs. He gasped as the water pressed his trousers against his legs. As he reached for the bridle, Spot snorted and lunged forward, dragging the sulky through the water like a small paddle boat. The clay bottom churned and turned the water to grey folds that slapped Mr Titterton's waist. At the top of the dam bank Spot paused, his passengers angled precariously and clinging to the dashboard. Streams of muddy water poured from his sodden mane and the waterlogged sulky. Spot braced himself to shake – Maude cried, 'Lord save us' – and shivered, sprinkling the air with arcs of water, shuddering the harness and rattling the sulky beneath the women. Then he sighed and plodded slowly up to the road.

Saluting Mr Titterton with her whip, Phoeba called, 'Thank you,' and left him dripping on the bank, slimy from the waist down. The women wrung their hems and loosened their wet bootlaces while Spot walked calmly on, a wet trail behind him.

The church was a small weatherboard building with a pitched roof supporting a wooden cross that leaned slightly to the left. Spot turned into the yard, passing a sparkling new Abbott buggy, its thin, black mare drooping in the hot sun outside the vestry door. The previous vicar had shattered his hip when he sneezed and fell from his horse outside Mrs Flynn's shop, and Bay View had endured a succession of stammering, blushing curates for months.

A moment later, the still slimy Mr Titterton stopped the britzka at the church door.

'We needn't go in,' whispered Maude, humiliated.

'We have to,' said Lilith, her eye on Marius Overton as he helped his mother from the carriage.

Spot drew up under the peppercorns at the end of the half dozen wagons and sulkies, next to the Pearsons' Hampden buggy, an old but superior upholstered six-seater with a removable top. Standing next to it was Hadley Pearson, a lanky young man with peachy cheeks and spectacles.

'Good morning,' he said, taking the reins from Phoeba. He was growing a moustache: it looked like a pubescent centipede had arrived on his top lip. 'Spot did his water trick again, did he?'

Phoeba ignored his offered hand and jumped to the ground, showing a flash of boot and stocking.

'Wait for me, Phoeba,' Hadley called, but she was already heading for the church.

Inside, the ten or so locals sat hemmed in by swaggies like train passengers experiencing an unpleasant odour. Henrietta, between her mother and someone with a grimy neck and greasy hair against his frayed collar, waved a long arm at Phoeba.

'See you later,' Phoeba mouthed, squashing in next to the mailboy, Freckle, and his mother, Mrs Flynn. Henrietta was not much like her brother; she was boisterous and cheerful, whereas Hadley was inclined to worry.

Outside, Hadley wrapped his arms around Maude's hard steel and whalebone middle while she searched with her foot through layers of petticoats for the sulky's small, wrought-iron step. The whole carriage groaned and tipped, but he managed to get her safely onto the carpet of dry peppercorn leaves. She seemed to be heavier every Sunday, he thought. Maude checked for insects caught in her dress's jabots and her hat feathers.

'You look smart, Had,' said Lilith taking his arm.

7

'It's my new suit,' Hadley explained. It was grey wool and he'd left the coat unbuttoned to show his father's watch chain. The shirt was new too, with a stiff, square-winged collar that grazed triangles of skin on either side of his Adam's Apple. The whole lot had cost over thirty-five shillings.

Hadley ushered them past the pile of swags – grubby blankets rolled in thick coils and blackened billies – that blocked the tiny vestibule.

'Crowded today,' said Lilith.

'They must have got wind there was a new vicar,' said Hadley. 'The last one chased them away because they drank too much altar wine.'

Maude had found a place in front of Phoeba next to Mrs Jessop, a toothless woman with six children and a newborn, and Phoeba noticed the back of her mother's dress was wet. A stain of sodden chocolate-brown serge circled her billowy bottom like a huge target. It was fortunate, she thought, that most people had their eyes closed in prayer or on the vestry door.

Lilith marched straight up to the front pew and sat next to Marius Overton. The Overtons always occupied the front pew exclusively. But Lilith just turned to Marius and smiled, wrinkling her nose and squeezing her shoulders together. He nodded to her, moving closer to his mother. Lilith leaned over and spoke to them. More front than the Exhibition Building, thought Phoeba. Hadley squeezed into a row with workers from Overton, scanning the pews for the cockatiel feather that perched on top of Phoeba's straw hat.

Phoeba wasn't praying. She was counting the sparrow chicks nesting in the truss above. The ceiling wasn't lined, and as the sun warmed the iron roof it expanded, creating tiny blasts that startled the chicks to squeak and dart out through the bell tower.

8

Last spring, during one of the previous vicar's sermons – 'Now the Serpent was more subtil than any beast of the field which the Lord God had made. And he said unto the woman …' – the congregation had sat transfixed as a brown snake slithered across a beam and ate the eggs from the nest before coiling over itself and sliding out the window. But no one could be distracted from the vestry door today.

Finally, the new vicar backed out, short, and fat from his low ears down. Swinging around to face them, he raised his arms so his angel sleeves hung. He saw the aristocracy, the local dowager and her heir. He saw Farmer Jessop, a staircase of dishevelled children, and his feeble wife with a babe in arms. Next to her was Maude, round and jowly with a feather forest on her head. Then the three fierce matrons from the Temperance society, Mrs Pearson, thin with a blue nose, and Henrietta Pearson, large and ruddy. Further back, Hadley Pearson, a slim, well-groomed strawberry blond praying among weathered farm workers and sunken-eyed swaggies and shearers. And finally, the Crupp spinsters – one plain with a pert feather in a sensible straw hat, and, sitting in the front pew, the pretty one with porcelain skin and dark curls.

The vicar opened his hymn book and so did the congregation and the church filled with the thistly sound of flicking hymnal pages. From the first note of 'Father, who on man dost shower Gifts of plenty from thy dower', it was clear the new vicar couldn't sing, but he sang anyway, and enthusiastically, his voice rising and his fat throat quivering. Finally, he snapped his hymnbook closed and cried like a small boy suggesting a game, 'Let us pray for relief in this time of scarcity.'

The vicar gave a passionate lecture that rose to whistle pitch: 'Increase the fruits of the earth by thy heavenly benediction. We must pray for a good season: drought, famine and hard times are

9

caused by improvidence, drinking and gambling – all of which are at the root of evil. Cast thy burden upon the Lord and he shall provide.'

The farmers shifted on their knees and Freckle nudged Phoeba: 'A bit of a letdown if rabbits is the best He can provide.'

Phoeba smiled. She didn't believe dry weather was caused by squandering money, and she knew the banks were to blame for the depression.

Turning then to the altar cup the vicar let out a mighty squeak: a sparrow was perched on its lip, splashing and preening in the wine. The bird flew back to the trusses, the swaggies charged down the aisle and the vicar had to refill the cup three times.

At the end of the service the vicar clasped his hands at his chest and, with his neck bunched above his clerical collar, said, 'I know you're looking forward to lunch as much as I would be if I had a nice roast and pudding to go to, but in the interests of the Lord, nature and the elements, I ask you to dig deep and offer donations to finish this roof. We are all in depressed circumstances but £50 would see the ceiling lined and the birds cast out.' Then he rubbed his hands together and rolled down the aisle towards the door. The Overtons followed hot on his heels, with Lilith nudging her way through the small dense crowd behind them. Phoeba fell in behind her mother to hide her wet bottom. At the door, Maude introduced herself to the vicar, already flanked by the Temperance ladies.

'Mrs Crupp has a vineyard,' said the largest Temperance woman. 'It's for alcohol.' She had low buns either side of her head which, combined with a mole on her nose, made her look like a koala.

'A vineyard?' The vicar's eyebrows shot up. 'I must come for lunch.'

'We'd be honoured,' said Maude. 'And this is Phoeba, my elder daughter.'

The vicar took Phoeba's hand in his with a grip like warm, raw chicken.

'The vicar will have roast rabbit with us today,' boomed the koala-like Temperance woman.

Phoeba extracted her hand: 'We grow Sweetwater and a few Glory of Australia grapes. For white wine.'

'Lovely,' said the vicar. 'I do get tired of red.'

Phoeba propelled her mother towards Widow Pearson and Hadley as they waited in the shade between the vehicles. Henrietta arrived.

'Happy New Year for tomorrow,' said Phoeba, squeezing her hand.

'Hadley has an interview at Overton this afternoon.'

'For wool classing?'

'Yes. But it's a secret.'

As the Overton carriage passed, the older women stood to attention. Mrs Overton hid behind her parasol, and Marius tipped his hat without actually looking at anyone. Mr Titterton captured the Widow's gaze and lifted his hat high, his lips stretched back from his wooden gums. Mrs Pearson giggled, then gasped, like an expiring canary, the rest of the group holding its breath until hers was restored. She suffered respiratory problems.

'You'd think the Overtons would donate an organ for Christmas, wouldn't you?' said Maude. 'The hymns are such a struggle.'

'At the moment everything's a struggle for all of us,' said Hadley, glancing across to the swaggies wandering to the foreshore.

'Of course, Mrs Crupp, I've always had to struggle,' wheezed his mother.

'So you keep telling us,' said Maude.

Maude and Widow Pearson endured the wary acquaintance of neighbours whose children had grown up together and who shared common experiences – middle age and the treacheries of rural life – but who actively despised each other. Maude's bulk could no longer be shaped by a mere corset, but Widow Pearson drew her small torso very tight in the middle, squeezing herself into the shape of a sand timer. As a result she wheezed like a burning gas lamp and the tip of her nose was blue. The three false ringlets she pinned above her ears and the small mourning bonnet she shoved on top made her look like a spaniel with a bunch of grapes on its head. She'd worn the same bonnet, the same black dress and the same large, elaborate bustle every day of the nine years since her beloved husband died. Hadley resembled his mother – fine and thin – but Henrietta was big boned, like her late father.

Widow Pearson pointed to the muddy watermark at Spot's flanks: 'I see you have been dragged through the mud again.'

'I thanked Marius Overton for saving us,' gushed Lilith.

'We were saved by Mr Titterton,' said Phoeba, impatiently. Her jacket itched and her feet were swelling in her boots. She just wanted to go home.

'My poor friend Mr Titterton,' said Widow Pearson. 'I don't know why you don't get a decent horse and for that matter, a suitable carriage. At least get lamp sockets.'

'Anything larger would be extravagant for the three of us,' said Maude, glancing at the Pearsons' sumptuous six-seater. The truth was that Robert said they couldn't afford a four-seater, even a wagonette. So that was that.

'It's good to see Marius out and about,' said Lilith, eagerly. 'He's obviously getting over his loss.'

12

Phoeba was about to ask why going to church indicated recovery from grief when Widow Pearson interrupted – 'They say he came back to Overton for Christmas,' – and pulled her mourning veil over her face. 'Anyway, Lilith, what would you know about losing a spouse?'

The vicar drove past in the wake of the Temperance women's buggy. 'Do you think he's … eligible?' asked Maude, and Phoeba felt her gaze.

'No,' she said.

Lilith and Henrietta, even Hadley, shook their heads.

'He has a career, a future,' said Widow Pearson, smoothing her son's lapel. 'But of course Hadley has a splendid future in wool ahead of him.'

Hadley bit his bottom lip and adjusted his spectacles.

'Well,' said Lilith, 'that won't be too splendid. All I ever read about is how the wool industry's about to collapse.'

Widow Pearson started panting and her sky-blue nose turned immediately purple. 'The world needs wool, Lilith Crupp,' she wheezed. 'What on earth else is there to wear?' And she lifted her skirts, put her foot on the step, held her elbows out and waited for Hadley and Henrietta to hoist her into the Hampden.

'Will you be in this afternoon?' asked Hadley, as Phoeba took her position behind her mother, found the rim of her corset through the folds of her satin skirts and pushed her into the sulky.

'No,' said Phoeba, panting. 'We're going to Melbourne.'

Hadley frowned, puzzled.

'It was a joke,' said Phoeba.

'Of course it was,' he said, and put his hat on. 'I'll drop in.'

Phoeba watched as he steered the old Hampden out of the yard. She always maintained she didn't believe in God, that she only came to church because she had to drive. But she said to herself, 'Please God, let Hadley get the job.' It would be his first job since finishing school and Overton must need a classer. It would lift Hadley, his mother and sister from a fading existence to comfort.

At the intersection Hadley waved and turned south to Elm Grove while Spot kept on towards Mount Hope. Home to the Crupps was a neat weatherboard nestled at the base of an outcrop which was actually just a gathering of boulders on top of a big, bushy ridge – a full stop to some distant, ancient ranges. The house had four rooms and a kitchen tacked onto the back, a lawn of stringy buffalo grass and some desperate petunias at the base of the front step.

'I don't know how the Widow can go out in public still wearing a bustle,' said Lilith. 'They went out of fashion in 1883!'

'Oh, I know!' said Phoeba with mock outrage, 'especially with the fashion around Bay View always of such a high standard!'

'Her friendship with Mr Titterton is unbecoming,' said Maude. 'She's only friends with him because he's stock overseer at Overton.'

'He looks after the sheep when Hadley's away,' said Phoeba.

'I'm sure that's not all he's looking after,' muttered her mother.

The competition between Maude and her neighbour had started shortly after the Crupps arrived at Bay View, when Mrs Pearson became a widow. At the wake, she had wailed, 'I am left alone to raise two children.' And Maude, trying to be encouraging, had said, 'We were very young when we were deprived of both parents, gone together, and my sister and I turned out splendidly.'

14

Convinced her new neighbour was practising one-upmanship, Mrs Pearson had been trying to outdo Maude ever since – skiting of plans for a grander house, purchasing a better horse and carriage, maintaining a thinner waist, all that despite her farm's and her family's struggles.

The only sign of Robert when the women got home was a note: 'Gone to see about a new horse.' It was anchored to the kitchen table by an empty wine jug.

'At last,' said Maude, pleased.

But then Lilith told her the back of her dress was wet, and she shrieked and ordered Spot immediately 'retired'. Phoeba unharnessed him, rubbed his shoulders boisterously with an old sheet where the yoke had rubbed, and led him not to the stables but into the dam paddock. At the gate she put her arms around his thick, black neck and pressed her cheek to his dense stinking hide.

'You won't have to drag us to church and back every Sunday and you won't have to wait in the stockyards at Flynn's while we shop in Geelong all day. But you and I will still go riding.'

She opened the gate. The resident rooster and the wild ducks stared as the new tenant walked straight past them into the dam and stood there, looking over to the sheltering peppercorn trees in the corner. He scanned the view then lowered his nose to the water and drank. Phoeba went to muck out his stable for the new horse.

At Elm Grove, Hadley unharnessed the creamy hack and saddled his tall brown mare before washing his face and hands to join his mother and sister at the kitchen table. Henrietta had made a tomato omelette and lemon flummery – Hadley's two favourite dishes. He said grace and Henrietta carefully slid a slice of omelette onto his plate and next to his bread: he didn't like the egg on the bread, it made it soggy.

The family ate in silence, but the second Hadley put his serviette down the women sprang to action. Henrietta checked his kitbag for his wool classing certificate and letter of recommendation from the Geelong Wool Classing School; his mother retied his necktie, slid it flat under his waistcoat and pinned a clean collar on his shirt.

'That's it,' she said and sunk into her wing-backed chair to catch her breath.

Hadley stood straight with his hands at his sides. Henrietta bent down and dusted his new boots with her handkerchief.

'Thank you, both,' he said. 'When I have my first pay packet I'll buy you a present.'

'A new dress and bonnet would do me the world of good,' his mother sighed, and they looked at Henrietta. A new dress and bonnet wouldn't do her any good at all. They would have to think of something else.

Henrietta's heart grew thick with pride and her eyes filled with jealous tears watching her little brother ride down the driveway, the shadows of the lush elms moving across his back as he went towards a new life. She was bound to Elm Grove, to a life tightening the strings on her frail, fierce mother's corsets, to endless days of tedious housework and, of course, to Hadley and his sheep. The weeks during lambing were always tense but she liked it when the hungry orphans rushed at her, bunting her skirt and bleating. She loved to feed them warm cow's milk and see them grow. And she was very handy in the pens, renowned for her knack of cornering the sprightly rascals then dragging them to Hadley for wigging and crutching. She knew Hadley would be

16

lost without her when it came to docking and castrating too. He appreciated her bravery, how she held them unflinchingly while he performed bloody tasks.

'I have a home where I am needed,' she reminded herself, unlike the swaggies tramping the lonely lanes. And things would improve. Hadley would get a job. He would sink a well deep enough to reach good water. He would fertilise the land, breed up the stud line and build the new house their mother boasted of. There might even be money to hire help and that would give her time to grow proper, prize-winning vegetables. At last they would be able to buy a cow, build a proper dairy and even fox-proof the old chook house. It would mean she would miss her rides to Overton for the hamper and her visits to Phoeba. But there would be time for friendship, not just hasty visits and brief conversations after church.

'I have a good friend in the world,' she muttered.

'Henrietta!'

'I am indeed fortunate,' she said, turning to go to her mother.

As he rode down the driveway Hadley looked at his land. It was a ghostly landscape of grey, dead gums. The majestic trunks were bare and bleached, jutting from the ground like stalagmites with angular branches that had twisted to a slow starved death and now pointed accusingly at him. His father had ring-barked them to make way for his sheep and now, years later, Hadley was battling salt-bog pastures clogged with rotting trees and supporting his mother and sister with money scratched from sparse, stunted grain crops and a few bales of wool each year. Not even rabbits, which plagued every other farm, bothered to eat his meagre patches of grass. But he still dreamed his father's dream – a flock

17

of prize stud merino ewes and rams. True, he had sold some of their dwindling stock to pay for his wool classing studies, but now he was about to embark on a career. He would plough his earnings back into Elm Grove and the stud flock, and when the drought was over, 'white gold' – that fine merino wool – would make them rich. He would make something of himself, improve life for his mother and sister, and marry and have a family. He had prayed hard in church that morning, and was certain God would help him.

Spurring his brown mare through the intersection, he glanced up to Mount Hope. Phoeba didn't believe in God. 'You just live and die and turn to dust,' she said. Sometimes he could spot her, a distant figure in a white blouse and dull skirt reading the paper on the front veranda. But none of the Crupps were visible now, just a group of swaggies making their way up the outcrop track – last year's shearers returning to Overton, hoping for work.

The lane led him through the outcrop pass to the Overton homestead, which sat on the plain like a wedding cake on a vast table. Scattered around it were stables and sheds, sheep yards and the shearers' store, workers' quarters, tank-stands and haystacks. The mare cantered through the gateposts, and Hadley, nervous but hopeful, tethered her to the yard gate at the back of the house. At the kitchen door he handed the cook an empty string basket. The cook was Chinese, so Hadley spoke carefully and loudly: 'Today for hamper I will have butter' – he mimed spreading butter on bread – 'and one leg of lamb. And six eggs.' He held up six fingers. 'Berry good,' said the Chinese cook, and Hadley walked around to the front of the house and knocked, standing back to admire the stained glass flowers bordering the door and its ornate brass knocker. A maid opened the door, a runt of a girl with a lazy eye. He asked for Mr Overton and she showed him to a low seat

18

in the hall. Hadley could hear Mr Guston Overton's voice as it filtered down the wide, sweeping stairs, but it was a different man, a broad, suntanned chap wearing jodhpurs who appeared up on the landing, and called, 'You're Pearson?' His accent was English and his coat – very flash – had never rubbed against a sorting table or pressed against a fly-blown ram. He came down the stairs two at a time, dark-haired, with strong, regular features, rugged for a Pom. The hand he offered was not marked by hard work, but his grip was firm: 'I'm the new manager, Rudolph Steel. Your reputation precedes you, Pearson,' he said, moving to the front door. 'I think we can find room for one more good classer.' He swung the door open and looked back at Hadley, who reached for the clasp on his bag, 'My certificate—?'

'I'll send word with Mr Titterton, but we'll start next week.' Rudolph Steel gestured at the wide veranda and the manicured garden beyond. 'There'll be a bunk for you in the workers' cottage.'

'Right,' said Hadley and marched through the door. His coat caught on the decorative brass doorknob and pulled him up violently, wrenching him so that his nose hit the edge of the door and his spectacles were dislodged.

'Looking forward to having you here,' said Rudolph Steel, and closed the door behind him. Flummoxed, Hadley followed the gravel path back to the kitchen door where the cook handed him his string bag and his account for the month: £2.0.6. Hadley felt rash, generous. He had a job. Henrietta could make a cake to celebrate. He held up six fingers: 'Six more eggs, please.'

When the cook returned with the eggs wrapped in newspaper, Hadley asked him to set aside ten chicks for him, next time the hens hatched.

Riding out through the towering gateposts he felt secure,

manly, somehow weightless. He had a job. He would sink a bore, fertilise his land, plant his trees and fix his fences. All he needed now was a wife and the only wife he had ever wanted was Phoeba Crupp. So now they would get married. What a surprise for everyone, and how happy it would make Henrietta! What a way to start the year – he even had a new suit ready for a wedding.

It was natural that Phoeba would marry him, a matter of course really, and that's what she'd say when he asked. 'Of course,' she'd say, and she would smile in her understated way. And Maude would throw her arms around him and say, 'I knew it! I always knew you would be my son-in-law!' And Robert would shake his hand and open good wine.

And there, bouncing towards the outcrop on the plain ahead of him, was Robert himself on his white horse. Just the man, a fortuitous chance. Robert was always easy to identify because his horse was white, like his hat, and an ex-pacer – a rough but swift ride for an ageing, round man. The hamper tied behind the saddle forgotten, Hadley spurred his mare on to a gallop: 'Mr Crupp!'

Robert's words, pounding up and down at derby pace, were punctuated by his mount: 'Had-lee-ee. Fan-ce-ee …' He had a wine-drinker's nose and it drooped a little over his large, tobacco-stained moustache.

Hadley's brown mare cantered hard to keep up. 'I wondered if I could have a word with you, sir.'

'No-ow-ow?' asked Robert.

'It's an important matter.'

Robert leaned back on the reins, the bit dragging his horse's jaw open. Gradually the gelding slowed to a walk.

'I have something to ask, sir. It's right to ask you first, I think.' His heart was pounding and his voice sounded high, so he cleared his throat and said, hoping for a lower register, 'It's an important matter so I've given it thought.'

Robert eyed the steep track that wound to the top of the outcrop.

'Phoeba and I have known each other for fourteen years now,' Hadley began. 'We have similar lives, went to school together, go to the same church—'

'The only one in the district.'

'—and I think we could make a good … partnership.'

Robert looked suspiciously at the eager, sweaty youth. He'd seen more imposing moustaches on the Temperance women.

'I think we should get engaged, sir.'

Robert pushed his straw hat back on his head. 'Holy mackerel,' he said.

'What do you think, sir?'

'Not much. I don't think much of it at all, frankly.' He pointed to the track. 'Ride on.'

Hadley, disappointed, nudged his horse. Mr Crupp followed him in silence. It was the surprise of it, Hadley decided, he was upset at the prospect of losing his elder daughter. He stopped his horse. 'I wouldn't marry her until I'd worked, invested money into Elm Grove, built a new house. I'd travel, work as a classer, breed up my father's sheep stud. And I have an idea for a ram emasculator.'

'Yes,' said Robert doubtfully, 'your marvellous invention.' Over the years he'd seen all the drawings. Robert couldn't imagine Phoeba marrying Hadley. Then again, he couldn't imagine her marrying anyone; she wasn't the usual type. Lilith was a different matter. The sooner she married the better, she was damned expensive to run. At the top of the rocky hill, he stopped his horse again and looked at the tremulous young man. 'Shouldn't you ask her?'

'I'll have to,' shrugged Hadley. He knew what Phoeba would say; Robert was the unpredictable one.

'If you ever put sheep on my land, Pearson, I'll rise up out of my grave and emasculate you with your own invention and put strychnine on your pizzle.'

'Right,' said Hadley feebly. They rode in silence towards the house, and a tiny shaft of doubt pierced Hadley's racing heart. But he dismissed it.

Phoeba saw the horses picking their way down the outcrop track and called to her mother in the cellar.

'Is he bringing a new horse?' she called back.

'No, he's bringing Hadley.'

By the time Hadley had tied his horse to the peppercorn tree by the dam gate Phoeba had a jug of lemon tea and glass cups waiting. Hadley came towards the small, hot weatherboard house, the knees of his new wool trousers bagging and his new boots squeaking. But he was smiling.

'You look as if you're about to melt, Had,' called Lilith, kicking the screen door open.

'Not really,' he said red-faced but cheerful, on their parched patch of lawn with his kitbag and his mother's hamper.

'Hadley again, so soon!' said Maude clattering out.

As he stepped onto the veranda the toe of his boot caught on the step and he lunged. Lilith, Phoeba and Maude said, 'Oh,' and thrust their arms to break his fall, but he caught the arm of the wicker lounge and settled himself on it as if nothing had happened. He dropped his hat on the floorboards, reached into his kitbag, brought out copies of the Melbourne newspapers and handed them to Phoeba.

'Thanks, Hadley, we haven't had *The Age* for weeks,' she

said, passing the social pages to Lilith, the *Ladies Home Journal* to Maude. She left the business section on Robert's chair, with its headline **DROUGHT WORSENS, MILLIONS OF SHEEP PERISH IN QUEENSLAND.**

'Oh,' gasped Lilith, settling on the top step. 'Paul Poiret, who dresses Mrs Asquith, writes that we should "return to our natural form and do away with corsets". Fancy that!'

'Your Aunt Margaret never wore a corset and look where it's got her,' said Robert, picking up his newspaper and settling in his chair. Aunt Margaret was Maude's poverty-stricken spinster sister.

'Your father and I rode over from Overton, where I've just come from a meeting,' said Hadley.

'My word.' Maude nodded meaningfully to Phoeba. 'A meeting.'

Phoeba poured lemon tea and Lilith asked, 'What was it about?'

'A position at Overton.'

'Such a perfect way to start the new year,' said Maude, clapping her hands.

'Well, Had,' chirped Lilith, 'you can't have got the manager's position. Mrs Flynn told us they'd employed a stranger, didn't she, Phoeba?'

The smile slid from Hadley's face. Lilith was pretty with her dark curls and bright eyes but she was bold and she liked spoiling things. She shortened his name to Had and always sat right in the middle of the wicker lounge, taking it all for herself. Phoeba was different. Her eyes were just a little too close together and her chin strong for a girl, but she made the most of her good posture. She was sturdy, sober and direct. You always knew where you stood with Phoeba Crupp, thought Hadley, and, unlike Lilith,

23

she didn't stamp her feet to get her point across. He stood up and moved to the veranda rail, his new boots squeaking.

Robert folded his newspaper. 'Righto then Hadley, thanks for dropping in—'

'I'm not going,' he spluttered.

'Hadley has news, don't you Hadley?' said Phoeba and winked at him.

'Yes,' he said, his chin rising. He placed his left hand, soft from working wool, carefully along the balustrade and looked at Phoeba. Then he cleared his throat and said proudly, 'I have a position wool classing at Overton.'

'Hooraaayyyy,' cried Phoeba, leaping up and throwing her arms around him. His face went red and his glasses tumbled from his nose but he was clearly enjoying the embrace.

She let go of him. 'Hadley, you deserve that job,' she said and poured him a cup of tea.

'A very good start to your career,' said Maude, tugging her boisterous elder daughter's skirt. 'Sit down and behave,' she hissed.

'It's just for the season,' said Hadley, sitting back on the couch. 'I met the new manager—'

'Really? Does he have a wife?' asked Maude.

'You'd think Marius would be the manager,' said Lilith.

'Marius is a dilettante,' mumbled Robert from behind his newspaper whose page read, **WOOL PRICES SLUMP FURTHER**.

'It must have been very distracting for him to lose his wife,' said Maude. 'Such a tragedy.' And they all looked out to the bay and thought about Marius Overton's young wife, dead after twenty-seven hours of labour, the baby gone with her.

'Still,' said Hadley, wanting to get back to his happy news, 'it is the new year tomorrow.'

'Here's to the new year,' said Phoeba, toasting with her tea.

'Hear, hear,' they said.

Then Maude brought the conversation back to marriage.

'A man of Marius's position will find a new wife. Someone will catch him. Marriage is natural, the right thing, especially for women, don't you agree, Hadley?' She flapped her jabot to fan her hot cheeks.

'Yes.'

'So do I,' said Lilith, emphatically.

Robert rustled his newspaper.

'Tell us about your new job,' said Phoeba trying to redirect the conversation again.

Hadley rubbed his knees with his hands: 'There are still sixty thousand to shear even though it's been very dry. They're mostly merinos – Tasmanian stock – Bellevue. A good sheep with a solid frame and the wool's from the Saxon lineage.' He kept rubbing. It was nerves. He'd done that for as long as she could remember.

'And I'll be able to put my wages into Elm Grove,' he said, brightly.

'Yes,' she said.

'My father's sheep have cleaner-than-average, first-class fleeces, you know. I'll shear three inches of fine, bright wool and it'll weigh at least twelve pounds per head, or more. They're beautiful sheep.'

'They are,' said Phoeba. Hadley felt about his sheep the way she felt about Spot. There was a silence then; Hadley seemed to have run out of plans.

'Very well, then,' said Maude at last, and stood up. Then Lilith stood up, then Robert and they all filed into the darkness of the house. Phoeba was left with the warm breeze, her lemon tea and Hadley's description of his meeting with Rudolph Steel – although he didn't mention how brief it was or that it took place in the front hall.

'His first name is Rudolph?'

'It is, but his surname's the worry – Mr *Steal*. A bad name for a banker.'

He launched into a lecture on the economy, the recession, the future of the wool industry and the power of 'white gold' to carry the nation, but Phoeba interrupted, irritated: 'I do read the newspapers.' As if Hadley, of all people, didn't know – right now she wanted to get her chooks to their roost before the sun went down and get cracking with tea so she could finish off *The Age* before bed.

She picked up his bag. The eggs had all broken and strands of yolk dripped from the strings. 'You'd better get going, Hadley. Your mother and Henri will be beside themselves with anticipation.'

Reaching for his kitbag, he walked towards the dam, Phoeba following with his hamper of eggs and butter. Behind them, Maude and Lilith watched from the parlour window, Robert hovering nearby with his hands behind his back and his pipe in his mouth.

At the brown mare Hadley turned to Phoeba, his expression serious.

'My future is set now, Phoeba,' he said.

'It is.' He seemed oddly nervous so she reassured him: 'You'll be the best wool classer they've had.'

'After the season I'll be able to get more work and build the new house at Elm Grove. I can develop my emasculator—'

'Yes,' said Phoeba.

Hadley adjusted his glasses. '—and I can get married and start a family.'

'Married!' She was amazed, thrilled, delighted for him.

His face lit up. 'You're pleased then?'

'Of course,' said Phoeba, picturing a handsome girl with spectacles who liked sheep. Then, suddenly, she wasn't sure how she felt about her childhood friend getting married. After all, she'd saved him once from Mrs Flynn's belligerent rogue gander, charging up to him with Spot at a slow half trot and dragging him off by the back of his coat.

Hadley sank down on one knee and she thought he must be feeling the heat.

She glanced up to the house and saw the parlour curtain move. Inside, Maude reached for a chair; Robert said, 'Damn,' and Lilith said, 'Henrietta and I will be attendants. We should wear white. It's all the rage.'

Phoeba looked at Hadley and his eyes shone up at her. A dread, a feeling like having eaten too much fresh bread and jam, grew large in the pit of her stomach.

'Phoeba, will you be my wife?'

Her immediate impulse was to laugh but Hadley's eyes, burning blue behind his spectacles, stopped her. She turned away and patted the horse. She'd never had any reason to think seriously about marriage for herself. No one had ever entered her world and prompted her to think about it. And, she'd never even had an urge to marry.

'Phoeba, we both want the same things in life.' Hadley started to panic and reached for her hand but she thrust his string basket at him.

'I hate sheep. They rot from the bottom up.'

'Not if you look after them properly!' he said looking truly offended. 'And anyway, you won't have to go anywhere near a sheep if you don't want to.'

27

He took the bag from her and got to his feet, round patches of dust on his knees. The yolk pooled onto his shiny, new boots.

'You must want children, a partner in life? You're a girl, surely …'

It was very strange, Phoeba thought as she watched the sticky yellow mess, to be talking to Hadley about getting married. It seemed … lewd.

'I don't think I ever wanted those things,' she said, struggling to compose her thoughts.

'That's just because you've never given it any thought.'

It wasn't supposed to be like this; he'd thought she'd say yes and now he was floundering. He hadn't thought about what to do if she said no. So he put his hat on. He'd give her time, that's what he'd do. 'Your father said—'

'You didn't!' she yelled, and he stepped back. 'Tell me you didn't ask him! Why, Hadley, why did you ask him? It's got nothing to do with him.'

'Promise me you'll think about it?' he asked, reaching for his horse, wishing he hadn't said anything, wishing he sounded stronger. 'There are lots of reasons to get married,' he suggested. 'It's about building a future …'

She shook her head at him, confused. Her eyes had turned grey and she was frowning.

'Will you at least think about it?' he said.

Phoeba couldn't gather her thoughts at all. And Hadley look-ed so desperate. She put her finger to her chin as if to ponder.

'Don't mock me, Phoeba.'

'I'm sorry,' she said. 'I will think about it.' She hadn't seen him this upset since she pushed him off the swing and broke his arm.

'Promise?'

'I promise.'

Hadley climbed onto his horse and looked down at her. 'You might find, one day, that marriage is the right thing.'

'Happy New Year,' she called feebly, watching him ride away. 'Blast,' she said. She felt irritated, sad and bothered. Nothing would be the same now; Hadley had always been like a brother, and of course she didn't want to hurt him. But she knew he would go home now to sit on his thin, boy's bed in its tiny room of books and plans and dreams. He would sit with his forehead in his hands and tears running down his lovely straight nose. Henrietta would be cross with her and when her mother found out she'd refused a proposal she'd be furious.

Spot whickered long and low from his paddock and she crossed the dry grass to him and rubbed his muzzle, the hot breath from his nose on her hand. Up on the outcrop, smoke wafted down from a swaggie's campfire. Phoeba turned back to the house, hearing three sets of feet rumble hastily up the hall towards the kitchen as she approached.

Hadley slowed his mare to a walk as soon as he was beyond the signpost, then he halted her and sat looking ahead to Elm Grove. Had he ruined everything? He knew Phoeba would think so. No, they would always be friends. And Phoeba would think about it and see sense. He screwed his face in agony. Such a fool. Fool, fool, fool. Obviously it was too sudden for her. Of course she wasn't expecting it; he'd never said anything, never even tried to be affectionate or tender. He should have brought flowers. Presents. He should have given her a book for her birthday last week. He would talk to Henrietta. No, he mustn't tell Henrietta. She might feel she had to take sides. He would keep it all close to his chest.

29

Maude was humming, 'I Hear Wedding Bells' as she set the table while Robert sat in the spot at the end of the table that caught the breeze between the front and back door and watched her slice cold meat and arrange pickle jars. Lilith asked her mother to order a yard of plain linen so she could make serviettes for trousseau boxes.

Phoeba ignored them all.

Finally, Maude asked breezily, 'Did Hadley bring any other news we haven't heard—'

'No!' said Phoeba, and stood up and went to bed.

The heat throbbed through the weatherboard, the crickets were in full voice. Phoeba opened *Far From the Madding Crowd*. Gabriel had just proposed to Bathsheba and she had refused, telling him he should marry someone with money who could stock his farm. Clearly, thought Phoeba, it was an omen.

It wasn't long before Lilith came in, undressed, chucked her clothes into the corner and flopped onto her bed. She tucked her mosquito net in and fanned herself with *Madame Weigel's Journal of Fashion*: 'What were you and Hadley talking about today?'

Phoeba ignored her. She'd been trying to ignore Lilith since she was born.

'I said, what were you—'

'Sheep.' She closed her book and turned down the lamp.

'Do you like Hadley?'

'How can anyone not like Hadley? He's lovely.' And Phoeba pulled the sheet up over her head.

'He's a dill,' said Robert untying Maude's corset. 'Fancy wanting to go off and start a sheep career in a drought, with strikers everywhere, squatters going bust left right and centre.' He loosened the strings and Maude's upper body sagged, her breasts pulling down so that her shoulder bones seemed to rise and push up against her skin. She dragged her rouleaux curl from her crown and placed it on the dressing table where it lay like a sleeping rodent.

'There are still sheep to be shorn, Robert, money to be earned for a wife and for my grandchildren. He's sincere and he's trying,' replied Maude.

'Trying indeed.' Robert sat gingerly on the edge of the bed as Maude removed her drawers, lifted them with her toe and dropped them into the basket. 'He can try all he likes but I doubt she'll take him on – and I don't want a son-in-law who thinks my vines are a waste of good sheep country.'

'Most people think your vines are a waste of good sheep country, Robert, including me. At least sheep eat the grass down.' She gestured at the door with her potty. 'Now off you go to the shed.'

'Come on Maudie, old thing, you can't throw me out just because Spot behaved badly. Mosquitoes eat me alive out there—'

'They could bother the cart horse instead, if we had one.'

Robert sighed, heading forlornly to the shed where he lay on a hard, gritty bed scratching at the mites which crawled into his armpits, slapping at the insects which flew into his ears.

In the dark, Lilith was still talking.

'You and Hadley are so alike, Phoeba. You're both old-fashioned and you like animals.'

How could they not be alike? They were formed next door to each other. Henrietta, Hadley and Phoeba interpreted the world entirely from a Bay View perspective. From the time Phoeba was ten they had fished, swam, played and gone to school together. They had shared responsibility for a blue tongue lizard, catching insects to feed it, taking it swimming in summer to cool it and warming it in the slow oven in winter until Henrietta left it too long and cooked it. For her eleventh birthday, Henrietta and Hadley had given her a red-back spider, which ran up the twig to the top of its jar for a live fly until she found it on its back, curled like a tomato stem, one day. She still had it, somewhere.

And Maude had spent many evenings teaching all four youngsters to dance, each of the girls taking a turn with Hadley. Phoeba **had never** thought about marrying Hadley, although it seemed that's what people did. They grew up and married someone suitable when it was time. Then they had babies, worked hard and made do, argued, and died.

Suddenly, Phoeba Crupp felt very tired.

The first wedding cake

Monday, January 1, 1894

Phoeba rose through the layers of slumber to hear bird-song in the still morning. It may have been New Year, but it was Monday – washing day. She would get up, milk the goat, light the copper, have breakfast and get to the wash-house before Lilith woke. After the wash she would ride to see Henrietta. Then she remembered: Hadley had proposed and now nothing could ever be the same again. She had hurt him and *the refusal* would always be there, lurking, like a thieving boy behind a hedge. She kicked back the sheet and hurried out, away from it.

It was a scorcher of a day and, and after a morning with boiling sheets, Phoeba sat on the veranda step to take advantage of the breeze from under the house. She removed her stockings, draped them over her boots, unfastened the buttons of her high-necked blouse and yanked her skirt up so high that the white work and ruffles of her drawers showed. Out on the bay a cargo boat with three steam stacks lurched out to sea. She put the looking glass to her eye and studied the flags: Dutch.

A few rabbits were grazing on the fine grass at the dam's edge and Spot stared at her, his bright eyes pleading in his long, black head. 'It's too hot for a ride,' she called, shaking her own head to rid her mind of Hadley's hurt face. Spot strolled back to the shady trees and gazed at the bay.

Phoeba focused the looking glass on the noon train, a line of square black boxes burning along the rail's thin line, slowing at the siding. Two swaggies tumbled from the guard's van, and scrambled off towards the bay. The mailman leaned out, flinging a mailbag onto the siding. As the train gathered speed again, he disappeared into his van then a square wad of newspapers flew out the door, knocking Freckle who fluttered off the siding into the scrub.

Good, thought Phoeba, papers to read.

While she waited for Freckle, she thought about marriage, as she had promised, but nothing came – apart from the dull brown shape of Freckle on his roan cob moving up Mount Hope Lane. Soon he rode through the gate past Spot and his ankle-height entourage – the ducks, the rooster – and eased up to the front step. Summer's sun ripened Freckle's freckles and they had massed together in one big smear that bridged his nose from cheek to cheek. He sat low in a huge saddle, his bare feet resting loosely in the stirrup irons. A damp cloth sack containing skinned and gutted rabbits hung from the saddle. Mrs Flynn's only child, Freckle was famous for turning up to school with crayfish sandwiches for lunch, much to the envy of everyone. Not that he attended anymore – he said he'd learned the alphabet so knew what the telegraph machine was spelling out. He handed Phoeba the *Geelong Advertiser* and a large hatbox addressed to Robert.

'Would you like a drink, Freckle?'

'I'll get tea and a biscuit at Overton,' he boasted. His horse sniffed the wiry, blanched petunias at the base of the front steps, lifting its head abruptly when Maude came out onto the veranda.

'Keep your animal away from my garden,' said Maude.

'Call that a garden?'

'We won't have a rabbit this week since we have lamb from Overton, but I was expecting a peach parer from Lassetters,' she said, frowning at the hatbox.

'If it had come I'd have brought it, wouldn't I?' said Freckle.

'Thank you. You can go now.'

'No, I can't.'

'Why not?'

'Your old man gives me a penny for bringing the newspapers from the siding.'

'He's not here.'

'His newspapers are.'

'Well I haven't got any money. Now off you go.'

The mailboy regarded Maude levelly: 'Your sister's crook. I hope she dies.' And he handed a post office telegraph to Phoeba and trotted away.

'Thanks,' called Phoeba.

Aunt Margaret, wisely, had written only three words for Freckle to interpret. 'Unwell. Arriving tomorrow.'

'Lovely,' said Phoeba. She would have good company for a few days.

Aunt Margaret came to Mount Hope when she was broke, lonely or starving. She lived in Geelong in the dank, shadowy house she and Maude had been raised in. The weatherboards slanted and the front veranda undulated, but Aunt Margaret spent her days at her easel in the sunny conservatory, a cracked and rusty construction now held together by blackberry bushes. She survived on handouts from Robert and a very, very small allowance from a fund her parents had started – before their tragic and unexpected deaths – as dowries for their two daughters. Every once in a while she sold an oil painting and for a long time she had taken in lodgers, but no one suitable wanted the room anymore. Maude often suggested she seek a position as a companion to someone rich, but Margaret said snappily that she'd rather catch hydatids.

'You could have at least buttoned your blouse,' said Maude, taking a newspaper from Phoeba.

'It's only Freckle.'

They both settled with their pages: STREETON'S PAINTING, THE RAILWAY STATION, REDFERN, EN-JOYS GREAT SUCCESS.

Robert arrived from the vineyard. 'My new hat,' he said, opening the box.

'There's nothing wrong with the one you've got on,' said Maude.

'I could have been blinded,' said Robert, pointing to a red scar on top of his head where a swooping magpie had torn the skin in the spring.

'If you had we would have moved straight back to Geelong and put you in a home,' spat Maude.

'I would have got you out, Dad,' said Phoeba. Her mother was always saying cruel things to her father.

Robert settled his new hat onto his head. It was a pith hat and looked very silly.

'Farmers don't wear pith hats, Robert,' said Maude.

'I am not a farmer,' said Robert. 'I am a vigneron.'

Maude put her hand to her temple. 'You are the cause of my headaches, Robert.' She drifted inside taking the social pages with her.

'I don't know what I did to deserve my lot in life,' he sighed, settling in his chair.

Yes, thought Phoeba, better keep Hadley as a friend. She didn't want to end up like her mother. She put her boots on and liberated Spot so he could follow her around the vines. At the top of the first one she carefully pulled the thin, rubbery leaves aside and there, at the end of a spindly stem, were the tiny clusters of green pellets, like baby broccoli at the end of pale, green peduncles. Beautiful, evenly spaced and laddering all the way to the end of the stem.

'Look, Spot, grapes!'

The pellets would be fat berries in a few weeks and then slowly they'd develop a bloom, a powdery coat to keep the water inside and transform them into sacks of dull juicy jelly. Every other farmer might look expectantly and eagerly to the skies to welcome the Autumn rain clouds, but the Crupps implored Pomona, Roman Goddess of fruit, to banish those fluffy pillows and summon them more warm, dry skies. No wonder the vineyard wasn't popular.

Grapes were easier to think about than Hadley.

Tuesday, January 2, 1894

Hadley was Phoeba's first thought on Tuesday morning when she woke. She nudged him gently from her mind and went out into the dry air, shooing birds from the vines just after sunrise. Later, eating breakfast with her father, they heard a floorboard groan under a heavy weight and Maude came down the passage holding her potty carefully in both hands. Robert smiled at his wife but she didn't take her eyes off the pot. Her grey-streaked hair was tied in loose, messy twists that hung down over her bosoms, and her cheeks were flushed. 'I still have a bit of a head,' she said, on the way to the outhouse. It was the one place outside Maude *had* to go. As much as she could, she stayed indoors.

'I'll make some fresh tea,' said Phoeba moving the kettle to the hotplate. The headaches had only started lately, but this one wasn't going to stop Maude settling at the kitchen table with Lilith, a box of dressmaking patterns and a stack of fashion magazines.

'I quite like a feathered aigrette on my bodice although they say the tailored effect is fashionable now in Europe,' said Lilith.

'And what's new in hats and veils?' asked her mother.

Phoeba headed to the orchard for some peace, but as she picked plums Hadley's hurt face came back to her. There was nothing she could do about it, she decided. Time would have to heal.

Sitting in the grass stoning the plums, she made a list in her head of alternative occupations: nurse, teacher, factory seamstress, librarian or governess. The options didn't seem too bad. But there was a depression, thousands of people were unemployed, she knew, and Bay View was a long way from anywhere.

After lunch she helped her father harness Rocket ready for the sulky.

'I hope he doesn't kill us. Why didn't you borrow a horse from Overton?'

'You're starting to sound like your mother,' said Robert looping the strap of his pith helmet under his chin.

'And you look as if you're about to go off shooting elephants.'

38

'Bloody women,' said Robert. 'Thank God for Rocket.'

Phoeba was smoothing her worn riding gloves over her rough hands when Lilith appeared dressed in her best knife-pleated skirt and jacket. Maude's finest bar brooch was pinned to her lapel and she wore her most sumptuous hat.

'Aren't you hot?' asked Phoeba, while Robert stared at the feathers waving about on top of his daughter's head: 'Ostriches will be cold this winter,' he mused.

'You never know,' said Lilith. 'We might meet someone.'

'Prince Edward is often at Mrs Flynn's shop,' muttered Phoeba.

As they approached the gate, Spot spread his front legs wide and dropped his big black head to the ground, sulkily. His nostrils were crusted with dust and his breath cleared two bare circles in the dirt. The rooster and duck stood supportively by his side.

'It's your own fault,' called Phoeba, but she made a mental note to give him an apple when she got back. She looked down to Bay View.

Fortunately, there was only one other horse in sight and it was two miles away, tied up outside Flynn's shop: it would have been impossible to stop Rocket at the intersection if there was converging traffic. Galloping pace was his only speed. Phoeba looped the reins between her fingers, squeezed the leather straps tightly and pulled back, restraining the white horse as he danced through the gate.

Lilith held her hat, Phoeba said gee-up and Rocket sprang, pacing all the way down Mount Hope Lane. Grazing rabbits scattered as they sped by and the intersection and the dam went by in a blur as they raced towards Bay View. Phoeba saw a man stride out of Flynn's to the tethered horse. She'd seen neither the horse nor the rider before.

'Oh no,' she said under her breath. 'Please let him stay put.'

The man got on his horse and saw Rocket racing towards the siding and, just as Phoeba feared, spurred his horse and rode to meet them. He was broad-shouldered and dark-haired and he turned his horse to ride alongside Rocket as he met up with them.

'I've got him,' he called to Phoeba and reached for Rocket's cheek piece.

'He'll stop at the line,' called Phoeba, but the stranger ignored her, tugging at Rocket's bridle.

Rocket charged on, the finish line in his sights, and they raced together, the wind on their faces, the harnesses creaking and tinkling and the horses panting.

Phoeba's grip on the reins was firm; she was in control although her arms were stretched. The rim of her straw hat was pushed back by the wind and the stranger noticed a confident, fearless glint in her eye and a firmly set jaw. Beside her, a fancily dressed lass held tightly to her hat and looked worried.

Rocket stopped dead, his way blocked by the siding, and the rider let him go. He circled on his horse, which was unusually thickset and stocky. 'Does he always race like that?'

'Yes,' said Lilith, looking vulnerable and helpless.

The stranger was good-looking, Phoeba noticed, in an unusual way. Not so much handsome as strong. It went through her mind that she should have worn her blue dress, or perhaps thought to borrow Maude's bar brooch before Lilith did.

'Our horse used to be a pacer,' she said.

'A very fast one.'

The man smiled and all Phoeba could do was smile back; she could think of nothing to say. His eyes were brown, his moustache shiny and the wax at its ends clean, not dulled like old string or clogged with bits of food. He got off his horse, took the reins from Phoeba and looped them through the wheel. Then he helped them down from the sulky.

'We're getting a new horse,' said Lilith, 'from Overton.'

'Indeed?' said the stranger.

'But thank you,' Phoeba stammered, and the man tipped his hat and rode away.

'Do you thinks that's the new manager, Phoeba?' asked Lilith.

'Possibly. Hadley says the new manager's name is Mr Steel,' she replied, a little breathless.

'I wonder if he's married,' said Lilith.

The two girls stood in Flynn's shop, their full skirts filling the room and their hems skimming the worn, flour-dusted floor. The shop smelled of dead mice and rancid butter and Lilith stood uncomfortably in the middle with her elbows pressed to her side, staying small to stop any part of her clothing from touching anything. She tried to summon her pleasant expression but she just looked as if she had a headache.

'Is there a parcel for us?' she asked, sweetly.

'Nup,' said Mrs Flynn, and smiled. Mrs Flynn was Irish and cheerful, and she controlled the mail, dry goods and the newspapers with a vengeful hold.

'It's a peach parer,' said Lilith, 'but Mother's hoping it'll do apples as well.' She lifted her hem clear of the chalky floor.

Mrs Flynn dumped Robert's papers on the counter: COLONIES GRIPPED BY DEPRESSION AS LONDON BANKS COLLAPSE, CRISIS PLUNGES PASTORALISTS INTO RUIN.

'Was that the new manager at Overton?' asked Lilith and Phoeba stepped closer to the counter to listen.

41

'That's him,' said Mrs Flynn, primping the curls at the back of her hair. 'Handsome chap for a foreigner, if you arst me.'

Mrs Flynn leaned on the counter so her breasts rested on her sun-dried forearms. She had two teeth – the front two – and they were straight and brilliant white. And although she pinned her hair up, fat, red springs always fell and rolled together over her bosom. Behind her the dusty shelves held very few items – a tin of Cadbury's Chocolate, boxes of dried fruits and nuts, dusty tins of biscuits, a few packets of tobacco, some nails, boot polish, a roll of wire, a lampshade, wicks, candles and a good stock of Rawleighs' Liniments. The walls were covered with paintings – Aunt Margaret always left a few when she visited, mainly vases of flowers, seascapes or faded landscapes. Mrs Flynn had hung *For Sail* tags from them that turned slowly in the musty air.

'Widow Pearson's got a package,' said Mrs Flynn. 'It could be a new corset. You know them corsets are killing her, slowly. Lack of blood to the head. That's why her hair falls out and she has to wear postiches.'

Lilith handed over a list and Mrs Flynn shovelled dried currants and sultanas, mixed peel, glacé cherries and almonds onto the same scales she used for nails, birdseed and butter. 'Bit late for Christmas, isn't it?'

'It's for the ploughing match,' said Lilith, quickly.

Phoeba looked up from her paper. 'Good grief. A plum cake.' Her mother was making a wedding cake. She would have to put a stop to this.

Freckle pushed aside the curtain that separated the gloomy residence from the shop and dragged a heavy mailbag through. At the front step he stopped, lowered it gently to the ground and then struggled with it towards the siding.

'I'll take that bag if you like, Freckle,' said Phoeba.

'I can manage.' But his brow creased with effort and he waited with them, a small boy with a big bag between two triangular girls, wide shoulders with bulging leg-of-mutton arms and tent skirts.

'We could do with a shelter on this siding,' said Lilith, holding her hat, like an island on her head.

'Wear a bigger hat.' Freckle rubbed his nose on his sleeve.

'She'd fold under the weight of it,' laughed Phoeba as the train rolled closer, like a burning house coming at them. It chuffed and thudded, the coaches rolling by in a cloud of smoke and steam. Passengers – workers, men in suits, mothers and children – peered out at the bay.

The mail van squealed to a stop in front of them and an old emaciated man with a crooked back leaned out and took the bag from Freckle, wincing as he swung its weight inside. Gleefully then, he raised the replacement mailbag and as Freckle reached for it he tossed it high into the air. It caught in the frame of the windmill above the stockyard and stayed there, draped over the crossbeam like a decaying possum. Then he slammed his door while Freckle pounded with his fist and yelled, 'You just wait, you dried up old cowpat.'

'Really!' huffed Lilith.

'He started it,' said Freckle. 'Chucking mailbags into the scrub and knocking me for a six with newspapers.'

A door in the middle of the nearest passenger carriage flew open, a carpetbag landed on the siding and out popped Aunt Margaret. Reed thin, she had facial hair on her upper lip and chin, which was why Robert had named his goat Maggie. As usual, Aunt Margaret was covered carefully by gloves and the dustcoat that her mother had purchased in 1824: she used this outfit to hide her paint-spotted clothes and hands.

'Yoo-hoo,' she said as if they mightn't have noticed her. A passenger handed her a newspaper-wrapped painting through the window.

'Good of you to dress up for me, Lilith,' she said, and gave her a paint box to carry.

'So good to see you,' said Phoeba and kissed her aunt's thin cheek. 'How are you feeling?'

'General malaise,' she said happily. 'But I'm better now.'

In the sulky, the passengers plunged one hand deep into their hats' decorations and with their other held fast to the armrests. Phoeba clicked her tongue, Rocket sprang from a standing start and they shot towards home.

A mile down the railway track the thin, bent mailman stood in front of his wall of boxes, feet apart, rolling with the rocking carriage. He up-ended the Bay View Siding mailbag over his sorting desk and a great chunk of wood fell out. It was a huntsman's nest that Freckle had found, and a hundred brown furry spiders trickled all over the desk and floor like spilled beads.

Maude's tea and scones drew the women to the kitchen table, where Aunt Margaret presented Phoeba with a package. 'Happy birthday for last week.'

'I remember the day you were born, Phoeba, as if it was yesterday,' her aunt went on ignoring Lilith. Phoeba unwrapped the parcel, untying the string and unfolding the paper.

'Did you sell a painting?' asked Maude, wondering where she got the money.

'I have been saving,' said Aunt Margaret.

'I'll be nineteen in June,' said Lilith, hopefully.

'It's perfect,' said Phoeba, holding the new blouse against

her cheek. It was white lawn with a bishop's collar and a pretty muslin insert down the front that matched the cuffs on its full-length sleeves. It smelled like the hosiery and lace department of a city shop. 'I'll wear it to the harvest dance,' said Phoeba – it was too fancy for the ploughing match. She folded it very neatly and carefully rewrapped it.

'You'll look very special for Hadley,' said Lilith, sarcastically. 'You know, Aunt Margaret, Hadley asked her to marry him and we think she said no!'

'Pipe down, Lilith,' sang her mother. 'There's plenty of time yet.'

'Well, it's not as if the area is rich with suitors.'

Phoeba had an overwhelming desire to stab her little sister but instead she said simply, 'Lilith's jealous because I got a gift.' She would deal with letting her mother down – and put a stop to the wedding cake – later.

'Now listen carefully,' said Aunt Margaret, 'I have news.' She threw two pamphlets onto the kitchen table; 'I have found the perfect solution for my poverty. I will sell the house and move to an artists' commune!'

Anticipating the reaction, Phoeba reached for her mother, who gulped her tea, her eyes watering as the hot fluid burned her throat. 'A what?'

Lilith was frozen, her teacup poised. 'You're not serious?'

'It's a very reasonable set-up actually,' continued Aunt Margaret. 'You pay a deposit and the dividends are invested—'

'In what?' asked Phoeba, now slightly alarmed herself. Banks were crashing at the rate of one a week. People were desperately trying to offload huge wads of pound notes for gold. There were strikes in every city and droughts and floods all over the country.

Aunt Margaret flapped her arms defiantly as if she was beating off small enemies, 'My favorite brother-in-law, Robert, can see to all that. There are dividends, from somewhere, and they pay for upkeep of the property!' Her eyes were gleaming and she was getting into her stride. 'I have to cook and—'

'You have never cooked a thing in your life!' cried Maude.

'—and I can stay until I die, unless I go mad, of course, and go to an asylum.'

Apart from the possibility of an asylum, thought Phoeba, it was a brilliant idea. Her aunt would paint side by side with other artists at their easels under gum trees resting with bright pallets on their forearms. There would be bohemians sharing picnic lunches with lyrebirds wandering peacefully on a dilapidated mansion lawn.

'Is it at Heidelberg?' she asked.

'Not the Impressionists,' said her aunt as if she was saying Leprosy. 'Realists and naturalists—'

'Lord save you, Margaret!' screamed Maude fanning her reddening face. 'A naturalist camp is no place for a respectable woman!'

'It is communal living, Maude. I will not be cavorting naked with nature,' explained Aunt Margaret, soothingly. 'The place is called Esperance and it's in Fairfield, by the river!'

'You have lost your senses,' sniffed Lilith.

'I am too old to go on starving, freezing in winter and frying in summer.' She shoved a second scone into her mouth defiantly leaving flour on her moustache.

'I think it's a good idea,' declared Phoeba.

Her mother regarded her as she would a traitor and snarled, 'Yes, but you would Phoeba.' She turned her attention to jam making.

Robert arrived and sat in the corner, his newspaper folded in his lap: **CRAZED SUFFRAGETTES STORM WELFARE OFFICE**. Aunt Margaret continued on about her potential new life. She had made an appointment to see the place the following Monday and Phoeba made a list of things she should make note of – amenities? And was there hot water? And what sort of food? And what if she decided she wanted to move out? Robert's only contribution was to tell her not to sign anything.

Finally Maude plonked down at the kitchen table and declared, 'I won't sell my parents' home so you can live like a … trull.'

'Mother!' gasped Phoeba.

'How dare you!' cried Aunt Margaret. 'After all, I'm not the one in this family who traded herself for creature comforts.'

Robert calmly put on his pith helmet, gathered up the newspapers and went to his cellar.

'It's her life,' said Phoeba. 'She should be able to do as she pleases.'

'You wouldn't like it if we sold your home!' cried her mother.

'But,' said Phoeba, 'isn't home here with us now?'

'It isn't right,' replied Maude.

'It might be right for Aunt Margaret,' said Phoeba.

'And anyway,' said Margaret, 'I can always burn the house down and sell the land. So you may as well sign.'

'We'll have nowhere to stay in Geelong,' moaned Lilith.

'Lilith Crupp!' said Aunt Margaret, slapping the table, 'the only time you ever stayed with me you told tales. You told your mother my house was a mess and that I only fed you sandwiches.'

'It was neglect,' said Maude.

'I stuck the letter you wrote me to the front door as a warning

47

to any other visitors.'

'I suppose you'll keep all the proceeds for yourself,' said Lilith.

'Mother already has a home, an income and a family,' said Phoeba, and dropped a teaspoon of boiling liquid plums onto a saucer.

'I don't care about the money,' wept Maude, 'but it's the only thing we have left of Mother and Dad.'

'Rubbish, Maude, you have the crockery set, the furniture—'

'Actually,' said Maude, suddenly lucid, 'I would like Mother's sewing machine so that way the girls can at least sew clothes for themselves since no one will marry relatives of a naturalist.'

'I hate sewing,' mumbled Phoeba, tilting the saucer.

Lilith said that Aunt Margaret simply should have married.

'And she could have married Archibald Treadery,' added Maude, 'but she rebuffed him, poor chap.' She fanned her red throat furiously with a pamphlet.

'I didn't love him.'

'Nonsense, he was a bank manager.'

'You can have the shed when Phoeba gets married,' offered Lilith.

'I'd eat cab-horse stew before I'd move to this wilderness.'

'You might have to,' said Phoeba, watching the skin crinkle on the cooling dob of stewed plums. 'The jam is cooked.'

Aunt Margaret drank too much of Robert's wine at tea and at bedtime she stripped off, flung her clothes into the corner and crawled under the mosquito net in her drawers and chemise. She looked over at the book Phoeba was reading. 'You won't like the ending of that story.'

'Why not?'

'Bathsheba abandons her self-reliance and marries for love; that marriage ends badly so she takes on the worthy character – the reliable sturdy one – presumably to be content for ever after.'

'Would you have married the bank manager if you'd loved him?'

'Oh yes. If I'd even liked him – but he was truly awful. I'm perfectly happy unloved and free to do as I please.'

'Providing you can afford it.'

Margaret sighed. 'People assume there's something wrong with spinsters, that we're missing out. But how can you miss something you never had?' She took a small, silver flask from her purse and drank, wiping her mouth with the back of her hand and checking the net around her for mosquitoes. 'In these modern times girls don't have to marry,' she said.

Aunt Margaret was right, Phoeba supposed, but Aunt Margaret's freedom to do as she pleased depended on her being able to join the family at Mount Hope at the slightest excuse. Phoeba thought of Hadley's expectant eyes, of Hadley rubbing his forehead when things looked complicated, uncertain … when someone said no.

'Anyway,' said Aunt Margaret, 'Lilith will snare a husband, there's nothing more certain. She'd sell her mother for sixpence if it meant she could have a new hat. Remember the dolly?'

Who could forget the dolly? Little Fanny, Aunt Margaret's neighbour, who used to play with Lilith and Phoeba when they visited, was sent to the corner shop for milk one day. She never came back. Gypsies, they said, or blackfellas. But when Lilith heard Fanny had gone all she did was race next door to ask if she could have Fanny's black doll.

'She has her eye on Marius Overton,' said Phoeba, an image

49

of the handsome manager at Overton, rather than its owner, flashing through her mind.

'Marius Overton, my, my,' said Margaret raising her flask. 'I bet you sixpence she gets him.'

'Either him or the new manager,' said Phoeba. 'What happened to your bank manager, Aunt?'

'He died,' said Margaret. 'Diphtheria. If I didn't die in childbirth I would have been a widow by now, possibly with a nice stipend.'

Wednesday, January 3, 1894

Phoeba rose extra early the next morning to enjoy the solitude while she could. She mixed her bread dough, rolled and kneaded it and then dropped it into tins and left the loaves to rise. She was turning her attention to the growling kettle when her father came walking down from the outcrop with his looking glass in his hand. In the kitchen, he cut a slice of bread and threw it onto the stove, then scraped dripping from the jug and spread it evenly on the warming bread, watching the flecked fat melt into the dough. He cleared his throat to speak: they never spoke in the mornings.

'Now, Phoeba, what about this fiancé of yours? Of course, your mother and I want you to be happy—'

'Good,' she cut across him, 'then I'll do what ever is going to make me happiest.' Robert said nothing and the subject was dropped. It was Wednesday, either Henrietta or Hadley would call in on their way from Overton with the hamper. Phoeba wondered if it would be Hadley.

'I think I'll take Spot for a ride today,' she said. She wanted to see Henrietta but dreaded it at the same time. Did she know? Would they all still be friends?

'Marius Overton is delivering the new horse at lunchtime,' said Robert.

'Marius Overton is coming here?'

'Yes.' He picked up his warm bread and dripping and said, 'now don't make a fuss,' but Phoeba had gone and the wake of her fleeing nightie lifted the edges of the curtains and even shifted the three remaining strands of hair Robert scraped across his shiny forehead.

Phoeba knew what must happen. Marius Overton must stay for lunch. Phoeba burst into her mother's room and prodded the mound under the cotton counterpane.

'Mother, get up.'

Her mother didn't move.

'Marius Overton is on his way with a new horse.'

The counterpane rippled and Maude's plump legs fell over the edge of the bed as her arm shot straight up in the air. 'Hand me my corset.'

Beside her, Lilith rolled over and raised her tousled head. 'I'll need to borrow your blouse, Phoeba.'

'You don't need my blouse, Lilith. Just bat your lashes.' And she headed in to her own room. 'Upsy-daisy.'

'You know I have not been blessed with a morning temperament,' said Aunt Margaret, wriggling deeper into the mattress.

'If you stopped anointing yourself with sherry you'd be blessed enough to paint sunrises. Now come Aunt, the squat-tocracy is visiting – the one Lilith's got her eye on. We need to be at our best if we want to unload her.' If she could just make that happen, thought Phoeba, the pressure would be off and life would be perfect.

Lilith ran into the room, grabbed Phoeba's new blouse from the wardrobe and ran out calling, 'The wands, Phoeba, put them on!'

Margaret pushed back the bed sheet. 'I didn't know Lilith could run.'

Robert milked the goat, left the bucket in the cool under the tank-stand, chopped some wood, liberated the chooks and then sat on the veranda with his newspaper and looking glass while the house rumbled with thrupping skirts, yelled instructions – 'Phoeba. We cannot serve rabbit!' – and doors snapping open and slamming.

He watched a group of swaggies jump down from the livestock trucks on the nine o'clocker and straggle up the lane towards him, and he nodded to the dusty men as they passed though his yard humping their swags. Shearers. They didn't ask for bread or tea and they were neater than itinerant workers, but not as neat as the fallen city men, the depression victims, the dispossessed bankers and factory workers, the shopkeepers and merchants. At least they would eat a few rabbits.

Maude called, ready for her final armouring, and Robert took himself inside to the bedroom where she waited, her large, cotton bottom hovering in front of the mirror and her whalebone corset in place. He took the laces, Maude placed her forearm under her very long, round breasts, lifted them and positioned a curved horsehair bustpad underneath. 'Right,' she inhaled. Robert pulled, pulled again and then tied the laces firmly. His wife turned to him, her high cleavage forced up from the satin and bone contraption like pink porridge.

'You must ask Marius Overton to stay for lunch,' she said.

'Must I? You only want to boast to old pigwidgeon Pearson.' But he held her long, chocolate brown serge frock patiently while Maude dived under the hem and manoeuvred it down over her now firm form.

'The ploughing match is on Saturday and the dance is coming up,' she said, forcing her arms into the dress's narrow forearms. 'We don't want wallflowers.'

'Certainly not,' said Robert, thinking of the available men in the district – dozens of farmers, at least sixty shearers and rouseabouts at Overton, not to mention stockmen and yardmen, swaggies and sundowners, boundary riders and city guests.

Maude dragged the last yards of gathered cloth down over her hips and twisted them about until they sat neatly where her waist had once been. She turned again and Robert adjusted his eyeglasses to button her frock at the back. But his fingers were too coarse to manage the small, cloth-covered buttons.

'Get Phoeba to do this,' he said at last. 'I'm too old.'

She bustled out, a rustling cloud of brown ruches and tucks, calling back to him, 'and clear out the dining room.'

Phoeba pulled her sister's corset strings. Lilith's face went red and the veins in her neck stood out. She leaned her torso sideways, reaching over her hip to her knee.

'One more,' she gasped.

'Lilith, you'll faint into your salad.'

'One more!'

The one thing Phoeba knew was that the day would only go well for everyone if Lilith was happy – she pulled once more.

By eleven she had a roast cooling in the meat safe and the smell of her hot damper was taunting the itinerants all the way up on the outcrop. She took creamy goat's cheese and a jar of blackberry jam from the cellar and went to raid the vegetable patch, where she came across Aunt Margaret propped against the mesh fence with sketchpad and pencil, studying a caterpillar on a lettuce leaf.

'Are you coming to lunch?' asked Phoeba, noting her aunt's grubby skirt and fingers.

'I'm progressing from landscapes,' said Margaret. 'I'm tackling nature.'

'Well don't let nature tackle my lettuces. Close the gate when you leave or we'll be eating fat fricassee rabbit with no carrots for the pot.'

Everyone was ready for Marius Overton by noon. Hopefully, thought Phoeba unkindly, Aunt Margaret would forget.

He rode down from the outcrop an hour later than expected on a tall gold and brown Arab. It was a majestic, lively horse with a sweet, dished face and flared nostrils. Trailing it, pulling against its lead, was the new horse; a short, ordinary hack – grey, a gelding. In the dam paddock Spot lowered his ears and walked to the far fence were he stood, dejected, with his nose against a tree trunk.

Phoeba put the carrots onto the hottest part of the stove, tied a thin black ribbon around her trim clerical collar, removed her apron and shepherded her mother and Lilith – both resembling rainbow lorikeets – to the backyard where they gathered around the new horse. Robert patted the grey horse's cheek: it swung its head away. He ran his hand down its shoulder to its thigh and hock, lifted a rear hoof. 'Ah ha, something's up.'

The horse wrenched its hoof free. Marius lifted it and dislodged a dirt clod with his penknife.

'Hello,' said Lilith in her sweetest voice, and swung her shoulders like a schoolgirl.

'Hello,' he said, warmly. He was pretty, rather than handsome, Phoeba decided. His face was brown but not wind-worn; his smart white moleskins were clean, almost new, and his riding coat was black linen. He tipped his boater – a city hat – to Maude and to Phoeba. 'Ladies.'

Lilith just stared at him, dumbstruck. Phoeba asked what the horse's name was.

'Centaur.'

'What does that mean?' asked Lilith, full of wonder.

'In Greek mythology, it's a wild creature with the head, arms and torso of a man joined to the body of a horse,' Marius explained, his gaze lingering on Lilith.

'How clever,' she said, and fluttered her eyelashes.

'How are your sheep this year, Mr Overton?' asked Maude in her most interested tone.

'Call me Marius,' he said, with another tip of his hat, 'and my sheep are thin and in need of a haircut.'

Maude laughed a little too forcefully and Lilith nodded sombrely. 'That's because it's been dry.'

'My word it has,' said Marius, nodding with approval of her understanding.

'Which is very good for Dad's grapes,' Lilith responded, seizing the opportunity to sound knowledgeable herself. 'Dad's got a bottle of last year's vintage especially for you to try.'

'I have?' Robert was confused.

'His wine is marvellous,' said Maude, who never drank it. 'You must stay for lunch.' She clasped her hands, her arms framing her large, lacy bosom and glared at Robert to support the invitation.

'You can show him your vines, Dad,' said Phoeba, helpfully.

Marius jumped at the chance. It would be nice to look around the place again, he said, as he'd hardly been there since his father sold it to the Crupps fourteen years ago and, he confessed, he was intrigued by the grapes.

'Last year we had the dust storm, of course, ruined half the vines,' Robert began, as he led the visitor away. 'The year before there was an early frost and of course, the birds ...'

Phoeba congratulated herself on how well everything was going and the three women hurried back to the kitchen.

The dining room, on the north side of the house, was hot and overflowing. Maude had brought everything – including her mother's sideboard and lounge suite, velvet drapes and matching ottomans – from their large home in Geelong and squeezed it into Mount Hope. On top of which the dining room was usually Robert's study, with his viticulture books and magazines, his correspondence, his dead and smelly tobacco pipes, used matches and dried twigs and leaves. All this Maude had stuffed under Phoeba's bed before she set the table with her mother's best service – pink gilt-edged Oxford including cheese and salad plates, a sauce tureen and gravy boat, a butter dish and a set of vegetable dishes with button roses on the lids for handles. The cutlery was silver and Maude laid it out to its full glory including butter knives, condiment sets and pickle forks.

When Robert's tour was over, Phoeba peeped through to the dining room to study the guest, sitting at the cluttered table and surrounded by Aunt Margaret's lush landscapes. There was no doubt Marius was a squatter: he dabbed his forehead with a serviette, talked to her father with an important air and quoted information he'd read about the internal combustion engine. 'It signals the certain demise of the steam engine,' he declared.

Where had he buried the fact that he hadn't been able to save his wife and unborn baby, Phoeba wondered. All she could see was a touch of the cavalier about him, but she pictured him holding Agnes as the light faded from her eyes and her body went limp, the poor child wedged lifeless somewhere in her. At some stage, thought Phoeba, he must have gone for a ride, far away, and bawled like a baby.

'Where is your aunt?' said Maude, scooping boiled potatoes into the Oxford tureen Phoeba held.

'She doesn't need to be here,' said Lilith from the porch where she stood catching a breath of the breeze. Suddenly, she primped her hair, wrenched her corset to push her breasts up, grabbed the potatoes from Phoeba and went to the dining room, where she set the steaming bowl on the table and sat opposite Marius, in Maude's seat. She placed one finger under her chin and listened intelligently to her father, who was asking about the new harvester at Overton.

'Well,' said Marius, making a steeple with his fingers, 'it will solve any labour problems forever.'

'Yes,' said Lilith, nodding gravely.

'Not that anyone has any shortage of labour at the moment,' said Phoeba, arriving with the beans.

'We get at least three beggars here a week,' added Lilith, brightly, but Marius hadn't time to respond because Maude arrived with carrots asking, 'Are you ready to harvest, Marius?'

Lilith started ladling carrots onto his plate.

'Yes,' he said, watching the pile of carrots grow, 'we've got a McKay Sunshine harvester on order, a new reaper-thresher. It winnows as it goes and then spurts out grain when it's full. We'll have our crop stripped and bagged in no time – when the thing gets here, that is.'

'So you're doing the thresher team out of a job?' said Phoeba.

'Well, of course, we still need stackers and chaff cutters.' Marius stared at her, startled.

57

'And,' said Robert, 'we'll need people for the grapes, by Jove.'

Lilith flicked her serviette loudly, but Marius still didn't look her way so she said, louder again, 'Perhaps old Captain Swing's men will storm over and ruin your new Sunshine.'

He looked at her, perplexed. 'Captain Swing?'

'Pipe down, Lilith,' said Robert.

'No,' said Phoeba, 'do explain it, Lilith. Marius is interested.'

Maude winced. She hated anyone mentioning Robert's convict past.

'Well,' said Lilith, leaning towards Marius, 'my grandfather was part of the Captain Swing riots and they were transported from Europe to Van Diemen's Land years ago for attacking threshing machines.'

'There's no such thing as Captain Swing anymore,' interrupted Robert and stuck his nose into his wine glass. 'What do you think of this drop?'

Marius sipped. 'It's strong, especially at the back of the throat.'

'Yes,' said Robert, 'a noticeable flavour.'

'They destroyed machinery and burned crops,' continued Lilith, defiantly, her voice rising.

'Why?' asked Marius, but Lilith didn't know why. She looked anxiously at Phoeba who said immediately, 'Because some were being replaced by the machine and those left had to work to the demands of the machine.'

'And so, you see, machines can't do everything, we still need people,' Marius said, as if that settled the matter. But Phoeba wanted the conversation to continue — after all, Lilith was just getting warmed up. 'You only need half as many people,' said Phoeba, provocatively.

'Yes. That's the point,' he said.

'Could you pass me the potatoes, please Marius?' said Lilith. Her eyes were brimming with jealousy and there was a desperate ring in her voice.

Robert pulled his napkin from his collar. 'Come, Marius,' he said, 'we'll find a better bottle in my cellar, something more subtle.'

Phoeba felt a slight dread: Lilith wouldn't like this.

'Hand me the potatoes,' snapped Lilith.

Phoeba handed her the potatoes.

'Robert, you haven't carved!' cried Maude, but Marius had discarded his serviette.

'Ouch,' yelled Lilith and the precious potato dish lid clattered onto the silver saltcellar and bounced onto the butter dish, knocking the pert rose handle from its top and leaving a pale shallow crater. For a moment there was silence. Lilith blew on her fingertips and said in her most wounded voice, 'Phoeba! The dish was so hot!'

Robert chucked his napkin at her and it landed on her head, covering her face. 'You dropped it.'

Lilith whipped the serviette down and wrapped it around her scalded hand.

Marius gazed at her hurt, pretty face.

'It was just so heavy …' she said, shakily.

Tears welled in Maude's eyes and she said weakly, 'That was my mother's tureen, Phoeba.'

But Phoeba didn't care. Marius Overton was completely captured by her irritating little sister: he was staring at her as if he had finally found something to interest him.

At that moment, Aunt Margaret appeared in the doorway, her green eyes twinkling brilliantly and her fingers black with sketching charcoal. 'Oh good, you haven't started.'

'It's just ended in ruins,' said Maude, her face flushing red and sweat beading her top lip. She bustled from the room waving a serviette at her crimson throat.

Aunt Margaret plonked down in Maude's seat and held her empty wineglass out to Marius.

He hesitated, transfixed by her startling appearance. The full glare of the midday sun was catching the greying hairs on both her chin and her top lip.

'You'd have to be the rich squatter,' said Aunt Margaret, returning the scrutiny. 'I'm the poor aunt.' She wiggled her glass and Marius poured the last of the wine into it. Robert went for more. Eventually they ate.

Aunt Margaret held court for the entire meal conducting a healthy discussion on the introduction of rabbits and the over-grazing of livestock which caused erosion, on the drought, on selective breeding and the eventual extinction of some breeds of common farm animals. From which she moved seamlessly to votes for women and, finally, the artists' colony at Esperance.

Lilith recovered. She smiled, she laughed, she said, 'How interesting' a lot. Marius, in between trying Robert's wine, was totally engaged by her. When he left at somewhere around four o'clock, he had the distinct impression that the Crupps were a generous lot with quite advanced notions and that their youngest daughter, Lilith, was a charming, bright girl.

Phoeba felt peaceful, as if she had finally finished a game of Patience without cheating. It wasn't until she was in bed that night that she thought of Hadley and realised she hadn't seen him for three days.

Henrietta had spent that afternoon chopping kindling for the

60

copper. She'd already chopped the day's wood, but when her mother's guest, Mr Titterton, after his tea and pikelets, had stood at the mantelpiece reading Shakespeare sonnets – 'When forty winters shall besiege thy brow, And dig deep trenches in thy beauty's field ...' – Henrietta had left.

She rested a pine log on its end on the chopping stump, eyed the spot between two knots where the grain curved, then swung the axe to split the log into two neat halves, which tumbled to rest at her boots. She split her halves again and again until she had a wheelbarrow full of sweet, pale woodchips with some medium-sized branches and a couple of good logs piled carefully on top of the kindling. Leaning against her axe, she caught sight of her brother, a figure in the distance, a man in shirtsleeves shepherding a small flock of confused rams through a dry paddock: strange, she thought he had moved them just yesterday. Life without Hadley would be tolerable when he went to Overton. She would ride with Phoeba to see him and there would be no more collars to starch or shirts to iron.

Taking off her felt hat, she wiped her forehead with her sleeve and set out across the yard towards the laundry with the wheelbarrow.

At the parlour window she caught a glimpse of her mother as she fell towards Mr Titterton, who caught her in his arms. Fainted again, thought Henrietta, those corsets – but then Mr Titterton lowered his head and opened his mouth and the Widow Pearson's bonnet tipped back. They were kissing, clamped together at the mouth, a corpse's teeth rubbing against her mother's. Henrietta's heart thudded and she felt like she had been dancing too long in a tin shed in summer. The wheelbarrow handles twisted in her hands and the barrow skewed and crashed, spilling her carefully balanced wood across the dirt. She plopped down on the wood

61

box, removed her hat again and fanned her cheeks as they flushed red.

'Erk,' she said.

She gathered up her wood and went to the washhouse. And as the serviettes and sheets swirled in the boiling copper, Henrietta worried. What would she do if they got married? Surely they wouldn't. Should she tell Hadley?

By the time the towels, smalls and finally the handkerchiefs were on the line, Henrietta had decided not to tell her younger brother. It would ruin his start at Overton and he already seemed preoccupied enough by that. But if old Mr Tit did marry their mother, what would become of her and Hadley? She would talk to Phoeba about it all. Phoeba would know what to do.

Thursday, January 4, 1894

Thursday was cheese day, so Phoeba milked Maggie early. Lilith, who didn't do cheese, took charge of the mending and fancy-stitching. She preferred less taxing duties on the whole – replenishing vases, plumping cushions and filling the kerosene lamps every day.

Aunt Margaret took herself to the vegetable garden with her sketchpad and when Phoeba arrived in the kitchen to make the cheese she found her mother there, soaking the dry fruit to make a plum cake.

'Why are you making such a rich cake in the middle of summer, Mother?'

'It's good for the digestion, everyone knows that.'

'There's no point making wedding cake for me.'

'The vicar may call,' said Maude, her voice rising. 'We need something to feed him.'

'The vicar doesn't need feeding,' said Phoeba and she dumped the milk bucket on the table.

Robert wandered through from the vineyard where he had been blotting dew from the berries with cotton rags. He picked up his newspaper, said, 'It's going to be 103 degrees by midday,' and went to the front veranda. Spot stood against the fence, his ears forward, watching small groups of surly, straggling people – more itinerants from Geelong, Robert supposed – move up the lane. They paused at the signpost then wandered towards Mount Hope and through the yard, a grubby lot, grimy and tattered, with their blackened camp gear slung over their backs. Robert watched the parade: the kids with boils and their mothers with green teeth; the men with beards stiff with matted knots.

'Campin' at the outcrop,' said the leader flatly. He was a small bearded man with ruptured blemishes all over his face.

'After harvest work, are you?' said Robert in his most friendly tone. He couldn't say that he didn't want them to camp there – because he knew if he did, they'd burn his house or crop.

The leader glanced back at the grapevines and spat on the ground near Maude's stressed petunias.

'You're not interested in grapes?' Robert asked.

'Fruit?' He shook his head. 'Grain is what we know.'

'Good luck to you,' said Robert. Here was a group that wouldn't like Marius's new Sunshine harvester.

The itinerants moved on leaving Robert with a sense of repulsion. Swaggies were the dispossessed, he knew, the down-on-their-luck and the unemployed. Itinerants were a different kettle of fish. Stray vagrants, sundowners, rogues, gypsies and ratbags – probably, he thought, without irony, from convict stock.

He would make sure the door was latched last thing at night, and keep his Collector handy.

Aunt Margaret saw them straggle through the yard and wondered if they'd sit for her. Then she dismissed the idea – they would ask for money.

Phoeba dropped the last thick curd into a cloth-lined vat, put its lid on, then placed a small, smooth rock on it to weigh it down. The kitchen reeked of rancid whey. She was putting the last of her cheese under the tank-stand when she saw the group halfway up the outcrop.

She cleared away her ladles, sieves and squares of muslin, washed down the table and removed her apron. It felt 103 degrees already, and she splashed cold water over her face, neck, arms and wrists in the washhouse before disappearing to the cellar to sit, flapping her skirts up and down, with her feet in a bucket of well-water. What she wanted to do was ride Spot to the foreshore, drape her skirt and blouse over a tea-tree and wade out into the green, salty water. Spot would stand up to his belly, his withers quivering and his tail in the air while Phoeba sank down to the peaceful sea world. But this was one of the sharpest ways the depression had affected them – swaggies now camped on their beach, fished and swam in their bay. So they couldn't swim there anymore. She thought of Hadley again. Loyal, sincere Hadley, ten years old and sombrely shepherding his mother and big sister to church for his father's funeral, then crying all through the service, his shoulders leaping about as she stared at them. It was strange not to have seen him for days.

Henrietta drove up at dusk, one foot resting on the dash and the reins loose in her hands. The dust behind her obliterated any sign of Spot, the rooster or the ducks as she tore through the gate and wrenched the brake lever and leapt to the ground before the

Hampden had fully come to rest.

A cloud of dust wafted over to the grapes and Robert called, 'Damned larrikin.'

'Nice evening, isn't it Mr Crupp?' said Henrietta coming towards the house, her long strides stretching the hem of her skirt and her shoulders swaying. Her blouse was pulled from her skirt at the back. She pointed up to the outcrop and said to Phoeba, 'They're turning the lights on in Geelong tonight.'

Phoeba was relieved. Hadley mustn't have mentioned the refusal to his sister.

Up on the outcrop a blue mist hung in the tree canopy above the campfires. Henrietta removed her battered hat. She had excellent hair, thick and auburn and the envy of many women who craved bouffant waves to support their enormous hats. But Henrietta wound it in a plaited coil around her head, like the base of a colander.

It was Maude who asked a series of questions about Hadley – why hadn't they seen him? He was packing for his new job and organising the flock, his sister explained. When was he going to Overton? Sunday after church. How long would he be at Overton? Until the end of season, of course. Was he entering the ploughing match this year? Certainly, Hadley always entered the ploughing match. He was, Henrietta said proudly, the neatest ploughman in the district.

'So dependable,' said Maude, tightening her eyes at Phoeba. The girls could go to the outcrop, she agreed, if they promised not to go near the camps, and they must take candles and matches or they'd surely turn their ankles in the dark and miss the entire season, as if they had a full diary of balls to look forward to. 'And,' she warned, 'be careful of those new electric lights – they cause fires.'

Phoeba and Henrietta climbed the track as the shadows faded and the view dulled. Mosquitoes sang in the hot silence and the sound of the evening express travelled up to them, its carriage windows faint orange boxes gliding through the dusk. Above them, clouds curled over the rocks, unfurling, long fingers that reached out and pooled together over the bay. Rods of silver pierced them making puddles of sparkling mercury on the dark water and the small lanterns on sailing ships winked.

They branched off the shortcut track along the path towards the spring, climbing through air that was thick with the stink of wood smoke.

'Swaggies,' said Henrietta, assuredly, but Phoeba was beginning to wonder about the scruffy men who had passed through her yard that afternoon.

Suddenly the smell of the air changed and Henrietta stopped. A chill ran through Phoeba. The atmosphere was eerie, stale, as though something vile had fled a split second before and left a foul curling wake. Human odour, human waste, burning tobacco. Phoeba and Henrietta reached for each other and turned to go but it was too late. The camp leader – the ragged man with skin dulled with black spots – slipped from a branch and landed behind them. Two more men crawled from behind boulders and women and children, wielding small branches, crept from the bush enclosing them, holding them with their gaze.

'Look what we have here,' said the ragged man as the circle closed in.

The skin on Phoeba's neck tingled. Henrietta's grip tightened on her hand.

'We've only come to look at the lights,' said Phoeba in her strongest voice. She stepped in front of Henrietta and could feel her friend's short, shallow breath on the back of her hair.

'What lights?' snarled the itinerant flicking his eyes to the trees. The skin on his cheekbones was raw with festering black pimples – Barcoo rot. The man was starving.

A scruffy, dull-eyed youth rushed from behind and knocked Henrietta's hat sideways on her head. The children laughed and waved the sticks they carried. Phoeba pressed against Henrietta and they stood back to back with their arms linked.

'They're turning the electric streetlights on in Geelong,' said Henrietta, her voice cracking.

'Doing the lamplighter out of a job!' screeched a thin, pregnant woman.

The crowd pressed in and Phoeba smelled rotted teeth and the rank saltiness of unwashed females.

The dull-eyed lad stepped closer, eyeballing Phoeba. He swung his clenched fists and Phoeba felt her guts sink. Then a woman shoved him aside and raised a warning finger. 'We know about the reaper coming to do us out of a job.' She pointed at her pregnant stomach, 'The bundles on us gleaners' backs is getting smaller.'

'It's the dry weather,' said Phoeba, gently.

'It's the machines!' the woman screamed, her teeth hanging like loose buttons. She drew her fist back as if to punch but Henrietta wrenched free of Phoeba and twirled, dancing on her toes, her fists winding and her chin tucked in. The men guffawed and hissed.

'Henri, no!' cried Phoeba.

Suddenly a familiar voice came out of the darkness, 'Girls don't know how to buy machines!' It was Freckle, looking down at them from a boulder. He'd been checking his traps and some fat, furry rabbits dangled lifelessly from each hand.

'And you'll all get work picking our grapes,' called Phoeba, pulling Henrietta back by her skirt.

'Grapes is no good to us,' said the woman, and the crowd pressed in again.

'There's already dozens of swaggies camped at the Overton creek waiting to shear and to harvest,' said Freckle, jumping from the boulder to stand between the girls and their assailants. 'The grapes are your only hope. Isn't that right, Miss Crupp?'

'And it's better work,' said Phoeba, 'no snakes and no machines.'

'Electricity will come out here one day,' said Henrietta. 'Everyone will have it in their houses and every swaggie will be employed to build the poles to carry the wires and they even say every house will have a telephone.'

'She's right,' said Phoeba. 'You'll get work building the lines.'

The ring-leader held up his hand and the group steadied.

'Where's these lights?' he demanded.

Phoeba pointed south. 'That way.'

'We don't like machines,' said the ring-leader holding his finger under Phoeba's chin. She stared straight back into his eyes. There were small balls of green in the corners and his lashes were sparse. He was the unhealthiest man she'd ever seen and she could only wonder what parasites his intestines harboured.

'We don't like machines either, that's why we haven't bought any,' she said, reasonably.

'You're camped on their land,' said Freckle.

The ring-leader swung on him. 'Putting a fence up doesn't make it theirs.'

'You'll have to scamper if you hurt them,' said Freckle.

'You don't hurt us and we won't hurt you,' said Phoeba.

'Gawn git,' said the ring-leader, and the girls hurried away, hand in hand, stumbling down the slope into the fading dusk. At the spring they sat down, breathed steadily until their hearts stopped thumping.

'I was afraid, Phoeba.'

'So was I.'

'You're not a squib though, are you?'

'We were both very brave,' said Phoeba.

'I don't know why people can't clean their teeth,' said Henrietta, and shuddered.

'They won't hurt us. They're desperate, that's all.'

They studied the darkening brown and blue patchwork landscape but there was no shine from electric light. Henrietta snapped a twig in half, shoved it in and out between the gap in her front teeth. After a moment she said, 'Speaking of teeth, I'm worried my mother will marry Mr Titterton. Yesterday they read poetry together.'

'Company for each other,' said Phoeba. 'We all need friends.' She glanced behind her but the bush was still and quiet.

'I saw them kissing.'

Phoeba laughed. 'I find that difficult to picture.'

'She acts like she's in love.' Henrietta inspected the twig, holding it just at the end of her nose.

'Then love must be blind, that's all I can say.'

Henrietta rubbed the twig up and down on a rock beside her, as if she was sharpening it. 'What will happen to us if she marries old Tit?'

'You'll have extra shirts to wash—'

'I'm serious. What will happen to me and Hadley?'

'You could always get married.'

'No one will marry me. I've got a face like a puffed apple at a dance and anyway, Mother won't let me. She'd have to do her

69

own washing and who would tie her corset? I'd worked out that she'd be dead by the time I was thirty and then I can just live on at the farm with Hadley.'

'What if Hadley got married, Henri, then what would you do?'

'I'd still stay there. It's my home too.'

Phoeba took Henrietta's hand, stopped her rubbing the stick up and down and made her friend look at her. 'Hadley wants to marry me.'

'Hadley's always wanted to marry you.'

'I don't think I can marry him though.'

Henrietta looked at her, astounded. 'He didn't ask you, did he? Gee whiz, Phoeba. That's perfect! We can all live at Elm Grove together. Mother and old Tit can retire to Geelong.' Then Henrietta's hopes faded, like the thread of black smoke from a candle flame. Phoeba was not happy. She let go of Phoeba's hand. So that's why Hadley had been working so hard these past days. Henrietta inspected the calluses on her palm.

'You don't want to marry Hadley—'

'It's not Hadley, Henri, it's ... I just don't think I want to get married. It's dangerous.' They were both thinking of Agnes Overton, young and privileged, writhing to death in a rich man's snowy sheets sodden with her own blood and sweat.

'Babies don't kill all mothers,' said Henrietta. 'Mrs Jessop had seven.'

'And no teeth left.' Phoeba pictured herself standing by Hadley with her lips folded in to hide the gaps where her teeth had been. Even more unsavoury was the though of procreation with Hadley, with anyone without love. He had given her measles once, that was intimate enough.

'Bathsheba, in the novel I'm reading, has taken over her

70

uncle's farm,' said Phoeba. 'Lots of women work. It's not necessary to marry. Please don't let it come between us, Henri. You're my best friend ... I'm sorry.'

But Henrietta looked away. Mr Titterton kissing her mother, and now this. It was all ruined, and they'd been so happy before.

'My mother married for security,' said Phoeba, 'and it's made her and Dad miserable. I think we're meant to live a happy life.'

'You would have made Hadley and me very happy,' murmured Henrietta.

The conversation was only making things worse. 'Anyway, I said I'd think about it.'

'Do whatever makes you happy,' said Henrietta.

But Phoeba was happy as she was: it was other people who urged her to change, to marry, to do the right thing.

Henrietta pointed off towards Geelong. 'Look.'

And there, for the first time, a very, very faint glow, like a bonfire that was thirty miles away, seeped into the sky to the south.

Friday, January 5, 1894

Early morning brought the thresher team to the district. As she milked the goat, Phoeba watched it move along the lane, floating through the golden mist that hovered over the crops. Six brown bullocks dragged a big round steam generator, its chimneystack and flywheel moving above the grain like two masts. Floating behind on a flat-bed wagon was a thresher machine pulled by a team of draughthorses. The fireman and tankerman, the bundlemen and stookers, all marched with their scythes over their shoulders. Behind them all came a lone boy on a draughthorse pulling a water cart. And last, the gleaners, their children gambolling beside them. They turned east and settled in the paddock next to the church. So much pomp and apparatus for such famished crops, thought Phoeba.

Summer was progressing as it should. Every year the same team came to Bay View and every year they harvested the church crop first – it was the smallest. Then, as the feed crops ripened, they moved around the small community – visiting Jessops', Pearsons', and Crupps', and then they decamped and moved everything to Overton for the last long stint. This heralded the harvest dance at Overton, usually held the first Saturday of the station's harvest.

After breakfast, Aunt Margaret took her paintbox and palette, her chair and her easel, and went out to sketch the new horse. Maude baked, tempering the stove fire with twigs and small logs, and when she pulled a perfect flat-topped, square brown cake from the oven the house filled with a warm fruity smell that made them all – apart from Phoeba – long for winter or a wedding. Lilith emerged for breakfast, then retreated to rest herself for the ploughing match. And Phoeba, the day to herself, spent it with Spot, in the vineyard, happy.

Saturday, January 6, 1894

On Saturday morning Phoeba roused everyone, including Aunt Margaret, early. Then she filled a jar with sweet black tea and packed a picnic basket – sandwiches, plums, apricots and, a great wedge of her mother's special cake. Aunt Margaret set about choosing one of her oils to display in the produce tent.

'Careful,' called Maude, 'huntsmen live behind them.'

Aunt Margaret selected a still life of a lace curtain billowing over a recently slain fowl and surrounded by an assortment of fresh vegetables and a pair of secateurs. Robert started his day tasting wine and Maude, over her porridge, said that it was too early to drink.

'Nonsense,' said Margaret, holding out an empty teacup. 'The upright classes drink at mass every morning.'

'Fragrant,' said Phoeba sipping her father's selection. 'Thick and mellow on the tongue.' One day, she thought, she would like to learn more about wine making, perhaps make her own and give it her own name. One day, when the recession was over.

'I've packed some of the cake,' she said to her mother, but Maude had other things on her mind.

'I hope this new horse isn't easily spooked,' she said. 'They may have a cannon this year.'

Robert gulped his wine. 'A cannon?'

'To start the match.'

'Mother, they've never had a cannon before.' Phoeba headed out the door with the picnic basket.

'Phoeba, you sadly know nothing of fanfare and hoopla,' her mother called after her. 'There's no telling what will be there. They had cannon for Prince Alfred when he visited in 1867 and one went off too soon and blew the gunner's hand off, very messy. And there were far too many cannon-volleys and kettledrums and trumpets.'

'Well Maude,' said Robert sucking wine from his moustache, 'there'll only be a bit of bunting and a brass band today.'

'I love a band,' cried Maude her hand on her heart. 'We so rarely see culture out here.'

They were about to set off when something terribly

73

important occurred to Lilith. 'I could wear Phoeba's blouse. She's not wearing it.'

Aunt Margaret objected immediately. 'I saved for a year to buy that blouse,' she said, 'for Phoeba.'

Maude patted Lilith's cheeks, assuring her she looked lovely in anything, but it was too much for her younger daughter. Her day was ruined, she declared, because her parasol didn't match her dress's polonaise. Lilith would not be happy until she had thrown her tantrum and everyone else was miserable, thought Phoeba, so they may as well get it over with. 'Every one will notice how terrible you look,' Phoeba said, 'so you'd better stay home. You'd have to travel in the back with the wine barrel anyway.'

'That's your fault,' said Maude, lowering her hat net, raising her chin and tucking the net between her thick wattle and her bishop's collar. 'Usually Hadley comes with the Hampden to take us.'

'I'll stay home,' she volunteered. She could spend the entire day by herself with a book, see Henrietta at church on Sunday and find out then if Hadley still liked her.

'You will drive,' said Robert firmly to Phoeba. 'Lilith, you're the smallest so you will ride dicky.'

Lilith stamped her foot. 'Phoeba can ride dicky for a change.'

'She'll drive.'

'I'll drive.'

'You don't know how, Lilith,' cried Aunt Margaret.

Phoeba offered to ride Spot; Robert insisted she had to drive; Margaret insisted she'd stay at home if Lilith drove; Maude said she'd do no such thing and that it was Robert's doing that they had inferior transport. Lilith stomped to her room and slammed

74

the door so hard that three of Aunt Margaret's landscapes fell off the wall.

Robert sighed.

Phoeba went calmly over to Spot and rubbed his poll, thick and greasy under her palm. His eyelids drooped and he pressed his nose into her skirt but she had no apples in her pocket.

There was always a scene, always. During their first winter at the local school, Lilith had been told to give her seat to Louisa Jessop, still frail from rheumatic fever, so that she could be closest to the wood fire. Lilith had bellowed all morning, so loudly that in the end Louisa had begged her to take her seat back. And here we are, thought Phoeba, still giving in.

Enough was enough. She marched back to the sulky, climbed into the driver's seat and yelled, 'I'm going. Anyone coming?'

Aunt Margaret joined her. Maude struggled, torn between her baby daughter and the prospect of the brass band. Robert headed through the gate on Rocket, and Phoeba made to follow, which propelled Lilith screaming from the house. She stopped in the middle of the yard wailing and skipping, like a marionette, with her skirts bouncing and her hat ribbons flying. Maude hauled herself into the sulky and Aunt Margaret sighed and folded her skinny bones into the dicky seat. Lilith settled herself, quite contentedly, and poor Centaur strained to pull the weight of them all.

'Please,' thought Phoeba, 'please let her find a husband today.'

When the new horse passed Spot, he stuck his nose in the air, suddenly preoccupied by the smell of freshly cut hay on the warm breeze.

At the intersection Robert reined the small convoy to a halt. Aunt Margaret looked around at the sweeping empty landscape and said impatiently, 'What's happened now?'

He was pointing down to the railway line where men unloaded wheat from a flat-bed wagon. They were using an A-frame and a chain-and-pulley system, their team of horses moving obediently forward and back to raise and lower the bags onto the square stack of bulging grain sacks that were growing at the siding. 'The grain co-op have acquired a mechanical device to haul those sacks, a conveyer belt elevator apparatus, I believe. It'll do the wool bales as well.'

'Marvellous,' said Margaret, flatly.

The sundowners won't be pleased, thought Phoeba.

'Now see Robert,' called Maude, 'there's traffic.'

The Hampden approached, overtaking three trudging swaggies who waved, begging a lift. Widow Pearson pointed forwards and Henrietta drove on.

'Gracious,' said Maude, 'she's got a new bonnet.'

Widow Pearson rarely went anywhere that required standing, walking or heavy breathing. It appeared she had abandoned her postiches for a new brown bonnet, which looked like an upturned purse on her head and, Phoeba noted, they had attached the fringe to the Hampden roof. Henrietta, in her best brown skirt and jacket outfit, still managed to look dishevelled.

'That bonnet is from Lassetters catalogue,' sniffed Lilith. 'The style was fashionable back in '83.' Her tantrum forgotten, Lilith said she would go in the Hampden if Maude came.

'I'm not going with her,' said Maude, waving at the Widow. 'She'll boast all the way about Hadley's job.'

'Oh for Mercy's sake! I'll go,' cried Phoeba, feeling itchy and irritated.

'If Lilith drives,' said Aunt Margaret, crossing her arms, 'I will walk back to Geelong, now!'

'Well then,' said Robert, 'why don't you go with the Pearsons, Maude, and you can boast that Marius Overton came for lunch.'

Maude and Lilith shot from the sulky at once and got into the Hampden, waving back cheerily as it moved off.

'Well done, Robert, now we have all the dust,' said Aunt Margaret. It was obvious Centaur knew where he was going, dust or no dust. When Phoeba turned him towards Overton he broke into a canter immediately. Margaret clutched the armrest and held her hat and Phoeba leaned back on the reins, trying to stop the horse from racing. They hurtled around the tail end of the outcrop and through the pass and there, laid out before them, was the tall square Overton homestead.

In the front of the house, tethered horses, buggies, traps, wagons and carts formed a disorderly queue beside the ploughing field and on the opposite side of the field the competing ploughs and their teams lined up in just as disorderly fashion. A brass band marched in between the two, its own warped lines oom-paaing and thumping while children in straw hats skipped behind. The crowd watched from under their hats and parasols or sat on picnic rugs. Bunting on the white and green produce marquee flapped in the hot breeze.

As soon as they could, Phoeba and Henrietta linked arms and escaped through the crowd. There were farmers and workers, and fancily dressed women from Geelong sauntered about in their city clothes – satin wing sleeves and matching collarettes, kid boots with ribbon laces, hats as big as wheat sacks and matching parasols trimmed with lace. Lilith would be green with envy. The country girls dashed about in their walking skirts and outdoor jackets, straw hats and sensible leather gloves.

Next to the produce marquee was a photographer. A crowd had gathered around the small tent where Guston Overton stood with The General, the new prize stud ram he had purchased for a record price of three hundred guineas. Guston had boasted in the papers and all over the district that the expensive ram would 'secure the future of Overton through sales of its progeny and infusion of good breeding blood into the stock'. The ram was a showy well-proportioned animal, symmetrical, with a long level back, and Guston posed with his prize against a painted backdrop of Kensington Palace. As soon as the image was taken, the ram was led into a small holding yard cushioned with hay for all to admire, and the photographer turned to the crowd: 'I'll take your photograph for sixpence … immortalised forever for your loved ones.' Phoeba and Henrietta had thruppence between them.

Beyond Kensington Palace, an engineer advertised a portable farm steam tractor – 'A Miracle Machine to Replace the Expensive Horse and Wagon' – and a man wearing a strap-on Cahoon's Patent Broadcast Seed Sower strolled through the crowd turning the handle on a box strapped to his chest so that a huge disc of seed sprayed around him, pounding the ground like hard hail and flinging it into the air to land on ladies' parasols and gather in hat brims. Passing on her way to the produce tent, Maude scolded the salesman. The seed spray would surely get stuck in a child's ear, she declared, and bumped into two women wearing badges, Australian Women's Suffrage Society. They stood either side of a sandwich board that obstructed passing pedestrians. One was well groomed, her hair cut short and neat. Her dress was bohemian, loose and sack-like but well made, and she held a signboard: VOTING RIGHTS FOR WOMEN IN ALL STATES AND TERRITORIES, NOW. The other was dressed similarly, only her hem was short enough to show the top of her boots.

Henrietta and Phoeba headed straight for them.

'Women in South Australia will be able to vote this year and stand for government as well,' they said. Curious, the girls took pamphlets from them, tucking them into their pockets and out of their mothers' sight.

They took their time in the produce tent, admiring the fine knitting and lace work, the preserves and fresh vegetables, the tumbles of wool clips and vases of wheat, the watercolours and oil landscapes – including Aunt Margaret's dead fowl – and eggs on their straw beds. Then they wandered out to the field. 'We should find Hadley,' said Henrietta.

'You go,' said Phoeba, lifting her skirt as if to flee. But Henrietta caught her arm.

'He'll be disappointed if you don't come, Phoeba.'

'Has he said anything?—'

'Not a thing.'

'Right,' said Phoeba, and braced herself. It would be worse if she didn't go; she may as well get it over with.

They walked along the line of thick, competent draughthorses, plaited and burnished with their harnesses almost gleaming, on through air thick with manure and pungent horse. Hadley was standing behind his team, the harness reins around his neck and his hands gripping the single-furrow mould-board. He tilted it from side to side, and made the soft noise of a blade carving through earth.

'Hello,' called Phoeba and he dropped the handles instantly, the colour in his cheeks deepening. He rushed towards Phoeba but the reins were still around his neck and they pulled him up, jerking his head so his hat fell off. Almost without missing a beat he picked up his hat and came towards her. He always recovered himself well, she thought.

'I knew you'd be here for me,' he said.

'I always will be,' she said, then regretted it and added, 'as any good friend should be.'

'Of course,' said Hadley, and gestured at the horses, 'My team—'

'Yes, they're lovely—'

'The furrow horse tends to race a bit.'

'If you win,' said Henrietta, 'we'll have our photograph taken.'

'We should have one taken anyway,' said Phoeba, 'to remember the good times.'

Hadley looked at her, levelly. 'Are the good times over, Phoeba?'

'Of course not, Hadley,' said Henrietta, quickly. 'Don't be a dill. She meant as a keepsake so we can look at it together when we're eighty.' She straightened his tie and slapped his shoulders. 'So, Had, what did the man say about your emasculator?'

'Oh,' said Hadley, and explained that he had spoken to the chap wearing the strap-on Cahoon's Patent Broadcast Seed Sower about his invention but that the man had said he'd need to see drawings. 'But I'm not silly,' said Hadley. 'He'd just steal my idea.'

'Of course,' said Henrietta. 'Now you must plough as well as you do at home and we'll see you victorious at lunch.'

'Righto.' He looked at Phoeba and opened his mouth to say something so she planted a quick, sisterly kiss on his cheek. 'Good luck.'

That was that over and done with: the first confrontation. She could relax.

The horse teams were always first away after the starting flag fell and drivers had until noon to complete their quarter acre. Traditionally, Guston Overton started off by ploughing the first furrow but this year it was Marius who began. A Scotsman named Jim who'd won £10 last year followed him, throwing up his hands in exaggerated dismay at the furrow and making the crowd laugh.

Phoeba and Henrietta climbed the windmill, as they did every year. From the top they could see Mrs Overton on the homestead balcony, her white skirt falling over her knees. Behind her three maids stood with their hands behind their backs, watching the smoke that curled from itinerants' campfires and from the shearers' camp on the creek bank. Behind the majestic homestead the shearing shed waited, its high stumps hidden behind a thousand yarded sheep. And way out on the western plain a thin curtain of red dust rose up – more sheep being shepherded in.

Widow Pearson passed beneath Phoeba and Henrietta, clinging to Mr Titterton's arm, her bustle behind her like a dwarf under her skirt.

'Have they been kissing lately, Henri?'

'I avoid them, just in case they are,' said Henrietta. 'It's no good for my health.'

The vicar trailed behind the Widow's bustle, his stomach jutting out and hiding his feet.

'It's terrible even eating with old Tit. There's an extra sound in his mouth when he chews. Imagine when the vicar comes to lunch. There'll be the sound of his chins slapping on his collar as well.'

They laughed and below them, Robert looked up. He was walking with Guston and Marius Overton, and the new manager was with them too.

'They say he's a bank man,' said Henrietta.

'A handsome bank man,' said Phoeba, thinking she must have looked a sight flying along behind Rocket.

Just then, he looked up, straight into her eyes, feigning an outraged expression at the two ladies perched on the narrow windmill ledge. Then lifted his hat. Phoeba smiled at him.

'Hadley's better looking than him,' said Henrietta defensively.

Perhaps, Phoeba thought, but Steel was different, more mature. She watched the group of men move through the crowd to the ploughing field. 'Do you think Overton has money trouble?' she asked. Henrietta shrugged.

There was a gunshot, Guston Overton firing to start the teams. Mr Titterton, who was one of the judges, followed a plough. He stepped from furrow to furrow measuring the depth and gauging the neatness of the dry brown wave. Hadley was proceeding steadily, carefully, way behind the other competitors. The bullock teams with three- and four-blade ploughs took up their starting position on the other side of the field.

Henrietta took the suffragettes' pamphlet from her pocket: 'Dress Review, by The Healthy and Artistic Dress Union'. It suggested she abandon her corset. Henrietta's mother made her wear a corset but she never tightened the cords, ever. 'I should show this to mother,' she said, but she screwed it up and threw it down onto the grass. Nothing would separate the Widow from her tiny waist.

Phoeba read hers aloud: '"Suffrage, marriage and women's rights. Marriage should protect your freedom, not make you a slave. Women should be able to get divorced and keep their children and property."' The first heading was Contraception. She took off her straw hat and slipped the paper inside, under the headband. 'I suppose we should go and find the picnic,' she said.

The Crupps and the Pearsons settled to eat lunch in the shade between their buggies, Henrietta and Phoeba handed out sandwiches while Maude propped herself against the buggy wheel, her corset rising to her armpits as the widow recalled Hadley's neat furrows. Hadley rolled his eyes in frustration.

'Ah! Some familiar faces.' The vicar's trousers strained across his thighs as he bounced towards them. He took hold of a buggy spoke and lowered his bulk onto the blanket next to Henrietta, eyeing her sandwich.

'I see I am just in time for lunch.' He leaned closer, 'And good morning, Miss Pearson.'

Henrietta pulled back.

They hadn't really brought enough for him but it was too late, the picnickers moved around with their tea and sandwiches to accommodate his spreading form.

'How nice to see you again, Vicar,' gasped the Widow, the tinge on her nose deepening. 'My son Hadley is the new wool classer here at Overton. He works with the stock overseer, Mr Titterton.'

The vicar took a plate of sandwiches from Henrietta and said to Phoeba, 'I must come to lunch one day and taste your wine.'

'She would enjoy that very much,' said Maude.

Hadley took his fob watch from his pocket as if he urgently needed to know the time and Phoeba quickly reached for the scones. 'Lilith made these,' she lied, 'please have one.'

'No cream?' said the vicar and he turned to smile at Lilith, scone dough clogging his gums.

'We don't have a cow,' said Lilith. 'Mrs Jessop has a cow but we've got a goat because they're cheaper. The Pearsons sold their cow because their soil is salty and their milk was always brackish.'

'If you say so,' said Hadley, mildly offended. Widow Pearson was speechless with indignation.

'She's looking for a husband to cook for, aren't you Lilith?'

83

said Phoeba. Lilith scowled, but Phoeba ignored her and offered the cake tin to the vicar. 'The plum cake is lovely too, Vicar.'

Suddenly there was a ruckus; the picnickers stood to see the fuss. The president of The Victorian Ploughmen's Association and three other gentlemen were marching two suffragettes to their buggy, gripping them by the elbows. They shoved the women up into their carriage, led them towards the driveway and let the horse go. The two women swung their buggy hard left, tearing straight across the ploughing field, their escorts hot on their tail. The buggy bounced alarmingly and the horse panicked, his head up racing. Pamphlets flew along in his wake while horse teams, bullocks, judges and competitors scattered before him. Spectators clapped, including Phoeba and Henrietta, who gave a long, loud whistle. The Widow Pearson lurched sideways at this, gasping, her complexion purple. But the daring suffragettes managed to circle the ploughing arena twice – and ruin it – before escaping.

'Well,' said Phoeba, 'that was worth a day out!'

Lilith said they needed to be doused with a bucket of cold sal volatile; Widow Pearson said it was a craze she hoped would disband, glaring at her daughter; Maude declared they'd ruin their families' reputations, 'the way they make a spectacle of themselves'.

'Henrietta does equal work with Hadley but she won't inherit the farm,' Phoeba pointed out and the Widow snapped, 'That is none of your concern.'

'And Mother,' said Henrietta, 'how would you feel if you lost us because Dad divorced you?'

'My husband died,' wailed the Widow and turned to tell the vicar all about her tragic life. But the vicar had left in search of better luncheon baskets.

'Gone to Mrs Jessop,' said Aunt Margaret, patting Widow

Pearson's hand. 'Mrs Jessop has fresh cream.'

'Ooops,' said Hadley, scratching at the dripped pickles on his new wool pants.

'Our new washing machine will get the stain out,' said the Widow, triumphantly. 'Did I mention, Mrs Crupp, that Hadley has ordered us a washing machine from Lassetters?'

'They say,' sniffed Maude, 'that those machines only wash as well as the person turning the handle.'

At three o'clock the produce tent filled with the babbling crowd. Henrietta and Phoeba stood with Hadley at the front. Patiently waiting on the podium were the judges from the Ploughmen's Association and Mr Titterton and Marius Overton. The vicar rolled up to the front uninvited and stood with the judges, his chins raised in anticipation. Marius spoke. 'Ladies and Gentlemen' – the crowd hushed, the air of expectation rising – 'the judges and I have inspected the furrows and reached our conclusion. But before I announce the winners, we will need someone suitable to present the awards.'

The vicar said, 'Of course!' and stepped onto the podium, but as he did so, Marius looked down and extended his hand to Phoeba saying, 'Miss Crupp?'

From nowhere, Lilith reached out and took Marius's hand. He had no option but to welcome her onto the platform. The vicar turned suddenly as if someone had called his name. Marius cleared his throat. 'The winner in section one, single furrow plough, two-horse team is, Mr Hadley Pearson.'

Thank goodness, thought Phoeba. Hadley entered every year but this was the first time he had won.

Lilith presented him with a silver-plated ham-bone holder and matching marrow spoon with the aplomb of someone who'd

85

officiated at ceremonies all her life. But it was Phoeba Hadley looked to, joy and triumph in his eyes.

The marquee had been dismantled and the bunting rolled away, The General returned to his comfortable enclosure under the shearing shed, the brass band was long gone and a child's cap blew along the plough ruts. Mr Titterton and Hadley rode back to Elm Grove between sweeping paddocks tinged with orange rays from the setting sun.

'The General is a remarkable ram,' said Hadley. 'He's thick through the heart and perhaps thirty pounds good wool on him, at a guess.'

They approached the intersection, Mr Titterton looking disapprovingly at the thistles and other weeds that grew thick along the boulder fences, spilling into the paddocks.

'City people just don't know,' said Mr Titterton. 'Raising hogs is the thing. Manageable animal, your hog, and big, lots of meat on 'em. People will always want bacon, but no good ever came from grapes. And sheep can be ruined in no time through scab or footrot.'

Hadley could have responded that good management would prevent these things but he was more concerned about the campfires that dotted the shadowy hill behind the Crupps' cottage: the workers, he thought. And no good would come of them if they couldn't get work.

That night at Elm Grove, the Pearsons and Mr Titterton settled around the dining-room table. Henrietta had baked rabbit and potatoes and she proudly placed the silver-plated ham-bone holder and matching marrow spoon in front of Hadley's place at the head of the table. But Hadley's mother turned to him. 'Let Mr Titterton take the head of the table tonight, Hadley,' she said.

Hadley's jaw dropped and Henrietta began, 'But mother—'

'You take your usual place near the kitchen, Henrietta.'

Mr Titterton said grace and an icy silence settled in the room. Hadley found the food difficult to swallow and Henrietta slid most of her potatoes into her napkin and shoved it in her pocket.

Mr Titterton breathed on Hadley's silver-plated prize, whipping out his creased and slightly stiff handkerchief and polishing it.

'I put in a good word for you,' he said, with a smirk to Hadley.

Widow Pearson smiled as if this was the greatest generosity, but Hadley looked destroyed.

'You did?'

'Think nothing of it,' said Mr Titterton, all graciousness, 'and your furrows were among the best—'

'They were the best,' said Henrietta, 'truly, they were.'

'Calm down, Henrietta,' snapped her mother.

Hadley put down his knife and pushed away his plate. He hadn't won fair and square. He wondered if everyone knew. 'I've had a big day,' he said. 'I think I'll—'

'No, Hadley,' gasped his mother. 'Mr Titterton has something else to say. Something important.' She fanned her face as if it might push the air towards her thin blue mouth.

Mr Titterton stood up, smoothed the shiny strands of hair on either side of his sparse middle part, and stretched one arm along the mantelpiece. He looked down at Hadley and smiled. Hadley didn't smile back; he focused his gaze on Mr Titterton's forehead, avoiding those dentures.

'Son,' said Mr Titterton gravely, 'your mother and I are to be married.' He lowered his mouth to touch Widow Pearson's hand as she reached out to him. 'Your mother will join me at Overton.'

'In the manager's house,' said the Widow happily. It took a second for the information to register.

Henrietta held her breath, wiping her palms on her apron. How embarrassing, she thought. What will people think? They'll share a bed.

Hadley stammered, 'Congratulations,' but the implications of all this were circling, waving at him like enemy flags over the crest of a hill.

'Thank you, Hadley, son.'

Widow Pearson pointed to the sideboard drawer where her precious house plans were kept. 'And while we are at Overton Mr Titterton will have the new house built for us.'

'To retire to,' interjected Mr Titterton, 'although my days as stock overseer at Overton are not over yet.'

Henrietta sat very still, trying to take it all in, trying to grasp what was truly happening. Could it be that she would stay here, with Hadley? Could it be that her mother would have maids at Overton, that Henrietta would be free? She was breathless with anticipated joy.

'Hadley, you must thank Mr Titterton for the recommendation too,' said her mother. 'He secured your position at Overton for you.'

Hadley frowned: had he achieved nothing on his own?

Mr Titterton pointed to him with his pipe. 'You must take advantage of your new career – travel, gain experience with all types of sheep in all conditions. In that way you can improve the land here at Elm Grove as you planned.' The enemy was marching down the hill; Mr Titterton would take over Hadley's inheritance, Hadley saw, while Hadley paid for the improvements to Elm

Grove that Mr Titterton would supervise to his satisfaction in order that the property would support him comfortably until his death.

'I will have a family,' said Mr Titterton, 'something I've never had the privilege to enjoy.'

'And,' thought Hadley, 'you will have a property, and my cash flow while I wait until you die to inherit my own future.' Hadley moved his gaze to the dull fireplace, his heart pounding. What about his future? What about Phoeba? Their future? And then it occurred to him: she might marry him if his mother lived at Overton! And if she did, he could work at Overton, save, secure the farm, build his own new house. For Phoeba and for their children.

Beside him, Henrietta crossed all her fingers. Please let Hadley ask if I can stay at Elm Grove with him. Please let me stay and care for him, mind the house when he's away working.

'Of course Henrietta will come with me,' said Widow Pearson and Henrietta felt something inside her sink. Everything was empty, pointless. She was to be maid to the overseer and his wife, her mother, in the manager's house.

Who would look after his sheep when he went away, Hadley wondered – and then he realised that was why Mr Titterton got him the job, was urging him to travel, to 'gain experience'. Mr Titterton wanted Hadley out of the way. Mr Titterton wanted Elm Grove. Hadley stood up to face him. 'I plan to marry soon too.'

Henrietta leapt up next to him. 'And I might get married as well … one day.' She wasn't sure how that changed anything, but it felt good to say something.

Their mother leaned back against her chair back while Mr Titterton took his pipe from between his dentures and stared at Hadley, confused. 'Who?'

'I have an … understanding with Phoeba Crupp,' he said, his confidence waning.

'He has,' nodded Henrietta.

'Nice piece of land, Crupps'.' Mr Titterton put his pipe back in his mouth.

But the Widow exploded, 'I won't have it!' Hadley winced. 'It is obvious Phoeba Crupp is not sweet at all – she has straight hair!'

It occurred to Hadley to point out that his mother had straight hair but, given that she wasn't prone to sweetness, he thought better of it.

'She is sweet,' said Henrietta, fiercely. 'And she's sturdy and she's a good worker. Like me.' Then wished she hadn't said it: it made them sound like plough horses.

'Pipe down!' hissed her mother. 'She's pithy. Her sister is flighty. Her mother is a ridiculous town woman and she has a mad aunt.' She struggled for breath.

'Dearest, I'm sure she'll mellow once she has children and family to consider,' said Mr Titterton patting her hand, 'and the love of a husband.'

'No husband will have her,' said the Widow Pearson. 'She rides astride.'

Henrietta flinched. So did she when her mother wasn't looking. She crept to the kitchen and began to plunge the plates into hot soapy dishwater. Hadley followed her, absentmindedly rubbing a tea towel over the sudsy china and stacking it in the kitchen cupboard. 'She hasn't said yes, yet,' he whispered.

'Phoeba's not the only peach on the tree,' Henrietta whispered back gently.

'But she's the peachiest.'

Hadley spent his last night at home lying in his old bed staring at his books about sheep, his albums of pressed leaves and grasses, his illustrated book of knots. On top of the bureau a tin globe caught the moonlight and the Pacific Ocean glowed dull blue. He must find a way to make it work, he hadn't waited so long to let it slip away. He would sink every last penny he earned into Elm Grove. At the season's conclusion at Overton he'd come home and move into his mother's room, change the house to suit a man with a job and a property, a future. He would take work close by, any kind of work – ploughing, harvesting, stacking grain sacks onto trains. Anything. He reached into his coat pocket and brought out the pamphlet: 'Women are for equal rights with men and we are fighting for the same laws and advantages, the same pay for the same work.'

Phoeba would marry him and build a future with him, as partners. Equal.

In her narrow bed next door, Henrietta twirled the end of her plait around and around her fingers. She wanted to ride bareback and throw away her corset. She wanted to sow oats and shear sheep like German women in South Australia she'd read about. She wanted Hadley to marry Phoeba so they could all live together, happily. She didn't want to be a maid at Overton.

Her mother would be happy there, happy as the stock overseer's wife. She would live on and on – it would be years before Henrietta was free. Tears slid down her cheeks pooling in her ears, and her large body twitched with misery.

Sunday, January 7, 1894

It was very early on Sunday morning that Aunt Margaret sat up in bed, turned to Phoeba and said, 'I heard creatures roaming in the night.' Her salt-and-pepper hair hung lank about her shoulders but her green eyes shone brightly in the morning sun.

'That's Mother,' said Phoeba. 'She gets hot in the night and goes out to stand in the front yard. She believes dangerous creatures sleep at night.' She threw back her sheet. It could also have been swaggies passing through, or shearers heading to Overton, she thought. The shearing would start the next day. She padded down the hall pulling on her dressing gown, vaguely conscious that something might not be right: the kitchen seemed strangely dark.

It took her a moment to comprehend that Spot was standing at the kitchen table, his smell crowding the small room. His rump in the doorway blocked the light and his nose rested on the table next to the saltcellar.

'Good morning Spotty,' said Phoeba, gently. 'What would you like, toast or porridge?'

He swung his head around to look out through the door and Phoeba placed one hand on his shoulder and the other on his nose and backed him out, his sharp hoofs cracking against the floor. The screen door had been torn off and lay on the back porch; the chicken coop gate hung open, the chooks happily scratching and pecking away in the vegetable garden. Maggie was not waiting on her milking table, chewing her cud. Fear crawled up Phoeba's spine.

'The campers,' she breathed, and her fear turned to panic. She ran to the front of the house, Spot lolloping after her. The dam gate was open too but the flowery green vines were still in their neat rows, the windmill turning in the breeze, and the bay beyond glistening.

It was then that she heard the faint tinkle of a bell – Maggie – and turning fast saw her father, in his dressing gown and pith hat, leading the goat down the outcrop's slope. She ran to the chicken coop, Spot still hot on her heels: all the eggs had gone.

'I don't know if they've taken anything from the house,' called Robert, 'because I couldn't get in past Spot.'

'You were afraid, weren't you Spot?'

'And Maggie's already been milked,' said Robert.

The goat bleated indignantly.

Up on the outcrop, smoke rose through the trees and Phoeba imagined the itinerants settling down to their breakfast of eggs and goat's milk.

'What can we do, Dad?'

'I've had words about them to Marius and Guston, and the new manager, Mr Steel. I think they'll leave us alone if we leave them alone but Steel seems to think they're up to no good.'

'What does this Mr Steel do at Overton?'

'Manager, apparently. He's a bit of a dark horse, but canny.' Robert went to check the pantry and cellar.

Why would the Overtons appoint a manager who was also a bank man unless something was wrong, Phoeba wondered. Pastoralists all over the country were going belly-up every day. She would ask Hadley what it was all about when she saw him. She caught the rooster and took him and Maggie to the dam paddock. Then she poured Spot's breakfast into his bin and left the trio standing together like orphans as they watched

93

her walk to the gate.

'I think you three should stay here until shearing and the harvest are over, she called back. 'It's safer, all right?' It didn't make them look any less nervous.

Robert counted the jars of preserved fruit and vegetables, the pickles and apples, the pumpkins and potatoes. Then he took the gate from the vegetable yard and screwed it to the cellar door, securing it with a lock. Not a good sign at the start of the busy season, he thought, and headed to the stables, where Phoeba had begun to harness Centaur. She needed to learn about this horse, she decided, because when she wrapped the girth strap under his stomach he filled himself up with air. It made it difficult for her to buckle the strap, so she walked him in circles until he had to breathe. His ears were small which, people said, indicated he had an ungenerous temperament. He pressed his tail down hard like a lid on a paint tin when she tried to ease it through the crupper and she stood in front of him and looked into his eyes. 'We will have no trying to race home today, Centaur. You live here now.' Then she rubbed his nose, checked his yoke and hoped she'd at least made one horse feel comfortable that morning.

They dragged the sulky from the shed and Robert backed Centaur easily between the shafts while Phoeba guided them through the tug stops. She attached the trace to the sulky, threaded the reins through the terrets and she and her father circled the horse checking his harness for firmness. She went inside to dress – and to prepare for the arguments about seating for the ride to church.

'The countryside is such a pretty hue at this time of year, all blue and purple,' said Aunt Margaret from the veranda, admiring the noxious weeds. 'I'll paint it after church. What crop is it?'

'Scottish cotton,' said Robert, puffing on his pipe. 'You

haven't made a special effort for the new vicar, Phoeba?'

'He's a galoot.' It was hot, and she dabbed at her forehead with her handkerchief. 'Given my druthers,' she said, 'I'd rather stay at home.' But she should go to say good luck to Hadley for his new job and to see if anything was known about the itinerants, if anyone else had been robbed. Besides, no one else could drive the sulky.

'Well you can't stay home,' said Maude. 'You know Lilith has never driven, Aunt Margaret has never owned a horse and I am afraid of them.'

'That's like being afraid of drinking water,' said Phoeba.

'I'm afraid of country water,' said Maude, pulling on her gloves. 'There are creatures in it. Right Robert, while we are away you can cut thistles and Phoeba, that handkerchief is too gay for church. Get another one.' Maude had slept through the eventful morning and had not noticed there was no fresh milk, or eggs, or that the gate was nailed to the cellar door.

Phoeba slipped her handkerchief up her sleeve. Lilith rushed onto the veranda and past her father.

'You have rouge on your lips Lilith,' he said, without looking up. 'Rub it off.'

'It's strawberry water,' said Maude, lifting her skirts to negotiate the front steps in her Sunday shoes. 'Now, where shall we all fit in this miserable sulky?'

The argument threatened to last all morning, until finally Aunt Margaret nervously took the reins and Phoeba saddled Rocket. She stood firm about riding astride, insisting it was better than being seen on Spot in the dam.

'You vex me, Phoeba Crupp,' scolded Maude. 'You deserve to get a nasty rash.'

Spot followed them along the fence as far as he could.

'I'll take you out tomorrow,' called Phoeba, leaning over Rocket and digging her heels in. She loved to ride Rocket – the speed of him – but her legs would ache because she had to stand all the way, or else have her teeth shattered. Spot turned his back and let his head drop. The rooster jerked his way over and stood supportively at the horse's heel.

Robert was kneeling between his vines, inspecting bunches of grape berries in case the nocturnal visitors had stolen any, when something dark caught the corner of his eye. A severe woman in a black dress with great circles of sweat under her arms stomped towards him looking uncannily like a koala. Two smaller creatures trailed behind her, firm-jawed and hostile, with black cotton-canvas hats perched on their foreheads, like birds. As they walked they snapped branches from the vines and threw them on the ground. The blood drained from Robert's face as the biggest one shook a green bouquet of plump berries at him, screaming, 'God has destroyed this evil industry once and he'll do it again!'

'It was bad weather and grape louse,' Robert shot back, advancing as fast as his roundness would allow. He felt his feet swelling and stinging with the speed. 'Now get to church,' he yelled, 'you're compacting the soil structure around my roots.'

'Alcohol is a sin,' said the koala, its voice rising. 'It corrupts good men, causes fathers to lose their jobs and abuse their wives and children.'

'Shoo,' yelled Robert, rattling a bunch of shade leaves at them.

'Total abstinence—'

'You don't approve of alcohol for medicinal use either?'

'No.'

'You know, if you drink it, it can actually cause smiling,' said

Robert, 'and that would benefit your marriage prospects with the vicar a great deal.'

The women didn't move. The koala-like one broke another branch from its trunk, freeing it from the wire trellis, and threw it on the ground. Robert reached down into his mulch and selected a clod of Spot's best manure from the edge of a thin irrigation groove. He heaved it at them and it landed on the woman's skirt with a soft phfft.

'Shoo,' he said again. 'Leave before you turn my grapes sour.'

The leader pointed a finger at him. 'Evil is within you,' she sneered. 'Punishment will be yours.' And they marched back to their buggy and climbed into the cabin, the springs flattening under their weight.

The vicar had left his horse in the sun again but a swaggie from a group waiting outside the church led it over to the shade between Rocket and Centaur. The swaggies kept their swags across their backs and stood in a hazy group, like people who'd travelled a long way for a banquet only to be told the food was eaten.

Hadley wasn't waiting to tether the Crupps' horses. He was just inside the door and he pounced on Phoeba when she came in. The pews were filled with the Crupps' new neighbours – the grubby but now well-fed seasonal workers – and the air smelled like campfires, bad teeth and pig flesh that hadn't stayed long enough in brine. Henrietta wiggled her fingers at Phoeba from the middle of the crowded pews. She was squeezed in on one side of her mother; Mr Titterton sat on the other side. It was the first statement of their relationship to the whole district. No wonder Henrietta looked so crestfallen.

'Stay here with me,' whispered Hadley.

'These itinerants,' she whispered back furiously, 'have violated

97

my goat, stolen my eggs and half my vegetables, and now they have come to church for free wine!'

Hadley nodded. 'They're desperate.'

'They could ask for food, or cut thistles, or something.'

She could feel his anxiety, could tell by his nervousness that he wanted to ask if she'd considered his proposal. But she wanted to ask him about Rudolph Steel – only to find out what was happening at Overton, she assured herself.

Lilith wriggled into a seat directly behind Marius and tapped his shoulder with her fan. He glanced warily at his mother before nodding to her. Phoeba, watching, smiled. Her sister really was very pretty. It was impossible not to take notice of her, especially if you were vulnerable.

Mr Jessop, a thin man with bandy legs far enough apart to drive a phaeton through, gave up his seat to Maude and Margaret. They squashed in next to Mrs Jessop, displacing her eldest boy at the other end of the pew. He joined his father to stand at the back of the church.

The itinerants murmured, fidgeted, dropped things and laughed at the birds bathing in the altar cup. They stayed seated during the hymns and murmured throughout the sermon. The vicar pressed on with a strong sermon on loving one's neighbours. Then he filled the communion cup and they flocked to him like seagulls to a picnic basket. It was then that Hadley took Phoeba's hand and dragged her outside.

'Hadley, please, people will think—'

'Bother people.'

Jamming his hat on his head, he led her to his horse and they stood between the carriages.

'Now, Phoeba …' he said and found himself lost for words.

Her heart sank. Hadley was staring so earnestly at her and

today was the day she knew she must really hurt him, put an end to all this. And it was the first day of his new career.

'I'm going straight to Overton now. We start in the morning, as you know.' His kitbag was tied behind his saddle. He straightened, held his lapels and looked her in the eye.

'Hadley, please—'

'Can't we just get engaged, Phoeba? We can be engaged for a long time if you like.'

But she couldn't say yes. She didn't feel love; she didn't feel that sort of attraction. Hadley was just a friend. She couldn't make him anything else. And the idea of marrying Hadley seemed to her like taking the highest paid job at the abattoirs. 'I can't,' she said at last. 'I think it would be … unethical.'

He gritted his teeth, looked up at the sky and rubbed his forehead. 'No it wouldn't, Phoeba. It would fix everything.'

'You'll meet a very lovely, very suitable squatter's daughter. Your whole future is ahead of you.' She wished it was night so she couldn't see his hurt. He took his spectacles off and rubbed them with his nice, ironed handkerchief. It was one of his father's.

'It's logical and not at all surprising that we should be a couple. And if we get engaged I can lay claim to what's mine.'

'Hadley! I'm not yours.' She spun around, shocked.

'No, I didn't mean … you misunderstand.' He sounded beaten then and his voice was wobbly.

'I can't, Hadley,' she said, miserably. 'It's not honest.'

She was right, he knew, it wasn't honest. And it wasn't honest to try to sway her by telling her if they were engaged he could claim Elm Grove, secure a place for a wife, for children, for the heirs to his father's dream. He could keep control of his farm away from old Mr Tit. But if she couldn't marry him, there was nothing he could do. He wanted to cry.

Phoeba felt wretched. Hadley was lovely, and she did love him standing there next to his brown mare in his new wool suit, and she loved his gallant moustache. He was funny and he was kind and she hated hurting him. But he had changed everything by persisting with this. It would always be there.

'It wouldn't be right,' she said, again.

He put his hands either end of the saddle and his foot in the stirrup and then suddenly stopped. 'We don't have to get married.'

'You'd expect that we would one day, wouldn't you?'

Hadley couldn't lie but nor could he tell her the truth. He got on his horse and pulled his hat down firmly. 'If you change your mind ...'

'I'll let you know.' Perhaps she shouldn't have said that, she thought, he might think she would marry him one day. It was all so wrenching and confusing. She would please almost everyone if she married Hadley – except Hadley's mother. Hadley would need a strong, plucky wife to cope with his mother. Phoeba didn't think she wanted to take that on.

The church doors flung open and the congregation rushed out as if a nest of bees had swarmed.

'Good luck for tomorrow, Hadley,' she called, but he was already riding on to Overton, his shoulders round and his feet limp in the stirrups.

'We're going to Pearsons' for tea,' said Maude, rushing across the yard and shooing her towards the horses. 'The vicar is coming so you'd better get going.' Her mother didn't want the vicar to know she rode astride.

Phoeba walked Rocket ahead of the small convoy – the Hampden, the sulky and the vicar's buggy – in the hot sun all the way to Pearsons' and rode up the drive under the gentle elm shade.

At the end of the grand arch of trees, she tethered Rocket in the stables and looked across the property: Hadley's inheritance.

When the Crupps had first arrived at Mount Pleasant, they had called on old Hadley, his wife and his two young children, driving up to the exposed house between two rows of small, green elm saplings. As Mr Pearson proudly told them, he'd ring-barked all of the trees for sheep pasture and cut the rest down to build his six-room house. It had sickened Phoeba's heart and brought tears to her father's eyes. Mrs Pearson, young and pink then, had pointed to the lines of elm seedlings and said, 'We'll call it Elm Grove.' Fourteen years later the house, gnawed at and frayed by the wind and rain, sat sagging in a swamp of saltbush and Widow Pearson still clung to the dream of the new homestead planned by her husband before he died. Robert always maintained Mrs Pearson had poisoned her husband – it was well known that she was a terrible cook – and that the last thing he saw, propped up in front of the window, was his great work, a salty bog eaten to the roots and punctured by the hooves of too many sheep.

Margaret climbed down from the sulky, saying to Phoeba, 'Such a bleak property, I would never paint it.'

'Paint the sheep,' said Phoeba, pointing to a regiment of fifty or so handsome erect sheep standing to attention in the paddock. They were square and straight-backed, standing on evenly placed feet with wool all the way down their straight legs. Chunky, thick neck folds tumbled down their wide chests and crinkly, thick cochlea-shaped horns wound at the side of their heads. She wondered why she had ever told Hadley she hated them.

Widow Pearson led them into her parlour. She sat in her Louis chair, her corset pushed up so that she looked like she had a book stuffed down her bodice. The vicar sat in the matching chair next to her and Maude, Margaret and Lilith perched opposite on the lounge. Henrietta and Phoeba went to the kitchen to organise morning tea.

Phoeba sensed something wrong: was it her? Was it the refusal?

'We know life isn't fair, don't we?' said Henrietta all of a sudden, tipping milk into a small jug.

'Yes,' said Phoeba, thinking she was about to be lectured on breaking Hadley's heart. 'There's good luck, misfortune and Mother Nature, Henri, but all things heal.'

'Not all.' Henrietta looked glumly down at her boots. They needed a good polishing.

'I'm sorry, Henri, but I can't marry Hadley—'

'No, it's Mother. She's getting married.'

'What?'

'Shhsss!' Henrietta bunched and screwed her skirt in her hands, tears welling in her eyes.

'Married?' hissed Phoeba. It was absurd. 'What on earth for?'

'He's a bachelor?' Henrietta suggested. 'Or he has savings? I don't know.'

Hearing Widow Pearson call from the front parlour they began to set the tray, loudly, then Phoeba put her arms around Henrietta and patted her back. 'Just remember, Henri, one day your mother will be in heaven.'

'Or hell,' said Henrietta. 'She'll have to empty her own chamber pot there.'

They took the tea tray in together and the Widow said, loudly, 'Put it on the sideboard above the drawer where the plans for the new homestead are kept, Henrietta.'

The girls served tea and sat together on the window boxes. Everyone sipped their tea then put their cups down in their saucers, politely: the milk was floating in blobs. It often curdled during the hot ride from Overton.

Sweat ran from the vicar's fringe, down his forehead, out over his cheeks and dripped onto his guernsey, as he spoke at length about his plans to finish the interior of the church. This prompted Widow Pearson to talk about the plans for her new house, 'which will be built sooner than anyone thinks,' she assured them.

She passed around Hadley's silver-plated ham-bone holder and matching marrow spoon before turning her blue nose to Maude.

'Mr Titterton tells me you let those anti-machinery people camp on your property.'

'Mr Titterton is a constant help to you, isn't he, Mrs Pearson?' said Maude, pointedly. 'A close friend.'

Widow Pearson drew herself up and placed her cup gently in its saucer. She smiled at the vicar, who cleared his throat. 'Indeed, Mr Titterton and Mrs Pearson have—'

'Mr Titterton and I are betrothed,' said the Widow. 'You will read it in the Geelong paper tomorrow.'

Lilith couldn't hide her astonishment. 'You're getting married?'

'Congratulations,' said Maude, faintly.

Aunt Margaret looked away, pressing her lips together and stuffing a handkerchief over her nose, but her snicker was still audible.

'It will be my first marriage ceremony at Bay View,' said the vicar and beamed at Henrietta. 'And I hope that it will not be my last! There is nothing more comforting to a man alone. These are excellent pikelets. You must enjoy cooking, Miss Pearson?'

'She hates it,' said Phoeba.

'My fiancé is the overseer, as you all know, but our home

will be the manager's house at Overton,' the Widow explained importantly. 'It has a staircase.'

'With your breathing problems it'll probably kill you,' mumbled Aunt Margaret.

'Pardon?'

'She said,' Maude hastily cut in, 'you'll probably take Henrietta, will you?'

'Of course, it will be good for her,' said Widow Pearson but Henrietta made a small involuntary squeak; Phoeba took her friend's hand.

'I will be mistress of the manager's house. It will be very good for Hadley too. New opportunities will arise,' said the Widow and looked directly at Phoeba. 'We'll be swept into a higher class of people. Hadley will find a wife. Someone suitable.'

Phoeba felt a great tightening loosen inside her. 'I couldn't be happier for him,' she said brightly.

'We must call,' said Maude, and the vicar said, 'Oh yes! We'll come for tea.' Then he turned to Aunt Margaret. 'Mrs Pearson tells me you are selling your house in Geelong to move to Melbourne, Miss Robinson?'

Aunt Margaret looked very pleased. 'I am!'

'Lodgings?' asked Widow Pearson. And Maude said hastily, 'Of a sort. Will you be honeymooning, Mrs Pearson?'

The Widow ignored her. 'What sort of lodgings, Miss Robinson?'

Maude looked afraid. Margaret put her teacup down gently. 'An artistic community, a sort of naturalist camp with seven free-spirited men and two other gay spinsters. It's most convenient, and we'll all have such fun together.' She winked at Phoeba.

'Gracious,' said Maude, fanning her reddening face with the end of her jabot, 'it's almost time for lunch!'

'You will stay, of course, Vicar,' said the Widow. She turned to Maude: 'Henrietta will see you out.'

The second wedding cake

Monday, January 8, 1894

Phoeba woke on Monday feeling unsettled. She had spent the night worrying about Henrietta. Fancy spending years running after Mr Titterton. She'd have to eat with him as well. All sorts of opportunities would be open to Hadley with a reference from Overton and Mr Titterton's influence. He would find the right girl. Everything was in its place. But there was something gnawing at her. She put it down to the windy day.

Her father rushed up and down between his vines, though there was no rain in the clouds and they blew rapidly out to sea. It was the dust and the thrashing leaves he was concerned about, but there was nothing to be done to stop it, so Phoeba left him alone. Her sense of unease was still there as she milked Maggie and harnessed Centaur to take her aunt to the train.

During breakfast, the itinerants moved stealthily down from the outcrop past the house along the bright lane to Bay View.

'They could be stripping the church crop today,' said Robert, doubtfully, 'but in such a wind …' The steam boiler would surely send sparks everywhere and confound the scythers, and the chaff would scatter as it fell from the thresher.

Aunt Margaret was dressed and chipper in plenty of time for her train, but Maude arrived at the breakfast table in her nightie. She was unwell.

'Margaret has given me a headache and palpitations,' she said. 'She was mischievous and provocative and now the Widow will tell everyone she's a naturalist and Hadley won't want to marry Phoeba.'

'Rot,' said Margaret. 'Your malaise is nothing to do with me. It's the change. You're the right age. And anyway, you can't really expect poor Phoeba to marry into that family, can you?'

'I don't know why you go there,' added Robert. 'You either come back poisoned or insulted.'

'Phoeba should marry Hadley,' said Lilith, arriving at the sulky in her Sunday best, 'if only to get the farm before Mr Titterton does. That would upset old Widow Poison.'

Phoeba paused: she hadn't thought of it like that. Then I can have what's mine, he'd said. But surely Elm Grove belonged to Hadley. He was a son, the land was his, and it wasn't as if Mr Titterton was going to retire there in the next week and start bossing him around.

'I don't have to marry anyone,' said Phoeba, tying her hat ribbon under her chin.

'Well what will you do?' cried Maude.

'I am already doing something.'

Aunt Margaret threw her carpetbag into the back of the sulky, looked at the huge clouds moving swiftly overhead and shoved an extra hatpin through her hat. She buttoned her old dustcoat all the way up to the top button and climbed into the carriage. 'If you had a barouche or a Hampden, Robert, we could have put the top on.'

'It would have blown off today,' said Robert, checking Centaur's harness again.

'More importantly,' said Phoeba, 'if we had a bigger carriage there'd be room for Dad and Mother would make him come to church, or worse, visit Widow Pearson.'

Lilith pulled her hatnet over her face and reached for the long cane prod, flicking it through the air so its tip bounced.

'Right,' she said. 'I have decided to drive. I need to be able to move about since Phoeba may get married.'

Aunt Margaret opened her mouth to object but Phoeba put her hand up. 'There's no point if you want to get to your train without a war.'

The two sisters climbed up into the sulky and settled their skirts across their knees. And with Robert calling warnings that the thresher was about, Lilith steered Centaur through the gate.

Spot watched them go, his soft chest pressed against the fence and his black mane lifting in the wind. At his ankle the rooster stood and beside him Maggie chewed her cud, her green eyes following the sulky down Mount Hope Lane. Spot whinnied lowly.

Hadley had woken at sunrise, was first at the kitchen for breakfast and first at the shed. Now he waited at the classing tables with his shirtsleeves rolled up and his apron tied neatly. No one came. The other classer, McInness, the pressers, wool rollers and rouseabouts didn't appear; no tar boy came, nor one single shearer. It was Mr Titterton who found him worried and alone in the vast shed between the two empty tables, a cage of sharp lightbeams boring down from nail holes in the roof. He patted Hadley's arm and said, 'Son, the foreman has called a meeting because the shearers

109

have suddenly decided they need five shillings more per hundred. I think they should be grateful in these hard times, but there you have it: plain greed.'

Hadley felt his heart skip a beat. He removed his glasses and polished the lenses with the apron Henrietta had so carefully starched for him, blinking away tears and trying to still his aching heart. Nothing was going right. Out on the loading dock he cursed the wind whipping across the dry, red dirt. He looked beyond the grain sheds and the haystacks to the gums lining the creek where the shearers camped, but they weren't coming.

'There are plenty more who will do the job,' said Mr Titterton, but Hadley knew skilled shearers were valuable, that itinerants couldn't do the job well and that things could easily turn bad if they tried to. Newspapers told him daily about sheds and hedges set alight, about riots breaking out and entire flocks stolen. He never thought those things would reach them at Bay View.

Mr Overton would pay the men what they wanted, if he wanted his sheep shorn and the wool sold, thought Hadley. Just as he himself must be able to plant trees at Elm Grove and sink a bore, and fertilise his land and start to show Phoeba how it could be.

Guston Overton had Marius stand by his side when he confronted the foreman and his crew, eighty lean, bearded men and a dozen Chinese.

'This is the way to deal with the rabble,' he whispered to his son, and offered them two shillings more, like it or lump it. The shearers turned away and went back to their swags.

When Marius and his father walked away, Rudolph Steel spoke to them. He spoke reasonably, reminded them that they had better conditions than most, that the cook was reliable and the tucker plentiful. Would they take three shillings? He left them to discuss it.

Hunger brought them dribbling across to the cook's hut at smoko. They lined up at the kitchen for sweat black tea, sandwiches and scones. At the sound of the first bell, they were on the board with their shears in their hands, facing the pens. At the second bell, they sprang to action.

Finally, Hadley was in his element, fist deep in greasy wool, the warm air saturated with sweet lanolin and foul sheep shit, and the sounds of the shearing shed. Bleating sheep, the patter of cloven hoofs on greasy floorboards, and the sharp shouts of shearers to the roustabouts, the scrape and click of metal shears slicing through tepid, moist wool – white gold.

The shed had sixty-four stands, the biggest in the district. Upwards of sixty men skirted ten slatted tables, quietly tugging dags and muck from fleeces flung artfully like eiderdowns of cloud. The low roof was suspended by thick eaves already snowy with wool fibre at the season's start, its corrugated iron heat bank pulsing hot waves onto the men that swelled the buttery atmosphere. At ten-foot intervals a door in the roof swung out propped on a pole, and letting in molten squares of hot light. The thermometer registered 114 degrees but the mercury shot to 142 when the foreman left it out on the iron for five minutes.

Hadley worked conscientiously, eagerly, a little too buoyantly. Mr Titterton had given him a lump of a fellow called Harry to work with, a slow, open-mouthed but constant lad who looked to Hadley for instruction. A rouseabout dumped a fleece onto the table and Harry watched Hadley take a small wool staple, snap it, study it, gauge the colour, crimp, length and tensile strength. He smelled it, rubbed it between his fingers and showed it to Harry, told him which bin to throw it in. Soon it was Hadley's table the rouseabouts came to more often than not to leave their fleeces. The other classer, McInness, was a hesitant judge and slow to fill the bins.

Hadley felt someone watching and when he turned, he saw Rudolph Steel.

'Good work,' he said, and walked away. A stranger, an Englishman, had just approved of Hadley. A warm glow spread through him; recognition, appreciation, success. He turned back to the fleece spread on the table and grabbed the warm blanket of golden wool in his hands.

Centaur had danced and shied as he overtook some of the sundowners on the road, and Lilith's confidence faded when she reached the church paddock. The big green and red steam engine puffed and cackled and a giant wheel turned a long, flat pulley belt that stretched to the threshing machine, driving the rattling, thrashing thing. Dusty straw spewed onto the brittle stubble behind it.

Around the turbulent machines, scythers stepped through the crop, their blades sweeping and the wheat collapsing into a thick straw mattress. Stookers paced and bent in a bobbing line behind them.

The vicar stood in the paddock watching the bundlemen collect the stooks and run with them to feed the thresher. Stackers waved straw bundles high on their forks, building a straw hill that caught the wind and rained stalks all around. Suddenly, the vicar's hat leapt from his head with a gust and danced across the field. Centaur threw his head back and skipped. Lilith tightened her grip on the reins.

'My train is waiting,' said Aunt Margaret but the wind whipped her voice away. There was a lot of activity around the carriages as they sat on the wayside track, well away from the siding. Shunters were uncoupling trucks, leaving them for wool bales or wheat sacks. Perhaps, thought Phoeba, that explained why the itinerants had grouped behind the church: they were waiting to load wheat or wool.

Another crowd, passengers and workers from Overton, assembled around a freight truck to watch the Sunshine harvester being unloaded; a team, harnessed to a flat-top wagon, stood ready to haul the machine away. The harvester rose high in the air and stayed there, swinging from its chains and dangling beneath an A-frame winch like a monster pendant, an odd contraption with a curved hood and two huge double-spoked metal wheels. It had belts and sprockets, levers and chains, a bin to collect chaff and a seat perched on a C-shaped spring. Across the front protruded a drum with sharp combs. Centaur threw his head again. Phoeba clutched the armrest and Lilith slapped the reins over his rump.

'That's enough!' she said in a thin voice. Surprisingly the horse settled, and she was able to guide him to Flynn's. She tied the reins through the sulky wheel twice, jiggling the brake lever, and said good morning to two young boys, one a tiny runt, grimy with dull straw-coloured hair, the other a large, dark-haired boy with a hanging bottom lip, but they just stared at her, apparently unaware they were witnessing her first drive. She turned her attention to a squat thing on legs like a cooper's barrel with a cog and flywheel and turning handle attached to one end. Aunt Margaret read the advertising sticker pasted to its top: 'Lily White Washing Machine will wash the finest lace or the heaviest articles absolutely without damage'.

The women crowded the shop in their wide hats and full skirts, a draught sliding up through the floorboards, disturbing flour dust around their hems. Still in charge, Lilith ordered butter, dried fruit, more peel, nuts and tea – another cake, thought Phoeba – then asked if the machine was for the Widow Pearson.

'Yes,' said Mrs Flynn rubbing her nostrils with the palm of her hand. 'Just one more thing to upset the Luddites if you arst me. They must be paying Hadley well is all I can say, but it wouldn't do me no harm if Overtons paid me.'

Phoeba read a newspaper. The headlines screamed: 'NEIGHBOUR BURNS BABY. In an increasingly dreadful situation of hunger and poverty, a distraught mother in North Fitzroy declared she had no food to feed the rest of her family, let alone a new baby, when a neighbour smelled something like meat burning and enquired about what she was burning.'

'What's the world coming to?' she said.

'Ruin,' said Freckle, loping through the shop and out to the boys waiting on the veranda, three fish dangling from his hand.

'He catches fish for them itinerants because they say they're tired of rabbit,' Mrs Flynn explained, 'but they don't pay either. Up to no good if you arst me.' She dropped a chunk of butter on the scales. One corner drooped wetly, avalanching onto the counter. 'Sun caught the side of the Coolgardie safe.'

Phoeba said nothing but Lilith said, 'You should get an ice chest from Lassetters.'

'That's a good idea,' said Mrs Flynn, sarcastically. 'We could have the ice sent out on the train each day, couldn't we? Pay for twice as much as we need so we've got enough left after half of it's melted on the way. You're very lucky to get any of this. There's a depression, y'know, and it's hard to get, is butter.'

She set about shovelling tea from a huge bag onto bench scales that were peppered with rolled oats. Phoeba asked if the peach parer had come.

'No parcels.'

They loaded their shopping behind the sulky seat and walked Aunt Margaret to the siding. Phoeba brushed chaff from the shoulder of her coat. 'Just be yourself, Aunt,' she said, kissing her and wishing her luck at Esperance. And Aunt Margaret bravely boarded the train, though her legs felt like jelly. It had been a very long time since she had been to Melbourne, and she wished she'd asked Maude if she could take Phoeba with her. But Maude would say no – cities were dangerous places for a young lady.

Across the railway line the new Sunshine harvester was on the ground, workmen securing it to the harnessed team. Lilith pulled her net over her face, smoothed her skirt over her knees and took up the reins.

'Lilith, I can drive back—'

'No Phoeba. You can't be boss all the time.' She slapped the reins over Centaur's rump, steering him towards the intersection.

Suddenly the air filled with shouting and yelling and a stream of angry men shot from behind the church waving sticks and sacks, trying to spook the wagon team. The driver held fast but the itinerants swarmed over the harvester, bashing at it with their sticks, tugging at its chains and tearing at its tin panels.

Centaur pigrooted, his hind hoofs slamming the sulky dashboard so the girls felt the sting of his metal shoes through the soles of their own boots. Lilith wrapped her calfskin fingers tightly around the reins and pulled back with all her might but the horse simply dropped his head and flattened his ears. The colour drained from Lilith's face. 'Lord save me,' she said and closed her eyes. Phoeba gripped the armrest. 'Hang on tight, Lilith, hang on.'

Centaur bucked and rose like a great hairy arc. As Lilith screamed, the horse bolted, jumping to breakneck speed and hurling the women back, their heads whipping so they bit their tongues and the smalls of their backs slapped the seat rest. Phoeba

115

felt her innards press against her spine and they shot off down the dusty road at thirty miles an hour, the wind blasting against her cheeks. Centaur's hooves pounded gravel, the sulky creaked and the reins slapped.

Lilith's face was like a mask, wide and vacant with enormous eyes and a mouth frozen wide. Her arms were pulled straight by the tight reins.

'Help me, Phoeba,' she screamed. 'Make him stop.'

Phoeba reached out with one hand. 'Give me the reins and grab the brake,' she said, but it was no good. Lilith let go of both the reins and grabbed the dashboard lace work. It went through Phoeba's mind that now was a good time to push her sister out, but she herd herself say instead, 'Just hang on, Lilith. Be brave.'

There was nothing else they could do.

The horse galloped around the thistles at the intersection, thundering towards Overton. Its ears were flat to its head, its teeth bared, and the harness worked hard against its shoulders, leather slapping and metal ringing. The sulky's iron-wrapped wheels, shaky and thin, razored through the air at Phoeba's elbow and when she glanced down at the roadside it was passing in a blur, faster than she'd ever seen. The wind roared and stung, slapping her with salty spots of sweaty foam from Centaur's mouth and chest. The horse panted, its bellowing lungs heaving, and still its hooves pounded onto the hard dirt. Phoeba's hat flew off. The sulky swayed, lurched, broad-sided from one soft side of the road to the other, and jumped and thudded over potholes, bouncing the Crupps high and then slamming them back onto the thin seat. The road will soon rise to meet us and grate our flesh from our bones, thought Phoeba.

It was lunchtime at the shearing shed. Hadley was in the cook's hut finishing his pudding when he noticed the wind drop, just like that, as if someone had closed a window. Outside, the clouds drifted silently overhead in a shiny sky. The shearers lounged in the shade of the yards, smoking, the discontent of the morning temporarily at bay. Some lay flat on the greasy floorboards, their black tea cooling in tin cups beside them.

'Rogue horse boltin'', cried a rouseabout sitting on a gatepost. He pointed across the paddocks and all eyes turned to the horse hurtling down the drive towards the homestead gates and the sulky springing along behind it and tossing its passengers.

Men uncurled and stood slowly. Someone called, 'It's two women!'

Hadley saw the sulky and raced outside. He dashed through the door and his heart gave a great lurch. 'Phoeba!'

Mrs Overton was pressing damp sachets of dock plant to her translucent skin when the horse and sulky clattered through the bluestone gates. She went cold as she saw the terrified girls, the reins dancing in the air beside Centaur's foaming flanks and the spindly sulky veering off towards the sheds. The two women bounced sideways.

'Marius,' she screamed.

Away to the west, Rudolph Steel was herding a flock of sheep, shorn to their pink skin. The faint sound of a screaming horse and men yelping came to him over the plain. He swung his horse around, speared the mare's ribs and sprang into a gallop across the paddock, scattering the sheep.

The girl in the vegetable garden threw down her basket and ran after the sulky. The kitchen maid abandoned the butter churn to follow and even the milking cow turned to watch as the shearers made a wall across the track to the stables. But Centaur bore down on them, sending them scrambling up trees, onto the tank-stand and over the fence into the sheep pens.

The horse tore on, making a beeline for the stable gate, his old home. Phoeba saw the narrow gateway coming. Beside her, Lilith lurched back and fainted.

And then Hadley was there, standing straight in front of the galloping horse, his arms wide, his teeth gritted and a look of calm determination in his eyes. Phoeba knew Hadley would save her. But then he disappeared, a marionette tugged off-stage by his strings – Mr Titterton had pulled him away. She felt Centaur cut too soon through the gate and knew, now, she was about to be smashed against the hard ground. She saw her father smiling in her mind's eye and Henrietta, dear Henrietta, dancing like a boy. She said, 'I love you,' and let go of the armrest, raising her arms and closing her eyes.

The wheel caught the gatepost and the judder was tremendous, a sickening jolt that pulled Centaur up hard at last and skewed him on his hind legs. He screamed like a birthing beast. The sulky wheeled, its wooden spokes splintered and the wheels fractured and flew away in pieces, as the sulky collapsed sideways and the metal axle knifed in the hard dirt. Phoeba flew out onto the hard ground and the air rushed from her. She was still, stopped, at last. A wave of pain took her to blackness.

The men watched the girls tumble out. They called 'Whoa-up' to Centaur, who heaved, pawing at the dirt, terrified. Behind him the cart lay like kindling, the tea, fruit, flour and butter splattered around the limp women in the settling dust.

Phoeba was on her side in the dirt, Lilith on top of her, trying to sit up and patting at her dishevelled hair with one hand. Mr Rudolph Steel reined in his mare, kneeling down in the dust. 'There now, it's over now, you're all right.' The wool presser lifted Lilith's hem as though he were handling a live snake and pulled it down to cover the bottom of her lace bloomers. Then Marius Overton appeared and took her outstretched hand, saying, 'Where does it hurt? Can you breathe all right?'

'Yes,' she said, her jaw chattering and her skin clammy. 'Such a bother.'

Marius said tenderly, 'You are very brave,' then scooped her in his arms and carried her to a gum tree where he settled her in the shade. He told the tarboy to stay with her.

Phoeba heard a great rushing in her ears, like the sea. Her arms, all the way to her elbows, were stinging, she was shaking, and great waves shuddered through her body. It felt as though icy winds were passing over her on a blistering day. The strength was all knocked from her. Around her, eager, desperate faces framed by white lace caps looked down – men hovered behind them. I will get out of this, she thought, and I will not die.

Steel appeared again and she tried to smile, but his face vanished behind a black curtain. Someone lifted her. She screamed in pain. It was her back, a white-hot poker in her spine. Then she couldn't feel it anymore.

'My legs are missing,' she said.

'They'll come back.' She opened her eyes and Rudolph Steel was grinning at her. Such a lovely smile, she thought, and he put a glass of something sharp-smelling to her lips. 'It's a draught, to make you feel better.'

She was in a room, a lovely room, and a sweet, warm potion was sliding down her throat. Steel leaned back but she clung to his neck. He was nice and she wanted to hang onto him but he pulled her arms away somehow and was gone. Her belt was unclasped, her skirt left her, her arms were raised and the blouse left, taking her undershirt. Her boots were unsnapped and her stockings slid off. She wore no corset; would they be shocked?

Fingers rummaged through her hair searching for snapped-off hat pins or punctures and her jaw started chattering. Then they washed and dried her, swabbed and dressed her arms and hands where they had been scraped raw. They put her into garments that felt like spun cloud and she lay stunned, staring at the ceiling, a dull hum in her ears and soft, white linen around her head.

The cook pressed a poultice to Hadley's shoulder. He had landed on it roughly and wrenched something inside: he winced. Behind him, Mr Titterton said, 'That'll see you right, Hadley, these chaps know what they're doing. The bruise will come out.'

'I'll see the doctor if he comes.' He would ask him about Phoeba.

'Of course, of course,' said Mr Titterton, and patted his shoulder making Hadley wince again.

The cook lifted Hadley's arm and he yelped, but the cook held firm; 'You do ebery day, put up put up,' and levered Hadley's sore arm up and down. He wound torn sheet around Hadley's shoulders and under his arm to secure the poultice. 'I change, tree days time. You come back I change.'

Hadley nodded and the cook helped him into his shirt.

'It'll smell like a stagnant scour pond in three days,' said Hadley, trying to be brave. He had wanted to save Phoeba.

Mr Titterton helped him button his shirt. The cook made him a sling from old sheet before he shuffled away, his long plait swinging.

'You'd better inform Mother, but don't alarm her,' said Hadley, thinking he should get back to the shed but wanting to go upstairs to see Phoeba.

'I'll ride home this evening,' said Mr Titterton.

Home, thought Hadley. Mr Titterton called Elm Grove

home already. Hadley screwed his face in pain, looked up at the kitchen ceiling, picturing Phoeba somewhere in the house, limp and grazed and bleeding. In pain. She is made of sturdy stuff, he told himself.

Robert whistled as he moved his lamp, pillow and pyjamas back to his room. The wind had stopped and his vines were still under the sunshine, quietly thickening, preparing to make their sugar and acid. In his shed he stacked empty barrels next to his small wine press and turned the handle to frighten the spiders. He swept out the bin and oiled the axle on the grape wagon. It was when he was making his way down to the vineyard, knowing it was far too soon for veraison – that magic change of colour that marked the grapes' ripening – but wanting to check anyway, that he saw Henrietta's short creamy hack cantering up the lane. He'd never seen Liberty canter before. It was a short-shouldered thing and Henrietta was jigging up and down enough to chip her teeth. The horse slowed of its own accord, its chest salty with sweat. Henrietta looked as if she'd seen a sea monster.

She handed Robert Phoeba's hat. The brim was torn, the net ripped.

'I can't find them,' she said.

'She's just lost her hat ...' But Spot whinnied, his ears forward and still, watching a dray travel down the lane from Overton. The draught horses trotted briskly, Marius Overton bouncing behind on his brown and gold Arab. When they turned at the intersection, Marius struck out ahead, cantering up the slope towards Robert and Henrietta. The hair on Robert's forearms stood up and cold fear turned in the pit of Henrietta's stomach.

'Where's Phoeba?'

'At Overton,' said Marius, tying his horse to the veranda

post, 'Centaur bolted. I'm very sorry—'

'Is she all right?'

'Yes, Mr Crupp, I'll go for the doctor as soon as we've seen to Lilith.'

The wool presser steered the cart to the veranda and Henrietta and Robert moved to the back of the dray. There was Lilith, supine and ragged. She opened one eye, recognised the sky as her own and then looked at her father standing over her.

'I thought you were a corpse, old thing,' he said and rubbed his chin with his hand to stop it quivering. 'Your sister?'

'How is she, how's Phoeba?' asked Henrietta.

'She's well and truly tucked up now, nothing broken we think. She was on the bottom, with Miss on top of her,' said the wool presser. Maude came out of the house, thinking she had visitors, and saw her daughter in Marius's arms, dishevelled, her jacket ripped and her skirt dust-covered. She screamed.

'An accident with the sulky, the horse bolted,' said Marius.

'This is a wretched, brutal place,' moaned Maude collapsing into the wicker chair while he told her about the accident. Lilith buried her face in Marius's neck, Henrietta hovering behind them.

Robert looked up to the heavens. 'Those ruddy temperance women have cursed us,' he said.

Fairfield railway station was quite a distance from Melbourne, at least thirty minutes, but Aunt Margaret found the entire trip from Bay View very pleasant; the flat, dun-coloured plains around Melbourne changed along the Yarra River to paddocks that lifted gently and sank, to thick bush and gum trees. When the train pulled into Fairfield, a tall man with a beard that reached his waist, wearing green boots and a red-checked suit, waited with a woman who was wearing a red sack dress. They watched, like characters from a light opera, as the carriage doors swung open and a carpetbag plopped onto the railway platform. A pair of paint-splattered boots stepped onto the small ladder and a thin older woman climbed down, backwards, clutching at the rails. Aunt Margaret stood next to her bag. A warm gusty breeze rustled the bush. All around her, bellbirds sang.

The man called, 'Margaret Robinson?'

Aunt Margaret beamed at them. 'Mr Spark?'

The couple smiled and clapped at her and Margaret felt a strange urge to bow.

The badly dressed man removed his boater and genuflected flamboyantly. 'At your service, mademoiselle.'

Aunt Margaret's mouth fell open. At last, she thought, I've met a real artist.

'May I introduce Miss Border,' he said.

Miss Border was Margaret's age but in better condition. She had a blossomy complexion and was immaculately groomed. 'Well bred,' thought Margaret. She picked up Margaret's bag and Mr Spark offered her his arm, smiling at her as if she was brilliant, famous, beautiful. He led her towards the river, pointing the toes of his green suede shoes as he walked, like a ballerina. Under an ancient pine tree they paused and spoke. They talked about the depression, about electric tramways and about the sea monster – a giant serpent that had chased a whale off Newcastle. People said it was the same sea monster that lived in Loch Ness, although Mr Spark assured them that a loch and an ocean were very different milieus. Then they brought up the topic of art.

'What do you think of Streeton's painting, "The Railway Station, Redfern"?' they asked Aunt Margaret.

Be yourself, she heard Phoeba say. 'I prefer a good still life.'

'What about figure painting?'

Aunt Margaret wasn't sure what they meant. 'There's nothing like a good portrait of a prominent figure.'

'Life drawing?'

She still wasn't sure. 'And nothing like nature and all its wonders!'

'So, you're not interested in painting the human form in all its naturalness, painting someone else, painting models?'

Aunt Margaret was flummoxed, 'I have lived alone for many years …'

'I think I know what you mean,' said Miss Border. 'At Esperance we feel we reproduce the ideal representation of things around us, we capture the beauty of a thing whereas the impressionists, well …' She screwed her mouth down at the corners.

Aunt Margaret said, 'That Redfern thing, so messy.'

Mr Spark leaned to Miss Border. 'Would you like some pineapple, Miss Border?'

'I like pineapples. Do you like them, Miss Robinson?'

'No.' Margaret could never afford fruit.

'It's our code,' said Mr Spark, smiling at her.

'We use the word pineapple if we approve of potential members,' said Miss Border.

'The last chap we had was on about "representation", how nature isn't always picturesque and how a studio portrait doesn't reflect the true, living form. He said it was the Impressionists who represented what is real. Utter rot.' Mr Spark winked at her. 'And of course, we must be careful in case you're interested in "nature camps". Now, we will transport you to Esperance.'

He rose to his feet and offered her his fine artist's hand. The next three beats in Aunt Margaret's neglected heart kicked, and she felt a little flurried.

Aunt Margaret pondered her day out all the way home to Geelong. She would be happy there, she would fit with them. She marched directly home from the railway station, dumped her carpetbag, and found the ancient sewing machine. Securing the lid she wound twine around and around it and wrote on a luggage tag: 'To, Maude Crupp, Bay View Siding, via Geelong, Victoria'.

On the back of the tag she wrote:

'Dear Sister, Hope deferred maketh the heart sick. Love, Margaret.'

In her dank kitchen she cut two slices of bread, spread them with butter and jam and sat in her mother's rocker by the cold stove. She chewed, remembering her mother turning from the stove and flinging a tea towel over her shoulder as she embraced her father. They had waltzed around the kitchen table and her father had kissed her mother's neck, called her his fair lassie.

It was memories like this that usually made her wish she had married Mr Treadery. Tears spilled from her eyes and she howled with her mouth full of chewed bread. In the backyard a pane of glass fell from the cracked conservatory where she had spent so many hours, alone, painting plants and dead fowl.

But now, at least there was hope. Margaret wiped her nose on her sleeve and said to no one, 'I will never be lonely again.'

The afternoon was fading and Phoeba lay on her back in a brass bed draped with lace and white muslin, her head supported by a fat, feather pillow and her mouth open. She could make out an elaborate ceiling with roses and small chandeliers for gaslights. The windows were hung with lace and velvet and the mirrored dressing table held tonics and towels and a washbasin with a floral jug.

She felt like a burst strawberry in cottonwool and her nose

snorted when she breathed. The skin from one side of her face wasn't there, she suspected, and her eyes were swollen, restricting her view. Her arms and hands were bandaged.

Her mother sat on a chair by the door with her face in her hands, crying: Phoeba could see the feathers on her hat quivering. Her father walked around the room tapping the walls and opening the cupboard doors. Henrietta was beside her, tears dripping off the edge of her chin and onto the bed sheet.

'Henri,' she whispered.

She felt a weight on the side of the bed, the hair brushed from her forehead and her father's whiskers on her forehead. She smelled his pipe tobacco and the sweet, stale smell of wine and dusty grape leaves.

'You're all right, old thing,' he said.

'You've got to rest,' said Henrietta and Phoeba wondered what else she could do.

'You have done some damage,' said her mother, and Phoeba said, 'It was Centaur.'

Then she was asleep again, exhausted, and Phoeba Crupp fell out of her days.

Wednesday, January 10, 1894

Freckle, his mother and a swaggie sat in the morning sun outside the shop. The swaggie, a well-spoken chap who used to be a jeweller, read the newspaper aloud.

'Another eighty-one people, claiming William Lane's "New Australia" wasn't egalitarian and that Lane was a despot, have left Paraguay.'

'Where's that then?' asked Mrs Flynn.

The swaggie pointed towards the bay's heads. 'Out there. "The first public telephone installed at Sydney's GPO last year has broken down."'

'Telephones are a fad,' said Freckle. 'They'll never replace the lightning squirter.'

'And,' said Mrs Flynn, 'look what happened when we got a mechanical harvester in the district. They say Phoeba Crupp will never walk again.'

'Nar,' said Freckle. 'It'll take more than a horse to bugger her up.'

In the distance the long toot of the ten o'clocker sounded and the swaggie rose. Freckle picked up the empty mailbag and the jeweller handed him a halfpenny. 'It's all I've got.'

'It's enough to stop a train,' said Freckle and headed off.

The swaggie crouched low in the scrub and Freckle stood on the platform holding the mailbag out on the end of the long hook. The mailman leaned from the van, Freckle waved his empty mailbag, and the train slowed into black smoke that folded around the carriages. The mailman lifted a bag, ready to throw and called to Freckle, 'Catch!'

Freckle dropped his mailbag and held up his arms. Almost too late he saw that the incoming mailbag was too heavy. It landed with such a thud on the platform that the sleepers jumped. Opening it, Freckle found a black thing with a solid wheel at one end for turning and a thick wooded base. It weighed as much as an anvil.

'Almost killed by a sewing machine,' he said, looking around. The swaggie had caught the train.

The long, distant hoot of the train chuffing its way up from

Geelong woke Guston Overton and he gingerly sat up in his mahogany four-poster. His desk calendar told him it was Wednesday and his fob watch told him it was late. He pressed his shaky brown fingers over his ears to block out the thudding he could hear, but found it was in his head. Sliding his hand under his pillow he found his whisky flask. It was very quiet outside; he could hear no stockwhips and no whistling stockmen. He tottered to the back balcony but saw no activity at the shearing sheds. There were no stockmen pushing his flocks in from the plains; the loading dock was empty and the bale winch over the wagon hung limply.

'Bugger,' he said. They'd only been shearing for two days. He went back to his bed and reached under for his chamber pot.

Later, he found the boundary rider and instructed him to poison every rabbit warren he could find with strychnine. Then he found Steel at the machinery shed. 'What the hell is going on now?'

'The rouseabouts want another shilling; they're on strike.'

'The rouseabouts?' bellowed Guston.

'Yes,' said Rudolph. 'How's our patient this morning?'

'I didn't see the coffin carrier in my travel here. Are you telling me, Steel, that those filthy fly-blown, board-rats want a shilling more for working a broom and picking up wool? How dare they! Where's Marius?'

Rudolph Steel pushed his hat back with the tip of his pliers. 'He's taken the brougham to Mount Hope.'

'So, Steel,' cried Guston, 'what are you going to do about these striking men?'

'They won't talk to me because they think I'm a bank man and they won't talk to you because you're a squatter, and they won't talk to Marius because he bought the harvester and they sympathise with the itinerants. They won't even talk to the vet or the farrier.'

'There must be someone they'll talk to,' said Guston.

The two men came across Hadley sitting on a low stack of empty wool bales in the corner of the huge, empty shearing shed. His forehead rested on the swollen fingers that jutted from the end of his sling.

Hadley had worked at his new job for exactly two hours. He had been of no use since Monday lunchtime, couldn't do anything except wander about the shed, watching Harry – and now the blasted rouseabouts were on strike. They really should be getting on with the harvest, too, but the stookers and stackers that belonged with the thresher team were afraid to upset the itinerants. The entire community, he decided, was being held to ransom by a bunch of Luddite ratbags. He was not earning any money, and he was so anxious to do something at Elm Grove. He would have felt better if he could say he was engaged. But Phoeba was injured and ill, and he couldn't even face her. He had let her down and couldn't rid himself of the picture of her with her hands in the air: catch me. She was the only true friend he had, apart from his sister, and he had failed them both.

'Please, God, don't let her die.'

'Parsons.'

Hadley jumped up, lost his balance and fell back onto the folded wool bales. He lay on his back like a turtle, grabbing at the air. 'My arm's not right yet,' he explained.

Rudolph hauled him to his feet and he spluttered, 'Thank you.' Damn the man for always accommodating him.

'Now look here, Parsons,' said Guston, 'I have a proposition for you.'

Hadley drew himself up to his full height.

'We're not getting anywhere with these bloody shearers and

129

rouseabouts. They'll have nothing to do with us. Titterton tells me you're a good sheep man and Steel says you're good with young Harry. Harry's my cousin's son and I appreciate your patience with the boy.'

'Thank you, sir.'

The gist of the matter, Guston explained, was two-fold: the rouseabouts were striking for more money, and the shearers and other men had gone out in support of them, leaving thousands of pounds worth of wool sitting at the property because no one would load it. He had ordered trucks to freight it to the docks and now the railways were threatening to haul the empty trucks away.

'You are a neutral person,' continued Guston. 'You have offended no one and you're a worker but if you're ever to be a manager you must develop a manager's wisdom and I am offering you a chance, Parsons. You won't let me down.'

'My name is Pearson, sir, Hadley Pearson.'

'I know that!' said Guston. 'I knew your father.'

Rudolph intervened. 'What we need, Hadley, is the men paid a reasonable price and the wool shorn and shipped out as soon as possible. Just see what you can do.'

'I will,' said Hadley, rubbing his shoulder confidently.

'For a reasonable price,' warned Guston, wagging his finger. He turned and walked away and it was Rudolph who thanked him.

'How's Phoeba?'

'Why don't you see for yourself?' said Rudolph.

But Hadley couldn't just go into Phoeba's sickroom on Steel's invitation. Phoeba was a dignified person, proud, and he had let her down. He would send a note. In the meantime, of course, he must find a way to placate the shearers and get the wool moving. It was his moment to achieve something great.

The air smelled of burned roast rabbit, and bush along the creek was hard and sharp. Ribbons of fallen bark crackled under Hadley's feet and he knew they were watching him, hiding in the bush. He sensed a faint din, the soft movement of a hundred resting men. His confidence drained: it would all go wrong. Was he being used or should he really be proud Mr Overton had selected him to negotiate? His blood moved reluctantly through his veins, slowing his progress. A hard, spiked branch leapt up like a striking snake and caught him on the soft plane inside his thigh and he fell, writhing on the ground and holding his leg. His face screwed in pain. All he had wanted, he thought, for the hundredth time, was to class wool, to earn money, to breed sheep, to get married, to grow old ... He opened his eyes, replaced his dislodged spectacles, and saw the perfectly round metal holes of a double-barrel shotgun an inch from his nose. Three shearers leaned above him and he put his hands at his ears, squeezing his eyes shut again. I am going to die, he thought.

'I come peacefully,' he said. His voice sounded like a piccolo and he badly wanted to piss.

They lifted him by the arms and marched him through the campers to the heart of the unhappy lot, past men lounging against trees and lying on swags, playing cards and smoking. They were weary and suspicious. The foreman, a thin-lipped chap with a massive beard and small eyes, didn't move from the log he sat on, didn't take his eyes off the boiling billy until Hadley offered the rouseabouts sixpence more. Then he gazed at him, incredulous, and threw his head back laughing.

'You're doing your master's bidding, but you know even the shearers deserve more than they get. The rousies won't work for less than a shilling more!' He was leaning close to Hadley. 'And if you try to recruit those seasonal workers,' said the foreman, pointing to the outcrop, 'you'll waste time and money scouring the country for teamsters willing to drag any bales away.'

Behind him, some men lifted branches to their shoulders, like spears. The ends had been whittled, shaved to sharp points, and some were bound with broken bottles.

'They have strychnine to put in the water as well,' said the foreman, softly, 'and they're eager to slaughter the prize ram and eat it.'

This couldn't go on. Hadley knew they could easily capture and eat The General, knew the flock were suffering in the heat and the men were suffering too. He drew himself up. 'If your men attack then they won't have any sheep to shear,' he said, his voice sounding more certain. 'They'll have to flee, hungry and hunted.' He rubbed his sparse moustache, hoped they didn't detect he was still quaking in his boots.

'It makes no difference where we starve,' said the foreman, 'but the squatters are up against time. They think they can have everything their own way.'

Hadley decided to try reason, starting to explain that the banks wanted money they loaned to the squatters to produce wool for prosperity for everyone. But it was no use: the foreman was laughing again. Still, eventually Hadley got them to agree to put their case to Guston, and asked if they would hold their attack for one more night.

'I'll put it to my men,' said the foreman, 'but I can't be held responsible for all of them. A few are fairly bloodthirsty.'

Hadley nodded, and made his way back skirting the camp and scuttling along the creek bank. He ducked behind a tree to piss, only too late noticing a shearer watching a string cast into the low amber water nearby. His cheeks were sunken and his eyes set deep in his head.

'Are they biting?' Hadley called, buttoning his fly.

'Fished out long ago,' said the man. 'I'm hoping for a tortoise. An eel would do. I'd make do with a leech.' He shrugged.

They weren't sinister, these men, thought Hadley. They were downcast and desperate, their self-respect eroded.

Voices in the distance came to Phoeba. Men whistled, dogs barked, footfalls came and went on carpeted wood. She even heard the rustle of passing satin and lace, smelled perfume and cigar smoke. In the blackest part of sleep Widow Pearson was in bed with her, prodding her ribs with a knife, her innards spilling like offal tumbling from a bucket. Then she rode Spot all over the outcrop searching for her lost legs, and the vicar followed her, calling, 'Come with me!' Alarmed, she forced her eyelids open to see the vicar's chins quivering behind plump fingers pressed together in prayer. His shut eyes made two puckers in his fleshy face.

I have been placed in soft sheets under ceiling roses in a grand house with servants to die, she thought.

Then she felt safe because Rudolph Steel came and sat by her, holding her hand. When he left the fear and pain ebbed and swelled and she was helpless again, waiting in the strange room slipping in and out of a soft, dark sleep. At times the dirt rushed up to her and Centaur bellowed. His hoofs thwacked and she flew, catapulted again towards Hadley's outstretched arms. But he didn't catch her and she woke abruptly.

'I haven't accomplished anything and it is so easy to die.'

Rudolph Steel was there again. He leaned close to her and smiled. 'But you will, Miss Crupp, you will,' he said and winked. She felt better.

That evening, Hadley put on his new suit, picked up a bundle of novels and flowers to leave for Phoeba and went up to the big house. He waited in the kitchen until the maid summoned him then followed her to the drawing room. Guston, Marius and Rudolph Steel stood waiting. Guston pointed to the chaise longue and Hadley sat, concentrating on his balance, on the backless end next to Marius. He steadied the books and flowers on his lap.

Mr Overton cleared his throat to speak but Hadley blurted, 'With respect, sir, you won't get anywhere unless you start at sixpence at least – and in the end, I think you'll find you need to give them a shilling and the shearers will probably ask for thirty shillings a hundred for the rams—'

'Humbug. We'll get the itinerants and swaggies.'

'They've burned sheds down before this, Father,' said Marius quietly. 'They've stolen wagon wheels and eat the oxen.'

'They will eat The General,' said Hadley. 'They plan to capture and eat your prize ram, tonight ...'

The colour drained from Guston's cheeks.

'They're just fighting for what they deserve, sir,' continued Hadley, amazed that he'd said it. But it was true. He sat up a little straighter.

'We cannot pay the rouseabouts a shilling more! We cannot afford thirty a hundred for the rams,' bellowed Guston, but he was bellowing at Rudolph. 'I won't pay it. I won't lose my property because a bunch of shearers and larrikins and ne'er-do-wells have bled me dry.'

Hadley shifted carefully on the couch, wondering if he should be listening to the fiscal secrets of Overton, seeing Guston so desperate, knowing the shearers were more desperate. Very well, he thought, he would solve this, if it ruined him, and he would solve it without bloodshed. It was no one's fault: these

134

were just bad times.

Rudolph Steel moved to the drinks tray and poured four glasses of whisky as if he owned the place. Hadley's nerves jangled with his new resolve. He took the drink.

'There's thousands of pounds worth of wool on the sheep's back not to mention the bales waiting to go to the siding,' said Rudolph, gently.

'We'll shoot them,' shouted Guston. 'We'll shoot the lot of the ruddy sheep and be done with it.'

Marius stood up and went to his father. 'Almost everything is riding on this wool, Father. I think we should do as Rudolph suggests.'

Guston thought for a moment, grinding his teeth. Suddenly his eyebrows shot up: 'They won't get a bloody concert this year, that's for sure.' Each year Mrs Overton played the piano for the shearers but Hadley doubted they'd miss it. Other pastoralists were better thought of anyway, for providing a fiddle and accordion.

Guston turned to the window, his whisky gone in a single swallow. 'Do as you wish,' he said.

'We'll go to them in the morning,' said Rudolph,

'The General,' said Hadley. 'I don't know if they'll hold off that long.'

They would take turns at the shed in six-hour watches, in pairs, Rudolph announced, with sheep housed in the yards surrounding The General so they would scatter if anyone approached. Hadley and the bookkeeper were allocated first watch; McInness, the other classer, could take the second. And in the morning, Hadley would offer the men a shilling. Hadley declined a second drink and stood up to leave, the books dropping from his lap.

'You read poetry, Parsons? Not too soft for this are you?'

'No, sir, these are for Phoeba.'

Guston looked at Marius. 'Who?'

'The patient.'

'Oh shit! The Crupp girl. God, what a bloody mess. It was the plain lass, wasn't it?' Guston held his glass out to Rudolph for a refill. 'Not the other one.' He smiled salaciously.

' "There is no excellent beauty that hath not some strangeness in the proportion",' quoted Rudolph to himself.

'She's a strong, smart girl and it'd take more than a bad tempered old rogue to dent her,' said Hadley, firmly, and went to find the maid to give her the books and flowers for Phoeba.

Guston frowned and shook his head. 'Shame about the horse.'

Hadley's partner, the bookkeeper, did not show up, so he found himself alone on the loading dock in the moon shadow feeling vulnerable, rejected and inadequately armed, with the rifle on his lap. When Guston had handed him the gun he'd said, 'We don't want a murder on our hands. You can do enough damage with this.'

But it was dark and Hadley's eyes were dry from straining to see movement among the silver and black blotches. The sheepyards stank, the sheep were in poor condition due to the dry season and they'd been housed for days. Some were flyblown and the hot air was thick with the stench and the thrumming of mosquitoes that bred in the puddles of urine and excrement. He couldn't hear well and his thoughts were preoccupied by Phoeba, in her bed, with her brown hair tousled on the pillow and curling about her small, pink lips. He would prove himself, show her, make her admire him. She wouldn't be swayed by an offer of a secure future. He'd have to think of something else.

Suddenly the sheep spooked, pattering in a circle, and he

thought he saw the moonlit shoulders of figures skimming from tree to tree.

He stood, his gun raised, and balanced himself on evenly placed feet, although his knees shivered in his trousers and his armpits ran wet. He imagined men driving sharpened sticks into him, belting him with clubs. But it was a lone figure that advanced, strolling, unafraid. 'This time, I will die,' he thought, but he summoned a menacing voice.

'Who's that?'

The figure kept coming, boldly, despite the gun at Hadley's eye.

'Stop!' he cried, his body quaking with fear. Then his finger twitched and a shot cracked loud across the night. Through the ringing in his ears he heard the sheep scattering, bleating, and then someone shoved him and seized his gun, laughing, and the nozzle was at the tip of his nose. Through the silence of Hadley waiting for his life to end he heard the bush behind the shed crackle as shearers retreated – a dozen men scampering over fallen bark and brittle grass. He had frightened them away – all but this one.

He smelled whisky on his murderer's breath and closed his eyes.

'Damned fool, it's me, the next watch.' It was McInness.

In her sleep, Phoeba had heard the crack, like a thick branch snapping, and she turned over.

Guston, Marius and Rudolph had heard it too, and they raced to Hadley, emerging from the shadows with their arms in the air.

'Steady-on, it's us,' called Guston.

Hadley lowered his reclaimed gun. In the sheepyard beside the loading dock a figure lay in a thick, green puddle, groaning.

137

'Shit, Parsons, is he dead?'

'No sir, he's … unconscious. Drunk.'

McInness lifted his heavy head from the slime. 'He hit me.'

Hadley's chin went up and his hands straightened at his sides. 'I repelled them, sir. I heard them run when I fired the shot. I saved The General.'

Wednesday, January 17, 1894

While Maude prepared the dried fruit again, Robert nailed jute scraps over the holes in the tin walls of his room: this time he knew his banishment to the shed would be a long one. When the cake was in the oven, Maude settled on the front veranda with the looking glass trained on the brougham. Her head ached and it felt like a barbed wire fist pressed down in her pelvis, but the intensity of her pain dulled as long as she watched the two chestnut Hackneys circling around the island of thistles in the middle of the intersection. Marius sat on the box seat with his arm around Lilith's waist; Lilith held the reins in her hands. Maude watched, delighted when her coquettish girl threw her head back laughing and the Hackneys shot off across the reserve. Lilith steered them around the dam and then around and around the dented Sunshine harvester that had been abandoned on the stock reserve. It was missing its nuts and bolts now and was therefore useless. The brougham turned towards Overton and sped towards the pass.

Maude flushed pink under her gown. She felt full of hope for her daughter and the gentleman beside her. Then she remembered her own gay youth, dancing with Robert when they were young and slim, and she felt fond for a moment before a searing rush of envy enveloped her and she was suddenly teary. 'This wretched change,' she said, suddenly craving something sweet to eat. She went inside for a comforting slice of the second plum cake, still warm from the oven.

Clean linen, wet roses and dusty sheep-manure floated on a summer breeze towards Phoeba, then the smell of lunch wafted in – roast lamb. Her head still seemed unevenly balanced and she had trouble lifting it. Her neck felt too weak and her body seemed to have been cast in barbed wire. At least she could wiggle her toes. 'Welcome back legs … thank you.' She blinked away tears of relief and tried to sit up but her back wouldn't let her. She flopped down and told the ceiling, 'At least I am alive.'

On the bedside table a bunch of chrysanthemums from Mr Titterton's garden and the mauve flowers from the jacarandas by the sheep yards sat in a vase, a note from her mother leaned against the lamp. The note assured her that the doctor had told them she would 'mend all right'. Her father had added, 'Mind when you first catch your reflection. You look worse than a flattened pomegranate.'

Behind the vase, leaning against the lampshade, was the photograph from the ploughing match – a brown and cream image of Hadley in his new wool suit and boots, a young and smooth-skinned youth with very round spectacles; Henrietta, ramrod straight, bonny, big-boned and grinning like a well-fed cat, her coat incorrectly buttoned; and a straight-backed, firm-jawed girl in her best skirt and jacket staring away from the camera, as if it was not to be trusted. Herself. Both girls had their arms looped through Hadley's; all three wore skin-tight leather riding gloves and there was not a frill, flower or ribbon between them.

A lazy-eyed maid appeared and Phoeba said, 'I'd like to go to the toilet and I'd like to clean my teeth, please.' They struggled together to the bathroom, its mirror reflecting a girl with a mess of lanky straight hair and one side of her face, as her father had said, like a flattened pomegranate. She looked away quickly and sat for a very long time on the commode, dabbing tears from her eyes and feeling sorry for herself. Life seemed so very precious – one chance, one time to live. Imagine if she'd been born an itinerant, she thought suddenly. No wonder they were upset. Their already sorry lives looked like they were getting worse.

Back in bed she pondered the things that were most important to her life. She was alive – there was nothing beyond that – and now she would stay in her safe home, her corner of the world at Mount Hope, away from floods or drought, the recession, strikers and rebels. Some stolen eggs and a milked goat were not such a threat, just a means of survival for the sundowners. Mount Hope would be her future. She would grow hectares of grapes and have the same, faithful travellers return every year for the harvest. Her wines would win awards and Henrietta, whose mother would die tragically – and soon – would come to live with her in a new, small house that she'd build up near the spring. They would stay together forever. Friends were, after all, essential.

Things were in perspective, thought Phoeba contentedly. Time would heal Hadley and he would marry a squatter's daughter with a generous dowry and they would breed champion ewes and rams at Elm Grove. He would see to the Crupps' grain crop, as he always had, and partner her for the progressive barn-dance at the harvest dance. Lilith would marry someone rich and live somewhere in the Yukon, or England. Even Melbourne

140

would be far enough.

Then the door opened and there she was. Lilith. She was wearing Phoeba's new blouse and holding a book and a bouquet – some daisies and a single geranium. 'At last, you're awake. You know if you hadn't made me nervous, Phoeba, I would have been able to stop that horse from bolting.'

'Hello, Lilith.'

'Mother's taken to her bed. She says she has fractured nerves and a headache. Under no circumstances are we to mention Aunt Margaret and her commune to anyone here at Overton. You didn't say anything while you were delirious, did you?'

'Have you seen Henrietta?' asked Phoeba, her voice croaky and unused.

'She comes every day to ask how you are,' said Lilith, shoving the vase of wilting flowers aside and sticking the fresh ones in Phoeba's glass of water. 'More flowers from Hadley. There's a note.'

'Dearest Phoeba, you are made of good stuff, you will be all right. May I visit?'

'Was he hurt badly?' Hadley can visit any time he likes, she thought.

'He's got a sore shoulder. Have you seen yourself? That nasty gash over your good eye will scar.'

'You're all right, then?'

'I had extensive bruising and very sore shoulders from pulling on the reins and, worst of all, a badly turned ankle. I couldn't walk. I had the doctor look at me all over, told him about my scarlet fever.'

Lilith plonked down on the bed and a pain shot through Phoeba.

'It was influenza, Lilith. Is anyone remembering to look after

141

Spot?'

Lilith dumped *Far From the Madding Crowd* on the bedside table.

'Marius had Centaur shot but he's teaching me to drive a brougham! I drove here! He said when he saw us tumble he thought of his wife.'

Lilith said Marius as if she'd been saying it for years.

'We have the cook's horse now. Her name is Angela,' said Lilith running her hands along the damask counterpane. It had small flocks of sulphur-crested cockatoos embroidered on it.

'Why can't they give us a decent horse?'

'And I can't wait to drive the brougham to church.' Lilith wandered over to the window. 'Marius says I make him feel alive.'

That was it, she thought suddenly. Hadley was honest and honourable but he didn't make her feel alive. Did she make him feel alive, she wondered, or just secure?

'They have running water and gaslights in the garden.'

'Lilith, can you bring my clothes—'

'No! You have to stay here. The doctor said your spine had moved, or something, and you must rest.'

'I'd rather be at home.'

'You are to stay until you're completely well,' cried Lilith.

'All right, I will,' said Phoeba calmly, 'if you bring me all Dad's books on grape growing.'

'I'll get Marius to bring them,' said Lilith. 'Have you seen Mrs Overton? She's so sophisticated.'

'You could learn a lot from her,' said Phoeba, falling back onto her pillow. Her body was very sore.

'I intend to,' said Lilith.

Thursday, January 18, 1894

Time and again the wool-rollers went to McInness's table with fleeces rolled against their chests. Hadley watched, disappointed and miserable, drumming his fingers on the classing table. He might have a bad arm but that didn't mean he couldn't gauge a fleece.

There was another two weeks shearing left and there were mostly rams to come. They were valuable animals, delicate and cumbersome. There was no shortage of willing men to shear but only the most experienced could be trusted not to ruin the priceless studs with a badly handled set of shears. Hadley knew the shearers would ask for even more money for this delicate task. And they had every right to ask. But would the work stop again or would Overton agree?

After the last bell, he headed upstream from the shearers' camp, crunching his way through the dry bark on the creek bank. The air smelled of wet clay and dusty eucalypts and occasionally, sickness – lot of the shearers were ill. First there was an outbreak of measles, and this last outbreak was from bad game, they said. He fancied he heard men moaning, although it was hard to tell as birds whipped and chirped and some shearers – the thin but healthy ones – sat peacefully on the ground, naked, or soaped themselves, waist-deep in the tan water. He dumped his towel and clean clothes and leaned on a stringy-bark to remove his boots and socks. Placing his spectacles on top of his clothes he stepped quietly into the water, feeling his toes in the slime on the creek bed and his thin, white limbs sinking. He slipped under the water to the murky silence.

He was towelling himself dry, wearing only his glasses, when Rudolph Steel popped up in the water in front of him.

'Good God, Steel!' He quickly covered himself with his towel.

'You like water, Hadley?' asked Rudolph scraping his dark wet hair from his forehead.

'I've nothing against it.' It occurred to him that he and Phoeba might go swimming at the bay again, if they were married. He'd shield her from the swaggies.

'We'd like you to take on the wool-wash,' said Rudolph. 'We're grateful for your negotiations with the shearers, and your guarding of the shed, and the scour would keep you on after the shearing's done.'

Hadley thought frankly that the scour was beneath him: he preferred the shed, the men working quietly, dignified among great baskets of tumbling wool. But the money from scouring wool would do very nicely.

'I'll think about it,' he said, reaching for his singlet.

'Let me know by the end of the day. There's £100 in it for you – however you divide that for men and equipment. Guston thinks you'll be good with the Chinamen.' The new Hadley – the Hadley who negotiated and protected – knew he could be good with any kind of man, Chinaman or not. He called after Rudolph, 'Can I ask … I'd like to return here next year, if I could.'

'And we will have you back, if we can, but there are sheep all over the eastern states. You can go anywhere with a letter from Overton.'

Walking back, he tallied up the cost of two pressers, pot stickers, soakers, first and second scourers, green hands and barrowmen. He reckoned he'd need £125 at the very least to scour the rest of the wool, pay the men and make a wage. He'd insist on £130.

Hadley appeared at Phoeba's door clutching the books and waving a handful of roses with his good hand. Petals fluttered onto the carpet. Quite pretty, thought Phoeba.

'Hadley. Come in.' She struggled up a bit and forced herself not to cry. It was lovely to see him, dear Hadley.

He came in slowly and rested his hand on the porcelain bed knob so that petals fell on the bed.

'Well,' he said, 'look at you!' His eyes were brimming with tears.

'I am very happy to see you, Hadley.' He was far better than Lilith. Hadley remained silent, grinning at her. 'I'm on the mend,' she said, and patted the bed next to her. Hadley dragged the pretty pink dressing table chair up to the bed and perched on it. Finally, he gave her the flowers and she sniffed them, so sweet and fresh, while he took *Great Expectations* and two poetry books from behind his sling and thrust them at her.

'I saw you trying to stop the horse. You could have been trampled.'

He shrugged and his painful shoulder made him wince. 'Titterton pulled me away, but I'd gladly have been trampled for you—'

'Don't say that, Hadley, I don't know if I'd do the same for you.'

'I know you'd do it for your children,' he shot back.

He took her hand and she wondered if another proposal was coming, but instead he opened one of his books and read her a poem.

"'I loved her for that she was beautiful,
And that to me she seemed to be all nature,
And all varieties of things in one;
Would set at night in clouds of tears, and rise ...'"

He closed the book carefully. 'You know, Phoeba, I'd do anything for you.'

'Please don't write me any poetry.'

He sighed and Phoeba told herself to take him seriously.

'Did you think I was going to die?'

'Yes.' He'd thought he was going to die too, facing those shearers, and guarding that shed. Phoeba didn't know how brave he'd been.

'I thought so too, Hadley. And you know, you paid me the furthest compliment, asking me to marry you, but—'

'But you promised—'

'I promised I'd think about it, and I have. I've decided to live life to the full, and as I want. I'm going to stay on the farm and grow grapes.'

'But you must want to do all the things life is about.'

'What is life about, Hadley?'

'Well, you do the right thing, you belong to a community, you have children ...' He picked up the copy of *Great Expectations* and turned it over in his hands.

'Had,' said Phoeba, tenderly, 'I don't have to do what everyone expects to have a full life. Life is about being how you want to be, doing what you want and being happy. I want to be free and I can't be free if I'm responsible for someone else's happiness. It's perfect the way it is. Out in the world I'd have to wear a corset to be a girl and do as I was expected.'

'You've had a bump,' said Hadley glumly, rubbing at his forehead. 'You should see a phrenologist.'

146

She looked him straight in the eye, those soft, blue eyes in his soft oval face – sincere and hopeful, and loyal. She didn't want to pity him, and she didn't want him to beg. She moved her gaze to the knot of his tie. 'Hadley, you need to marry someone who enriches you, who'll give you a full life. I don't love you like I'm supposed to—'

'Romantic love, Phoeba, humbug. It's only in books.'

'Books are true, Hadley, embellished a little, perhaps, by authors, but they are true. And you and I want very different lives. So I'd give up all my instincts and you'd give up all that is natural to you. You'd have to make do with hope and it would ruin you. I want to work on the farm so I can live and contribute, achieve. I don't want to compromise. And I think I deserve better.'

'We all think we deserve better,' he said. 'I'd give you friendship, and independence. I would make you happy. We would build something fine together.' He followed a twist in the turned brass column of the bedside lamp with his long finger. It was a beautiful banquet lamp with an engraved glass shade. 'And who will look after you and your awful horse when you're old?'

'I just don't want to look back and say, "Gosh, I compromised all the way,"' said Phoeba adamantly. 'Now, read me something else; I feel like a bit of satire.'

He put the poetry aside, crossed his arms and looked at the cockatoos on the bedspread. But she egged him on and drew him out of his sulk and he agreed to read her *Great Expectations*, until she yawned. When he was sure she was asleep he pressed the sheet around her chin and crept out, feeling his way through the great, silent house by soft gaslight.

Thursday, January 25, 1894

D r Mueller, a short and yellowish man, arrived on the next
Thursday to check on Phoeba. He tied the wall-eyed,
skewbald hack that grudgingly towed his coffin carrier to the
garden arch and left him to sniff the wisteria. Tottering into
Phoeba's room unannounced, he found her swinging her legs
over the side of the bed. 'Stop!' she cried. 'I'm better, truly I am.'

A vial of iron and quinine citrate dropped from between
the shredded seams of the doctor's leather case where a scalpel
protruded. His jacket was burnished with stains and three flies
hovered over his head. Sitting on the edge of Phoeba's bed, he
blew his nose into a stiff, crinkly handkerchief, then poked it into
his top pocket – he'd been battling a cold since anyone could
remember – and dragged a stethoscope from his trouser pocket.
The small circles of cold from its metal cone pierced Phoeba's
nightdress, and she shivered.

'Ah,' said Dr Mueller, wrapping his similarly cold, flat hands
around her ribs, 'fever. Influenza?'

'No,' said Phoeba.

'What day is it?'

'Sunday?' She had no idea.

'Hmmm.' He looked worried. 'Your sister was up and about
so quickly because she was wearing a corset. It kept her spine and
internal organs in place.'

And because she landed on me, thought Phoeba. 'When can
I go home?' she asked.

148

The doctor looked at her, puzzled. 'You are at home, Miss Overton.'

'My name is Phoeba Crupp.'

The doctor patted her hand. 'I'm sure it is.' He shook his head and walked forlornly to the door. 'Please God,' she said, though she still didn't believe in Him, 'may I not have caught hydatids.'

Later, sitting in the wicker chair at the small table by the window reading *Rules for Vignerons on Grape Cultivation and Harvest*, she heard noises come in waves. Horses coming and going, the grind and jangle of carts, maids struggling up and down the back steps. Someone played the piano and she listened, her head resting on the back of the chair and her eyes closed. Such a beautiful sound – she felt sad that she and Lilith hadn't learned. If they'd stayed in Geelong they would have. Instead, she thought, she had Spot – and the vineyard.

Henrietta burst through the door.

'Do you know who I am?' she said.

'You gave me a spider once called Betty and you can hit a tin can with a slingshot from fifty yards away.'

Henrietta flung her arms around Phoeba and pressed her cheek to her head, 'Dr Mueller said you didn't know what day it was.'

'Dr Mueller knows less than his horse.' She tried to move but Henrietta held her fast. 'Henri, you're squeezing me.'

'Sorry.' Henrietta dragged the dainty chair from the dressing table and cupped Phoeba's hand in hers. 'Did you think you were going to die, Phoeba?'

'Yes, but the worst part was lying here waiting. I couldn't even roll over.' She felt tears welling.

'I would have looked after you. I'd walk over broken bottles to make you all right, Phoeba.'

'You'd cut your feet.'

'I'd wear my boots.' Phoeba laughed and Henrietta held her hand to her tear-stained cheek.

'I've come to a decision, Henri.'

'What about?'

'My future. I will not marry your lovely brother, much as I like him. I will be a vigneron. I will be free and I won't compromise. I am going to live this life the way I want.'

'Oh, you're awake?' said a light, refined voice and Mrs Overton, soft and ethereal, floated in looking just like someone notable from *Madame Weigel's Journal of Fashion*. The sleeves of her dress were slim, tight over her wrists and covering half her hand. She was fine-boned, her neck long enough for a stand-up collar and three bar brooches. The lace was cotton, finely ruched, and she smelled sweet.

'Dr Mueller says you can go home,' she said, looking at Henrietta.

Henrietta bobbed. 'My name is Henrietta May Pearson. That's Phoeba.'

Mrs Overton glanced at Phoeba but her raw face and blue, swollen eyes were too confronting, so she said instead to Henrietta, 'You have a beautiful complexion, dear. I've always admired auburn hair and brown eyes.'

Henrietta patted the plait coiled on her head. 'Thanks.'

'I'm ready to go home, thank you Mrs Overton,' said Phoeba.

She continued to stare at Henrietta, now perplexed. 'But how will she get there, dear?'

'Your stock overseer, Mr Titterton, has arranged for us to have Angela, the cook's horse,' said Phoeba.

Mrs Overton's fine brow creased, just a little, and she said, 'That isn't suitable at all. What will the cook do for a horse?' and wafted out, the two girls quite forgotten and her mind on something else.

'She's been at the laudanum,' said Henrietta.

'What day is it, Henri?'

'Thursday the 25th, but it's 1904. You've been here ten years,' she joked.

'It feels like forever.'

'It does,' said Henrietta, 'but you're right now and we'll look after each other much better in future.'

Friday, January 26, 1894

First thing Friday morning the lazy-eyed maid placed Phoeba's skirt on the end of the bed, neatly folded undergarments on top. She headed for the bathroom, saying, 'You don't wear corsets or petticoats, I see.' Emerging from the bathroom with the commode pot, a grey towel draped over it, she saw Phoeba reaching for her clothes. 'What? Not having a bath?'

'I had a bath yesterday.'

'I'll tell Polly not to bother with the bucket of hot water then.' At the door she paused. 'Mrs Overton has a bath in warm water every day, all over, completely in it.'

'We'd all have one if we had a maid to bring us hot water and soap our toes,' Phoeba said.

The upstairs hall at Overton was as wide as Phoeba's bedroom at Mount Hope. Making her way cautiously to the stairs, she ran into Mr Overton holding a looking glass almost the same as her father's. When he saw her he stopped.

'Christ,' he bellowed, 'you've got a nasty rash on your face.' His suit was made of something fine with a soft furry sheen, like

151

velvet. With a lurch Phoeba realised it was platypus. She knew she should have said, Thank you for looking after me, but instead she said, 'It's better than being dead.'

'Here,' said Mr Overton, 'come and see this.'

Phoeba paused. She could say, 'Don't tell me what to do you cruel rude old drunk' – but that would be cruel and rude. She sighed. It wasn't going to be easy to live your life exactly as you felt.

She followed him into a room, a rich man's study with dark green walls and deep red rugs. There were mounted guns over the mantelpiece, crystal decanters and Huon pine pipe-holders on the lowboy, and papers scrawled with figures almost covered the polished mahogany desk. In one corner stood a solid, carved four-poster bed with a red silk counterpane.

'Come on,' he said, standing against the wide, white-blue sky.

Mr Guston Overton had a shiny red face and whisky seemed to soak through the deep pores of his ruddy complexion. No wonder Mrs Overton kept a separate bed, thought Phoeba.

She negotiated the slight decline of the floorboards towards the balcony rail, feeling a little unsteady. Beyond the large, neat garden and its ornate gates the dirt road led across the plain to the narrow pass in the outcrop. 'I never get tired of looking at it, knowing it's all mine,' said Mr Overton. 'It's a world-class view. Bet you've never seen one like it?'

'I have. I've seen it from the other side and it's better. The plains stretch on and on and you can feel your insignificance, your place in the great world.' He didn't appear to have heard her.

'I only own half the outcrop now,' he said, regretfully. He'd sold the land he once owned on the other side of the outcrop, thinking it was useless. Hadley's father ruined his section,

152

but Phoeba's father made excellent use of his sloping terrain. 'I sometimes see people up on the cliff, sometimes horses,' said Mr Overton, grinning and exposing his tobacco-stained teeth to her. 'I have a telescope for bank managers and blacks,' he continued, 'although the boundary rider says he's run them all off or shot the ones who wouldn't behave.'

'Shot them?' said Phoeba.

'Yes,' he said. 'There are hundreds of them out there in the wilds.' He handed her the looking glass. 'Have a look.'

'But that's so … surely the blacks are just people living as best they can, as we all should be able to.'

'You know nothing of life, girl; you don't know what you're talking about.'

'But I do,' she said. 'I know the value of life. I know what's important. Looking after the land is important. Friends and family, freedom, and being fair to those less fortunate.'

He must be deaf, she thought as he ignored her words and walked slowly back into his office, leaning to open the door.

'Please thank Mrs Overton and the maids for taking care of me,' Phoeba called, but he waved his hand about his ear as though moving a moth away.

Wondering where she should go, she trained the looking glass on a wool truck rolling down from the shearing shed to the sheep wash. She picked out Hadley's long thin frame and focused on him.

He was standing on a narrow wooden bridge that bordered a steaming pond, poking at clumps of wool floating like scum on a steaming soup in the hot pond. There were Chinamen in the water up to their chests and wearing tar-lined barrels as they moved and stirred the grease and dirt from the wool. Smoke from a fire heating a great water tub clouded the air and Hadley smacked at the cinders wafting onto his clothes.

'Gracious,' said Phoeba, 'what a job.' She imagined standing over that hot pond, the steam pumping the stench of sheep dirt and ammonia up her nose. He was struggling to lever the sodden wool onto the floor to drain; it kept slipping from the long stick back into the hot, acrid pond. The Chinamen chattered and the carts of wool kept rumbling down from the shed on small, metal tracks, slamming up against each other.

Then, because he was Hadley, he lost his footing. Phoeba watching in horror as his legs circled in the air like a ragdoll's and he slapped onto the wet bridge. He lowered his forehead onto the filthy slime-iced boards.

Phoeba put her hand to her heart for her clumsy friend and smiled, but her face felt like it was coated in hot tar too.

'You've no idea how happy I am to see you in one piece.'

She jumped. It was Rudolph Steel, in a suit of pale linen with tufts of wool caught in his shirt buttons. He stepped very close to her and took her hands in his, turned them over. His touch was firm but delicate.

'Hadley said you'd mend,' he said. She could see each of his lashes and remembered his eyes, close to hers, when she was ill.

'Hadley and I have been friends since childhood,' she blurted. It seemed urgent that Rudolph Steel know she wasn't Hadley's *paramour*.

Steel inspected her scabbed cheek, running his fingers lightly over its tight, red flesh. It was like being sprinkled with falling wattle dust.

'I don't think your face will disfigure.'

'I don't care if it does, really,' she shrugged. 'Anyway, it's not as if I'm looking for a husband, Mr Steel.'

'Call me Rudolph.' He smiled and led her down the staircase

and out onto the front veranda where her father's sulky waited, mended and oiled. The coach-painters had decorated the dashboard and body with gold swirls and loops and there were even fine lines tapering to the end of the shafts. Steel's dark Holstein was tethered to its back and Angela, a shiny, slim mare with terrific forelegs – short, strong cannons and straight rear quarters – waited in a harness that shone dark and lustrous. Phoeba felt suddenly apprehensive. She stopped, flooded by images of the road racing beneath her, of the gravel rising to slap her. It would take courage to drive again. She wished she had Spot to take her home.

'You drive,' said Rudolph, 'get your nerve up again. Your sister was back behind the reins in no time.' And he took her hands and tugged her gently towards the sulky.

She heard steel wheel rims whirring and the sound of splintering wood.

'I'll be next to you.'

He pointed to the small iron step, but her feet wouldn't move. Then she was airborne, scooped up and placed on the seat, as if she were a child. He climbed in next to her, untied the reins and she found them in her hands. The horse seemed a massive beast, all muscle at the end of two flimsy strips of leather. But Rudolph Steel wrapped his hands around hers, pressed them firmly to the reins and then let go, holding the backrest behind her and pretending to be absorbed by the shorn rams that shuffled across the plains. He smelled hot – smelled of saddle wax and freshly shorn wool.

'Off we go,' he said and pressed his elbow to the small of her back.

She flipped the reins lightly and Angela walked easily along the road. The sulky felt sloppy beneath her, as if it wasn't attached to anything, but the further they went, the more she relaxed.

'They say you're a bank man but I think you're very kind.'

'"They" say I'm a bank man, do "they?"'

'"They" do.'

'Let them say it but I'll tell you the truth. I'm part owner of Overton. I don't throw people off their land. I try to manage it so that they can be saved.'

'But you'd still be part owner if you were from the bank.'

'I invest. I try to help people in strife through a bad time. Droughts end. Shearers behave if they're paid correctly. There'll be plenty of money to be made from sheep in the future.'

'You invest in other people's misfortune and turn that into a fortune for yourself.' She didn't mean to sound so confronting but she couldn't think of anything else to say. The last thing she wanted him to think was that she was silly, like Lilith. But in his presence, she did feel silly – and girlish.

'You could see it like that,' he said, 'but I prefer to see it as an investment in the future of the rural industry. The drought has done a lot of damage in places. And there is mismanagement.' He looked sideways at the thistles, the Salvation Jane spreading through the Crupps' feed crop. 'Some are worse than others.'

'I know,' she apologised, 'the thistles …'

'And,' said Rudolph, 'some people prefer a partner to the bank.'

'How many pastoralists and farmers have you saved?'

'None of your business,' said Rudolph, grinning at her.

She felt as if she had been punctured by something pleasantly rude. Her arms wanted to reach out of their own accord and wrap around his nice, big shoulders and she wanted to drive on for hours with him, to never get out of the sulky. She could feel the pressure of his arm along the backrest enveloping her and there was a shimmer from his fingers as they rested near her own. This

156

was something to tell Henrietta. Aunt Margaret should know about it too. This felt like being alive.

They turned at the intersection and passed the Harvester still sitting by the dam, dented but shiny.

'Did the itinerants ruin your new Sunshine?' she asked, trying not to grin. She didn't know why she was grinning.

'Not completely,' he sighed, and for a moment, just a second, his hand cupped her arm and there wasn't enough air in her lungs.

'An engineer is coming to fix it and then we'll get on with the harvest.' Again, she felt his hand at her arm as he gestured to their small feed crop. 'We'll do yours to start with,' he said. 'It'll only take a day.'

She almost said, 'That'll upset the itinerants,' but she couldn't. The idea that she might spend a whole day with him was too pleasant.

'Do you save English farms?'

'No. I've just had four years there but I was born and raised here.'

'What brought you back again?'

'Unfettered liberty, or the illusion of it. It's a long story.' He said it lightly but she saw something in his expression that told her that it was sad. 'I disembarked in Broome, a wonderful place, and hiked my way down here.'

'So, you're a bit of a swaggie.'

'There's a lot to be said for the life of a swagman, the freedom and camaraderie, the way they look after each other. All you need is a swag, a billy and a pocket knife and you can please yourself.'

'I've decided to do whatever I like now instead of trying to please everybody.'

'You can never please everyone,' said Rudolph, ruefully. 'I've

157

tried but I ended up displeased myself.'

She smiled, but it made her face hurt. She held it with her hand.

Spot whinnied to her from his paddock. His soft chest was pressed against the gate and she saw he'd lost weight.

'Spot!' she cried her voice high and silly. 'That's my horse, Spot.'

'I've heard about Spot,' said Rudolph.

She opened her mouth to defend him but he touched her arm again and said, 'They say he's a remarkable horse. And you are a remarkably brave woman.'

Spot threw his head up, walked in a circle and came back to the gate. Her father sat on the veranda, two plump legs jutting out from under a newspaper. Lilith stood at the top of the steps – thankfully, not wearing Phoeba's new blouse, although she did look very pretty with a ribbon in her hair and her curls just so. Maude was next to her, wringing her hands.

'Hello,' sang Lilith, flicking her hair.

Rudolph nodded to her. He placed two hands at Phoeba's waist and lifted her down from the sulky, holding her for a second until she had caught her balance.

'Thank you,' she said, then added regretfully, 'I'll just say hello to Spot.'

'Of course.'

Maude bowled down the steps calling, 'Just in time for tea, Mr Steel. Please come in out of the sun.'

'Well, I really should—'

'Nonsense, it's very hot, you must have a cup of tea,' said Maude, and took him by the arm.

Spot pressed his long, flat nose against Phoeba's chest and she rubbed the stiff greasy hair between his ears. 'You're thin, Spotty,

158

have they neglected you? You'd never try to kill me, would you?' She fetched some oats for him and left him, his nose deep in his feed bin.

Maude fussed over Rudolph and asked far too many questions. Where had he come from? The north. Was he staying forever? He wasn't sure. Would he like to have his own property one day? He would. Around here? Possibly. Did he read an advertisement for a manager at Overton in the paper? Not quite.

'We live in fear now because of the swaggies stealing from us,' said Maude.

'They were dispossessed,' said Phoeba, 'itinerants.'

'They're all the same – dangerous. I will never go anywhere again without the Collector.'

'Very wise,' said Rudolph, looking at his hat to hide a smile. He rode away as soon as it was polite to leave. Maude said, 'I didn't expect him to be as well-mannered as Marius.' She put her finger under Phoeba's chin and turned her head to inspect her cheek. Phoeba waited: her mother would say it was lovely to have her home, or ask if she was tired. But instead Maude asked, 'Did you see Mrs Overton?'

'I did.'

'What did she look like?'

'She was wearing an ermine trimmed silk ballgown threaded with gold and a crown on her head. She never wears anything else.'

'Such lovely people.'

'Except they gave us a horse that nearly killed us and they shoot the natives.'

At least her father said he was glad she was back. But then he looked over at Spot up to his ears in his feed bin. 'Spot's been on a hunger strike and the last thing we need is to be upwind of a dead horse in summer.'

Finally, Maude patted her hand sympathetically. 'I expect you were longing to get back home, to life as it was.'

'Actually,' said Phoeba, 'I don't think life will ever be the same again.'

'Life goes on,' said Maude, glaring at Robert. 'If I can survive every day of the fourteen years I have endured this wilderness, you can. The harvest dance is coming up too so you'll need to be at your best. You must put this accident behind you. I have.'

Lilith had swapped the beds around, shoving Phoeba's close up against the wall and moving her own to the window. Phoeba found her bloomers and cotton combinations in the bottom drawer of the bureau and her blouses and skirts shoved to the far end of the wardrobe. Normally, she'd have tried to ignore such behaviour. But not anymore.

'I will have the life I want,' she said to herself.

She couldn't move the bed because her back hurt, but she threw Lilith's clothes out onto the floor, cutting the laces on her sister's best corset in the process. Satisfied with her new start, she went out to Maggie.

The goat was indifferent to anyone unless it was morning and they carried the milking pail or her breakfast, which made her indifference quite comforting. But then Phoeba saw that her vegetable garden had been plundered and half her chooks were missing. They had slaughtered her beautiful Leghorns with their lolling combs and small, sagacious eyes! Poor, poor trusting hens, she thought, murdered after the months she'd spent teaching them to trust her hands, to let her pick them up, even though from time to time she chopped someone's head off to cook and eat them. She gathered the last of her now-wary hens and ushered them into the cellar. They'd be safer behind lock and key, she

160

informed her parents.

'We hardly get any eggs these days,' said Maude from behind her sewing machine, 'and the outcrop reeks of roasting chickens.'

'Or fish,' said Robert, stuffing Maude's second wedding cake into his mouth. 'Freckle gets crayfish for them. I've been asking him for years to catch me a crayfish but he won't, says he gets top dollar from Overton. And the itinerants get them for free!'

'I doubt it's his choice,' said Phoeba, glumly. No one seemed outraged about her poor chooks. No one was going to do anything about the itinerants. Everyone was so … resigned.

'You know Mrs Pearson's washing machine arrived? And Lilith has a new friend,' said Maude, trying to get the sewing machine needle to shunt up and down. 'It's Marius Overton no less! She is such a comfort to him in his mourning. And he's such a thoughtful man.'

'Such a ditherer,' mumbled Robert scraping butter onto a second slice of cake.

Maude wrenched the material caught under the machine's foot and it tore. The sharp rip made everyone stop. She covered her eyes with her hand.

'Wretched, useless machine,' she hissed, then turned her anger on her husband. 'Robert! I did not say anyone could eat the cake.'

'It's very good,' he said, 'rich. Far too good to be wasted on gluttonous vicars or widows.' He opened his mouth wide and bit down, his teeth sinking into the thick, even spread of butter.

Maude burst into tears, snatched up the delicate cotton and lace nightie she was making and rushed out.

'Your mother,' said Robert, through his half-chewed cake, 'is heading for the asylum.'

'It's a woman's lot,' said Phoeba, sighing. Why was it that men had an easier life, she asked herself.

Lilith wandered in, her nose pressed into a small frond of eucalyptus flowers. Robert wiped his buttery fingers on his trousers. 'Where have you been, Lilith?'

'Out walking.'

'You? Exercising?'

Just then, they heard the looking glass shut with a sharp thwack. 'Here she comes,' called Maude rumbling down the hall, 'and she's got the vicar with her.'

Robert grabbed his pith hat and rushed out the back door. Phoeba moved the kettle to the hotplate and Maude sniffed. 'We may as well eat the rest of the cake, Phoeba. The ants will get it before there's a wedding in this house.' She rushed off to move the sewing machine to the middle of the table so Widow Pearson would see it when she peered down the hall.

Henrietta circled sharply in the yard and parked under the peppercorn. Her mother and the vicar clung fearfully to the armrests and an arc of dust wafted down to settle on the vines. Henrietta helped her mother from the Hampden then skipped across to Phoeba, swinging her hat in her hand, with her smile as wide as the bay. 'Welcome home!' she said, then whispered, 'I don't want to sit next to the vicar.'

'I feel a bit like I'm made of marmalade,' said Phoeba, 'but I'll mend.'

Widow Pearson, wearing a new mustard-coloured dress, made her way up the front steps and fell into Robert's large comfortable chair, gasping. The vicar paused in the middle of the yard, his hands behind his back as he gazed at the vineyard.

'So this is Mount Hope! My word, look at those lovely vines!' He headed towards the front veranda. 'You must show me the cellar and press as soon as we've had tea, Miss Crupp.'

162

'Margaret has painted you a sea-scape,' said Maude thrusting a brown paper package at the widow, 'since your land is low and you won't have a sea view at your new house.'

'I know how you felt when you fell from your sulky, Phoeba,' Mrs Pearson began, dumping the gift by her chair. 'I've had a terribly bumpy trip over. The road is very pitted because of traffic from those Luddites you invite to camp on your hill.'

'They're waiting for work at Overton—' started Maude and the Widow pounced.

'Speaking of Overton, we will have gaslights and tap water inside at the manager's house.' Her breath came in short wisps.

'We have a sewing machine now,' said Maude.

Phoeba nudged Henrietta indicating they should sneak away but the vicar picked up the cake plate and held it in front of them.

'Mrs Crupp's cakes don't agree with us,' said Widow Pearson. 'They're very heavy. The cook at Overton makes a nice sponge. He's a Chinaman you know, but the food was quite good the last time we lunched there.'

Henrietta rolled her eyes, and Phoeba realised she was surrounded by people who had strong feelings about nothing that mattered and the wrong opinions about things that did matter. 'Lunch?' she said. 'You lunched with Mrs Overton?'

'Hasn't it been dry, Vicar?' said Maude and looked out to the windmill.

'When did you lunch?' persisted Phoeba. She couldn't help herself. Henrietta nudged her again.

'Mr Titterton took us to the horse race to celebrate cut-out and to thank the shearers last year,' said Widow Pearson, and slammed her cup into her saucer. Maude gasped.

'We all went,' said Phoeba. 'Everyone in the district went. We all bought lunch for a penny a plate and we all ate it on the lawn. I did not see Mrs Overton on the lawn.'

Henrietta cleared her throat and Maude put her finger to her lips to silence Phoeba. She was staring out at the long neat vines, lush and glinting in the sunshine. She inhaled, smelling warm leaves and fructose. She felt she should go and check her grapes but couldn't. At that moment she didn't like anyone on the veranda, except for Henrietta.

'No races this year?' asked the vicar, innocently.

'No,' said Henrietta, seizing the opportunity to deflect the brewing argument. 'The shearers went on strike so Mr Overton put a stop to a bit of good fun.'

'I've called to have tea at Overton,' said the vicar, reaching for more cake, 'but Mrs Overton was not in.'

'By Jove,' said Phoeba, and slapped her knee, 'I bet she was over visiting Mrs Flynn.' She laughed but no one joined in and even Henrietta stayed tactfully quiet.

'The maid brought Phoeba something different for dinner every day,' said Lilith.

'You ate in your room?' said the Widow. 'Mind you, with a face like yours. You'll be scarred, you know. I don't suppose you saw much of Mrs Overton?'

'Mrs Overton wears a crown,' said Maude, dreamily, and Phoeba cringed.

Widow Pearson slammed her cup into her saucer again. 'I've never seen her wear a crown.'

Maude's said, shakily, 'That cup and saucer is Oxford, part of a set. It belonged to my mother. Phoeba will inherit the entire set, intact, I hope, when she marries.'

'I'm getting the furniture,' said Lilith.

'The cake was very good,' said the vicar and licked his thumb.

'We can see the cellar now.'

'Right,' said Phoeba, and stood up taking Henrietta's hand.

'Where are you going?' Mrs Pearson slammed her cup in her saucer again. 'Sit down, Henrietta. You must stay here. We're taking a risk just by visiting these people, harbouring itinerants and highwaymen up behind their house. You should run them off your property, Mrs Crupp, that's what I think.'

'They are starving, Mrs Pearson,' said Phoeba, evenly. 'And frankly, no one cares what you think about anything.' And she whipped the saucer out of the Widow's hand before she could slam her cup down again.

Maude spluttered, 'She's had a bump on the head—'

'And it's unleashed her true nature.' The Widow's eyes narrowed and her lips puckered like a tight buttonhole, but she didn't quite know what to do.

The vicar put his flat, round hat on. 'I'll find the cellar,' he said and rolled down the front steps and around the side of the house.

'Phoeba, dear,' her mother reached out to her, 'you cannot just say things—'

'Why not?' Phoeba pointed at the Widow. 'We've endured her barbed comments for years. And Lilith says whatever she wants and everyone just dismisses it because she's bird-witted.'

'I am not!'

'You are,' said Henrietta, then slapped her hands over her mouth.

Maude's face turned red and she fanned herself with her jabot. Lilith was open-mouthed, struggling against her indignity, her face wobbling like half-set jelly and her eyes brimming.

'Henrietta!' said Mrs Pearson, turning purple, 'you have been influenced by these people for long enough.' She held her elbow

165

out for her daughter to take. 'We're leaving.'

'She can stay if she wants to,' said Phoeba. 'She is not your slave.'

'If she doesn't come with me,' hissed Mrs Pearson, 'she can join the line at the welfare offices to eat horse soup.'

Henrietta winked at Phoeba, mouthed, 'Well done,' and helped her wheezing mother down the front steps as if she was manoeuvring a leaking weather balloon.

Lilith ran inside, crying.

Maude took the saucer from Phoeba and held it close. 'I don't think the wretched woman should get married, it's indecent.' She put her palm to her right temple and said, 'And, Phoeba Crupp, this Oxford saucer is cracked. I don't think you deserve to marry Hadley, or anyone. You ride bareback, you don't wear foundation garments and you're rude.'

The vicar appeared at the side of the house, waving a dusty bottle of wine. 'I found the cellar, thank you …'

A great wailing, like a birthing cow, came from the bedroom. Lilith had found her clothes all over the floor and her corset strings cut.

Phoeba escaped to bed early. She was enjoying the solitude, *Great Expectations* was open on her lap and Rudolph Steel was on her mind. She saw his face before hers, felt his presence lingering the way the smell of hot scones did. He had called her Phoeba, touched her, and seemed genuinely concerned about her. He'd be at the harvest dance, surely. A knock at her door interrupted her thoughts and her father came in.

'There you are!' he said, as if he'd been searching for her for days. He wore his pyjamas and dressing gown, the cord tied high on his tummy. 'Well, well.' She put her book aside and smiled at him with the good side of her face. He sat on her bed and patted her hand. 'After you'd fallen out of that sulky and were stuck at Overton, I sat down and asked myself why I'd brought you here. And it was because I thought this was a safe place that offered a more wholesome life and good air for your sickly sister. Turns out she'd rather spend her life shopping in Melbourne and your mother was right, the accident would never have happened if I hadn't brought you to Mount Hope. There's nothing here for you.'

'You were right to bring us here, Dad. There is everything here.'

'Your mother says you don't want to marry your suitor. Of course, you must do what is right – and I'm not entirely sure he is – but what if you end up an old maid?'

'I'm an old maid already and anyway, Aunt Margaret's an old maid and she's all right.'

'She wouldn't be without handouts from us.'

'I want to stay here, Dad, I want to grow grapes.'

He patted her hand again. 'If only your mother had made you a boy.'

'If only,' she agreed.

'You want to be the only woman growing grapes and making wine in a prime sheep- and wheat-growing area, laughed at by your neighbours and attacked by hostile Temperance women?'

'Yes, Dad. I want to learn to make wine properly.'

'Right. But what about your sister?'

'Lilith will get married and have a grandson for you and I will leave my lot to him when I die.'

'Seriously, Phoeba, if she doesn't marry or if she marries a farmer and you're single—'

'I know, there's a risk her husband would want Mount Hope,

167

or at least Lilith's half and he might even insist I pay him out. But you could prevent any of that in your will – specify that I'm to manage it, for grapes. I planted them; we planted them. I've pruned them every year and harvested alongside everyone else and I would do more only I have to the make cheese and milk the goat and cook … don't worry about Lilith,' she finished, 'I'll be fair.'

'You could make her live in the shed,' he suggested. Then said, 'I'll see about it.'

'I will never run sheep or tear out your vines for wheat, oats, apples, anything.'

'It's an awful lot of work and your mother will object.'

'She'll be pleased when I'm here to care for you both in your dotage.'

His face brightened and he leaned close to her, whispering conspiratorially. 'A few more years, all going well, just a few more harvests and if we reinvest the returns we will triumph. Mark my words, Phoeba Crupp, one day this whole area will be covered in vines. Covered in them! My grandchildren, your grandchildren, will be rich.' His face was ruddy with joy. He kissed his fingertips and placed them lightly on her cheek. 'You are my cornerstone, Phoeba.'

Later, Lilith came in and tore off her clothes, threw them in a pile on the floor and settled into her bed.

'Turn the light down, Phoeba. I've gotten used to going to sleep in the dark.'

Phoeba ignored her. Lilith turned the lamp down herself. Phoeba turned it up and as she opened her mouth to call out to her mother Phoeba snapped. 'You are an incomplete person, Lilith. You have no tolerance, grace or generosity. You are motivated by your own superficial needs and sadly, it seems, you are indestructible.'

She waited for Lilith's wail, but there was silence.

'And why, Phoeba,' asked her sister very quietly, 'do you imagine that you're not all of those things too?'

'And you're not very clever either.'

'I don't pretend to be,' shot Lilith, tugging the sheet up to her ears. 'You've got no sense of humour, Phoeba, and you're … ungenerous.'

Phoeba felt her equilibrium slightly rattled. She knew it was true. She could be sour – but only, she was sure, when she was around Lilith. Her sister brought out the worst in her. She went back to thinking about Rudolph and wondering what 'unfettered liberty' implied.

Saturday, January 27, 1894

There was a calm between the sisters when they woke on Saturday morning, and Phoeba did something she rarely did. While she laced Lilith's corset – with its new strings – she asked her sister's advice: what should she put on her face and skin.

'Lemon and cow's milk,' said Lilith, with great authority. 'Actually, Phoeba, you could look quite attractive if you put in some effort.' Lilith sat her at the dressing table and stood behind her in her under-garments.

'Now look,' she said, pulling hairpins from the tight bun at Phoeba's crown. She brushed her sister's hair out then twisted it to a loose bun at her nape. 'You look less like you've got a tomato stuck to your head now.'

'Thank you,' said Phoeba, and wondered if Rudolph thought

her bun looked like a tomato. Her hair did look nice, she thought, but it wasn't appropriate for vineyard work. She wound it back into a tight bun and went to find her father at the start of the first row.

'Right,' he said, looping his thumbs into his vest pockets. 'You must listen very carefully to everything I say, understand?'

She nodded.

'We have just gone through the stage of—'

'Berry set. The tendrils have grown long and the flowers turned to berries.'

'Correct. The grape is a conservative plant, it does not rush to growth in spring and it takes time to ripen. So deciding when to harvest is our most difficult and important task during the entire grape-growing and wine-producing process.'

'Yes, Dad, and grapes must have good composition. Harvested too early, grapes will lack sugar. Low sugar means low alcohol content. In cooler climates grape sugar and flavour develop slowly. Overripe grapes lead to coarse taste and slow fermentation.'

Maude called. They ignored her.

'Right then, Miss know-everything, you can tell me when ripening has commenced.'

Maude screamed from the veranda.

Robert handed Phoeba the Collector. 'You're so good at everything – you shoot all the birds.'

'I will,' said Phoeba. Her father went to his wife, large and pink in her dressing gown, her corset strings dangling. Phoeba obediently shot at birds, then she harnessed Angela.

Maude arrived at the sulky bound and strapped in her best brown silk taffeta carrying an overnight bag, a parasol and jacket, a purse and a handbag. Behind her, Lilith held a basket of Phoeba's scarce eggs, cold meat and goat's cheese for Aunt Margaret – Maude was off to help her empty the house in Geelong. But Lilith wasn't dressed for town.

'I offered Lilith new threads and embroidery patterns but she won't come,' sniffed Maude in her most hurt voice. 'I'll have to travel alone. And only last year a stoker was killed while they were crossing a particularly unstable bridge.'

'He leaned out too far and fell from the cabin,' said Phoeba.

'Are you suddenly paraplegic, Lilith?' asked Robert, perplexed.

'On the contrary,' said Phoeba. 'Lilith has taken up walking, haven't you, Lilith?'

'Yes,' she said, 'I'm strengthening my ankles for the harvest dance.'

Phoeba rolled her eyes.

'Don't look like that,' said Lilith, sounding hurt. 'She thinks it's rot.'

'It is not rot, Miss Impertinent!' said Maude. 'There's nothing more debilitating than having a turned ankle. Why are you being like this, Phoeba? You are rude to our neighbours, you act like a boy working outdoors – so much so you'll end up looking like you wash with harness soap. All I have done is try to bring you up to be a dutiful daughter and a nice young lady and you repay me by being pertinacious.'

'Let's get back to discussing why Lilith isn't going to Geelong, shall we?' said Phoeba, narrowing her eyes at her sister. 'The focus has passed from Lilith to me.'

'It's that bump on the head!' said Maude, turning her bottom to her husband so he could heave her into the sulky. 'The dangers of country life. And I'll need £10, Robert.'

'Ten?'

'For longcloth combinations – and the girls need undershirts. And while I'm gone you must do the thistles; the countryside is puce!'

Robert drove. Spot neighed loudly at them as they drove through the gate but the rest of the trip to the shop was very quiet. They found Mrs Flynn uncharacteristically glum. She put her hands on her ample hips and said, 'Well, you look a fright, don't you, Phoeba Crupp?'

'Yes,' said Phoeba, gaily. 'Just one ticket for Mother, please.'

'Lilith not going? Sick is she?' asked Mrs Flynn sticking her tongue behind her front teeth to concentrate on writing out the ticket.

'Has my peach parer come?' asked Maude, fanning herself with a medical pamphlet advertising cures for biliousness, constipation and urinary ailments.

'Na.'

Robert walked around the shop, his hands behind his back, peering behind coils of wire and lifting tins on the counter. He walked out on to the veranda, looked up and down and came back again. There was not a newspaper in sight.

Feeling a scene brewing, Phoeba sat on a flour sack. Once, a long time ago, her mother had displeased Mrs Flynn by mentioning that there was rat dirt in the rolled wheat. A week later Robert had rushed to the shop and threatened legal action because Freckle wouldn't deliver newspapers or mail. Mrs Flynn simply crossed her brown arms over her grubby apron and said cheerily, 'Well you just tell me when I have to be at the law court and in the meantime you can ride to Geelong for your papers.'

Robert had relented, apologised on behalf of his rude wife, declared that there must be rats in their own larder. Mrs Flynn had magically found a pile of newspapers a week old and Freckle arrived with a sack of mail that afternoon.

'Mrs Flynn,' said Robert, lightly, 'we haven't had any papers this week?'

'There's been a flood.' She snatched the fare from his hand.

'I know nothing about a flood.'

'Well, you wouldn't. You've had no papers.' She fanned herself with Maude's train ticket, one hand on her hip.

In the distance, a faint train whistle screeched.

'Do we owe Freckle money for papers or rabbits?' suggested Phoeba.

'They're rabbits from our outcrop,' hissed Robert.

'He's the one what traps them and skins them,' said Mrs Flynn, indignantly.

'And sells the skins,' muttered Phoeba.

'But it's not money,' said Mrs Flynn, putting her other hand on her hip, 'it's your sewing machine. It nearly killed him.'

'I am deeply sorry,' said Robert removing his pith hat and placing it over his heart. 'I'll make sure it never happens again.'

'Killed him how?' asked Maude, and as Mrs Flynn told them the story of the guard throwing the machine, a crimson flush crept up her throat and spread across her plump cheeks.

'Surely,' said Phoeba, 'it's between the guard and Freckle, it's their war—'

'But it's your machine and machines is nothing but trouble if you arst me!'

'Absolutely right,' said Robert, 'absolutely right. No more machines for us.'

Mrs Flynn handed over the ticket and the newspapers as Freckle struggled past, heading for the siding and dragging a very large supply cart. It was a heavy, cumbersome, two-wheeled old thing with two thick shafts. Two lads Phoeba recognised from the

173

itinerant's camp walked behind the cart, their hands resting lightly on the back of it.

'Do you want someone to help you pull, Freckle?' called Robert, wobbling quickly from the shop.

'Come,' said Maude, bustling from the shop, 'the train is arriving.'

'Do you know,' said Phoeba as casually as she could, 'if the new manager at Overton gets mail from England?'

'He does,' said Mrs Flynn, 'but you're too late for the stamps. Freckle collects them.'

'I see,' she said, wondering how to get Mrs Flynn to tell her more. Did he write back? To a woman? His mother?

'Mysterious chap,' said Mrs Flynn, sinking on her elbows to the counter. 'That wagon Freckle's got's for a new stove. The guard telegraphed to say there was a great big iron stove had to be picked up and delivered. And it'll be trouble too.'

The subject of Rudolph had ended.

The three boys lined up along the siding to watch down the line, their bare toes clinging to the edge of the sleepers.

'The stove must be a wedding gift for Mrs Pearson,' declared Maude.

'You should get Mr Titterton to pick it up,' said Phoeba to Freckle. 'A stove's a very heavy thing.'

'We can make sixpence a mile,' Freckle said, triumphantly.

'Tuppence each,' said the straw-headed kid with the grimy neck.

The train appeared, the engine slid by and the carriages screeched to a stop.

Robert boosted Maude up the steps and Phoeba handed the baskets and parcels to her through the window. Her mother looked nervous.

'You'll be all right,' said Phoeba, cheerfully.

'You could have offered to come,' said Maude, turning away.

She could have, and probably would have once, but not today. A middle-aged woman with her daughter sitting opposite Maude was staring at Phoeba's face, so Phoeba smiled at her. She commented that the weather was unseasonably hot.

'Yes,' said Maude, 'it always is in this wretched place. I'm actually from Geelong, are you?'

The mailman popped his head out of the goods van, looked at Freckle, his two friends and the cart and said, 'Why did you bother bringing that big old cart across for?' He waved his flag laughing uproariously, and Freckle was speechless with fury.

There was no stove. It was one of the mailman's tricks. Then Freckle's face changed, revenge on his mind.

The straw-headed boy said, 'You still gotta pay us.'

'We didn't make any money.'

The other boy shook his head. 'We'll have to burn your house down then.'

'You're a bunch of bloody extortionists,' said Freckle. He threw his hat in the dirt, dancing in the dust, with his fists circling in front of him. 'Put your dukes up, come on then.'

'Right,' said Robert looking at his fob watch, 'we'll have three rounds at a minute each, no hitting below the belt—'

'Dad!' cried Phoeba, grabbing the two itinerant boys as they squared up to Freckle. 'Violence will get you nowhere.'

'Bugger off, missus, this is business,' said the straw-headed boy, and kicked Phoeba's ankle.

She biffed him over the back of the head; Freckle took a swing at his mate but he missed, and Freckle copped a punch. There was a terrible sound like cracking porcelain and blood ran from Freckle's nose.

Mrs Flynn came thundering across the lane and clouted the itinerant boys with a straw broom, sending them running.

'I told you,' she hissed, dragging Freckle by the ear. 'Modern conveniences only bring trouble.'

Robert and Phoeba arrived back at Mount Hope to find the last of the apricots and peaches were stripped from the trees and in the vegetable patch, carrots ripped from the soil, an entire row of lettuce gone, the bean bush torn from its trellis and lying in the dirt and a dozen rabbits grazing on the remaining radish seedlings because the gate had been left ajar. The sound of a fiddle wafted down from the outcrop.

Lilith was nowhere to be seen.

The itinerants were taking everything, bit by bit, but there was nothing she could do. She reminded herself they were unfortunate: the shearers didn't want them, nor did the threshers. Her father needed them to harvest the grapes but they weren't ready to harvest. And the vineyard looked so lush, so promising against the stunted grain crops and the rest of the parched country. In her mind's eye Phoeba filled the entire landscape with great squares of vines. She imagined travellers returning each year to pick her grapes. They would help each other. She knew her family had done nothing to threaten their existence – on the contrary. She imagined an enormous corrugated-iron winery next to the dam, and outside it, the cart overflowing with fat, green bunches of grapes. Spot would be harnessed in front of it. He would be her first employee. But this theft, this pillage: this couldn't go on.

Below, in the yard, her father made his way to the house from the shed carrying his pipe and tobacco, wine jug and slippers. She smiled. With Maude away, he would throw her pillows on top of the wardrobe and put his ashtray on her dressing table.

Lilith was late for tea, rushing in and plopping down, flushed and breathless. The top button on her blouse was missing.

'I've been out walking,' she declared, spreading a napkin on her lap.

'You've got grass in your hair,' said Phoeba.

Robert stopped, his mouth open, a fork full of mashed potato and peas in his hand.

'I lay in the grass to read a book,' said Lilith, brushing the back of her head.

Robert put his fork down. 'I don't believe you.'

Lilith paled. Phoeba played nonchalantly with the saltcellar.

'You've never read a book in your life,' he said, and ate his vegetables.

Phoeba checked the animals before she went to bed and her father locked and latched the doors, then took the Collector with him to his room. He leaned the gun against the dressing table and snuggled into bed with his pipe in his mouth and a glass of wine. He pulled the sheet up to his chin and farted long and luxuriantly.

Next door, Phoeba lay in bed with her lamplight low, listening, waiting for the itinerants to come for more provisions – and raid their cellar, steal their goat. Spot would call out to her, she was sure. She looked over at her sister, angelic in the tousled white sheets, her pretty curls spread across the pillow. Phoeba knew what Lilith wanted and knew that nothing would prevent her from getting it. It occurred to her that, in that regard, they were not unalike.

Sunday, January 28, 1894

They woke to find nothing amiss. Spot followed Phoeba around the grapes and she discussed going to church with him.

'I should go to support Henrietta and Hadley. It's Widow Pearson's wedding day. But people will stare at my face and I'll have to talk about the bolting horse and describe the accident. Besides, we haven't been invited, so Mrs Pearson will think we're just coming to stickybeak. Or is that being too petty, Spot?' She looked into Spot's dark eyes but saw only her own reflection, long and top-heavy. 'We'd better go and break the news to Lilith.'

Robert was back in bed with his pipe and the newspapers. Lilith sat at the stove with her cold curling irons in her hand, rocking and wailing, 'But I need to go.'

'You can pray for your soul here,' said Phoeba, knowing it was the pain of missing the wedding – and Marius Overton – that had upset her. 'Why don't you harness Angela and go?'

'I don't know how to drive the sulky!' Lilith spat.

'It's the same as a brougham only there's half as many wheels, horses and reins, but the church is the same as it always was and it's still opposite Mrs Flynn's shop.'

'You just wait until Mother gets back, Phoeba. I'll tell her —'

'You will do no such thing!' Robert stormed into the kitchen, threatening to tie Lilith to the sewing machine and throw her in the dam if she didn't shut up.

'I hate this rotten place,' screamed Lilith. 'I can't wait to get married and leave!'

'Neither can we,' said Phoeba and followed her father to the vineyard. His thumbs poked in his waistcoat pockets, Robert gave her her second lesson, on sampling.

'Sampling is a means of testing the sugar, acidity and taste of grapes about three to four weeks before harvest.'

Phoeba eyed the hard, green berries. 'But it'll be weeks before they even start to ripen.'

'And you, Miss Grape-Expert, will then begin sampling. Avoid collecting grapes from end vines and outside rows. Always select berries randomly from various parts of the vine, for example ...' He pointed to one grape berry from the crown of a top bunch, one from the outside of a bunch, one at the bottom of the vine, and one from the inside of a middling vine. 'Place it in your mouth, burst it over your tongue then write down for me exactly what it tastes like. We'll compare notes.'

He issued her with her instructions for the day; she was to scare birds, make lunch, cut thistles and at sunset turn the irrigation on for one hour.

'What will you do?'

'I have a sign to make,' he said, and went to the shed.

When the general congregation had left the church, Mr Titterton led his fiancée, wearing her mustard frock and green hat, to the altar. Hadley and Henrietta sat tight-jawed in the second pew. Mrs Overton, Marius and the three Temperance women were the only other guests.

The vicar took his place and looked down at the bride and groom. Henrietta felt unwell, like she had when she'd tried to get drunk with Hadley and Phoeba by eating grapes. Hadley lowered

179

his forehead into his hands. Please God, don't let Mr Titterton retire and breed swine at Elm Grove.

The vicar placed his finger on the open page of his prayer book.

Mr Titterton sensed his fiancée next to him trembling with emotion, so he took her small hand and looped it through his elbow. She was, he felt, such a frail, helpless little thing. For the first time ever, Widow Pearson wanted to loosen her corset. But Henrietta had tugged it very firmly that morning. The Widow felt as if her ribs had met under her breastbone and were grating against each other.

The vicar read: '"Dearly beloved, we are gathered together here in the sight of God, and in the face of this small congregation to join together this man and this woman in Holy matrimony".'

A sob laced with spittle burst from Henrietta and the vicar paused. Hadley, looking as dignified as he could under the circumstances, put his arm protectively around his sister and rubbed his knee with his other hand. He prayed: Please God, don't let Mr Overton go broke and sack Mr Titterton.

The small convoy headed back to the manager's house for the wedding breakfast. Mrs Overton excused herself but Marius attended. He stood against a wall behind a frond of potted Phoenix palm on a walnut canterbury. As soon as he could, Hadley excused himself from the Temperance women and joined Marius, turning the conversation to the strike.

'Yes,' he said, bouncing on the balls of his feet. 'It was a rum affair but we showed them, didn't we?'

He knew it was he who'd shown them and he wanted to be acknowledged for his bravery again. Marius had done nothing to confront the troubled shearers: he'd gone driving to see Lilith Crupp. The man's heart didn't seem to be in being a pastoralist, thought Hadley.

'Of course, negotiation is a matter of engagement,' he said, but suddenly Henrietta and Marius disappeared and Hadley found he was talking to a potted palm. He turned and saw why. The vicar was heading towards him to discuss raising funds to line the church ceiling. Hadley suggested he raffle one of Maude Crupp's plum cakes.

'They are,' he said, 'rich – and she's making so many these days.' But though the vicar knew Mrs Crupp's cakes were very good, he wasn't sure about the family: the oldest girl was inclined to be pithy.

Later, as the honeymooners waved from their departing train, Hadley and his sister pondered their future with a new father – he would build a new house to retire to and if Hadley went away classing, as both his mother and Mr Titterton seemed to want him to do, then Mr Titterton would run Elm Grove. And as long as Mr Titterton was at Overton, Henrietta had her instructions to adhere to customs in the manager's house that reflected the high standard in the main house. She was even supposed to see the housekeeper for a uniform that afternoon.

'My life is over,' she said.

Hadley patted his sister's shoulder as if he was testing wet paint. 'We will look out for one another, Sis,' he said, but his voice was cracking.

Spot moved to the gate, took the apple gently from Phoeba's palm and chewed, the woody noise echoing in his long skull. He sniffed her pockets for more while she bridled him, then she stood in front of him and showed him the scythe.

'You may come to cut thistles, Spotty, but if my hem gets wet I will give you to the itinerants and they will slice you into thin strips and toast you over their campfire for dinner.'

She rode him bareback but only at an amble – he kept pausing to take in the view or to sniff green tufts of grass. He stepped sideways, giving the Sunshine harvester a wide berth, but kept on, his pace suddenly quickening, heading for the dam.

'No,' said Phoeba, pulling his head the other way. But Spot walked on. She begged, kicked and threatened, cursed and told him he was mean but he just turned circles, reversing and then going forward, until he had worked his way to the water. Resigned, she raised her boots to his rump and lay flat with her arms around his neck as he splashed into the water. She surveyed the thistles and Salvation Jane. She watched the Melbourne ferry steam across the bay. She pondered Robert's new sign: Please travel slowly dust ruins grapes, R. Crupp.

She was watching dragonflies hover over the dam surface, her cheek against Spot's hot, smelly neck, when she heard a horse neigh softly.

Rudolph Steel and his sturdy mare sat on the dam bank. Phoeba felt a rush of delight at seeing him.

'Good afternoon, Miss Crupp,' he said formally.

'Good afternoon, Mr Steel.' She rested her head on Spot's mane again.

'I see the hot dry weather continues.'

'Yes,' she said, 'so it's reassuring that the stock dam is quite full.'

He smiled and shook his head. 'Why do you think he does it?'

She was suddenly conscious that she was wearing her father's socks and that her skirt was riding up, but there was nothing to be done.

'He's always liked water,' she said, 'but the older he gets, the more he likes it.'

'How are his shoes?' said Rudolph.

'The farrier at Overton does them.'

'That farrier should have been a coach painter.'

They waited in the hot sun discussing this and that and Spot didn't move.

'How's Angela?' asked Rudolph.

'We didn't go to church today so I don't really know.'

Steel nudged his horse towards the dam, Spot suddenly splashed through the water to the sweet grass by the inlet. Rudolph followed, got off his horse and put his hand up to Phoeba – she could have easily swung down on her own but she accepted it. His coat smelled of sun-warmed wool.

Rudolph ran his hand down Spot's neck, across his sloppy breast and down to his front hoof while Phoeba tried to think of something to say rather than just staring at his nice hands and admiring the way he touched her horse. There were feathers poked into his hatband.

'Did you collect all those on your walk down from Broome?'

'Some.'

'What breed is your horse?'

'It is a Holstein, German. They're renowned for their excellent legs, and good, hard feet.' Rudolph stood up, wiped his hands together and smiled at her. She smiled back, like a small girl on her birthday.

'Your horse has got an inflamed pedal bone,' he said to her, and her smile fell. She felt very silly.

'We thought he was just vengeful.'

Rudolph was nonplussed. 'You didn't check?'

'Dad was an accountant,' she shrugged, 'but I've looked at

them and they never look any different.'

'I suppose you checked before you rode him.'

'The rest of the time he stands in dams.'

Rudolph laughed and rested his hand on her shoulder lightly, just for a moment.

'To be fair,' he said, 'it's only his front feet and pedal foot is only evident after certain distance. The dam is cool. We can ease it by adjusting his shoes.'

She slapped Spot's neck sadly. 'He's been trying to tell us.'

They walked together towards Mount Hope, Spot and the German horse clopping along behind them, and Phoeba struggling again for something to say. But Rudolph seemed happy with the lack of conversation, so she luxuriated in walking along with a nice man who wasn't Hadley or her father.

'Have you managed to please yourself so far?' he asked.

'Yes. And I've displeased almost everyone else.'

He laughed, and then there was another silence. She watched the tips of her boots poke out from under her skirt as she walked.

'Do you think Marius Overton will marry again?' she blurted.

'Yes,' he said, 'but it's ... there's a respectable time people should wait, isn't there?'

'I suppose. If you care what people say.'

He knows, she thought: the whole district must know.

He seemed to read her thoughts and said, 'There are some things we can't control. Things happen and they can be untimely.'

'Sometimes people marry for the wrong reasons.'

'Yes. Or they marry for the right reasons and it turns out to be wrong. You never know the future,' he said, almost to himself.

She wanted to ask him if he'd had a broken heart but decided it was best not to know. She pointed to the vines. 'There's my future. I'm going to grow excellent grapes and make wine.'

'You are going to grow the grapes?' He stopped walking and looked slightly taken aback.

'You don't think I can?' said Phoeba.

'I'm sure you can. It's just I didn't realise that your future depended quite so much on Mount Hope.' But he seemed suddenly preoccupied. 'This area is perfect for grape growing for wine but it's a lot to do. Still, you will need help,' he said, as if that solved some sort of problem.

'I can hire help. And swaggies always want work. What about your future, Mr Steel?'

'I just want to get this harvest started. It's very important for the future of Overton.' He frowned and looked up to the house, worried. He needed a haircut, thought Phoeba, and toyed with the idea of telling him that Lilith would cut it for him. No. Not Lilith.

'Won't the itinerants—'

'No,' he said, waving his hand towards the grounded harvester. 'They refused because of that.'

The thresher team was still at the church cutting chaff. It could take a week to reach Overton, Phoeba knew: too long to wait when a lot depended on the crop. She laid her hand on his arm and he turned and smiled at her.

'It's good to see you're recovered.' He handed her the scythe. 'Hadley Pearson is on the veranda waiting for you.'

Hadley was looking straight at them. His bespectacled face was passive, his hat on the couch beside him and his long fingers wrapped over his grey woollen knees. Resting on his thin thighs was the looking glass.

A rush of fury shot through her, then a wave of terrible pity.

185

'Hadley,' she sighed. She turned back to Rudolph Steel. 'You could stay for tea—'

'No.' Rudolph took Spot's lead, 'I'll take this old ungulate to the farrier.'

He got on his horse and nudged the mare but she was anchored fast by Spot, who leaned back, his ears screwed around to Phoeba and the whites of his eyes showing as he pulled against the reins.

'Off you go, Spot,' she said, patting his rump. He didn't move. She whacked him so hard that her hand stung but it didn't dispel her mood. Bother Hadley, sitting like a spy on her veranda. Spot gave her another, reproachful, tragic look then haltingly followed the dark mare. Phoeba walked up to the house.

'Hadley,' she called, through gritted teeth. 'How was the wedding?'

'Very ordinary,' said Henrietta, clattering out onto the veranda with a tea tray, her mouth already full of plum cake. 'There's no one here so we made ourselves at home ... since we are without a home now. And there is your mother's excellent cake.'

Phoeba took a seat next to Henrietta. Hadley feigned great interest in the tea in his cup.

'Spot has pedal foot,' she announced. 'Rudolph helped me—'

'I saw,' said Hadley, waving the looking glass. 'You call him Rudolph, do you? You must be on good terms.'

She wanted to be on better terms with Rudolph Steel, she thought. When she was with him she felt elated. The air was fresher, the clouds were whiter, the road was interesting and everything seemed of greater value.

'Would anyone like wine?' she asked, feeling celebratory, and ran to fetch a jug. When they were settled with a glass each,

Hadley said, 'You know he's a banker.'

'He's not,' she said, a little too defensively, 'he's an investor.'

'Tarred with the same brush,' warned Henrietta. 'He's sent the scullery maid, the house maid and the housekeeper away—'

'—and put the cattle on the train to the abattoir,' added Hadley.

'Overton must be going bad,' said Henrietta, leaning back and resting her foot up on the veranda post.

'No,' said Hadley, 'the wool's gone to be sold and there's the crop yet.' He cleared his throat, 'Speaking of scandal, they say Lilith is having trysts—'

'With Marius Overton?' said Phoeba, her voice brittle. So it was true. Lilith was probably with him at that moment. Well, thought Phoeba, it would either make them or break them. He would either marry her or abandon her – and then Phoeba would be stuck with her forever.

'Even the boundary rider knows about it and he's hardly ever back here!' said Henrietta, her brown eyes bright and her cheeks flushing red. Wine always made Henri shine a bit.

'Well then,' said Phoeba, 'he has to marry her.' She raised her glass.

'Mrs Overton has expectations for her only son,' said Hadley sounding strangely like his mother, 'but I just want you to know I won't be swayed by it, Phoeba. My regard for you stands and my … expectations for us will never change.'

'Mine too,' said Henrietta and beamed.

'How's shearing?' Phoeba asked, wanting to move on from marriage.

Henrietta spoke on her little brother's behalf. 'Hadley's nearly finished the scour. He hates it, but he'll get almost £100 for it.'

'I wanted more,' he muttered.

'Did you know he repelled a hundred strikers on his own, Phoeba?'

She shook her head.

'Well,' said Hadley, sitting a little straighter, 'a pack of them. I repelled them on my own. They were armed with pikes carved from saplings, and strychnine. They could have thrown it in my eyes! And they had shears strapped to the end of spears.' He got up and moved to the veranda rail, as if he was under a proscenium arch, and by the time he'd got to the end of the saga he was animated. He acted out the scene where he shot the bullet with an invisible rifle, '... and they fled, and The General was safe.'

He was no longer Henrietta's little brother, a small, orange boy bearing a dead lizard tearfully to a neat grave under the persimmon tree. And when she saw them off, Phoeba knew he was happy. He'd had three glasses of wine and he felt he'd impressed her, but it made her sad for him. She sat on the front step and pondered Rudolph Steel. Her heart felt faint when she thought of him. Perhaps that was how Lilith felt about Marius, but did he feel that about Lilith?

There was one way to find out.

Phoeba walked up through the boulders to where the trees thickened, careful not to stand on fallen branches. A third of the way up she saw the Arab horse. She stepped behind a tree. Did she really want to know what they were doing? They'd be reading poetry, or something. Holding hands perhaps? Or would it be worse. Through the bush she spied Lilith's skirt and fought an urge to run away. What if they saw her? What would that do?

Her stomach churned. Then her curiosity got the better of her. She crept closer, staying behind the bushes.

Lilith was pinned against a tree, Marius kissing her and

grinding his mouth to hers. Phoeba felt vaguely nauseated and the hair on her neck crawled. Then Lilith jolted, her head falling back and her curls shuddering. She raised her knee and Marius's hand searched up under her skirt. The white of her petticoat folded back over her hem. Suddenly, Phoeba wanted to flee, but Marius looked up and saw her – looked straight into her eyes – and she went cold.

He stepped back, wrenching up his trousers. Lilith's skirts fell and she turned and saw her big sister. Her expression settled into one of challenge.

'Stickybeak,' she spat. Phoeba felt rude and ridiculous. 'How dare you,' said Lilith, her lip curling.

Phoeba stayed behind the bushes, paralysed, embarrassed.

Marius called, 'It's not what you think.'

It's not what you think? That was exactly what it was. So ridiculous, she started to giggle. 'Then what is it?' she asked, stepping from behind the tree.

'She won't tell,' said Lilith, 'and anyway, if she does they won't believe her. They never do.' She backed into Marius's arms. 'Plain old Phoeba.'

'Everybody knows, Lilith. You're the talk of the district.'

'Are we?' said Marius, horrified, struggling to button his fly.

'Yes,' said Phoeba, crossing her arms. 'Are you going to do the right thing?'

Lilith's chin went up. 'We're getting married.'

'We can't!' cried Marius. Then, 'Not yet.' He looked like a naughty boy, shoving his shirt into his trousers.

'We can, when the time is right,' said Lilith, in a reasoning tone.

Marius stood beside her, guilt all over his pretty face.

Phoeba shook her head slowly, like Maude had done when

189

they'd been mischievous as children. 'What about your reputation? What about Mother and Dad's standing in the community? Those things are important to them.' Marius began to wilt a little, flinching under her words. 'You're so selfish! What will you say to Mother and Dad when they hear about it from Mrs Flynn or Widow Pearson? And what if Marius's parents don't approve?'

'You think you're so important,' screamed Lilith, 'but you're sour and you're selfish. You're just jealous because you're plain. You should marry Hadley, because he's the only one who'll ever ask you.'

'Now now, Lilith, Marius doesn't want to know what you're really like,' said Phoeba, but it still stung. She felt her plainness acutely: her waist was a little too thick, and her hair was straight. But, she reminded herself, she was clever – and Rudolph Steel liked to converse with her.

Lilith's words hung in the air and Marius would remember them. But he wrapped his arms around her, protectively, and Lilith turned and buried her face in his chest. Phoeba had exposed a fraction of her sister's worst and decided that it was the right thing to do. She walked away, her emotions swinging between fear and elation. It was all so brutal, lewd. And Lilith had seemed over-powered, but yet willing. She hoped she hadn't destroyed whatever it was, hoped she had pointed them in the right direction.

That evening, at the tea table, Phoeba watched Lilith eat heartily. She was willing to trade her reputation, her chastity and her parents' expectations for something she wanted; Lilith wanted Marius Overton. It was worthy of respect, thought Phoeba, and with a jolt, she realised that she wanted something just as much. She wanted Lilith gone, life on the farm without her and the freedom that went with it. Someone else supporting Lilith … forever. But she doubted she would compromise those she loved to make it happen.

She would confront Marius again.

In Geelong, Maude and Margaret were cleaning out their family home, now signed over to the Chinese vegetable gardener next door, for £105. Maude was weeping – she didn't seem to be able to stop herself – blubbering quietly into her sodden handkerchief. She was having another hot flush and she felt bulkier than usual, her thighs chafed from rubbing together under her skirts. Her lower back ached and she felt like sewing pins were stuck in her pelvis. She'd been chucking things from the window boxes into a rubbish bin when she pulled out an ancient, moth-eaten black doll. It was the doll Lilith had taken from the little girl who'd disappeared from next door.

'Is this your dolly, Margaret?' she sniffed.

'I refuse to believe I ever played with dolls,' called her sister from the kitchen.

'I'll keep her for my grandchildren,' said Maude, as its head fell off and hundreds of tiny silverfish ran out of its neck. She let out another sob, tossed the doll away and furiously brushed the tiny creatures from her hands.

Margaret came running. 'What on earth is the matter?'

'You wouldn't understand,' Maude snivelled. There was no use trying to explain it to Margaret – she was unfulfilled, hadn't been awakened to the pain, the pathos, the gall and wormwood that marriage, bearing and raising children yielded. And then to find yourself redundant and neglected, forced to travel alone to endure the sad business of selling your childhood home. No, thought Maude, Margaret had only half lived. She wouldn't understand.

At the bottom of the window box she found an old

photograph and scraped the dust away. Her hand went to her bosom and she wept: 'Mummy and Daddy.'

It was a very old print of a rigid, serious couple surrounded by stiff, over-bustled and bearded attendants against a backdrop of drapes and Roman columns. Her parents glared back at her. Phoebe and Rufus Robertson, 1843, she read on the back.

'Deary-me,' she winced, 'it's hard to imagine that people loved each other back in the olden days. Do you remember, Margaret? Did our parents love each other?'

'Yes!' cried Margaret, 'they did. Unlike you. You got your come-uppence, seizing on Robert for security and ending up in the wilderness.'

Maude pressed the photograph to her bosom and cried.

'It was sad for them to end that way,' said Margaret. She frowned at her big sister. 'But aren't you being a little dramatic, Maude? At least they were together when the buggy crashed.'

'Actually,' said Maude, 'they were crushed by a load of hay. A passing wagon went into a pothole and the load shifted. It fell right on top of them. I've never felt safe outside since.'

She placed the photograph carefully in the box labelled, Maude Crupp. If they had lived, she thought, I might have got the life I deserved.

Monday, January 29, 1894

Spot came home by himself on Monday wearing new shoes. The farrier had bathed his feet, given him a pedicure and new built-up shoes to ease the pressure on his pedal bone, and then put him in the holding yard. Spot had promptly nosed the wire from around the top of the post and gambolled across the plain like a big black foal on a spring day.

Robert and Phoeba had just settled on the front veranda to wait out the afternoon heat; Robert was smoothing his newspapers across his knees and Phoeba had let three shots off at the birds when Spot trotted around the corner and stood with his new feet on the bottom step.

'Right then,' said Robert, 'Angela can go back.'

'No,' cried Lilith, running down the passage. 'We should keep them both and buy a barouche.'

'More horses means more manure, Lilith! I'd have to start each day shovelling it all over the vegetable patch. There'd be more diseases and more bills. We'd have to buy another harness and I'd have to spend an hour each day fitting the horses so you could drive over to have tea with Widow Pearson and gossip. If you want a barouche, marry someone rich.'

'Look,' said Phoeba, as the Hampden trotted through the intersection and headed for Overton. It sagged under a load of wing-backed chairs, lamps, a writing desk, dressing table, the mahogany box containing the fine lace duchesse runners and afternoon tea cloths, the good crockery and the silver cutlery, and the washing machine. Hadley was driving and Henrietta jigged along behind on Liberty. She raised her hat and waved up to Mount Hope. They all waved back.

'I'll ride Angela back,' said Phoeba, eager to see Henrietta and her new home. She might see Rudolph, and then she could thank him for Spot's new shoes. Then she would confront Marius, tell him he must marry Lilith. And Robert and Lilith would collect her later in the sulky – a test run for Spot in his new shoes – and she would announce it to her father. She had the whole encounter planned, and ran to the stables.

Underway, Angela coughed once or twice but kept on. Then she stumbled and slowed.

'Whoa,' said Phoeba, patting her dark neck. The horse wobbled to a halt, swayed gently, coughed again and crumpled. Her great, shiny head dropped and her soft nose rested in the gravel, blasting away two scoops as her lungs emptied. Phoeba was left sitting on top of the mare like a stork on a hippopotamus, one foot still in the stirrup.

'Gracious,' she said.

Angela's innards shifted, moving the centre of balance sideways, and Phoeba jumped up and stepped back quickly as the horse rolled onto her side, her legs kicking out from under her and scattering the dirt.

Angela was dead.

Phoeba stood next to her in the middle of the road, stunned. She felt the breeze touch her injured cheek through her hat net, heard the blood rushing in her ears. All around her, birds cawed and crickets and geckos tickled in the dry grass.

'Gracious,' she said again, and crouched down at Angela's head to peer into her cloudy eyes.

'I'm sorry, poor thing.'

She stepped over the front legs, undid the girth strap, wrenched the saddle out from under the horse and was working the bit from Angela's mouth when Freckle arrived. He regarded her as he would a masked man outside a bank.

'Your mother's coming home tomorrow on the four o'clocker.'

'Thank you, Freckle,' she said, shakily. She stared at Angela. 'I didn't do anything. She just sort of—'

'Fell down dead,' said Freckle, flatly. 'Horses can live up to thirty-six years old, or more, unless you kill them of course.'

194

'I wasn't … she's not even sweating.'

They looked at the great mound of static horseflesh on the gravel.

'You better stick to Spot, missus. He seems to like you, wants to stick with you.'

'Can you carry the saddle up to the house, please?'

Freckle looked doubtful and patted his horse's neck.

'I'll give you a penny when I've got one,' said Phoeba.

His horse stepped away from her.

Phoeba nodded towards the static horse. 'It's just bad luck, I suppose.'

'For the horse,' said Freckle reaching out for the saddle. 'I hope she made the best of it while she was here.'

'Yes,' Phoeba said, and started up the lane, perplexed and dismayed. Angela must have had a bad heart, or something. It was another omen, she decided, a sign that it was prudent to make the best of life.

She stumbled through the front gate to find her father still on the front veranda reading the paper. 'Freckle charged me standard freight fares to transport that saddle and bridle!' he called. 'You could easily have put them behind the fence until later.'

Phoeba lowered her face into her hands and cried, her tears sliding through her leather gloves. She'd wanted to see Henrietta, to talk to her about Lilith and Marius, to tell her about the itinerants stealing her fruit and her poor chickens. What if they stole the winter preserves? She'd just wanted someone she could talk to. And was Overton going bad and what would happen to everyone else if they did?

Robert came down the steps, his arms spread. 'Now now, Phoeba, this isn't like you. It isn't as bad as it seems.'

But it was. She felt sure it was.

He gave her a glass of wine and decided to cheer her up by reading her the paper. 'John Makin was hanged after the discovery of seven murdered babies who met their fate under Mr Makin and his wife Sarah's baby farming practices … Martha Needle was hanged today for the arsenic poisoning of her husband and three children and her new fiancé's brother…'

Lilith arrived, smoothing her riding gloves. Her hat was perched at a jolly angle and her driving coat featured a sprig of gum blossom on the lapel. Her weeping sister stopped her short.

'Oh,' said Lilith. 'Does this mean, Dad, that you and I are not going to Overton?'

Tuesday, January 30, 1894

It was while she waited for the four o'clocker that Phoeba decided she would subject herself to curling irons for the dance on Saturday night. Naturally she would wear her new blouse. And if Rudolph didn't ask her for a dance, then she would ask him. And if he couldn't dance, then she would strike up a conversation with him. They had discussed the obvious things – the drought, banks and swaggies. She would search through the newspapers for something fascinating. And she would tackle the Lilith and Marius dilemma. She perused the papers, but there was hardly anything: NEW TIVOLI THEATRE OPENS IN SYDNEY – that didn't give her much of an opening. When the train drew into the siding, a window shot up and her mother leaned from the window, waving away the smoke and steam.

'Take these,' she called, shoving some brown-paper wrapped paintings at Phoeba and gathering her bags and packages.

'What a surprise,' said Phoeba. 'Paintings.'

Behind her, perched on the edge of her seat, Aunt Margaret was tight-lipped with anticipation and looking very small. She pulled her carpetbag and boxes closer to her.

'Two hours from your new life, Aunt,' said Phoeba, sounding jolly.

'Mr Spark will be there to meet me,' said Aunt Margaret confidently, but it was clear she was terrified. 'Do you think I have made a mistake, Phoeba?'

'I think it's a perfect opportunity for a new start, Aunt. We'll hear all about it at the dance?'

'Yes,' said her aunt.

The mailman put the last of Maude's packages and boxes on the platform and the guard blew his whistle.

'Remember. New challenges,' said Phoeba, reaching through the window to squeeze her aunt's hand.

'Has my peach parer come?' asked Maude. 'Are there swaggies about? Have we got the Collector?'

'No, no and yes,' said Phoeba, loading the boxes onto the sulky.

Behind them, the mailman bent to pick up the single mailbag left on the siding. He tugged, screamed, and grabbed the small of his back. Freckle had nailed it to the platform.

'I'm ruined,' he cried, shaking his fist at Flynn's shop.

Maude prattled on about the perils of her sister's new life all the way home. 'It will fail,' she said, 'and she will end up on the streets, or at Mount Hope with us. She's supposed to cook, so I hope they like sandwiches!'

Suddenly Maude wrenched her gloves off and shrugged her shawl from her shoulders. 'This change of mine,' she said, 'dreadful business. They put some women in asylums, you know, but they say if you have children it's not so bad.' She opened her knees, flapped her skirt up and down. 'Let that be a warning to you, Miss Phoeba Crupp.'

Phoeba didn't care about children. She'd never felt an urge to have them and wasn't the type to stop at a pram and goo-goo over babies, like Lilith and Maude. There was nothing wrong with her. Henrietta was the same, so was Aunt Margaret.

There was activity at the intersection but this time it had nothing to do with the dented Sunshine harvester that still sat there. It was Mr Titterton, riding postilion with a team of four draught horses.

'I have bought you cleminite for your face,' continued Maude, 'and you will scoff, Phoeba, but I also have some lace and serviettes for your trousseau. I worry that you're unbecoming and now your aunt has ruined your chance of marrying anyone other than Hadley—'

'I've been telling you for weeks,' Phoeba cut in, 'I'm not marrying Hadley.'

'Well who else will marry you? You'll end up like Margaret, living with strangers in Melbourne and it's such a dangerous place ...' Maude fell silent and her damp handkerchief froze in mid-air. Spot led them casually around Angela's carcass in the centre of the intersection. It had been attached to Mr Titterton's team by a rope looped around its stiff hooves and head. Mr Titterton lifted his hat to Maude and Phoeba.

'Good evening,' said Maude.

Mr Titterton nudged the draught horse and the team trudged across the tufty common, with Angela leaving a wide, dark groove and a wake of flattened grass.

Wednesday, January 31, 1894

On Wednesday, the thresher team unlooped the engine from the thresher, gathered its scythes and forks, left Jessops' and set up on the edge of Hadleys' neat feed crop. The water boy filled his tank from the tower near the siding which meant Freckle had the news to spread on his mail round.

Thursday, February 1, 1894

Hadley wore his new white moles – 7/6 from Lassetters, plus postage and tuppence to Freckle. Now that they had a washing machine, white moles were no longer a great hardship for his sister. He was feeling successful and in charge. He was feeling manly. He had quelled a strike and received a wonderful letter of recommendation from Marius Overton. He would have preferred one from Guston but that would risk a letter recommending Mr Parsons instead. His grain crop filled the morning air with sunny ripeness; and Phoeba, tidy and sensible in her plain brown skirt and hatnet, was driving towards him with her leather gloves, scythe and knife. Her face and hands were still scabbed, but healing, and she walked now without stiffness.

'You can do stooking,' said Hadley, firmly. 'Scything is too hard for you.'

She didn't object and joined the rakers and stookers moving

steadily behind the scythers. He watched her pull on the fine chain attached to her hem brooch and he admired her firm shins emerging as her hem rose. She moved along at once, scraping stalks together, then tying them into a neat bunch that she leaned against a neat stook.

'She's a grand girl,' said a voice next to him.

'Stubborn though,' Hadley answered before he'd considered who was next to him admiring Phoeba. It was Steel. 'I've known that since I was ten years old,' said Hadley.

'She'll make a good vintner, one day,' said Steel.

'She's good at anything once she makes up her mind about it,' said Hadley. 'The trick with Phoeba,' he continued, his confidence swelling, 'is to get her to set her mind to it. Once that's done …'

Again, Steel was conciliatory. Hadley sensed no competition from the man over Phoeba, so decided to boast. 'I haven't told you about my ram emasculator, have I, Steel? It's an idea I've refined over many years. Come and see the prototype.'

'I'm interested in anything innovative,' said Rudolph following Hadley towards the machinery shed.

The emasculator was solid metal, like a squat guillotine, with a dull, round-edge blade. 'First,' said Hadley, lifting the guillotine handle, 'you sit the ram in the appropriate position and drape its testicle sack over the base of the guillotine.' Hadley let go of the handle and the blade thudded heavily on the base. 'Strike the blade once or twice without making a tear in the sheep's skin.'

Rudolph winced.

'Then,' continued Hadley, 'you pull the testes purse and you will feel an internal severance. Both testes and the purse will slowly shrivel until there's just a sack as small as a walnut.'

Rudolph adjusted his trousers and Hadley clapped his hands together. 'What do you think?'

'I think it's a very clean, safe procedure. Whether you'll get Freckle to post them off for you is another matter.'

Hadley laughed. 'I'd better add sixpence to the price. Now, Steel, what can I do for you?' said Hadley, putting his hands deep into the pockets of his new white moles.

'I've come to speak to the thresher team,' said Rudolph, glancing over to the workers. 'The Sunshine is still missing drive chains and we need to get this harvest underway.'

The stubble clogged Phoeba's nose with spiky dust and flies found their way under her net and stayed there, trapped, gathering about her eyes and lips. The sun burned through her blouse and sweat dribbled down between her thighs. The sharp end of the stubble scraped her skin and punctured her fingertips, and straw dust bit into all her wrinkles. She stood, arched her back to ease its dull ache, and ripped her hat off to liberate the flies. She was fanning her face when Rudolph arrived at her side. 'This is hot and gritty work,' he said. 'Spot still might take you for a swim on the way home. You never know, it might not have been his feet.'

She laughed, knowing her face must be the colour of beetroot, even though she'd bathed it in water and cleminite. She couldn't think of anything to say, so they moved through the stubble together, bundling the oats and leaving sheaves in neat stooks in their wake. Rudolph gallantly took straw from Phoeba's row and made bundles for her. She knew Hadley was watching from the top of the stack – Hadley was a first-class stacker – but she pushed him from her mind and talked to Rudolph about the shearers and the battling pastoralists, the ongoing depression and the National Bank of Australasia, which had just gone under. Yet another ruined *nouveau riche* had walked into the Yarra River and vanished under the Hoddle Street punt. Rudolph blamed it on Argentina. The country had crashed in 1890, and then Barings of London had failed.

'That's true,' said Phoeba, 'but if the government hadn't over-borrowed the banks wouldn't have crashed and people wouldn't be so desperate. And if they'd had their wits about them the banks would have seen it coming.'

He smiled and shook his head, and when lunchtime came he put his finger under her chin and inspected her angry cheek. 'You're mending well, Phoeba, starting to look your old self.' He had noticed her *before* the accident! 'It's been a lively and interesting morning,' he said. 'I'll see you at the dance.'

'Yes,' she said, watching him walk away towards his Holstein. It was tethered under the elm trees next to Spot, but Spot was in the sun, straining at the end of his lead to get as far as he could away from the foreign horse.

Phoeba walked over to the haystack, and sat at its base next to Hadley with her sandwich and her jar of cold, sweet tea.

'How's Henrietta?' Hadley shrugged, screwed the lid off his water bag and drank. 'I'll see her at the dance.'

'Yes,' said Hadley, wiping his mouth with his sleeve. 'I'll collect you at seven?'

She looked straight down into his keen blue eyes. 'People will think we're courting.'

'I always take you all to the dance,' said Hadley, then added gently, 'you haven't gone soft for Steel, have you? You like your life, Phoeba. You like the farm and things in their place. He's so ... unsettled.'

'Mind your own business.' Hadley stared at his knees and she

202

knew his heart was aching. 'I'm sorry,' she said.

They ate a sandwich in silence.

'Your moustache is getting thick,' said Phoeba after a while.

'Thank you,' said Hadley, and added jokingly, 'So is yours.'

Friday, February 2, 1894

On Friday morning, most of the people in the district arrived at Hadleys' again wearing sun hats and carrying canvas water bottles and lunches. As Phoeba and her father drove she scanned the crowd, but Henrietta was still not there.

Henrietta was in her new kitchen. It was lovely, the stove was a Leamington with lifting handles for its moulded hot plates and two ovens with a dish rest each. And it was brick-lined, so the kitchen was much cooler than the one at Elm Grove. The kettle had a wooden pouring handle as well, and there was a view to the homestead through the front window to remind her of her new *station*. A pot of potatoes boiled on the stove and Henrietta pushed cold roast mutton and raw onions through a mincer. Tears were streaming down her cheeks and she sneezed every few minutes.

The new Mrs Titterton, breathless, and just returned from a brief honeymoon in Geelong, stamped her small, tight shoe on the floor of her new house. In the kitchen, Henrietta stopped turning the mincer handle and went to her, wiping cold mutton and raw onion on her new uniform.

Coming carefully down the stairs, carrying three of her new husband's collars to be washed and a bundle of cotton stockings to be soaked, the stock overseer's new wife noticed a pale blue envelope stamped with a golden 'O' under the front door. It was terrifically exciting and she had to stop and concentrate hard for a few seconds: 'deep breaths, slow breaths.' The envelope was addressed to Mrs Pearson. Mrs Titterton pursed her maroon lips in mild annoyance and bent to pick it up but her fingers wouldn't reach it. Now that she was married she had thought it might be unnecessary to pull her corset so tight, but her new husband, in charge of tying her corset these days, had reminded her that Lilith Crupp was only alive because of her corset. 'And,' he said, 'there's nothing more becoming than a nice, straight back. They say it shows good breeding.'

Mrs Titterton tried to bend again but her face turned purple and her toes and fingertips started to tingle. She flicked the envelope with the toe of her shoe, sending it skipping across Henrietta's beautifully buffed floorboards to wedge under the oak what-not.

'Get that envelope, Henrietta, it's from Mrs Overton. It'll be an invitation for morning tea.'

But it wasn't.

'She's forgotten,' said her mother as she tore the note into tiny pieces. 'Hadley will be a manager one day and you'll enter society. We all will. You can't be a maid. Now pick up that washing for me and when you've washed it you can set the table. Hadley will be tired after the harvest and he'll need lunch straight away.'

Henrietta pieced the note together in the laundry. It asked if Henrietta would like a job in the homestead – for five shillings a week. Five whole shillings a week. Of course her mother would have taken her money … unless Henrietta moved across the road to live at the homestead! Perhaps she would ask Mrs Overton – but why was she hiring someone when Rudolph Steel was letting everyone else go?

She tipped a bucket of water into the new washing machine, shoved the sheets in with a handful of soap flakes and fixed the lid shut. Gripping the handle with two hands she turned it with all her might, groaning with the effort.

'Infernal thing,' she said, looking despondently into the empty copper. If she moved to the homestead she'd lose any chance of going back to Elm Grove. Her mother would punish her forever. Was it worth it? But she hated working for nothing, being dependent. No one ever asked her opinion. No one, except Hadley and Phoeba, ever took any real notice of her. She was always just there, a useful chattel. Only last week it had been possible to ride for the hamper or even to the siding for the mail. In the past two days she'd gone as far as the homestead kitchen, and Phoeba hadn't been to see her at Overton once! And now Henrietta had missed the harvest for the first time ever – she and Phoeba had always harvested together. It wasn't fair.

Phoeba was right, thought Henrietta: there was no God.

Saturday, February 3, 1894

On Saturday, Aunt Margaret stepped from the carriage onto the Bay View siding on the arm of a man. In under a week she had bloomed. She was rounder, her skin was smoother and she was glowing. She clung to Ashley Spark in rapture over this tall, thin man in his red-checked suit and black cummerbund. His

205

beard was impressive – it shimmered all the way to his waist – but Phoeba didn't care for fancy Dans. And when he said, 'I heard you fell victim to a homesick horse; I'm delighted you are survived so that I could meet you,' she knew he was a pretender.

'You won't be delighted for long,' she replied, tersely. 'You'll have to sleep on the parlour floor.'

Just then, a dense canvas bag thudded onto the siding dangerously close to them, the small, bent mailman glowering behind it.

'A tent,' Mr Spark explained. 'I am a pantheist. Nature is God so I prefer the natural outdoors.' He spread his arms to embrace the sheep nibbling at the short dry grass, the regimented vineyard, and the bald paddocks and cultivated crops tinged with Scotch thistles and Salvation Jane.

Aunt Margaret turned pink with adoration and Phoeba's heart sank. It was lovely that Aunt Margaret was in love … but with a Dandy?

'The pretty blue crop is Scottish cotton,' said Aunt Margaret with authority. Phoeba smiled, but her heart sank further when Ashley laid eyes on Lilith: he was a philanderer too.

'I see Eros, Venus, Aphrodite,' he said, nibbling her knuckle. 'You must let me sketch you!' Aunt Margaret's chin went up with pride at his learned knowledge, and after lunch Lilith happily reclined in Robert's big old wicker chair, gazing wistfully out to the bay, while Ashley captured her profile on a sketchpad.

Phoeba left the artistes for the sanctuary of the washroom, where she spent several minutes dressing her scarred face with a cleminite poultice. She gathered a camisole, bloomers and her good skirt – blue linen with a red waistband – and then reached for her new blouse. She pulled it from Lilith's end of the wardrobe, suddenly cold with anger. Lilith had unpicked the bishop's collar and cut a new low, square neck which she'd trimmed with white guipure lace. The sleeves were now three-quarter, trimmed with the same guipure lace, and there were new Japanese silk bows. Very calmly, she sat at the dressing table for a few moments; Ashley's rounded vowels, Aunt Margaret's giggles and Lilith's charming flirtatious squeak all trilled down the hall. Finally, she put the blouse in a large, brown paper bag then went outside, climbed the peppercorn tree behind the outhouse and hung it on a high branch. The sticky pungent smell of pepper surrounded her, the clusters of small hard seeds rattling in their thin red shells, like tiny castanets. A few cloud wisps reached in from the sea and she studied the blue heavens. That was it then. Marius had to marry Lilith. She went back to her bath.

Her mother pounded on the washhouse door but Phoeba stayed in the tub, up to her chin in hot soapy water. She used everything in the copper without bothering to refill it from the well or stoke the fire for her sister and mother. They could wash in the dam.

The tantrum that preceded the dance was one of Lilith's best. First she complained about the lack of hot water, then about her hair, which she said had gone frizzy.

'Now now,' soothed Maude, 'there's not a drop of moisture in that sky.'

Next, she complained that no one had put the curling irons on to warm. Then she went to get the blouse. With the strength only summoned by lunatics, Lilith upended Phoeba's bed, tore everything from the wardrobe and even took up the floor rug. All over the house she stormed, screeching, yelling, demanding to be told where the blouse was.

'It's my blouse,' said Phoeba, quietly and calmly. 'You had no right to alter it.'

Lilith stamped her foot. 'You ruined my best corset.'

'I only cut the cords—'

'Well done,' said Ashley reaching for Lilith's slim waist. 'You needn't wear those unhealthy things.'

'I have had to wear hand-me-downs all my life, Phoeba. Once, just once, I wanted something new.'

'You're fibbing, Lilith Crupp. You haven't worn anything of mine since you were six and the blouse is mine, Lilith. My blouse.'

Lilith grinned. 'Did you know, Mother,' she said, 'that at the ploughing match Henrietta and Phoeba climbed the windmill and watched from the top. Everyone saw right up their skirts.'

Phoeba laughed. It was so petty, and before she could stop herself she said, 'Does Marius Overton know that you're a liar, a thief and a tell-tale now that you're meeting him at the outcrop for your trysts?'

'Phoeba!' said Maude, in disbelief.

But Lilith was only momentarily lost for a retort. 'We are seeing your true colours now, Phoeba!' she spat and stormed to her room.

Aunt Margaret told Ashley to put his fingers in his ears, as Maude and Phoeba had. They waited, then the bedroom door slammed and the kitchen window fell with a thwack to the sill. Its glass shattered into the kitchen sink.

'Phoeba, that is a truly disgusting exaggeration. How could you?' said Maude, cupping her cheeks.

'Everyone's talking about it,' Phoeba said, feeling a surge of daring.

Suddenly Lilith was back, pointing at her. 'Phoeba's always been jealous, mother, always.'

'What are they saying?' asked Maude, reaching for a chair.

'He'll have to marry her,' said Phoeba. 'I've seen them, mother. Together. In flagrante.'

'Mind your tongue in front of strange men, Phoeba,' said Maude, jerking her head at Ashley.

'Ashley isn't a stranger,' said Margaret but Maude said, 'I said strange men, Margaret. Now get a glass of water with a teaspoon of sal volatile for Phoeba.'

'Is it true?' asked Margaret hastily pouring a glass of water, her eyes shining with intrigue.

'It's true. They meet at the—'

Maude threw the glass of water over her. 'You're hysterical,' she said, fanning her reddening neck.

Ashley put his arm around Maude's shoulder. 'It's just passion.'

'You are a maiden's prayer and my sister will be hurt,' said Maude, shrugging his arm from her shoulder.

'I am an artist,' said Margaret and stomped her foot. 'It's essential I unleash my passions. "She who has never loved has never lived." It's a shame you've never lived, Maude.'

'I have never lived?' said Maude. 'I'd prefer to be dead at this moment.'

Good, thought Phoeba, now they will watch and see. She went calmly to her room, dried her face on Lilith's best petticoat, dressed in the blue frock she wore to church every Sunday, and strolled with Spot through the vineyard.

'I hate them all,' she said, and turned her thoughts to more pleasant things; Henrietta, who she hadn't seen for days, and Rudolph Steel.

As the sky darkened and the moon appeared low in the grey sky, she went to retrieve the blouse. It was still in the brown paper bag, but Lilith had discovered it – and shredded it. The guipure lace was torn off and the Japanese silk bows hung in tendrils. Phoeba left it in the tree and said nothing. A calmness washed over her and she wondered if a sense of conclusion was building.

Her mother and sister had worked quickly, for Lilith sat at the stove in Maude's blouse, the sleeves cut to the elbows, the neck square and lined with lace from a petticoat. Maude put down the curling wands and pinned a floral posy behind Lilith's ear. 'After all that fuss, Phoeba, you choose not to wear your blouse. You are a spiteful girl.'

She could have re-ignited the argument, said she wasn't tizzy enough for lace, told her mother the blouse was destroyed, told her mother she could ask the boundary rider about Lilith's affair. But she didn't. It would be better if Lilith felt victorious. She would dance all night with Marius Overton and everyone would see, including Marius's parents.

The party assembled on the veranda to wait for the sulky. Maude, coiffed and curled with an over-sized ostrich frond shooting from her crown and the family pearls straining around her plump throat. Margaret, startling with her equine beauty wrapped in black and white stripes and a red rose behind her ear. Lilith, still fuming – but pretty in her curls and lace. Phoeba, in her Sunday blue with a white ribbon looped through her loose bun. And Ashley, looking like a gnome in his red checks and green slippers. With a flourish, he presented Phoeba with a sketch of Spot. Her horse resembled a wavy-locked steed fit for bearing archangels in a rococo painting. Ashley could not even draw.

Spot looked at the five people on the veranda, dressed and waiting, then swung his head to look pointedly at the three-seater behind him.

'You cannot wear that blouse, Lilith,' said Robert. 'Go and change it at once or no one will go to the dance.'

'Very well, we won't go.' Lilith sat down, her arms crossed and her lips pressed to a pout.

Her mother sat down next to her. 'And you cannot wear that hat, Robert,' said Maude.

Robert had dressed in his accountant's suit complete with bowler hat, which looked like an upturned pudding bowl on his head.

'Well,' he said, flushing with anger, 'a mutiny.' He held out his hand out to Phoeba. 'You can be your old dad's partner tonight.'

'With pleasure,' she said, and lifted her skirt to climb into the sulky.

Margaret and Ashley lined up behind her and as Maude and Lilith began to look anxious, Hadley swung into the lane in the Hampden.

In the manager's house, Henrietta brushed and plaited her hair and wound it in a neat coil around the top of her head. Then she pushed small jacaranda flowers in between the plaits, stepped back from her bureau mirror and smiled, satisfied. She pictured herself, swirling around the woolshed with Phoeba to the pumping beat of an accordion and a piano, and felt a ripple of glee. Dancing was terrific fun.

Her mother stepped into the room.

'Your father has finished his bath,' she said. 'You look like you've walked under a shedding jacaranda.'

Soap scum clung in a rough line to the side of the tin tub. Henrietta scooped out a bucketful of water and took it to the homestead vegetable patch, pouring it all over the rhubarb plant. A small stone, brown and slimy like the seed from a stewed plum, fell onto a green rhubarb leaf. Henrietta leaned closer, wondering what it was.

Behind her, from the window, Mr Titterton called, 'Is that my molar? Bring it here, will you?'

Henrietta decided she would run away. She would go home with Hadley after the dance.

Spot picked a place at the end of the line of tethered horses within earshot of the music. Overhead, the sky was darkening: a great sheet of cloud slid in from the sea and a light wind whipped swirls of dust on the ground.

The harvest dance signalled that the district was nearing the end to the toil and the tension of gathering wool and grain, the end to days spent anxiously scanning the skies for signs of threat. Instead, farmers would begin to look hopefully for autumn rains, luxuriating in the lull, the tinkering and maintenance chores, fencing, the mechanical repairs, the weeding, ploughing, scarifying, sowing.

Robert joined the farmers and workers and Phoeba waited on the loading dock for Henrietta. Shiny red farmers arrived in wagons, work carts, sulkies and carriages with their wives and families, pressed, scrubbed and smiling. The itinerants wandered across from the outcrop and gathered under a tree near the sheepyards, where they would have their own dance. The women from the thresher team, their hair brushed, their faces scrubbed, stood with their weathered husbands in a group. Mrs Flynn and Freckle arrived in their cumbersome supply cart. He wore a clean shirt buttoned all the way up to his chin, and gallantly offered his mother his arm to escort her to the shed.

The homestead glowed in the sunset and the wide front-door stood open. But no figures moved inside and spider-grass skeletons gathered against the hedge. The feeling Phoeba had had earlier, that this was a culmination of some sort, crept over her again. She sensed this would be the last Overton dance for a very long time and felt a desolation worming through her bones. In her mind's eye she saw the French windows boarded up, sheep sheltering on the veranda, the arbour collapsed under a tangle of blackberry bush. She heard the kitchen screen door thudding on its hinges.

'Hey!' Henrietta ran towards her, her forehead white where her hat had sat too long in summer. Dear Henri, in her clean brown skirt and her plain white shirt, running like a boy through the sheepyards, climbing the fence when everyone else politely ambled the long way around. Her desolate feeling left her and she felt warm seeing her cheerful friend again. They would dance. It was a happy time.

They found a seat together inside on a hay bale close to the piano. The floor had been swept and washed, bales placed about the walls for seating, and behind them, straw had been spread for sleepy children. A long trestle table was stacked with punch and sandwiches, cakes and sweets, all covered by netting.

'I'm going to dance with Rudolph tonight,' said Phoeba.

'He's very nice, Phoeba. He stacked wood for me the other day and told me I was the best wood-chopper he'd seen. But there's something elusive about him.' Henrietta thought for a moment. 'Don't you want to be a vigneron?'

'Yes.'

'If you married Hadley, you'd get me too.'

'I had hoped, Henri, that if I did or didn't marry anyone you'd still be my dearest friend.'

'You want everything, Phoeba,' Henrietta said.

Lilith passed and said, 'Well if it isn't the frowsy sisters.'

Henrietta watched her circle the shed, her shoulders back, thrusting out her bosom to show off her blouse. 'It's a shame,' said

Henrietta. 'She's actually quite a nice girl, but she's spoilt, and she's about to fall.'

'Hopefully, she'll fall on her feet,' said Phoeba, and told Henrietta about catching Lilith with Marius at the outcrop. Henrietta wasn't surprised.

'Lilith always wanted to play weddings when we were kids,' said Henrietta, 'but you never know, Phoeba, Marius might do the right thing.'

'I bet as far as Mrs Overton is concerned Lilith is the wrong thing altogether.'

'He seems an honest sort, and being honest can never be wrong,' said Henrietta.

Maude arrived on the vicar's arm and Hadley followed, looking quite sober and important, a brand new pipe between his teeth. Gradually the shed filled with dancers.

Henrietta took Phoeba's hand, squeezed it and whispered: 'I've come to a decision, Phoeba. I'm running away tonight. I'm going home with Hadley. Mother will have a conniption but if she begs me to come back, I'll make a stand. If it all goes really wrong I'll get a job in Melbourne.'

'Henri, there are no jobs!'

'I know what you mean about having half a life, about marrying my brother being a compromise. And Phoeba, I want to be free too.' Mrs Flynn rolled proudly past wearing a new frock, still creased from where it had been folded in its brown paper parcel. 'Mrs Flynn has a perfect life,' said Henrietta, watching her.

'Yes.'

The vicar took up a spot at the centre of the dance floor, clapping his hands, his belly jumping. The crowd hushed and the vicar informed them that a plum cake – which Mrs Crupp had kindly donated – was to be raffled to raise funds to line the church

214

ceiling. Then he asked them to bow their heads.

'Let us pray for relief in this time of scarcity, Cast thy burden upon the Lord: And he shall nourish thee …'

That was as far as he got as the lamplighter turned the lamps down and the floor started to fill. Aunt Margaret and Ashley were first up along with Freckle and his mother, Lilith and the farrier. Hadley swept Phoeba onto the dance floor as the pianist sat on the piano stool. She adjusted her spectacles, struck a chord and the other musicians – fiddle, an accordion, a jew's harp and a concertina – arranged themselves to tune their instruments. The vicar made a bee-line for Henrietta, who quickly grabbed the tarboy and carried him to the floor. The vicar turned abruptly to Maude, who declined, saying a polka would make her fruit water repeat, and Mrs Titterton said her bunion was playing up. He made his way to the refreshment table instead.

The band struck up and the dancers moved off as if they'd practised together all through winter and spring. Lilith swung in circles with the farrier, then a stockman took her and the farrier took Phoeba from Hadley for a quadrille. But there were no spare partners, so Hadley fought his way through the galloping dancers to the edge of the dance floor, where Mrs Flynn clapped her hand on his shoulder. He turned to see her broad, two-tooth smile and away they went.

During the second bracket the atmosphere was ardent and joyous, the floorboards bouncing and the flames in the kerosene lamps blinking. The dignitaries – Marius and Mr and Mrs Guston Overton – had arrived.

Rudolph wasn't with them and Phoeba couldn't see him anywhere. But it didn't matter. She was dancing with Henrietta, rollicking around the shed like a couple of boys while Maude watched grim-faced with anger.

Hadley abandoned Mrs Flynn and approached the Overtons, but the pipe between his teeth turned upside-down and ash fell onto the hay-scattered floorboards. Hadley tap-danced to smother them, slapping ash from his coat.

It was very early for anyone to be making a spectacle of themselves but Henrietta and Phoeba didn't care. They bounced on, Ashley and Mrs Flynn, her fat red curls springing round her bouncing breasts, joining them – leaping high and clapping like frolicking barmaids.

It was then that Lilith lost her footing. The vicar, earnest, red and sweating, jogged her past Aunt Margaret, who was kicking her feet and singing along, and she tripped, flipping over the hay bales and landing on her back with her shoes and petticoats in the air. Maude struggled to her feet and concealed the spectacle from the onlookers with her bulk. The vicar fetched punch. The dance ended, and Henrietta stepped away from Phoeba with a wink and a grin. Rudolph Steel was at Phoeba's side.

'I don't normally dance so I hope you'll understand my feet.'

She wiped her damp palms discreetly on her skirt and felt his hand on her waist. She couldn't think of anything to say.

'How's Spot?' he asked.

'Much happier,' she said, but it came out in gusts as she paced in circles. She had to concentrate; he wasn't a practised dancer. It was like dancing with her father – you just had to go where he pushed you and keep your feet tucked in. The fiddle whipped into a sharp reel and Rudolph grimaced at her and they laughed, shuffling about the floor and ducking and weaving to avoid collisions. She wanted him to take her to the far end where it was quiet, but Hadley was there, watching.

'I like your blue dress,' he said. 'It's becoming.'

'Thank you.' She felt his breath on her hair as Marius danced past with Lilith. Such a pretty couple.

'What do you think will come of Marius and Lilith?'

Rudolph held onto her even though the music had stopped. 'She has a lot to offer someone in his position.'

'Like what?' said Phoeba.

'Constancy, affection, security …'

The pianist struck up and Rudolph waltzed her, the room behind him circling. She felt safe, as if there was no one else there – what did he mean, 'security'?

'But what about Mr and Mrs Overton?'

He shrugged. 'In these times people have to adjust their expectations.'

She sensed there was something he wasn't telling her, but she felt so good dancing to lovely music in the warm shed that she didn't pursue it.

'I mean,' he said, 'wealth isn't necessarily a secure thing; a friend and loving partner is – to most people.'

They found themselves dancing in a corner and Rudolph concentrated on shuffling them out again. She wished they could stay on their own and just dance in very small circles.

'To most people?' she asked, looking him in the eye, but he looked over her shoulder and wound her around and around. She thought about Mr and Mrs Overton who didn't love each other. Her mother had married her father for security and neither of them appeared to like anything about the other. Widow Pearson had married for prestige. Mr Titterton had married for company, home comforts and perhaps land. Her aunt was no longer lonely and poor but smitten, glowing and enslaved to her strange, new romantic love. And there was something in Rudolph's past, thought Phoeba, a sadness that made him restless, something that sent him away from England. She wanted to know what, or who, it was that made him wary of a loving partner. Maybe Henrietta was right. Perhaps Mrs Flynn was the happiest person they knew.

The music began to wind down and Rudolph danced her towards the refreshment table.

'Your feet are doing well,' she said.

'Thank you, Phoeba.'

Everybody seemed to get whatever they wanted. Lilith would get what she wanted. Phoeba would get what she wanted, in time. Why not marry and have children and have everything else as well – the grapes, the farm, a life.

'I've enjoyed this dance,' he said. 'I don't normally risk it.'

'People get married for lots of reasons, don't they?' she said, following her own train of thought and wanting him to stay and talk to her – keep his hand on her waist.

'They do.'

The music was slowing to a shuffle.

'I could only marry someone who let me do as I please,' she said, boldly, 'and I would let him do as he pleased.'

'Naturally,' he said, at they stopped moving. 'It's only right and fair.'

She sighed, relieved. At last someone, a man, who thought like her. Henrietta would be impressed.

'Phoeba, would you like a drink?' It was Hadley, standing with a glass of punch in each hand.

'Thanks, Hadley, but I can get one myself.' It came more sharply than she'd intended and Hadley flinched, just a little, but enough for Rudolph to step back. He let her hand go and said, 'It's been a pleasure.' She watched him wind his way through the crowd, felt cool air on her empty hand.

'Why is it, Hadley, that everywhere I turn you're there?'

'You're my friend, Phoeba, and tonight there's danger around. I've told Henrietta, and the fire truck is full. Just keep your wits about you.'

She had no idea what he was talking about and she wasn't interested. She was furious, wanted to cry, didn't want to be protected. The shearers had gone, the itinerants were outside, there was no danger. The only person she had offended was Lilith, and Lilith didn't matter.

'Hadley, let me be!' she said icily, and picked up her hem. She marched across the dance floor towards the loading dock and the summer night, trembling inside, cross and disappointed, and longing to dance with Rudolph again. Was that it? Was it over for the night? Four dances?

The caller announced a barn-dance: it was the one dance she always started with Hadley. They'd had a game when they were little to see if they could get back to one another before the music ended.

Freckle was sitting on the edge of the loading dock watching the crops glow silver under the full moon. She sat down next to him, and swung her legs to the music as the dancers behind them shifted across the dull floor. Under the tree, the itinerants danced too, one two three kick, back two three kick, swing, slide, slide, under, turn and onto the next …

'Smells like rain,' said Freckle.

Phoeba looked up. The stars had vanished and the full moon shone through clouds like a lantern behind ruched muslin. But Phoeba wanted to know about Hadley's 'danger'. Was Overton in trouble? And did Freckle know anything about Rudolph?

'Tell me, Freckle, is Mr Overton in trouble?'

'Everyone's in trouble, missus,' he said, his forehead twisted in worry. He stood up. 'I'd keep my ears and eyes open tonight.'

219

She followed him. 'It's the itinerants, isn't it?'

'I'm sorry, I've done everything I can,' he said and held his cup out to Mrs Overton, who stood stiffly behind the refreshment table. She was only in attendance because the staff had been let go.

'How are ya', Missus?' said Freckle brightly, dipping his cup into the punch bowl himself.

'Good evening, Freckle,' said Mrs Overton. She held the ladle between two fingers but didn't seem to know what to do with it.

Phoeba had never heard the word 'Freckle' said so fluently. Then Mrs Overton recognised Phoeba.

'My dear,' she said, 'how lovely to see you recovered from your accident. I have vanishing cream. You must come and see me. It will make the redness go. Come tomorrow after church?'

'Of course.'

Suddenly, Mrs Titterton was beside Phoeba, and Lilith was there too, nudging Phoeba aside and holding her cup out to Mrs Overton. Here they are, thought Phoeba, the competitors.

Mrs Overton picked up the ladle again, turned it over in her hand then passed it to Lilith.

'Please help yourself to refreshments,' she said.

Maude leaned close to Mrs Titterton. 'Have you been to tea since you moved to Overton?' she whispered.

'No,' said Mrs Titterton, her voice like fizzing acid. 'You'd think she'd have better manners. But then they say she arranged for Marius to marry Agnes for her money. They say he didn't love his wife, say he went on a holiday after she died.'

Lilith's blue eyes narrowed and her lip curled. 'That's a vicious lie, Widow Poison.'

'I am Mrs Titterton now and they say—'

'They? Who are they? I think you are they. Marius loved Agnes when she was alive.'

Mrs Overton put her hand to her cameos, and Maude started flapping her handkerchief furiously; guests were beginning to stare.

Mrs Titterton began to swoon, falling towards Henrietta, who caught her mother by the upper arm and held her. Hadley picked up an empty cup for punch but Lilith pushed it away. 'Marius did everything he could to save them.'

Mrs Titterton rallied, hissing, 'I suppose Marius Overton told you that on one of the occasions you met him at the outcrop?'

Mrs Overton's eyebrows raised and she placed three fingers on the table, steadying herself. Maude gasped; Phoeba steadied her. It wasn't meant to be this brutal – a revelation like this might ruin everything.

Ashley rubbed his hands and said, 'Montagues and Capulets!' The vicar put down his plate of sandwiches: 'Ladies, please …' but Lilith turned to Mrs Overton. 'The Widow's got no right to repeat lies.' Mrs Overton closed her eyes, put her fingers to her temples.

Mrs Titterton made a squeak as if she'd sat on a frog. 'Everyone knows what you two get up to at that outcrop!'

The farmers and workers standing around murmured and nodded and Mrs Flynn said, 'Oopsy-daisy.'

'Mr Titterton only married you for your farm,' continued Lilith.

Henrietta held her mother – she was buckling and gasping for air but she still managed a comeback. 'You can talk, gold digger. You're a common strumpet.'

'We are in love!' cried Lilith, and the crowd was silenced.

Mrs Overton calmly lifted her hems, stepped away from

the refreshment table and marched towards her son. The crowd shuffled along behind her. Margaret led Maude outside where she leaned forward as much as she could in her stiff corset and retched. Her punch and cream cake splattered the spokes of someone's buggy.

Hadley and Henrietta grabbed an arm each and dragged their mother away, the toes of her shoes leaving two sharp lines in the lanolin-soaked floorboards. The vicar picked up his plate of sandwiches.

The first sprinkle on the iron roof didn't register. People were still stunned in the wake of the spat. Then, from outside, low shouts filtered in. Raindrops crackled across the roof and the shed filled with the smell of wetted dust. As if someone had dropped a tiger among them, people fled to the doors. The rain gathered tempo pushed by a long, slow rumble that rolled up and over the outcrop from the shore and across the plain. The shed started to ring like the inside of a piano. The drops got fatter, pounding in sweeping sheets across the roof, and a breezy chill swelled. Drops slashed against the walls and the noise grew and grew.

'The grapes,' said Phoeba, and beside her Freckle said, 'The crops.'

In the doorway to the loading dock, Marius and Guston stood looking out at the water. It was pooling in dry depressions and small rivulets ran in wheel ruts.

Phoeba went from group to group looking for Rudolph. She couldn't find him, then pushed through the swinging gate into the pens behind the shearing stands and down in the far back corner she saw him, leaning in a doorway, one hand on his hip. A lightning flash cracked like a fizzing Catherine wheel and lit him.

She went to him and without even looking his arm reached

out and gathered her in. She nestled against him while outside the dry season broke and it ruined everything. Another lightning bolt lit the landscape and they saw the silver figures of men fleeing across the plain, like flickering daguerreotypes.

Outside, under the tree where they had danced, Hadley stood with a gun at his shoulder, aiming at the fleeing backs of the sundowners. At his feet were their bottles of kerosene and their rags. Secretly, he had wanted to capture one of them, just one of them – to drag into the shed in front of the crowd, in front of Phoeba. But the rain had stopped them throwing their flaming bombs. And then, in the flash of silver light, he saw her enclosed in Rudolph Steel's arms. Yes, thought Hadley, the rain had ruined everything.

'The itinerants were going to set fire to the shed tonight,' said Rudolph. 'We found matches and newspaper. All that wool grease, it would have exploded like a crisp eucalypt. We could have been burned alive, but Freckle warned us.'

'What will happen now?'

For a while he said nothing, then he untangled himself from her and walked towards the shed, and Guston. Through the shattering rain she heard him say, 'There's no future in it now, Phoeba,' and something icy tightened around her hopes. A white finger of lightning reached down and touched the flat plains, electrifying the boiling clouds and bathing the homestead in blue and silver beams.

She stayed watching the violent storm. It was brilliant and pretty and she clung to the feeling of Rudolph, felt a yearning for him, wanted to feel his breath on her hair and her body harnessed by his hard body. So this was passion.

Sunday, February 4, 1894

She didn't sleep at all. How much destruction had the rain done? As soon as the room was tinged with light blue she was up and dressing. Aunt Margaret sat bolt upright in her bed. 'Did anyone see you come?'

'You're at Mount Hope, Aunt, with me.'

'Oh,' said Margaret and flopped back.

Her father was in the kitchen, still in his tight suit, its waistcoat open. He kept his eyes on his warming bread. He had aged, overnight, his nose withering like a ripe passionfruit and his eyes opaque. An empty jug of wine and a cup sat on the table.

'That blasted vicar,' he growled, 'praying for seasonable weather!'

'There was no hail,' said Phoeba, her enthusiasm thin.

Her father was not encouraged. 'We'll lose our feed crop,' he began and sighed, shaking his head. 'There's no space to take risks when you're just trying to survive.'

They cruised the vineyard, washed green and dripping, and as they walked they rustled raindrops from the flat, rubbery leaves and wriggled the small, hard bunches up and down the rows. They could at least save some of their grapes from being tarnished by the sun, and reduce the risk of mould on the bunches just starting to develop a pasty bloom. Leaves had been stripped and berries ruptured but they would lose only about a third of their fruit.

They could live with that.

Next, they stood in their sodden feed crop. The pungent

odour of new compost clogged the air as it heated under the rising sun, and the damp seed heads swished softly, muffled. Phoeba's skirt hung damp and heavy.

'It'll be shot and sprung by tomorrow,' said Robert. 'Overton will be lucky to salvage enough for seed grain.'

Mid-morning, the sun rose and faint steam saddened the already water-logged crop. The entire district was like a hothouse.

Phoeba climbed through dull scrub to the outcrop and sat on a washed boulder to study the damage. Around her, clumps of dry grass and bushes bobbed with brown and beige movement – rabbits. Unharvested crops along the foreshore, as far as the looking glass would show her, were marred with great patches of flattened stalks as though a giant had waltzed through them. At Overton, Rudolph and Guston kicked through their sodden crop under a pastel sky. She closed her eyes and shouted to a God she now knew didn't exist – 'Please don't let them go bust,' – and then went to find Lilith.

Lilith was sitting on the back porch pushing pins into a heart-shaped pincushion.

'Well?' said Phoeba, her hands on her hips.

'He'll come,' said Lilith and shoved another pin deep into the cushion. The pinheads formed the initials M&L.

In Maude's room Aunt Margaret and Phoeba watched the shuddering lump in the middle of the double bed. 'I can never be seen at church again,' she cried. 'I can't even enjoy a simple drive to Mrs Flynn. The shame …'

'You're attributing far too much importance to a spat at a country dance, Maude. Now sit up, Phoeba has made you a boiled egg and toast.'

Maude struggled out from under her eiderdown dabbing

her tears with the bed sheet. Phoeba placed the tray on her mother's lap.

'Our reputation is lost forever. But you, Phoeba, are a great comfort to me. I hope you always will be.'

'You called me a liar yesterday.'

'And,' said Margaret, 'you told me she was ungrateful and defiant.'

'You hardly help us cavorting with you coxcomb popinjay friend, Margaret, and where is Lilith?' Maude smashed the top of her egg.

'One could assume,' said Margaret, 'that she was at the outcrop with her dalliance.'

'He's coming,' said Lilith coming into the room with the pincushion for her mother to admire. 'You'd better get up, Mother.'

'If you'd held your tongue, Lilith, Mrs Overton might have been more amenable—'

'You always think you know best, Phoeba.'

'It's galling, Lilith,' said Maude, pressing her palms to her temples. 'All these people think you are sullied.'

Lilith gazed back at her with blue eyes that were clear, constant and quite sincere. 'You can expect a different life now, Mother. The front pew at church, the theatre, shopping in Melbourne—'

'I think you're getting more than you expect, my dear,' said Maude, sucking the egg from her spoon.

'And I think,' said Phoeba, 'that we will all get a lot we didn't expect.'

Margaret and Ashley, Lilith and Marius, and Phoeba sat at the kitchen table in the humid silence. Maude marched down the passage and stood in the doorway – the back of her dress was unbuttoned and her powder was applied in dusty pink smudges.

She glared at the squatter's son.

'You have ruined our reputation,' she said, but her livid resolve softened. She didn't want to scare him off.

'I know we should have been open,' Marius began, 'but it was so soon after Agnes died. My parents have come to terms with my … with Lilith now—'

'You'll find Mr Crupp outside with what's left of his wretched grapes.' She turned on her heel and thumped down the passage. In the girls' bedroom, she clenched her fists, screwed her face in glee and whispered, 'Thank you Lord.' Then she eased herself to the floor and reached under Phoeba's bed for the trousseau box.

'That's the worst of it over, son,' said Ashley, slapping Marius's shoulder.

'Are the grapes ruined?' said Marius.

'Not all of them,' said Lilith, and Marius looked relieved.

Phoeba wanted to feel deliriously happy that Lilith was getting married and going away, but she couldn't be sure yet. What if Overton had gone broke?

'We, that is Dad and I, planted the grapes,' she said, folding her arms, like Maude. 'We've lost some and we've lost our feed crop. But we'll manage. One day I will run Mount Hope. I'll be a vigneron.'

'I see,' said Marius, weakly, as Lilith dragged him down the passage.

'My God,' whispered Aunt Margaret. 'What a coup, Phoeba! Lilith is marrying the squatter from over the hill. You've got to hand it to her, haven't you?'

'I'm not handing them anything,' said Phoeba. For Marius, ten acres of grapes meant he could establish an independent life, he could settle in the two-bedroom house his father had built before he married well and built a mansion. Mount Hope was the

227

perfect place to start, in his own right, and succeed. Phoeba shook her head. It was an impossible thought.

Robert squinted at the thermometer nailed to the trellis post. It was 97 degrees, and rising. He was hot and the ventilation promised by the manufacturer of his pith hat was letting him down. Mopping his brow, he removed his waistcoat and noticed Marius Overton walking towards him with Lilith on his arm.

'Good of you to come,' called Robert, 'but there's nothing to be done. If I had a few more acres we could have made a profit this year. But it'll be a lean winter.' He gestured to the emptied outcrop. 'They've gone. I could have used them to strip what's left of my feed crop.'

'Yes,' said Marius. 'I noticed their camp was deserted.'

'This was my best crop of grapes to date, a beauty.'

Lilith kissed her father on the cheek and headed back up to the house.

'Something's up,' said Robert. 'I only ever get a peck on the cheek when she wants a solid gold safety pin or an embossed bamboo bracelet.' He shook his head at his grapes, squinted up to the sun. 'It was no good last year, remember?'

Marius was watching Lilith walk back up to the house. Sweet, Lilith who snuggled into him and adored him just as he was. She was a girl who thought the front pew at the local church, a few fancy hats and a carriage ride through Melbourne were pinnacles of achievement. He could live up to her. She wouldn't ride him or needle him to conquer anything. He realised Mr Crupp was still talking to him.

'A dust storm cut the buds to pieces, just one miserable gust of dust. Then in '91 it was frost, and now this! If it stays dry and

228

warm we'll get a ton or two for the winery and a hogshead to drink.'

Marius glanced out to the bay twinkling under the sun. 'You have water to reflect light, a sea breeze to dry the grapes, the gradient to drain, altitude, good soil—'

'Heat in spring to stir the vines from their winter slumber.' Robert stopped. 'Know a bit about grapes, do you?'

'I've been reading a bit.'

'How's your wheat crop?' said Robert,

'Shot and sprung,' said Marius, and shuddered. 'We'll nut something out ...' He slid his hands into his pockets and made a small half-moon depression in the dirt with his boot. 'There's another matter I must discuss,' he said, still looking at the ground. 'Perhaps you've heard something?'

'Heard what?' asked Robert, then something dawned on him. He thought of Lilith clinging to Marius's arm, the kiss on his cheek, some sort of cat-fight at the dance, Phoeba terse and preoccupied. Up on the veranda, the women stared at him, like a group in a photographer's studio. Maude's hands moved quickly, working some small white woollen thing with needles. That fop in the tartan suit, Ashley, gave him a thumbs-up and Phoeba had the looking glass trained on him. Even Spot and the ducks were peering at him from the dam paddock.

'I feel the need for a glass of wine,' he said. 'How about you?'

'I'd like to marry your daughter, Lilith.'

Robert took his pith hat off and steadied himself against a trellis post, the words churning in his head. He thought he'd heard Marius Overton say that he wanted to marry Lilith.

'I don't have any money, Marius. The bank lost most of it and I'm chipping away at what's left to keep us alive.' He jerked his head at the watching women. 'They don't know about our financial strife; they just think I'm mean.'

'I may have a little money of my own but I don't think money is everything. You have your land, sir, and a wonderful future in wine – and I'd like to help.'

'You'd like to help me?'

Marius nodded. 'There's a great future in wine.'

In his mind's eye, Robert saw a bounteous grain crop in the front paddock and the slope covered in neat vines all the way up to the outcrop. He put his hat back on his head and eyed the young man suspiciously.

'You did say Lilith?'

'Yes, sir.' He squeezed a vine leaf.

Robert clasped his hands behind his back, looked out at the sweep before him; this siding halfway between two important cities on a major train line, this bay between two sea ports that glittered on a day perfect for sailing; this land – a hopeful future for his daughters and the next generation. Marius a dilettante? Marius a ditherer? Robert pushed it from his mind – Marius had vision, Marius had capital. 'I'm the last to know, aren't I?'

'I'm sorry.'

Robert headed for the veranda then he stopped and turned. 'Are you sure about Lilith? She's not the brightest sud in the wash bucket, but then I don't suppose she needs much savvy to fathom silk bandeaux and hat ospreys.'

'On the contrary, I find her captivating—'

'And I'd be careful with your cheque book.' Robert took his hat off again, scratched his bald patch. 'As one man to another, I'm being honest. It'd be wrong to sell you a bolter or something that drops dead under you when you're under the impression you're getting a serviceable mare.' Now it was Marius who was speechless. 'Right then,' said Robert and held out his hand. As he approached the veranda he was smiling from ear to ear; one less mouth to feed.

At Elm Grove, Hadley sat on a wooden chair in his sparse kitchen composing a pamphlet for his ram emasculator: 'Improve the sheep of the Empire, prevent loss of blood, tetanus, septic poisoning, fly-strike and needless cruelty and suffering.'

He threw down his pencil. What was the point? It had all come to nothing. He had lost Phoeba to a ruddy Englishman who'd held her hands and danced her away in the Overton wool shed, his banker's palm on her strong, fine back, his smallest finger resting on the little ledge where her skirt came lightly off her blue bodice. It ached inside his chest. All he had left were his father's sheep and a failed dream to make something of them, of himself. He had a future without a wife ... or even a farm if Mr Titterton had his way. Bother the rain that was bound to ruin Overton. Bother Steel with his thick, shiny moustache and his English wool suit, and bother Titterton in his two-storey house telling his dear sister how to do things she'd been doing forever and looking lustily at the new house plans. He'd probably fill the paddocks at Elm Grove with pigs.

'He is a louche man,' Hadley said, his voice bouncing in the empty house. He wished his sister had run away and come home with him.

The vicar sped through the landscape between brown boulder fences and flattened yellow crops, now worthless. He slapped the reins over the bony rump of his trotting black mare and inhaled the aroma of humid hay cleansed by quenching rain. The air was rich with nature – curdling ditch water, ripe manure and fertile

231

mud. 'One day,' he assured himself, 'I will be a rural dean.'

He waved to Mr Jessop who was loading a bag of grain – reaped from the bounteous crop the Lord had provided – onto the back of a wagon, stacked high with furniture. Mr Jessop ignored him. This was the second family the vicar had seen packing the contents of their house that morning. His smile fell – the Jessops' creamy Jersey cow was tied to the back of the wagon.

He stopped his horse outside the vestry door, climbed down backwards from his buggy, looped the reins through the wheel and went inside, leaving his thin, neglected horse staring wistfully at the shady fence where the congregation usually tethered its horses.

Wriggling his toes into his sanctuary slippers, he hummed, 'Come, ye thankful people, come; Raise the song of harvest-home; All is safely gathered in …'

He scratched out a few words for a sermon thanking Him for ending the dry season. He smiled at Mrs Crupp's magnificent plum cake wrapped and tied with ribbon on top of the empty crosier cupboard. His grateful flock would buy lots of raffle tickets and the ceiling would be lined before the next blistering summer hit. He cleared his throat, raised his chins and made his entrance. Mrs Flynn smiled brightly from the back of the church and, right at the front, his three reverential Temperance worshippers leaned forward a little on their pew.

'Where has everyone gone?'

'Bankrupt,' said Mrs Flynn.

'Oh,' he said, crestfallen, his flaccid neck lowering.

Outside, his horse leaned towards the shade; the reins tightened around the buggy spokes. The horse sighed and shifted back, lowering her head – the reins slackened. The mare shifted her weight forward again, then took a step back, stepped forward and back, forward and back. Finally, the reins unfurled and slid like heavy ribbons to the ground. The horse walked towards the shade.

At the end of the brief service the vicar emerged into the scalding sun to find his horse gone. He glanced up and down the siding, up to the intersection and he walked around the church. There was no sign of her, just the faint cloud of dust from the Temperance women's vanishing buggy. Shoving a chunk of Maude's cake into his mouth he sauntered towards the shop, where he asked for credit.

Mrs Flynn crossed her arms and shook her head. 'Nobody gets a free ticket. It's against railroad rules.'

'I only have the collection money – seven pence.'

She thought about Freckle, getting ready to leave home from fear of the vengeful itinerants whose plan he'd foiled. She thought of Mr Overton, his unpaid bill, the rain and the ruined crops.

'Only sometimes some people get what they arst for in this world.'

The vicar's next hope was the guard on the train. Perhaps he would take seven pence and fruitcake.

The third wedding cake

Monday, February 5, 1894

On Monday, Phoeba woke and didn't know what to do. She waved Aunt Margaret and Ashley onto their train and went about her chores, not knowing if she should be happy, or relieved, or heartbroken. She tried airing her woes to Spot but it only brought them more to life. In frustration, she joined her mother – who was suddenly crocheting babies' booties – on the front veranda while watching down the lane to Bay View, waiting for the dull brown form of Freckle and his horse to appear.

Robert ambled down the passage with his pillow and pyjamas intent on claiming his bed back again but Maude had other ideas. 'You make me too hot, Robert. Stay in the shed,' she declared.

'Anything you say,' said Robert, then added mumbling, 'anything for peace.'

Eventually, Freckle rode away from the shop, turned north to Overton and then, an hour or so later, appeared from the outcrop.

Maude put aside her crocheting and went to the top step and Freckle handed her a plain blue envelope with a gold 'O' on the front and waited, unusually forlorn.

'We'll take one rabbit this week,' said Maude, ripping the envelope open.

'I didn't bother with them today,' said Freckle, and his roan cob sniffed the petunias.

Maude read the note, the powdery pink planes of her face falling in small stages. Her eyebrows creased into a small furry M at the top of her nose. Wordlessly, she handed the page to Phoeba.

The note, written and signed by Guston Overton, stated that the ecclesiastical authorities had been telegraphed instructing the banns of marriage not be published and demanding that a marriage licence be sent by the Superintendent Registrar immediately. The vicar would formalise the union between Lilith Crupp and Marius at Overton the following Saturday.

There it was, but Phoeba felt flat as a millpond. Lilith had what she wanted: marriage and Marius. But what of Overton? No verdict had passed around the district, no swaggies were headed north for its harvest and the outcrop was as still as a photograph. It was eerie, like the sea before a cyclone.

'There's no reply, Freckle,' said Maude, regally, lifting her skirts and turning away with as much dignity as she could muster.

'Would you like a drink, Freckle?' asked Phoeba.

'No.'

'Cake?'

'The cook at Overton gave me coffee and marzipan.'

The horse sighed and shifted its weight; its saddle creaked.

'We know you didn't do anything wrong, Freckle.'

'I dobbed.'

'It was the right thing to do.'

'Right for the rich squatter with his machines. Them other poor bastards didn't deserve the life they got, I don't reckon.'

He took his hat off and held it over his heart. His red curls were squashed flat on top and looped out in a gutter big enough for birds to bathe in. 'I only got food for them. And only because they made me.'

'We believe you.'

'Not everybody does.' He put his hat back on. 'So I think, missus, I have to go away.'

'No, Freckle! Why?'

'The itinerants, and the snake.'

'Snake?'

Freckle nodded. 'A red-bellied black snake. Fell out of a mail-bag.'

'I see,' said Phoeba. 'But the rain stopped the itinerants from lighting their fire.'

'They know I dobbed. And I know they cleared out – but they could come back anytime and hang me.'

'Where will you go?'

'I got a job as an assistant guard. On the train,' he said, glumly.

'Life's a funny thing, Freckle,' said Phoeba, and watched the cob lower its head, rip Maude's petunias from the ground and eat them.

By the time Phoeba got to the kitchen, Maude had the sewing machine out and all Robert's possessions were shoved under her bed again.

'At last, I can change my surname from Crupp,' said Lilith, humming as she moved about the house plumping cushions and straightening doilies.

'I'd have liked a big wedding, but I suppose a marriage is a marriage,' said Maude, spreading the contents of the trousseau on the floor.

'We'll put a notice in the *Southern Sphere*, in the "Social Chronicle" section,' called Lilith.

'Along with the Countess of Tankerville and the Governor,' said Phoeba. It was convenient that Maude could ignore the circumstances of the betrothal.

'Right, Phoeba,' said Maude, rubbing her hands together. 'We'll go to Flynn's and buy the ingredients for the cake.'

'I'm more than happy to do that, Mother.'

'And we must drive over and visit Mrs Titterton.'

'Of course,' said Phoeba. At least she would see Henrietta and Rudolph. And she would find out what was happening with the crop, with the Overtons.

Maude wore her chocolate brown church dress, her best hat and her mother's pearls. Lilith wore her knife-pleated skirt and matching neck scarf. She pinned Maude's best bar brooch to her lapel and wore her most sumptuous hat. Spot behaved impeccably and as they passed through the majestic Overton gates and rounded the homestead, their proud mother sniffed. 'You will be so happy here, Lilith.'

'For heaven's sake, Mother, don't cry,' said Lilith, impatiently. 'Mrs Tit will think you're afraid, or not up to it. And it's not dignified.'

'Engaged one day,' said Phoeba, 'and you're setting standards and issuing instructions the next.'

Lilith smiled.

Overton homestead looked very quiet, almost deserted, as they drove past towards the manager's house. Henrietta opened the door, her sleeves rolled up and her white apron stiff as paper.

Her skirt underneath was crushed and stained where she'd dried her hands. She looked at Maude, at Lilith, dressed as if they were going to a coronation. 'What's happened?'

Mrs Titterton called from the front parlour, 'This is hardly the time to come and make amends—'

'We're not making amends,' trilled Maude and pushed past Henrietta.

Mrs Titterton crept slowly across the floor, strapped tight and extra gaseous. She seemed to be vaporising, day by day.

Phoeba held Henrietta in the entrance hall. 'Where's Rudolph?'

Henrietta pointed to a window in the far corner of the homestead. It was closed, the curtains drawn. 'The cook says he's gone to Melbourne.'

'Will he be back?'

Henrietta nodded. 'He only took a kitbag. But the crop is ruined.'

'Ruined?'

'Shsss,' said Henrietta, squeezing her shoulders gleefully together and smiling at the ceiling. 'I might get to go home!'

A wave of panic washed over Phoeba and she felt her cheeks smart. In the parlour Maude boomed triumphantly, 'We've come to inform you that there is to be a wedding. Lilith is getting married.'

'Who's marrying you?' said Mrs Titterton, confused.

'Why, a vicar of course,' said Lilith, haughtily.

'No, you silly girl, who is to be your husband?'

'She will be Mrs Marius Overton,' said Maude, and looked to the homestead through the parlour window. 'It's wonderful for Phoeba; it increases her prospects considerably.'

Phoeba's mind was racing. She desperately wanted to talk

239

to Marius, to Rudolph, to anyone who could tell her what was really going on.

'We must get back,' said Lilith, fingering her bar brooch. She'd had her moment, no point wasting any more time with the overseer's wife.

'We've another cake to make and ice,' said Maude.

Phoeba began, 'But I wanted to—'

'So much to do, Phoeba!' snapped Lilith.

That evening, Phoeba sat between her vines, listening to them rustle and sigh as they settled in the dusky air. She threw her head back and watched as silver-tipped clouds floated in the endless, azure space. Please, let her go to Overton. And let Rudolph save me.

Tuesday, February 6, 1894

Phoeba read about grape growing; she did her chores. She made her cheese on Tuesday instead of Thursday, had the ironing done before morning tea and then weeded her depleted vegetable patch and turned the soil for her winter vegetables. She was mucking out Spot's stable and loading the wheelbarrow with manure when Lilith strolled past with Marius, heading for the outcrop, 'Here comes your sweetheart, Phoeba.'

Her heart skipped a beat and she let the pitchfork fall, but it was only Hadley driving up the lane. On the wagon behind him was his single-blade plough. He had come to turn their fallow, as he did every year.

He tied the mare under the peppercorns next to Marius's horse and came wearily across the yard, carrying a homely bunch

240

of geraniums and dahlias.

'Hadley,' she said, feeling a pang of guilt and sorrow. She had made him feel so forlorn. 'It's lovely to see you.'

He nodded, glumly, and reached for the handrail.

'You needn't have brought your plough, Had,' said Lilith, gaily. 'Marius will turn our fallow. He has a three-blade.'

Hadley's progress up the steps faltered, just a little, but he continued on.

'Congratulations,' he said, handing her the flowers.

Lilith kissed his cheek and said, 'Had, you're a dear. You'll come, won't you?'

'Oh,' said Phoeba, thinking she'd prefer to have Lilith's wedding day with Rudolph. 'I don't think the Overtons want—'

'Rubbish,' said Lilith. 'Hadley's my oldest friend too. And anyway, we won't all fit in the sulky.' She hummed her way down the hall in search of a vase.

'You've heard nothing about Overton?' asked Phoeba.

'No. I've been busy.'

'Nothing at all?'

'No, Phoeba. I have been busy,' he repeated pointedly.

'I think Marius is marrying Lilith to get our vines because Overton is ruined,' she blurted, hoping Hadley would say it wasn't true.

'I think the wool will fetch enough to keep Steel content,' said Hadley, reassuringly. She chose to believe him – for the time being.

He settled carefully on the wicker couch and said, 'I know that I've lost you, Phoeba. I know that your heart belongs to Steel and I accept that you don't want to marry without your notion of love.' He pushed his spectacles a little further up his nose. 'Your aunt seemed very happy, at least, and it's wonderful

241

that Marius is going to do the right thing. They'll have each other ... companionship.'

She sat next to him then and took his hand in hers. 'You're very alone at Elm Grove, I know, but I have to stay now, Hadley, I'll have to help Dad.' He took his hand back. 'Now, Had, my oldest friend. You're a fine man – and an excellent sheep expert – and you need to marry someone who'll support you – someone who wants to breed sheep.'

Hadley nodded at his lap. 'I suppose I must say now that at least we still have each other, Phoeba, that we have always wanted each other to be happy, and that we will still care for each other, no matter what.'

'No matter what,' she said, and meant it. She did love him so much, and probably would stand in front of a moving train for him.

He pushed a seed around his hat brim with his finger, her rejection of him swelling in the silence. She knew she was meant to say she was sorry but she wasn't. She was sure that she wanted to stay here, at Mount Hope, on the farm.

Abruptly, he stood to leave, reaching for the veranda post and swaying a little, as if the hurt had made him weak. Phoeba wanted to run to her bed and weep or scream with rage and frustration. It was all so tense. Please just let Lilith get married and go, she thought urgently. Let there be some sort of progress, some relationship for me and Rudolph. Let Hadley continue to be my dearest friend. Let things go back to the way they were just a few short weeks ago.

'Hadley, I'm sorry, I don't want to hurt you.' He stopped. 'Please stay for tea with us, please. Marius is here.'

'Very well,' he said, and she could see him push his unhappiness aside. He sat down next to her again and said proudly, 'I have been busy. I've applied for jobs. I've even been to Geelong for an interview with a chap called Mr Williams.'

'Hadley! Have you?' She was surprised, even a little shocked that he had been to Geelong and back without her knowing.

He looked at his hat on his knee. 'I may get some sort of position, but manager is what I want. It's ambitious, I know.'

'Now all we need is to see Henrietta right,' said Phoeba. 'I think she's lonely at Overton.'

'She is not alone there,' he said, and Phoeba sighed.

'Come and help me set the table,' she said, standing up and offering him her hand.

Inside, they found Lilith had set the table and she was sitting Marius at the head – in Robert's spot. Robert arrived and pointed out the error and Marius went to the other end of the table, right near the heat of the stove.

Maude, feeling worse than ever before, staggered around the room dumping bread, butter and jam on the table and then shoved a plate of cold meat into the centre upsetting the saltcellar. Her face was red and greying wisps matted her damp hairline. Her eyes were puffy. She lowered herself onto her chair and said, weakly, 'Forgive my appearance.' A new son-in-law might be a new son-in-law but she felt wretched.

Phoeba sliced bread and Lilith served a salad. It was only the third time Lilith had ever made a salad.

'Tell us about your new job, Hadley,' said Phoeba.

Lilith laid a napkin across Marius's lap.

'I haven't got it, Phoeba! I've only applied.'

Marius put down his knife and fork. 'I may be able to help.'

'It's a manager's job,' said Phoeba. 'The property is up past the Murray …'

'The drought,' said Marius, 'difficult to get staff.'

243

'At least he's not in the welfare lines,' said Phoeba.

'They're very long,' said Hadley, shaking his head. 'I saw women and children sleeping on the street in Geelong.'

'You'll see wonderful landscape up on the Murray,' said Marius.

'We hope Phoeba will see it,' interrupted Lilith. 'We're all busting for Hadley to propose again.'

'Not all of us!' yelled Robert and throwing his napkin at her so it stuck to her curls and hid her face. She threw it back at him.

'It's wrong for a woman to move away from her family even in this day and age of rapid transport,' said Maude, coming to life. 'Women and children perish out there alone. You can't tell me it isn't the same as murder, taking a girl into the bush and making her fend with dozens of children while her husband falls off his horse in some distant valley and dies, or she gets abducted by timber-getters or blacks while he's off shearing.' She glared at Robert. 'No responsible man in his right mind would take a woman to live in the bush!'

They were silent. The only sound was Robert chewing. Lilith ate her salad, Marius sawed at his tomato and Hadley lifted the pepper mill and looked at the bottom of it.

'It does sound very pretty up around the Murray,' said Phoeba, to break the silence, but the comment set Maude off again.

'That it may be, but all that means is the dangers are harder to see!'

They were silent again.

Maude suddenly excused herself and crept back to her dark, quiet room.

Robert shifted his salad about with his knife, as if he was

searching for rat dirt. 'For the life of me I cannot fathom women. I am extremely vexed by the lot of them.' He looked at Lilith. 'This salad has pips in it.'

'Almonds,' she said, 'they're new.'

'New?' said Phoeba.

'Your wife, sir, is losing a daughter,' said Hadley philosophically.

'That's not it,' said Lilith buttering another slice of bread. 'She's going through the change.'

Marius nodded, but looked puzzled. Hadley wasn't sure exactly what it meant either but he'd heard men at the sheds talk about women going to asylums for a time.

'So,' said Phoeba, 'tell us Marius, is your crop ruined? Are you broke?'

'Not that I know of,' he laughed.

'What will you do if you are?'

'Phoeba,' said Robert sternly. 'You are being very intrusive.'

'It would be very crowded if you came here,' said Phoeba.

'I don't think,' said Hadley gently, 'that this is the time or the place.'

'And,' continued Phoeba, 'you wouldn't like taking direction from me, a woman.'

'He won't,' said Lilith, and the corner of her mouth twitched almost imperceptibly.

February 7, 8, 9, 1894

Lilith and Maude happily checked the contents of Lilith's trousseau against the 'Approaching Marriage' article in

245

the *Southern Sphere*. They packed fine white cotton drawstring bloomers, collarettes, nuns' veiling nighties, suspender straps, corsets and silk flowers, garters, ribbons, a selection of lace hand-kerchiefs and far too many petticoats. Together they altered Lilith's best frock, then trimmed her hat and covered her shoes with the discarded material. Lilith was threading her shoes with ribbon when Phoeba asked her again if Overton was in financial strife.

'You can't ruin this for me, Phoeba. It's impossible. I'm too happy.'

'The rain must have ruined the crop, Lilith, and they were in dire straights before Rudolph bailed them out.'

'Marius has said nothing to me.'

'Well, he wouldn't,' said Phoeba. 'Why would you tell the woman you were about to marry, after only three or four short months of widowhood, that you were broke and wanted to live at her house and work for her father?'

Lilith paused, letting the ribbons slip onto the floor and curl beside the ottoman. She gazed out through the heavy drapes as if there was a miracle outside. She smiled. 'But if they do lose their property to the bank then we will go to Melbourne. And I will live in Toorak!'

Maude carried in a plum cake encased in smooth white icing and set it on a huge silver tray in the middle of the dining table. 'There were no almonds left,' she said, standing back to admire it. 'Mrs Titterton may have a machine for washing clothes, but I think I will have grandchildren before her.'

'I think you will too,' said Phoeba, remembering Lilith had risen in the night and leaned from the bedroom window to retch, and her usual afternoon nap had stretched from half an hour to almost two.

Robert polished the sulky and harness and then found Lilith.

'Give us a trim, Lil?'

He sat on the back porch with a tablecloth around his shoulders while Lilith trimmed his receding hair, his eyebrows and the spikes jutting from his round, dark nostrils. As she snipped the last fine fronds curling on his sagging ear lobes Robert said, 'If you find the mansion too draughty and don't feel useful, Lil, you can always come back home to your kerosene lamps,' he said, reaching around to pat her hand.

'I can be very useful if it suits me,' she said, removing the tablecloth and shaking the hair from it. 'And I will continue to cut your hair for years, until there is none left.'

'I should have clouted you more often,' he said, 'but I think this will be the making of you.'

'And I think that you'll miss my presence very much,' said Lilith. 'You underestimated me, Dad,' she said and threw the tablecloth at him covering his head.

He laughed and pulled the cloth away just as Henrietta came riding down from the outcrop with a basket of roses from Mr Titterton's garden. 'For corsages,' she called, 'and the bouquet if you like.'

'Henri, you are priceless,' said Lilith. 'I look forward to having you as my neighbour at Overton.'

Henrietta found Phoeba in the vineyard. 'Rudolph's back,' she said quietly.

'Do you think—'

'I can't tell, Phoeba. Perhaps after the wedding …' Henrietta looked pained.

By Friday evening, Maude was in bed, wrung-out and aching. Phoeba gave her a cold marjoram compress for her throbbing forehead and a warmed sack of lavender and oats to ease her cramps.

247

'There are ants in my veins,' she said.

But for the first time in days, Phoeba felt wonderful. Tomorrow was Saturday, Lilith's wedding day. And Rudolph would be there.

Saturday, February 10, 1894

It was a glorious day. Maggie blinked and stopped chewing her cud when she saw Phoeba coming at dawn. She walked hesitantly on sleepy legs to her milking stand and sprang up, and together they watched the sunrise push a sheet of cloud back to reveal a brilliant sky. A breeze wafted in carrying the smell of dew on stubble, sheep manure and dusty eucalyptus leaves. Today must go smoothly; there must be no scenes, no hitches. Lilith must get to Overton on time, composed and radiant.

Phoeba shook her awake at seven with a cup of tea and said, 'The water in the copper is hot and the bath is waiting.'

Then she went to Spot. By eight o'clock, he was curry-combed to a glossy black hue, his mane and fringe trimmed and his hoofs polished. Only then did Phoeba lock herself in the washhouse – and stayed there half an hour. She stepped into the kitchen dressed and ready in her blue frock with her best hat, her hair looped in a loose nape coil that draped around her bow-tie collar. 'By Jove, Phoeba,' said Robert, who wore his small suit and pudding-bowl hat, 'we'll lose you today as well.'

Maude looked like a frilly barrel under a massive hat. It was almost a yard wide and so laden with satin and feathers that the brim drooped and touched her high Juliette sleeves.

'When you make an effort, Phoeba, you can actually look quite pretty. Is that strawberry water on your lips?'

248

'And I have scent behind my ears.' Her face had dulled to a more agreeable shade of rash and she felt quite beautiful.

Lilith emerged from Maude's bedroom, pale and trembling. Her skirt was hemmed to the new length to reveal her white shoes and stockings. Her hat was also very modern – white, low over her head, its oval brim reaching out to her shoulders while pink roses crowded the hatband. She was all pastel and creamy with brilliant blue eyes, and she clutched a bouquet of gum flowers and bottlebrush, roses and fern leaves.

She looked truly lovely, so Phoeba told her so.

'You know, Phoeba,' said Lilith, 'you have never once, not ever, said anything nice to me. You have disliked me for as long as I can remember. It's in the tone of your voice.' Phoeba was about to say that that wasn't at all true, but realised it probably was. 'I have always had to sleep with the lamp turned up.'

'You had no trouble sleeping; you snored,' said Phoeba. 'And why shouldn't I read?'

'You don't think of others as much as you suppose, Phoeba. You like everything your way but you think that you don't: at least I'm honest about myself. You never let me ride your big fat horse and you never let me drive the sulky. You never played with me or let me be friends with Hadley or Henrietta—'

'We didn't like playing at mothers and fathers—'

'How do you know they didn't? You never let them. Mother has been my only friend.'

'Now, now,' said Maude, fussing with Lilith's bouquet. 'We won't cause a scene today. You're just different to each other, that's all. Margaret and I are unalike, and tragedy forced us to be good sisters.'

'Which brings me to the subject of sulkies,' said Robert, taking a penny from his pocket. 'It would be an inconvenient day

249

for both of us to die in the manner of your parents, Maude, and it would look bad for Marius if he lost another bride. So let's flip a coin to see who gets to go with Spot.'

'Heads,' said Lilith, winning herself the seat next to Robert in the sulky with Spot. Hadley drove the Hampden into the yard right on time, helped Phoeba heave Maude into the front seat and they followed, travelling via Bay View to collect Margaret from the siding.

Spot gave a superior sideways glance to the ducks as he stepped proudly through the gate, the shiniest horse with the most sparkling sulky in the area, and the Crupp convoy travelled – slowly so as not to cause dust – without incident all the way to the intersection, where they turned towards Overton. Then Spot stopped dead and wrenched his head, stepping sideways and trying to turn around.

'No!' shrieked Phoeba from the Hampden.

Robert leaned back on the reins. 'Not the dam, Spot, not today.'

Lilith sat grim-faced and frozen next to him: the dam was low, the banks slimy and the sulky would bog up to its axle and sink, the bridal white turning putrid with mud. Spot dug his shoes into the ground and groaned, the metal wheel rims twisting in the dirt as he dragged them, inch by inch, and Robert battled all the way with the brake handle calling, 'No Spot, bad horse.' But Spot wasn't heading for the dam; he was trying to get closer to the signpost.

Phoeba leapt from the Hampden and grabbed Spot's bridle, and there in the middle of the intersection, slumped on her carpetbag and hidden by the thistle bushes that surrounded the Mount Hopeless sign, was Aunt Margaret, weeping. Her smart new purple jacket and slim, striped skirt were flecked with thistle spikes and her bowler hat was cast aside. Her nose was mahogany and her mouth was dry and stuck together. She couldn't seem to get her words out.

Maude said looked down from the Hampden, rolled her eyes and said, 'Tsk.'

Lilith cried, 'I haven't got time for this.'

'Margaret, old thing,' said Robert, 'this is supposed to be a happy day.'

Phoeba knelt down in the sharp thistles next to her bony old aunt, put her arms around her quaking shoulders and said, 'Ashley?' and Aunt Margaret brayed like a mule.

'Chin up, Aunt Margaret,' said Hadley, helping her into the Hampden – she was the only aunty Hadley had ever encountered. He stopped beside the water tank at Overton so Phoeba could press a cold, wet handkerchief to her aunt's dry, burning cheeks.

It was a wedding without much ceremony – no grand entrances, no gasps of wonder. Henrietta and the Tittertons arrived at the same time as the vicar; Mr and Mrs Overton appeared with Marius. And they all stood on the lovely carpet – surrounded by crystal decanters and mahogany mantel mirrors, the upholstered drawing room suite (ten piece), the vases and exotic flowers, and the sumptuous pot plants that curled from pot stands and hung from the walls. Lilith became Mrs Marius Overton of Overton. Maude used her best accent throughout – and didn't seem to notice that Mrs Overton spoke to none of them, didn't even look at Phoeba's face to see how it was mending. Phoeba drank three glasses of sparkling wine and wondered if Lilith would inherit the big, black pearls threaded through Mrs Overton's bun, or the matching pearls that dangled from a belt slung loosely around her waist. Perhaps the diamond on her wedding finger and its matching drop earrings. Mrs Overton's décolleté, powdered and painted with faint blue lines to give it a delicate hue, was too low for someone of her age, thought Phoeba, and her wrists were heavy with girlish gold bangles and bracelets. Perhaps Lilith's daughter would inherit them?

It could have been the wine, but Phoeba allowed herself to believe that all was well. This was the way it would be. As the remaining single girl, as the spinster, she was bound to help her mother, help her father – she was released from the need for marriage. She took another sip: her future was resolved. She would be able to stay at Mount Hope, free. It would do very nicely.

Still, she couldn't help imagining Rudolph Steel coming down the staircase at the big house, or working behind the heavy closed doors, and she glanced at the gilt mirrors now and then just in case they reflected him. When he finally did step out of the shadows, looking very European in a mid-length vicuna suit with silk trim, Phoeba's happy freedom dissolved: she was like a jittery country girl in a hand-made dress. He shook Marius's hand and placed a kiss on Lilith's cheek. 'Congratulations.'

He turned to Phoeba, took her hand and kissed it. 'And, you have a brother,' he said. 'He will be an asset, I know.'

In the days he had been away she had forgotten how brown his eyes were, so velvety that their pupils were almost indiscernible. The back of her hand hummed where his soft lips had touched. Hadley hovered after Aunt Margaret, refilling her glass often and discussing the paintings with her, keeping to the fringes of the room: Phoeba knew he was only pretending not to watch her every move, and she was sad to think she was making him behave so. When he went to stand with Mr and Mrs Overton they looked as nonplussed as three Quakers witnessing a bar brawl – but

252

Phoeba decided she must push all these disgruntled people from her mind. This was a happy day, and she was standing between Henrietta and Rudolph Steel.

Robert nudged her aside to talk to Rudolph about land-owners planting vineyards across the peninsula to the south. 'They're put in riesling grapes at Pettavel,' he said, worried about the dangers of the new vignerons and outbreaks of phylloxera like the one in the 1870s. The cake remained uncut and Robert was still talking to Rudolph when Mr and Mrs Overton senior drifted upstairs without a word. It seemed to signal the end of the occasion.

Rudolph leaned close to Phoeba. 'They don't like me much either.'

As she snuggled deeper under her quilt in her room, Phoeba heard her father walking softly by and saw his lamplight pass as he made his way to his bedroom. Apart from Aunt Margaret snoring in Lilith's bed, she felt all was right with the world. She even al-lowed the truth that had been incubating at the back of her mind to blossom. She had gone soft on Rudolph Steel. She felt it when she stood next to him and she felt it again now, imagining him in his satin-trimmed coat on one knee at the outcrop in a golden sunset, holding her hand – she could even feel his firm fingers around hers.

It came quickly then, a strange sinking feeling: Lilith was now living at Overton. Phoeba could never live there with Rudolph – she'd be stuck with Lilith forever! She pushed her daydream out. It was silly. Then she thought of a solution: she'd have to build a house on top of the outcrop, halfway between her vines and her husband's work.

There, she had thought the word – husband. But she knew

her dream was far-fetched. Anyway, she reminded herself, she was happy on her own. She didn't want anyone interfering with her or with the vines. She wanted to run them. She wanted to be a vigneron. Why didn't the Overtons like Rudolph? Money, of course, she thought. He owned half of them. So he would run Overton and she would run Mount Hope. They would meet somewhere in the middle.

Sunday, February 11, 1894

On Sunday, Aunt Margaret arrived at the breakfast table irritable and cranky while Phoeba hummed as she dressed and prepared breakfast. 'Stop making a din,' Margaret snapped, so fiercely that Robert asked if her gout was acting up.

'Why would I have gout, Robert? I don't overindulge in wine, like you!' she said, but Phoeba knew her hip flask was empty. She fed her aunt bread and dripping and then her mother arrived, teary and snivelling.

'For pity's sake, Mother, what's the matter now? Will you never be happy about anything?'

'You just wait for this time in your life, Phoeba!' said Maude, shakily. 'I can't control it. And I am concerned that Lilith will move to the city.'

'Lilith will make sure she's all right no matter where she is but I don't know what's to become of me,' cried Margaret, dramatically.

'Oh for heaven's sake, Margaret,' said Maude, wiping her eyes, 'it's just a broken heart. You made your bed. Remember that ridiculous quote? "She who has never loved has never lived." You have lived.'

'You are a cruel and selfish sister, Maude.'

'Me? You sold our home—'

'Enough!' said Robert, throwing his newspapers aside. 'All I ever hear is whining and complaining! You are wearing me out and if it weren't for the rabbits I'd be dead from working to feed you all!'

Maude crept back to her bed and Aunt Margaret left, her footfall hard on the back porch. In a fit of pique, she attempted to harness Spot to the sulky. Spot stood patiently while she placed the collar over his head and then found she could not thread the trace straps because the collar was on back-to-front. He lowered his head while she removed it and replaced it properly, then he sighed and looked hopefully to the house while she failed to join the girth strap again and again. Eventually, Phoeba came, and when Spot was correctly attired, Aunt Margaret re-buffed Phoeba's offer to drive. 'I can drive,' she snapped, and wriggled the reins over Spot's rump. 'Take me to Mrs Flynn, Spot,' she said with great pathos, and Spot obediently loped out the gate.

An hour later, he strolled back up the lane again. Behind him, Aunt Margaret was up to her waist in her dusty paintings while at the shop, Mrs Flynn leaned on the counter and wondered what to do about the square patches on her wall where the green paint had not faded under the canvasses. It all looked very bare.

Spot stood respectfully on the dam bank while Aunt Margaret constructed a clumsy pyramid of oil paintings in their cheap frames and threw a lit match at them. As each one grilled and melted she took another from the sulky and placed it on top. She took every canvas from the walls of the house and burned them, and finally chucked her sketchpad onto the blaze.

255

Phoeba was reorganising the bedroom, spreading her garments evenly through the drawers and shelves vacated by Lilith when her aunt came in and shoved all her things into her carpetbag.

'I am, once again, extraneous,' she spluttered, tugging her bowler hat on and stomped off down the passage. She kicked the screen door open, thumped down the front steps and out the front gate leaving a small wake of curling dust.

Phoeba and Spot followed her.

'No one is ever extraneous, Aunt Margaret. Everyone has a place,' she called. Of course her aunt must stay at Mount Hope – it was obvious, Phoeba knew, even though she was compromised again. She'd still have to share a room, and she'd have to cook and wash for one more person – chauffeur one more around. She invited her to stay anyway.

'I'd rather eat a sundowner's toenails,' spat her aunt and threw her carpetbag into the back of the sulky. They drove silently to meet the twelve o'clocker, her aunt glaring out at the bay.

Mrs Flynn asked as she wrote out the ticket, 'Where's your flash friend?'

'Probably with one of his other friends,' said Aunt Margaret, her voice like wire grating on tin.

The shopkeeper nodded knowingly. 'If you want your back scratched use a doorjamb I say.'

'Hear hear,' said Margaret.

'Have you heard from Freckle?' asked Phoeba.

'It's a secret,' said his mother, looking about in case there were vengeful itinerants behind her flour bins. 'He's seeing the whole of Victoria way up to the border. A lightning-squirter's job isn't easy but it was the snake in the mailbag that finally made up his mind.' Mrs Flynn studied the floor around her feet. 'It had twelve little babies and they all crawled off in here somewhere.'

'You won't ever tell Mother that, will you?' said Phoeba.

'Not unless I need to – for some reason.'

As they waited on the siding for the train, Aunt Margaret said grandly, 'I will not be ruined by some fickle, capricious man, Phoeba. It isn't dignified. What every woman requires is a loyal friend to bury you when you're dead, bring you a cup of tea when you're ill and scratch your back when you're without a suitable doorjamb. Romantic love, what humbug.' She thought for a moment then added, 'Mind you, the intimate thing was something I'm glad I didn't miss out on.' And she shivered, still delighted.

'Good,' said Phoeba, 'but one man shouldn't dash your hopes. As the suffragettes would say, "Men should protect your freedom, not make you a slave to their whims".'

The light in her aunt's green eyes switched back on, 'The suffragettes, of course!'

Phoeba tried to read late that night, tried to relish having her room to herself, but she was soon asleep, exhausted. Her dreams brought rain, thunder, weddings and Rudolph Steel.

Monday, February 12, 1894

She woke feeling tense. A cold air eased up under her skirt as she walked along the hall. She kicked the cloth snake against the gap and stood at the window in its squares of brittle morning sun to eat her porridge, a shawl wrapped around her shoulders. Robert came in from the outhouse, threw a slice of bread on the hot plate, poured himself tea, and then moved his chair to the other end of the table by the stove.

'Place is dull without Lil, isn't it?'

'Yes,' said Phoeba, cheerfully, not missing her at all. 'But we'll have grapes, Dad, fat pale grapes. And next season will be a bumper crop and we'll make wine.' She would make it herself, all going according to plan. She put her bowl in the sink and said, 'I think I'll ride to see Henrietta.'

She had decided to confront Rudolph, to find out about the crop, and find out what would happen to Marius and Lilith if it went bad.

But before she could finish her chores, Henrietta rode down from the outcrop astride Liberty, her skirt screwed under her thighs and her shins exposed where her stockings had come adrift from her garters. She flopped at the kitchen table.

'Have you run away?' asked Phoeba, pouring her a cup of tea.

'You can always have the shed, Henri,' said Robert removing his shoe to inspect his gout toe.

'I won't need it,' she said. 'Mr and Mrs Overton left on the ten o'clocker to Melbourne. Lilith is in a state because …' Henrietta was having problems getting the words out. '… I'm happy to go home. But I don't know what Hadley will do. He may stay at Elm Grove now …'

'Tell me, Henrietta,' said Phoeba, her knuckles white around the teapot's handle.

'Guston Overton has gone bust. Rudolph Steel has bought them out.'

The teapot dropped with a wet crack and several, brown-stained ceramic slices skidded across the floor leaving a starburst of tea-leaves. Phoeba gathered the mess into the tea-cozy.

Spot cantered as fast he could to Overton, so fast that Henrietta was left far behind. She tied Spot to the back gate and ran into the house, bursting through the back door to the cavernous kitchen. Rudolph Steel was at the stove in his shirt and trousers and knee-length boots, a cup of tea in one hand and a slice of bread in the other. He didn't look surprised to see her.

'Tell me what's happening,' she gasped.

'Would you like some bread? I've been dreading this scene for days, Phoeba,' he said, sitting down slowly. 'And I'm sorry about this. I believe you will make your vineyard viable.' He watched her carefully – he liked her particularly now, standing in the kitchen after a fast ride, vibrant, a little breathless. She was pretty, he thought, but there was something else in her, a substance that would grow with age and knowledge, and he admired that. Sometimes he'd seen her eyes blue and sometimes grey. Today they were dark and challenging.

She sat down in front of him, folded her hands on the table. 'Go on.'

'The London Bank of Australia foreclosed on Overton's liens. I have paid them out—'

'You've bought Guston Overton out?'

He didn't pause. 'Mr Titterton has been let go and is packing up as we speak. I'm sorry it's come to this but your sister and Marius can stay in the manager's house for as long as they need …'

For as long as they need – until they find somewhere else. Marius had been dispossessed.

In the short, piercing silence dread sank Phoeba's heart then hope lifted it just as quickly. So Lilith and Marius would go to Melbourne. And Rudolph would take over Overton. Which would keep him next door to her.

'But Marius has refused,' she heard him say. He took a breath

259

and she held hers. 'They say they will go to Mount Hope.'

Very quietly, her ambitions, her plans for her whole life flaked into pieces on the floor around her like paint falling from an old ceiling. Rudolph drummed his fingers on the table next to the slice of bread in which his single bite had left a small bay. She looked at him squarely. He could have warned her.

'You didn't tell me.'

'I wasn't sure—'

'You knew though. You knew and you let Marius marry Lilith.'

'What could I do about it? They had to marry, didn't they?'

He was right.

'You can save me now,' said Phoeba desperately. 'Let them stay as manager.'

'I am the manager. He has been manager.'

'And he managed to ruin Overton.'

'To be fair, a lot has to do with his father—'

'And the banks,' she spat.

'And the banks and workers, the dry season. Marius could stay as caretaker, but he won't.'

'He'll manage Mount Hope though. He was happy to marry Lilith for the grapes,' Phoeba shrugged. 'What about me?'

He gestured helplessly to the ruined crop, the sheep in their poor condition, the low green water in the dams. She knew that he had seen it all coming. 'You will need help …' she remembered him saying.

'You knew.'

'I hoped it would come right.' He turned his teacup on the table and she reached and put her hand over his wrist, stopping him.

'Rudolph, they'll move in over there and I'll be … I don't

know what will happen to me. I'm like you. I don't want to be anyone's possession.'

'I thought, like me, you had someone … a commitment.'

She took a moment to catch her breath. 'Hadley wants a wife who's devoted, homely, who likes children – and sheep. I'm not right for him; I'm the same as you.'

'I have a wife in England—'

'No!' she screamed, startling herself. She stood up, the chair behind her tipping over. 'But I thought …'

He turned to look at her. 'I have been honest. I have never approached you … romantically.'

'But it's there,' she said, simply. 'I feel it, and so do you—'

'I did. I do.' He looked directly at her. 'I thought my wife was the right person to marry, and she is the right person. Anyone is if you want them to be. But it's not the person, it's the condition of commitment, of compromise. It's impossible just to be as I want to be – that's what I discovered. If I could be with you, I would still hurt you if you said, be as you want, I won't stop you. You would still hope for something, an obligation—'

'I want my freedom – you know that. I would have no expectations.'

'It wouldn't be honest.'

Which was what she had said to Hadley: 'It wouldn't be honest to marry you …'

'I would know that you were waiting,' said Rudolph. 'It would tear at me.' He gathered her into his arms and said, 'I'm sorry,' and she fell against him. He smelt like cigars and bath soap and she felt she was entirely safe, felt the sensation of a body so close, being enveloped. She was miserable but thrilled, standing there with her tears leaving wet stains all over his shirt. But if he said, stay, be with me, she thought, I would. She would. It was

261

cosy, lovely. The things she'd often imagined that men and women did, the things she'd thought would be uncomfortable or lewd, now they were natural. So this was attraction, this was why Lilith risked everything to be with Marius. Rudolph pulled her tighter against him and she knew she could easily live in hope, for this – she could truly do anything, say anything, be what she felt. And she knew that was what he felt too. It was like a net around them. No one need ever even know.

She looked up at him and pressed her lips to his but he pulled her back. 'I will not tie you to me,' he said gently. 'I would not do that to a friend, to you.'

She took his hand, 'But I want you to—'

'No.' He stepped back, became a manager again. 'The place will be left until it can be worked up, the sheep will be sold, a caretaker will stay here. It will be worth its weight in wool and grain one day but the land has been flogged ...'

'I don't care what anyone says, we could just be together sometimes.'

He took her hands and pressed them to her sides. 'No. It will be years before I come back and do anything with Overton and when I do, my wife will come with me.'

'I'll live here, in the house until you do,' she said, nonsensically.

'Waiting? With your sister and brother-in-law over the hill in your house, in your vineyard, and you exiled and standing on the balcony watching for someone to come – someone who will come with someone else.' Hadley would say this was like something from a book, she thought.

'It will be all right, eventually,' said Rudolph. 'Things change. You must sort it out with your family, your friends.' And he let her go and walked away. She felt cold and wished she'd brought a wrap. Now she knew how Aunt Margaret's heart felt. It had all come to nothing.

Lilith was not crying, stamping her feet, slamming doors or screaming. She was tense with fury, marching about in a quilted silk morning gown, pitching white lacy things at her trousseau trunk.

'It's not fair,' she said through gritted teeth. 'I have lost everything.'

'You've gained, Lilith,' said Phoeba. 'You've gained a husband.'

Lilith put her hands on her hips, narrowing her eyes at her sister. 'A husband who has lost his land, his future. Poor Marius …'

'Why don't you take the manager's house?'

'I'm not going to replace old Mrs Tit.' She pointed her finger at Phoeba. 'Marius has to do something and he's interested in wine.' Then she strode to the hallway, screaming, 'and I am not staying here with that … that … banker.' She slammed the door, hard, the noise like a cannon shot. When it swung open again, slowly, there was Rudolph, his brown eyes angry. As he walked away Lilith screamed, 'This is Marius's home, he can't live next to it as a … servant.' She looked at Phoeba. 'And you thought you'd got rid of me, didn't you?'

'Well,' said Phoeba, 'I thought that if this happened you and Marius would go to Melbourne. She paused. 'Lilith, what will happen to me?'

'Phoeba! That man, Steel, has seized Overton, and you're worried about where you will sleep?'

Lilith had always twisted things, Phoeba knew, but wondered if this was the way life worked? You took what you could and if you weren't forceful, others took it from you. There was nothing for it, she thought: it was time to please herself.

She turned on her heel and went to the rooms at the corner of the house, Rudolph's rooms. He was putting on his riding coat but paused, frowning when he saw her. She leaned against the door, shutting it, and he heard the key turn and lock with a clack. He eased his arm from the coat's sleeve and threw it on a chair.

Henrietta jigged around the corner of the house on Liberty, her jaw clenched to stop her teeth chattering and her plait unravelled. Spot was tethered at the back gate, straining against his reins to get to the vegetable garden, a pile of manure behind him. She had a good mind to let him off to eat all Rudolph Steel's vegetables, but she didn't. She went to Lilith's room to find Phoeba, but Phoeba wasn't there. Phoeba wasn't anywhere in the great home-stead that she could see – though she didn't go far. It felt wrong to be snooping in a house so recently abandoned.

She found Hadley in their mother's parlour, wrapping Mr Titterton's epergne in newspaper.

Henrietta said, 'Careful, it's an heirloom,' sounding just like her mother.

'You can carry it then, on Liberty.'

'Very funny. Have you seen Phoeba today?'

'No.' He carefully put the parcel in a box with all its little hanging bowls and plates and carried it outside to the wagon, his sister shadowing him. It was the movement that caught their eye. The bare arm grabbing the drapes in Rudolph Steel's rooms, wrenching them together, and Phoeba's face. Hadley and Henrietta looked straight back into her bold dark eyes as she looked down. Then her head fell back and the drapes closed.

The box tipped in Hadley's hands but Henrietta reached and caught it. Inside, the epergne tinkled. Hadley straightened himself, gesturing, it's all right, I am all right. Henrietta put the box safely on the wagon.

'Go and start lunch, Henri,' said Hadley, 'before Mother comes down.'

'Hadley, Phoeba's—'

'Just leave me.'

He led Spot to the stables, gave him a bag of oats, filled his water trough, slapped his rump and said, 'Patience, old boy.' Then he sat on the feed box and watched his tears drop into the powdery dust among the wheat grains and dry stalks, the flecks and chaff, the stalks and wisps of wool.

Phoeba felt herself locked with Rudolph Steel and knew this was what life was all about, being entwined, flesh on flesh, limb through limb. What a bizarre and ridiculous thing to do, she thought. And how glorious it was, how undignified, messy and soft. The ugliness of men, but so beautiful if you loved them. This was delicious.

Later that afternoon, Robert was pottering in his wine cellar. He slapped a pair of leather gloves together to shake out the spiders, and placed them next to the grape bins. He gathered up the shears and secateurs and turned to his sharpening stone as Phoeba's shadow slowly filled the door. Her expression was strangely hard.

'Lilith wants to come home. But the vineyard will still be mine, won't it?' She was calm, precise.

'Everything we have and everything we could be – the future – depends on the grapes, Phoeba.' He took off his pith hat and brushed something from the top of it.

'Dad, look me in the eye and tell me what will happen to me if Marius lives here.'

He looked at her. His nose was purple against his smoke-stained moustache. She saw him now, clearly, a pressured man, a drinker, fast-hearted, the kind of man who had apoplectic fits and fell dead.

'I have spent everything, given everything for these grapes. My neighbours think I'm mad, my wife hates me for them and you tell me you are the best person to make the most of them. Someone must make the very best of them because I have nothing left to invest in them.' He pointed at the vineyard. 'The money we'll get from these grapes is the only money we have. Now Marius has a bit, which we need, and contacts too. We're on the edge here, Phoeba. I can't afford to turn him down.' He pushed his foot to the treadle and the sharpening stone revolved. The blade pressed against the stone filling the shed with an abrasive noise that put her teeth on edge and made her fists clench. Her father was selling her out.

At least she could lie in her bed reliving every gesture, every touch, the tumbles and the kisses. Her skin was rough with goose-flesh and she tossed as images came to her, flashes of skin, the smells and sounds, textures and wetnesses. She wondered at the human body and smiled and buried her head in her pillow and groaned knowing how bold she had been. She had been very, very reluctant to leave when it was clear they could stay no lon-ger. But Marius was banging on the door, thumping up and down the halls searching for Rudolph, and Lilith was screeching in her room. She had known Marius would go to the stables to check for the Holstein, and that he would see Spot. And she hadn't wanted Lilith to know she was there.

Rudolph was more than she had ever imagined.

Tuesday, February 13, 1894

Maude shot from her bed on Tuesday to be at her spot on the front veranda with a cup of tea, her knitting and the looking glass when the tabletop wagon, piled high with Mrs Titterton's belongings, travelled back to Elm Grove. Hadley led in the Hampden and Henrietta bobbed along far behind. At the intersection Henrietta raised her hat and waved up at Mount Hope. Maude whipped the telescope behind her chair and said in a cheery voice, 'Well, Mrs Titterton has made her bed.'

Phoeba stayed quiet with her wrap pulled tightly. Birds lifted and fluttered behind her father as he moved unsteadily along the vines. He picked grapes at random and held them up to the light, rubbing them on his lapel and peering at them closely. He ate one and spat it out, his face screwing from the bitter taste.

'Sampling,' said Phoeba, quoting her father, 'and you, Miss Grape-Expert, will begin sampling.'

'What?' said Maude.

'Nothing.'

The noon train came and went and a huge passenger steamer rolled gently out to sea leaving a black smear in the sky. Spot lifted his head and studied her down his black nose – she wondered what he thought about all the coming and going.

The world moved along as always, yet everything had altered. Some people only ever got some of the things they wanted, sometimes. She'd had two days of everything she wanted; a room of her own, a future growing grapes, Rudolph, and now she wasn't sure if what remained would still remain tomorrow. She might become extraneous.

Her mother put a sandwich in front of her. 'Your face will stay creased if the wind changes,' she said, retreating again behind the screen door.

But Phoeba's brooding hadn't run its course. In the afternoon she watched a swaggie come up the lane from the siding and then suddenly the Hampden turned at the intersection and sped up the lane, Henrietta at the reins and Hadley by her side. The trailing dust floated gently and settled on the vines. Phoeba sighed, bracing herself for Hadley's hurt, Henrietta's disapproval. She had spent one day with a married man, right under their noses. If that had ruined everything, if they hated her, then that was the way it would be.

It was when they didn't stop to give the swaggie a lift – he jerked a clenched fist at them – that she knew something else had happened. Henrietta circled the yard sharply. There was a weary slump to Hadley's shoulders as he came towards her but his face was calm. Henrietta strode across the yard, the rim of her felt hat pushed back and her boots kicking her hem. 'Hadley has been disregarded. Mr Titterton has taken Elm Grove. He's going to build a new house and everything.'

'It's all right, Henri, really it is.' Hadley looked straight at Phoeba and she saw no judgment in his gaze. 'I have my wool classing certificate and …' – he took his hat off and slapped it on his knee – '… and I have a position up north.' His moustache was thicker than it had been at New Year, waxed now and twisted at the ends.

'But it's only for a year,' cried Henrietta, desperately. And 'there's a drought up there —'

'They may keep me on if I'm satisfactory,' said Hadley defensively.

It was all so unfair. Phoeba let her head drop, her tears rolling down her nose onto her folded arms while Hadley and his sister sat miserably on either side of her on the battered wicker lounge.

'No matter what,' said Henrietta, taking Phoeba's hand, 'we'll look after each other.' Hadley took her other hand and said, 'No matter what.'

Aunt Margaret was right when she said all you needed was a friend.

They were still there, a short time later, and looked up as one when the britzka turned into the yard with Marius at the reins and Lilith beside him. She was wearing a ridiculous new hat with a nautical theme and she sailed up the front steps. 'You three look as if the world's about to end. You should count your blessings: at least you have a home.'

Marius hesitated as he passed but no one, not even Hadley, greeted him. Without a word, they followed him to the kitchen. Maude was eating a sandwich. She fussed over Marius: did he want tea? Coffee? Cake?

Robert told her to pipe down and poured everyone wine.

They sat around the kitchen table. Marius and Lilith, so familiar for two people married only three days; Maude, bewildered, fussing to cover the tension she didn't understand; Robert, his expression pragmatic. But Phoeba could see he was timorous, like an accountant with a bag of murderer's money to invest. She kept her eyes on him as she sat between her friends. In this room, she knew, the truth of her fate circled closer and closer.

Lilith put her hand on her abdomen and raised her head. 'We have nowhere ...' she declared, and looked to her mother. 'We have been … we will come home.'

Immediately, Maude reached out for Lilith, her handkerchief in her hand. 'Of course you will.'

'No,' said Phoeba, 'you got what you wanted, Lilith, and now you can live with your husband in Toorak.'

'What would I do there? How would I make a living?' asked Marius, his empty hands raised in despair.

'Anyway,' said Lilith, 'we can't live there until his mother dies apparently. She lives on marzipan and sherry so that won't be—'

'Lilith, dear,' said Marius. He looked at Phoeba. 'I can do a lot with the grapes. I'll have money to plant more acreage and improve—'

'No!' cried Phoeba, leaping up, 'Dad promised me! I will be a vigneron! You can stay in the manager's house at Overton as long as you like – Rudolph said you could.'

Marius placed a hand on his wife's shoulder. 'We won't stay over there as a banker's caretakers, as chattels.'

'But the farm is to be Phoeba's,' declared Henrietta, uncertain.

'Quite right,' said Hadley.

'If I thought anyone would put stinking, fly-blown sheep on my good vineyard soil, even when I'm dead and buried a hundred years …' Robert shook his head.

'Sheep do feed the nation,' said Phoeba huffily, and Robert stared at her. Tears started to fall from her eyes and she felt her knees shaking. Hadley gave her his handkerchief.

'This is nonsense. We are not throwing you out, Phoeba,' said Lilith slapping the table and taking control. 'You can stay, we'll fix up Dad's room in the shed, and you'll have your cherished privacy. And you can help with any babies.'

Phoeba twisted the big, white handkerchief in her fingers.

'You've taken a bribe, Dad.'

'And you're being uncharacteristically hysterical, Phoeba,' he replied, but without meeting her gaze.

'You brought me here,' she said, 'and I am happy here. You said that I could have Mount Hope. I planted those vines with you and I nurtured them. You have betrayed me for Marius's money and I thought, Dad, that you were better than that.' He seemed to grow smaller under her words. She knew it was because inside, the truth was withering him. And she was pleased.

If she stayed, she thought, she'd have Henrietta at least. But was that friendship enough to compensate for a life of servitude to a sister she couldn't bear and her demanding infants, to her drunk father and her bossy, empty mother on a farm she was no longer entitled to? A farm that was given to her idiot sister and her failed husband? Her sister, as she realised terribly, as the head of the house?

'I'll go to the city,' she said, shakily. 'I'll live with Aunt Margaret, somewhere.'

'Well there's a solution,' said Lilith, sarcastically. 'You can apply for a job in a corset factory along with a thousand other people who can at least sew.'

'And sixpence is as much as you'll get in those sweat shops, standing on your feet fifteen hours, sewing all day in a back room,' said Robert, unhelpfully.

'I could be a governess.'

'Governesses are slaves to squatters. You'll have to go miles from home and anyway,' said Robert, 'there are not many squatters alive that are rich enough to pay a governess these days.'

Marius flinched.

Maude said, 'Your family needs you here, Phoeba, and you know you would rather be home than anywhere.'

'Not as everybody's servant! I'll end up looking after Lilith and her children, then you two in your old age and Marius would get my vines. I'd sooner get paid and be independent.'

'There's no work in the cities,' said Marius. 'There is nothing for anyone there. You're better off here where there's food, shelter, friends and at least it's healthy.'

She looked pleadingly to her father. 'What happened to being your cornerstone?' she asked – but he turned his moist eyes away and held his hand up. He could do nothing.

She couldn't, wouldn't be a spinster, a companion relying on handouts from her own property with none of her opinions heeded and no say in anything.

She looked from Hadley to Henrietta, all three of them lost together dispossessed. 'I'll go away to the Murray with Hadley.'

Hadley and Henrietta nodded, once, as one.

'Perfect,' said Lilith. 'That's settled then.'

'Solves everything,' said Marius.

'You hate sheep,' Robert howled. 'You have a brother-in-law here who will look after you.'

'No!' cried Maude. 'You can't go to the wilderness.'

'But marriage is natural,' said Hadley, crossing his arms. 'I've heard you say so a hundred times, Mrs Crupp.' Phoeba knew, in her heart, that she hadn't actually meant she would marry Hadley, but that was what Hadley expected. And in the face of everything else it seemed a small and irrelevant thing. What had Rudolph said: 'anyone' is the right person if you want them to be. 'Well, all right, she thought. Henrietta reached over and took Phoeba's hand and Hadley scratched his moustache to hide his quivering chin.

'And, Mother,' said Phoeba, feeling nasty, 'it is an opportunity to be seized … isn't that what you did?'

They sat on a log under the peppercorn tree, Hadley in the middle, where the swing used to be before it was removed. Phoeba and Henrietta had pushed Hadley too high, trying to get the swing to loop around the branch, but he flew off landing badly and shattering his arm.

'I love you Phoeba, always have, no matter what.'

'He has,' nodded Henrietta, 'ever since you saved him from Mrs Flynn's goose.'

'It was a gander,' protested Hadley.

'You're good for me, Phoeba, and I know I can bring a calmness to you. It's sort of a fate.'

'But Hadley,' said Phoeba, 'there's fate and there's being different. And you don't know any other girls; there are no other girls around, you're used to us. And, Rudolph and I have—'

'Don't,' said Henrietta and jumped up, waving as if she was deflecting attacking magpies. Then she stopped. 'Don't. It's not really important, is it Hadley?'

Hadley shook his head.

'So then, what about me?' asked Henrietta. 'Will I be left here, alone? Will I lose you both, do mother's bidding and cook for old corpse teeth?'

'Henrietta could come with us,' said Phoeba taking Hadley's hand.

'Mr Titterton would love me to go; he says I'm disrespectful,' said Henrietta, smiling wickedly. 'It wouldn't seem right if I had to help old corpse tooth with the birthing ewes instead of Hadley.'

'Yes,' said Phoeba, feebly, thinking she would have to help in New South Wales, feed the whining orphans plodding lightly on their thick snowy legs.

'We've all been passed over, dispossessed,' said Hadley.

'No,' said Phoeba, 'your home is still yours, Hadley. Your

273

accession has merely been postponed.'

Later she sat on her bed looking at the photograph from the ploughing match, Hadley between herself and Henrietta. Hadley would bring her cups of tea when she was poorly, would bury her when she was dead. And she had lived … loved, even so briefly. Bother her disappointed mother and father! They could struggle without her … and she smiled, knowing Lilith would have to do the washing, the ironing, the milking, the cooking – the caring for everyone else.

There was a quiet knock at the door and it pushed open, tentatively. Her father stood there, half-hidden. He didn't look at her, his pillow under his arm as he stared down at his slippers. 'You are a good friend to me, Phoeba, my only one, and I am sorry, very sorry you feel betrayed, but you have not been cast out. This is still your home and always will be. If you marry Hadley, you will betray yourself by not being honest with yourself. Now, you can stay and help—'

'No! Mother settled for less, didn't make the best of it and is disappointed. I will make the best of it. And you have a son-in-law with money for grapes to prove a point to her.'

'You should learn by our mistakes.'

'I have learned.'

'Have you, Phoeba? Aren't you disappointing yourself now? The grapes will see you right, in the end.'

Mrs Titterton was propped upright on her bed when Hadley decided to tell her the news. Several pillows, judiciously placed under each arm to steady her brittle, birdlike ribs, prevented her from crumbling sideways. With Henrietta firmly at his side, Hadley stood up very straight and declared, 'Phoeba Crupp has agreed to marry me. Her father has given us his blessing.'

'He has,' said Henrietta, 'and we're all going to New South Wales.'

'Excellent,' said Mr Titterton, slapping Hadley on the shoulder. 'We'll travel to see you there, won't we dear?'

His wife was silent, her small eyes flicking from Henrietta, to Hadley to her husband, trying to process the sentences. She thought she had heard them say they were all going to New South Wales. Her feet in their tight pointy slippers turned blue and her heart struggled under its lacy sternum.

'I am seeing yellow stars,' she breathed.

Mr Titterton pushed another pinch of snuff into her small hard nostrils, replacing the tin of Menthol Snuff next to his carved Russian wood denture box.

'We will have grandchildren,' said Mr Titterton proudly, but his wife screwed her pointy little face and squeaked, 'They'll be in New South Wales.'

'With me,' said Henrietta, nodding her head and rubbing her hands.

Wednesday, February 14, 1894

Wednesday was not an ordinary day for anyone. Robert patrolled his grapes then took Maude a cup of tea.

'A very tepid effort,' she said and put it aside.

'You'll have to make do. I am all you have now,' said Robert.

'Make do, make do,' hissed Maude, and pulled the sheet up again.

Phoeba milked her goat and left the milk on the chopping block with the day's firewood. If they wanted fresh bread for tea, Maude could make it but they would need a fire. Her father could chop the kindling.

She rode Spot to the very top of the outcrop and while he dozed in the shade, swishing flies with his tail, Phoeba watched Overton through the looking glass.

Mid-morning, Rudolph rode away with the boundary rider, the two figures vanishing into the endless plain. Above them in the white-blue heavens, two eagles hung in the breeze. Phoeba lay back over a warm boulder and turned her thoughts to her new life in New South Wales. But her childhood interrupted. She turned her years over and over in her mind, searching. How had it come to this? But she couldn't find anything to explain why her father broke his promise and betrayed her in favour of Lilith.

Her hours with Rudolph took over, but she nudged him from her mind.

'Come, Spot,' she said, sitting up. 'Our new family is waiting.'

At the bay, while Spot paddled, Hadley spread a map of New South Wales at the edge of the muddy shore and they hunched over it on their knees. Their home would be a very small dot on the railway line fifty miles from the Murray River.

'Good,' said Phoeba, 'the town's small but there will be shops and people, perhaps even a doctor.' And there was a thin blue line snaking past the town. It had to be a flowing creek, not just wet-weather water, since there were people and sheep. She would grow vines.

'And only three or four days by train from here,' said Henrietta.

They splashed on the salty shore, threw shells at the water, and planned. There was insufficient time to organise a civil service, as Phoeba had hoped. She would settle for holy matrimony.

New South Wales was rushing at her like a fallen log in a treacherous current of the Murray River, but Henrietta would be there to help her. She squared her shoulders and looked to the future. She would not close the gate to life; she would live it. She might even have children, if everything was agreeable.

Thursday, February 15, 1894

Life passed almost as it always had. Phoeba got up, milked her goat, fed her horse, then did as little as she could around Mount Hope. This forced her mother to venture into the backyard for water and to the clothes line. Sometimes swaggies passed asking for tea and sugar, inquiring when the grapes would be ready to harvest. But Robert and Marius thought it would be weeks yet, so their campfires burned on the beach at night. And every day, Phoeba found her wedding planned around her.

Maude stood over the vicar with her round arms wrapped under her bosom and her lips pursed. Robert was at her side. The vicar agreed to set the wedding for the fourth Sunday in February, just two weeks away, eight weeks into the new year.

'So rushed …' he said.

'Not really,' said Hadley, happily. 'I've known since I was ten and Phoeba's been thinking about it since New Year's Eve.'

'It's all so very modern,' complained the vicar. 'Why does no one have nice matrimonial services with celebrations and generous wedding breakfasts these days?'

'Because they're a waste,' snapped Phoeba. 'We'll end up married no matter how much food is eaten.'

When Marius and Lilith visited, Phoeba fled with Spot, and each afternoon she rode to meet Hadley and Henrietta at the bay. Hadley mentioned Rudolph Steel only once: it was during their last week at Bay View.

'Steel has installed an unemployed gardener from Geelong in the manager's house as caretaker and the homestead has been boarded up. He says he's going to England for a while.'

Hadley watched his fiancée for signs of regret, defiance, a broken heart. She thrummed with life and vitality but it was morose, and she rattled with a suppressed anger. She was more guarded than he'd ever seen.

'Your father has done what he has done—'

'For the grapes, so he says, but he's also done it for Lilith, and for himself. He's done nothing for me.'

'Just wait,' said Henrietta, working her bare feet into the mud and sinking up to her calves at the water's edge. 'Wait until we're in New South Wales, Phoeba, then you won't be in such a mood!'

'No,' she said, half-heartedly, and Hadley put his arm around her, tugging her closer to him. She must get used to Hadley's arm, she thought; she knew she would learn to like it and wondered if her mother had said the same thing to herself.

'We will be there soon,' he said, as if he was promising her a garden paradise with cauldrons of gold.

He could barely contain his anticipation. Phoeba, all to himself, all night. He longed to kiss her properly and he smiled when he imagined her standing at the stove when he came in late from work. She would put a plate of lovely food in front of him – oxtail stew with rice or her steak and kidney pie with home-made tomato sauce – and they would read the paper by the fire before going to bed, together. Someone to hold.

Lilith stayed resolutely at Overton, swanning about the mansion, humming and dancing with Marius in the ballroom, playing two-fingered tunes on the grand piano, drinking sparkling wine from the cellar and making eggs and toast for breakfast and dinner, and salad for tea. Marius prepared for the clearing sale and rode to Mount Hope almost every day. Phoeba studied him from the veranda, watched him trailing Robert up and down the vines parting leaves and peering closely at the ripening grapes.

Once, she lined him up through the sights at the end of the Collector, trained the gun on him as he walked – but pulled the barrel to the sky before she squeezed the trigger. The gun would only graze him anyway, at that distance, or maim him.

In the evenings, Phoeba, Robert and Maude ate in complete silence. Maude seemed to be in some kind of torpor and Robert was generally slightly drunk. It took every bit of what concentration he had to manage his food. After a week of icy meals, Maude took to her bed completely and would not come out.

'It's all so wretched,' she mumbled from under her blankets.

In the end, Robert was forced to ask Phoeba to make bread, pointing to his belt buckle, pulled in one extra notch, and imploring her with sodden eyes. She wondered if he had thought to save any money for her wedding – suddenly realising that she might make it through the event without a wedding cake. She almost laughed.

'Please,' he begged.

'Lilith won't make bread,' she sniffed triumphantly, dragging the flour bin from the pantry.

'I'm sure I'll grow to like salad with almonds,' said her father and sat at the table to watch.

279

Her mother staggered down from her darkened room and said, her voice croaky and strained, 'Please, Phoeba, please drive to Flynn's and send to Lassetters for Codeine powder. The veins in my head are shooting with hot acid and I fear they will burst.'

She wanted to say no. She wanted to say, you have betrayed me, you can suffer. She wanted to make them say, 'Stay, you can run the vines.' If they said that, then she would look after them forever.

She went to the stables, bridled her slow, black horse, rode to the shop and collected the papers. She still missed Freckle.

The *Geelong Advertiser* headlines read: '**NEW VINEYARD AT WAURN PONDS**. The farmers and quarrymen at the community of Waurn Ponds, which was badly affected by phylloxera in the 1870s, are buoyed by plans to establish fifteen acres of vineyards which promises to become the Victorian Halle aux Vins ...'

'The place is going ahead, be vineyards everywhere soon,' said Mrs Flynn and handed Phoeba a picture postcard.

'I'll grow vines in New South Wales,' said Phoeba. The postcard was a reproduction of a van Dyke painting of the lavishly dressed child groom, Prince William of Orange, and his opulently coutured child bride, Princess Mary Stuart. William's reluctant fingers bent warily to hold three of Mary's succulently unused fingers and the timid couple gazed uncertainly at Phoeba. Aunt Margaret had rubberstamped the happy couple with the Fairfield Women's Progressive League emblem and wrote, 'Can't attend your marriage, busy with my true calling – first exhibition.

Good luck,

Always your favourite Aunt, Margaret Robertson,

Artist and Treasurer, FWPL.

PS. Women can rule monarchies so why can't they vote?'

Mrs Flynn raised herself from her counter and put her hands

on her hips. 'You stopped arsting ages ago,' she smiled, 'but here it is.' She passed the peach parer across the counter.

Unfortunately, Maude found it would not do apples.

Thursday, February 22, 1894

The Overton sale was a disappointment. Most of the good machinery was not for sale and no one in the area had any need for three-furrow ploughs or a damaged Sunshine stripper. The sheep had already been sold along with the cattle and the pigs, and there was a surplus of horses so the draught horse team was split up and sold to various neighbours – Mr Titterton took the two Hadley had always used for ploughing. Robert looked longingly at the huge, docile beasts but Maude reminded him that there would probably be grandchildren before long and a new room would be required. No one needed a team of twenty oxen either, and the blacksmith's bellows were left. Nor had anyone the time or money to make use of stained walnut platform rockers, folding carpet chairs, oyster knives or oil landscapes of the Colchester Downs. But Maude did pick up an apple parer that also cored and sliced for two shillings. New, they cost two and six.

Mrs Flynn bought two draught horses, the harness and the flat-top wagon. She loaded the Overton washing machine and mangler, a sewing machine, a very modern kerosene refrigerator, a mechanical butter churn and Patent Milk Sterilizer, a Silicated Carbon filter to make fresh water, a coffee grinder and roaster, a counter milkshake machine, the chickens and a canary cage complete with fittings and tethered a milking cow behind before setting off home.

'Bay View is going ahead, if you arst me,' she said.

The new farmers at the Jessops' place bought the second milking cow and some strangers from a far-flung district bought candle lanterns and lamp fittings, maids' aprons and soup ladles, sausage machines, turnip cutters, chaff makers, portable forges, tyre bending machines and Forest Devils. No one needed julep strainers or canopy bedsteads.

Phoeba strolled around with her arm looped through Hadley's and Hadley walked inches taller. She flinched, though, when they encountered the people who had taken over the Jessops' farm as they loaded their wagon and Hadley introduced Phoeba as his fiancée. The formal finality of the title, the implications of it jolted her. But she dismissed the reaction. This was 'nerves'. They would be all right, she and Hadley and Henrietta; they would muddle along together. Anyway, a brilliant satisfying life would always be rendered meaningless with death, just as a less than satisfying life of compromise would. In the long run it needn't matter. It could all end the same way, no matter what. It was then that the light of reason came to her: she would simply make the best of it.

At the height of these nihilistic thoughts, she turned and saw Rudolph in the stables, leaning against the door with his legs crossed in his moles and knee-high boots, and his lovely vicuna coat. He was studying her with a look that seemed to hold affection, regret and sadness. Whipping her arm from Hadley's she felt as if she was outside herself, watching another Phoeba walk towards him. He tilted his face away, as if in pain, and raised his palm: Stop. He even began to walk away but Phoeba followed.

'How are you?' She couldn't think of anything else to say.

He didn't answer her, just picked at a bit of paint flaking from the shaft of an ancient trap.

'I'm going to New South Wales,' she offered.

'So I hear.' He rubbed the paint between his thumb and middle finger and let it fall to the ground, then he reached out and she stepped into his arms. She would have stayed there, entwined, for a fortnight – forever – but he untangled himself and walked away without another backwards glance. She sank to a stack of chaff bags behind rows of looped harnesses, reins, stirrups and saddle blankets, put her head in her hands and cried, a wrenching silent cry that stretched her jaw and hurt her ribs.

What had she done?

She had seized an opportunity because she had to. She was marrying her friend. She was making him the 'right person' – and Henrietta would be there too. She was making a life.

She was being silly. And it was the right thing to do. The hours in the days would be hers while he was out working. But she would help him with his sheep. In spring he would bring the baby orphans, hungry and bleating to her, and she would wrap her arms around their tiny, rough curls and feed them and send them wobbling on their thick snowy legs. And one day they would return to take over Elm Grove … or Mount Hope. At the end of her life she would be able to say, 'I did the best I could, I did the right thing.' At the end of her life, she'd be back here, one way or another.

Her shuddering eased. She gathered herself and peeped out. Marius passed leading a pair of horses that dragged a dray. It was stacked with candelabra three feet tall, floor-to-ceiling gilt mirrors, glass cabinets still packed with crockery, Huon pine hatstands and a bath – a large, heavy, claw-footed thing that would take up most of the Mount Hope washhouse. Lilith was perched on the edge of the dray like a model in a furniture advertisement. Mount Hope would be a crowded museum for the relics of lost fortunes and dashed expectations.

Saturday, February 24, 1894

On the eve of her wedding, Phoeba packed her favourite things into her new carpetbag – a wedding gift from her parents – and when the sun sank and a cool shadow crept over the warm brown paddocks she went to Spot. She crawled onto his back and lay with her cheek on the wobbly ridge of his mane with her arms around his neck.

'One day, Spot my dearest friend, when Hadley has his first pay cheque, I'll come and get you. I'll grow an apple tree that will be exclusively yours. You will have your own dam and you can eat breakfast in my kitchen every day if you like.' She slid from the pungent comfort of her horse and looked deep into his bottomless elliptical pupil. 'I will come back, Spot.' He rested his cheek on hers, like a suitcase on her shoulder. 'I love you, Spotty,' she said.

She walked up though the vines, tears falling from her chin like raindrops from a leaf, her fingers running over bunches of the pale green grapes. Spot stood with his brisket pressed against the fence and his lovely ears pricked forward. Her sister and brother-in-law watched from the wicker couch.

At tea, Lilith complained.

'I have to do everything at Overton, Mother. I've only got the laundress. We're only using the parlour and one bedroom.'

'And the kitchen,' said Marius, piling his plate with shepherd's pie and bottled beetroot.

'You've made your bed, Lilith. Lie in it,' said Phoeba,

wondering what they would do when the preserves ran out.

'I may not be able to come to your big day tomorrow, Phoeba,' said Lilith, huffily.

'What a shame,' said Phoeba, sarcastically. 'And pass me the pie, Marius, unless you're going to take all of it for yourself.'

'He can have my share,' said Lilith, quietly. 'I'm unwell.'

'So much has changed for you,' said Maude, dropping a pat of butter onto the mashed potato, 'of course you're tired.'

'Scarlet fever, is it?' asked Robert, flippantly.

'We have news,' said Marius looking nervously smug.

Maude's hand froze, the butter lid in her fingers. Lilith assumed her stricken expression.

'Mummy, I think I'm … I could be expecting.'

'Already?' yelled Robert, his mouth full of half-chewed bread.

Maude glared at Marius.

'We'll have to get a barouche, Dad,' said Lilith, and pouted.

'We should make enough to buy a nice little wagonette in the next year or so,' said Robert, pointing his knife at Marius, 'don't you think?'

Lilith rested her hand on her tummy. 'We'll need something by September: the baby will be here by then.'

Phoeba watched her mother turn ashen. The butter lid fell from her fingers and clattered onto the table. Lilith and Marius must have known, she thought.

'September,' she repeated, pointedly. Barely seven months after the wedding day.

Robert whipped his napkin from his collar, threw it at Marius and took the wine jug from him.

'I'll have the relish, Marius,' said Phoeba.

Sunday, February 25, 1894

The fourth Sunday in February was an unseasonably flat day. There was an icy tint in the air and the bay was as still as a bowl of whey.

Marius arrived early with Lilith, who wore a Canton silk crepe shawl and a fur busby with a matching muff.

'You'll be nice and warm,' said her mother.

'It's last season's but no one will know,' she said. 'Mrs Overton didn't take them with her.'

Marius took a bridle from the shed and went to Spot. 'Come on, you old mule,' he said affectionately, 'let's get you harnessed.'

Spot swivelled one ear and leaned away from Marius as he stepped towards the horse with the bit ready in his hand. Spot turned his head away, shifting his weight and raising his front hoof. He let it fall onto Marius's boot then shifted his weight back again. A searing pain exploded in Marius foot. He froze, silent with pain and dread before the sharp edge of the horseshoe bit. A fragile bone in the top of his foot started to bend. In desperation he pushed against Spot's thick, warm shoulder, but found himself too weak and watery from pain to budge the horse. Then the thin metatarsal in the crown of Marius's foot cracked and Spot twisted, turning his head, pricking his ears towards the empty lane and screwing his hoof down on Marius's shattered foot.

Phoeba heard the scream as she dressed and there was quite a ruckus as her brother-in-law was helped to the bed in the front room. They left him with a jug of wine, a bottle of Maude's headache powder and Lilith sitting at his side fanning his bent and purple foot.

Phoeba wore her blue frock, wound her bun tight, looked at her reflection in the dressing table mirror for the last time before the wedding and said, 'Fetching, even with a tomato on your head.'

She closed the door to her room – Lilith's and Marius's room now – and found her father waiting at the sulky in his small suit and silly bowler hat. Her mother wore the family pearls and her brown taffeta frock strained at the seams. Robert would have to drive Maude everywhere now – and how on earth would they manage to milk the goat, make bread and cheeses, clean out the guttering, fill the copper, harvest the orchard, grow the vegetables and slaughter the chickens?

At Elm Grove, Hadley's withered mother tied his necktie and breathed, 'My baby boy.' He looked fine in his suit and he turned his soft eyes down to her; they were blue like the middle of the sky at noon.

'I am getting married, Mother,' he said.

'Are you sure?' she asked, clinging to him.

'You've asked me three times and yes, I want to marry Phoeba Crupp.'

'Why? You're too inexperienced to know what you want.'

'You have betrayed me,' he said, his anger rising. 'The farm was mine and we could have all stayed here. Now Mr Titterton wants it and Henrietta and I, and Phoeba, are cast aside.'

'No,' she whispered, 'I did it for you, for a guiding hand. Mr Titterton has means, he will build the new house …'

He gently took her hands from his shoulders.

Phoeba drove to the church squeezed between her parents, a rug

287

over their knees and gloved fingers over their ears. It was cold for February, even though the sun was full and bright. Her teeth chattered, her porridge churned in her stomach, her feet were sweating in their boots and she felt disappointed when Spot trotted straight through the intersection without even a sideways glance at the dam. For the first time, the vicar's horse was tethered in the shade.

Spot pulled up as usual under the peppercorns next to the Hampden. Hadley wasn't waiting, so Robert helped Maude from the sulky. The sulky, unburdened of her bulk, sprang and rocked.

The walk across the yard to the door went far too quickly. Inside, the church was dusty. Cobwebs laced the pews and the floor was scattered with straw from the birds' nests on the beams. Sparrows darted overhead.

Hadley's face lit up when he saw her at the end of the aisle. Henrietta, her cheeks rosy from the chilly drive, beamed at Phoeba and waved. She and Hadley wore gum flowers on their breasts and together, Hadley and Henrietta took one long step to the altar.

Hadley's hands were stiff in his tight leather gloves, his striped worsted trousers pressed lovingly to a razor crease by Henrietta and his wool coat steamed until it was shiny. He assumed his serious expression and a fond, caring feeling swamped Phoeba and she wondered when he had changed. Why hadn't she noticed? He had 'filled out', as her mother would say, his ranginess had thickened to firm, strong limbs and a long, deep back.

She had strong desire just to go home. She had always done what everyone expected, and even in defying them by marrying Hadley, she was doing as everyone expected.

But Hadley had cantered up Mount Hope Lane on his tall brown mare, come to her as he had as a freckly ten-year-old, then a peach-faced adolescent, then a sensitive youth. And now, as a gentle, strawberry-haired man, he had rescued her.

She raised her bouquet of gum flowers, wrenched her arm from her father's grasp and went alone to stand between Hadley and Henrietta.

Like Lilith's, this was not a moving ceremony. When the vicar said, 'Keep thee only unto him, so long as ye both shall live,' Phoeba looked into Hadley's sincere face and said, 'I will' as if she'd just been asked to feed the chickens on her way past the coop. Hadley mispronounced her name as 'Phoebe' and struggled with his vows because his mouth was very dry. Just as he was about to place the ring on her finger a bird flew in and splattered Mrs Titterton's green bonnet with bird dirt. She squeaked. The plain gold ring slipped from Hadley's slickly gloved fingers and fell to the floor with a small ping. Proceedings halted while the two Pearsons searched on their hands and knees between the pews. Henrietta found it, wedged against a knee-rest with dry flies, grain seeds and dusty fluff, and Hadley and Phoeba became man and wife in the eyes of God and the law.

Mrs Flynn cried, 'Whacko!' and threw bruised geranium petals at Hadley. They settled on his shoulders and in his hair.

In the churchyard, lit by silver sunshine through the white clouds, Henrietta passed Hadley a cylindrical leather case with a small flourish and he presented his wedding gift to his new wife. It was a pair of binoculars. He pecked her on the lips then – but not for the first time. He had kissed her just like that once before, but she was twelve at the time and he was ten.

There seemed to be a general sigh in the air, a sort of resigned acceptance, as they made their way to the siding. Robert dropped in to Mrs Flynn's and collected his newspapers.

Mrs Titterton and Maude, her face as stunned as a barn owl

under a gas lamp, stood at either end of the siding, separated by their husbands and children, all looking south to Geelong and the noon train like luckless punters watching the starting flag for the last race.

Phoeba and her new husband and sister-in-law didn't speak, didn't meet even let their eyes meet. The silence hung between them.

Maude pulled her shawl close and said, 'I suppose the coming autumn will be wretched and bring no rain with it.'

'Rain is the last thing we need for the grapes,' muttered Robert, and no one attempted to speak again, so Robert opened his newspaper: **RABBITS REACH PLAGUE PROPORTIONS IN NEW SOUTH WALES. ONE HUNDRED RABBITS TO EVERY ACRE**. When the train appeared – a steaming monster rolling out of the horizon – Phoeba felt a burden leave her. 'The future,' she said, but at once a dread descended and she hoped with all her heart that the choices she had made would be bearable.

The others shrugged, tidied their lapels, rubbed their cold hands. Maude pulled her shawl tighter again and Mrs Titterton teetered in her slight heels. Mr Titterton held her. Robert cleared his throat and Phoeba waited for him to insist she stay, to say he'd send Marius and Lilith to Melbourne, anything – but he just clutched Phoeba's hand, squeezing it until it hurt, and said, his voice cracking, 'Well, old thing, you'll write, won't you?'

She removed her hand.

The train sounded its long, loud whistle and suddenly Maude sobbed, 'I shall miss you, Phoeba,' as if it had only just occurred to her.

The smell of burning coal, steam and engine oil engulfed them. Smoke clouded the noisy black engine, the wheels went thunk and the brakes screeched.

No one saw Mrs Titterton crumble, but in the din, as the train exhaled and shuddered, Henrietta heard her mother's little squeak and turned. She was hidden behind Mr Titterton but as she buckled towards the edge of the platform Henrietta shouted and lunged, knocking her stepfather aside. The train lurched to a standstill and the doors were flung open just as she pulled at her mother, wrenching her so that she flipped over. She landed on her side on the platform, her small head bouncing once on a rough sleeper. There was a sound, like something snapping inside a cushion and Mrs Titterton lay on her side, flailing her tiny arms like an up-turned beetle, her skin turning purple. She stared up at her husband and reached out with her pleated, maroon fingers, but no sound came from her mouth.

'Shit,' said Robert.

'Help me, that's what she's saying,' said Mr Titterton standing perfectly still.

'No,' said Hadley, kneeling. 'Mother no.'

A small patch of blood grew on her bodice, just above her waist, and there, poking through the torn, green material of her new dress, was a snapped steel corset stay. It was rusty, the pink material of her corset perished and brown around it.

A crowd was gathering. The emaciated guard, the decrepit mailman, and some passengers who held parasols to shade her.

'She can't die here, not now,' hissed Maude, indignantly. Phoeba and Henrietta stood holding hands, speechless, looking down at the injured woman among their hems.

'Perhaps we will have to stay,' thought Phoeba.

'At least get her to the Hampden,' urged Maude. The guard and some passengers helped Hadley and Mr Titterton take the wounded woman, like a shot sparrow, to the Hampden.

'It's only a wound,' said Mr Titterton. 'It'll mend.'

'Something snapped,' said Hadley.

'A corset stay,' said Henrietta, hastily, and Phoeba felt Henrietta start to tremble. 'I didn't mean to hurt her.'

'Of course not,' said Hadley.

Mr Titterton grabbed Henrietta by the arm, 'You'll have to stay and nurse her.'

The guard dragged his watch from his waistcoat and checked the time. The passengers started to climb back into the carriages.

'I won't stay,' said Henrietta, and crossed her arms.

'We'll all stay with you, won't we Hadley?' said Phoeba, her voice a little too shrill.

Hadley looked directly at Phoeba. 'Henrietta will have to nurse her.'

It took a full heartbeat for her to understand. She put her bag down. 'We'll wait until she's better.'

'We have to go—'

'Henrietta must come—'

'Later, yes.'

Phoeba and Henrietta stood frozen, but Phoeba's mind was racing. If she stayed she would break Hadley's heart, and she would have to wait on a mother, a sister, a brother-in-law and, in very short time, a baby. If she went she would be without Henrietta. There was a pain – she might have inhaled a handful of barber's razors for its sharpness. Her heart was labouring and her breath coming in short gasps. Hadley stood up and took her bag. 'The contract for my job is signed, Phoeba. We have to go.'

'Why can't Mr Titterton look after your mother?'

'I'd have to sell the farm to pay for a nursing home,' said Mr Titterton. 'It isn't necessary. The girl pulled her mother too hard.'

'She was falling in front of the train,' said Henrietta, bunching her skirt in agony.

Hadley put his hand around her shoulder. 'You saved her, Henri, you saved her.'

There was just one moment while the train huffed and a carriage window slammed shut, that Hadley, Phoeba and Henrietta looked at each other and thought, how everything would have been different if she hadn't.

'I'll send a telegraph to Doctor Mueller,' said Mr Titterton heading for the shop.

'Good,' said Maude, smoothing her gloves, 'he can see to Marius's foot.'

Phoeba looked at her father. He stared back at her, silent, and she thought she heard Lilith say, 'You have made your bed.'

'Phoeba, please, the train—' said Hadley, and the guard blew his whistle.

'Wait,' said her mother, and Phoeba's heart quickened. Her mother was going to forbid her from going to the wilderness; she would send Lilith away instead. 'You must take the Collector. If Hadley is away with his sheep you must have some protection.'

Phoeba crossed her arms and looked over at Spot, his head high, his ears sharp and forward as he stared at her from the churchyard. 'I won't go without Spot.' It didn't make sense, but it was all she could think of.

Hadley said, gently, 'There's no time just now,' and held his hand out to her.

It was all wrong. Henrietta was supposed to come.

'I'll send Spot,' said Robert, trying to be helpful. 'I'll go and see Mrs Flynn later and book his passage.'

Her father took her hands in his again, held them tight, and made her look into his rheumy eyes. 'Almost everything you will ever be was taught to you from this place and it will always be here for you.'

She looked at them evenly; her father the betrayer, her fat mother in a tight brown dress and a hat the size of a pillow. At home her pretty sister would be pouting over her costumed husband, like an actor in a rural play. She never wanted to see them ever again.

She reached for Henrietta and as they held each other fast Henrietta's voice came into her ear above the rumbling of the engine and the spurting steam. 'We will see each other when one of us is free. And I will always love you both, no matter what.'

Then, as she turned to the train, Phoeba vowed that she would make a satisfying life. She would create a worthwhile future – a good life, and when she was old she would look back and say, I did my best.

Phoeba whispered to her teary friend, 'You'll be free one day,' then let her go and turned to the train. She reached out to Hadley and left Henrietta standing on the small wooden platform, her skirt still screwed in her hands.

Henrietta watched until the train was a black smear in the distance and then drove carefully towards Elm Grove. Mr Titterton cradled her whimpering mother in the back seat. At the intersection she reined in the horse. The thistles scratched together in the breeze and two eagles circled above the dam.

Maude and Robert were sitting in the sulky, up to its axle in muddy water. In front of them knelt Spot, brown muddy water lapping his shoulders, his eyes closed and his nose high, like the monster in Loch Ness.

Epilogue

The young woman pulled her motor vehicle up at the railway crossing and looked about her. She wore dark glasses and a large straw hat secured with a wide scarf and her passenger, a young man with spectacles, clung to the dashboard. The vehicle was dark blue with a golden 'O' painted on the small door.

'Why have you stopped, Roberta?' said the young man. 'There's nothing here.'

'As my dear departed Grandmaudie would say; nonsense.' She stood up behind the wheel and cried, 'Just look about you!'

Beyond the beach, which was actually just a salty slice of seaside mud, the bay glittered and the smokestacks on ships sliding out through the heads left plumes of smoke across the clear sky. It was low tide and the jetty pylons jutted from the mudflats, like thin legs without trousers.

Roberta gestured inland to a gathering of boulders on top of a big, bushy ridge. 'Up there, above the vines, is Mount Hope,' she said, and the young man turned to inspect the neat weatherboard nestled at the base of the outcrop. Around it, acres of grapevines covered every slope, like a green chenille blanket.

'The vines are Mother's,' said Roberta, 'but my Aunt Lilith and my Uncle Marius live in the house and their children, all six of my cousins, were born there. You'll meet everyone this afternoon. We all gather at the homestead for the ploughing match.'

Roberta tooted the horn and waved to a tall, broad woman on the railway station reading a newspaper. The headline screamed, **WAR LOOMS**. The woman looked up and saluted, then flung a long, thick grey plait over her shoulder.

'That's Aunt Henri,' said Roberta. 'She runs the railway station and the shop. Dad bought it for her when he made all his money on the ram emasculator. He bought himself Overton, and over that outcrop, there are thousands of first-class sheep.'

'I hate sheep,' said the young man.

'As far as I'm concerned there's nothing more pleasing than a mob of first-class merinos with fine bright fleeces, closely crimped and three inches deep,' declared Roberta, and leaned down to kiss the young man's cheek. 'And my brother runs the winery so you needn't go anywhere near a sheep. You can just stay in the office with your sums and balances and your adding machine. As soon they can, my parents will retire to the manager's house with Aunt Henri. They'll rattle around together until they all join my grandparents in the family plot at the outcrop.'

Roberta threw her arms open wide. 'There is everything here for me. What about you?'

The End